Y0-BYZ-399

"FIRE THE MK-70!"

The hull of the USS *Swordfish* quivered as the MK-70 shot out of the torpedo tube and rocketed downward to intercept the Russian torpedo. Also known as a mobile submarine simulator, or MOSS, the MK-70 was designed to simulate the sound of a fleeing submarine. Sonar technician Brad Bodzin was in the best position to monitor the *Swordfish*'s desperate tactic.

Brad hunched over the console, his eyes tightly shut, the headphones pressed over his ears. The high-pitched whine of the MOSS rose distinctly as it initiated a wide preprogrammed turn. The throaty muted roar of the Russian torpedo gained in volume as it adjusted its course and surged forward in a sudden burst of speed. As the two signatures appeared to merge, Brad ripped the headphones from his ears.

A split second later the depths were filled with the sound of a deafening explosion . . .

CRY OF THE DEEP

RICHARD P. HENRICK

ZEBRA BOOKS
KENSINGTON PUBLISHING CORP.

ZEBRA BOOKS

are published by

Kensington Publishing Corp.
850 Third Avenue
New York, NY 10022

Fifth printing: January 1996

Printed in the United States of America

*Special thanks to Commander William S. Brown,
U.S. Navy retired, and the staff of the Mote Marine
Laboratory, Sarasota, Florida*

"The ability to synthesize—to derive a new idea or concept from seemingly unrelated facts—is usually considered one of the hallmarks of intelligence . . . It follows then that "intelligence" is a very imprecise term . . . If we encounter so many problems in trying to pin down what is meant by human intelligence, consider the much greater difficulty of assessing the intelligence of other animals. For we have no insight into their minds."

> —*Marine Mammals and Man—The Navy's Porpoises and Sea Lions* by Forrest G. Wood, Luce Books

"There is at present no way in which a meaningful rating of porpoise intelligence can be made."

> —"Behavior of the Captive Bottlenose Dolphin, Tursiops truncatus," by A. F. Mcbride and D. O. Hebb, *Journal of Comparative and Physiological Psychology*, Vol. 41, no. 2.

"Modern Soviet submarines, operating undetected in Cuban waters, would offer far more of a threat to the U.S. than all the medium-range missiles in Cuba with which Khrushchev sought to improve Russia's strategic posture."

> —Donald W. Mitchell, *Soviet Seapower in the Caribbean: Political and Strategic Implications*, Praeger Publishers.

Chapter One

October 27, 1962

The view from the DC-3's forward cabin was a spectacular one. From an altitude of fifteen thousand feet, Theodore Anderson sat forward and watched as a large pod of dolphins gracefully cut through the crystalline-blue Gulf Stream waters. This was the young ensign's first visit to the Florida Keys, and he was immediately impressed with the utter clarity of the surrounding ocean.

A mild pocket of air turbulence shook the lumbering aircraft, and Anderson readjusted his line of sight to take in the various islands that formed the Keys themselves. Most of these masses of sand, mangrove, and palm were minuscule affairs, connected to each other by a single roadway that he knew to be Route U.S. 1. Its terminus was his current destination also, the city of Key West.

An abrupt change in the pitch of the DC-3's engines was followed by a gradual loss of altitude. It was obvious that they were preparing to land, and Anderson instinctively pulled his seat belt tighter. Oblivious to the constant, muted snores of his seatmate, a weather-worn Marine who had been sound asleep ever since leaving Jacksonville, the newly commissioned naval officer yawned widely to clear his blocked eardrums. Once this was achieved, he turned his attention back to the window.

With their decrease in altitude, Route 1 was clearly visible, and he was surprised to see it filled with a large convoy of green-and-brown-painted Army vehicles. Many of these trucks were flatbeds loaded with tanks, while others were completely filled with troops. Seconds later, they were flying over a central staging area, and Anderson spotted several Nike and Hawk missile batteries, surrounding a massive encampment filled with thousands of dark green tents. Armed soldiers were everywhere, and only then did the recent Annapolis graduate comprehend the true scope of the crisis that currently faced them.

When President Kennedy had addressed the nation only days before and revealed that Soviet nuclear missiles were being secretly placed in Cuba, Anderson had been genuinely shocked, as had been the rest of the country. The mere idea of having such weapons of mass destruction only a scant ninety miles away from the U.S. shoreline was particularly upsetting. Thus the nation stood solidly behind its dynamic president when Kennedy demanded that the Soviets immediately remove these weapons and announced a naval quarantine to enforce this ultimatum. The heavily armed encampment that passed down below, and in a sense his own recent call to duty, were prompted by this same crisis. For if the Soviets refused to meet Kennedy's demands, the U.S. would have no choice but to invade Cuba and remove the missiles themselves.

Anderson shuddered to think what such a drastic operation would entail. Untold thousands would surely die, with the world brought to the very brink of nuclear devastation. He could thus only pray that the Russians would come to their senses and remove the missiles before it was too late.

The plane made a wide turn over the coastline as it initiated its final landing approach, and Anderson caught his first glimpse of the naval facility that had called him here. A line of sleek gray frigates floated beside several troop ships and a single tender. Barely visible in the water, immediately beside this last ship, was a black, cigar-shaped vessel, whose characteristic rounded hull and streamlined sail caused the young ensign's pulse to quicken. Though he had seen photographs of this very same vessel before, sighting it with his own eyes only served to verify the reality of his current circumstances.

Three days ago, when Anderson initially received the orders sending him down to Key West, he looked upon his new assignment with great anticipation. Submarine duty had been the reason that he had enlisted in the Navy in the first place. Now, to actually see the boat on which his childhood dream would be fulfilled, made the moment all that more unforgettable.

The sub's name was the USS *Swordfish*. Commissioned in 1960, the two-hundred-and-ten-foot vessel displaced over fifteen hundred tons. The ship's

11

diesel-electric propulsion source allowed it near-silent operating capabilities, while its rounded hull permitted high speeds and great maneuverability. Combined with a sophisticated electronics array and fire-control system, the *Swordfish* was a first line man-of-war that was ready to take on any operational commitment. Proud to have been selected to serve on such a vessel, Anderson turned from the window when a gruff voice suddenly broke in from his left.

"Where in the hell are we, anyway?"

The grizzled Marine was in the process of yawning and stretching his massive limbs as Anderson replied, "We should be landing at Key West any moment now."

As if to emphasize this response, the muted whine of the plane's engines decreased and the DC-3's landing gear made contact with the runway with a bare jolt. As the pilot expertly applied the brakes, puzzlement flavored the leatherneck's words.

"You've got to be kidding me? We can't be in Key West already! Why, I could have sworn that we just took off from Jacksonville."

Pointing out the window, Anderson answered, "See for yourself. I guarantee you that those mangroves out there signal the end of the line."

The Marine took in the distant collection of willowy trees that his seatmate was referring to and rubbed his beard-stubbled jaw. "Brother, I must have really been out cold. Was my snoring bad?"

"I've heard worse," retorted the young ensign lightly.

"Thank goodness for that. When I'm in form, they say that I can wake the dead."

12

Continuing to gaze out the window as the plane taxied to the gate area, the Marine commented, "That's some collection of military hardware out there. I haven't seen this much action since the closing days of Korea. It's about time that this country woke up and started playing hardball with the Russkies. It's strength and determination that those Red bastards respect. Never forget it."

Anderson nodded and the Marine added, "This your first assignment, son?"

The ensign shook his head that it was and the Marine smiled. "Well, you picked one hell of a time to get your feet wet. Though I must admit that my own career was no different. Two weeks after completing basic at Pendleton, I was on my way to Inchon, where I landed with the second wave. Shit, that was one hell of a place to become a man, but I had little choice if I wanted to survive.

"You'll do fine, son, if you'll just listen to the veterans and then follow your gut instincts. And remember, in a shooting war there is only one rule to go by, and that's to survive above all else. Everything else is bullshit."

The DC-3 braked to a final halt and Anderson watched as his seatmate stood and prepared to exit. The muscular Marine seemed to fill the entire aisle as he looked down and winked. "You know, I was a week away from retirement when they called me down here. I could have mustered out early, but the way I look at it, my country needs me, and I'm not about to let it down now that the Russkies have us up against a wall. Each one of us has to do his sworn duty, or freedom will be but a dream in a history

13

book. So take pride in that uniform, and never doubt that what we do is right."

Issuing a crisp salute, the Marine then pivoted and disappeared out the forward hatchway. Anderson was strangely affected by this brief encounter, and wished that he had more time to better know the veteran leatherneck. Inspired by his patriotic rhetoric, the ensign stood and followed the other passengers out the exit.

Outside, he was met by a gust of hot, humid air, rich with the salty scent of the sea. A gull cried loudly overhead as he climbed down the stairway ramp. Waiting for him on the tarmac was a familiar blond figure, smartly dressed in the khaki uniform of a U.S. Navy lieutenant commander.

"Welcome to Key West, Ensign!" greeted the officer warmly.

Genuinely surprised by this unexpected reception, Anderson saluted, then stepped forward to exchange handshakes. "Uncle Pete, what in the world are you doing down here?"

"What's the matter, isn't my favorite nephew glad to see me?" returned Lieutenant Commander Peter Anderson, who took his nephew's hand in his own and then hugged him as well.

"Of course I am," retorted the red-faced ensign. "It's just that I thought you were permanently stationed at the Pentagon."

"Even us pencil pushers have been called out from behind our desks for this one, Ted. I've been down here for almost a week now. Naval Intelligence is playing a key role in determining the degree of our military response, and the CNO wanted me on the

14

front line to see things like they really are.

"And by the way, congratulations on your assignment. When I learned that you got the *Swordfish*, I couldn't resist coming down here to personally greet you. Now, how about a lift down to your ship? I'd offer you lunch, but I understand that your new skipper is a stickler on details. Wouldn't want to hold you up, now that he's expecting you."

Of similar height, build, and coloring, the two blond officers walked over to an awaiting jeep.

"How's your mother and sister?" quizzed the senior Anderson as he climbed behind the wheel.

"The last I saw of Mom, she was soaked in tears. I think the reality of my career choice really hit home the moment I received my current orders. Susie took it all in stride. She's talking of enlisting herself once she's of age."

"That's all your mother needs," said Peter Anderson, who guided the jeep out of the airport. "I'll call her tonight and let her know you arrived safe and sound. I was going to call her anyway to suggest that she take Susie out of school and go up to the cabin at Big Bear for a couple of days. I'll sleep better just knowing that they're out of Los Angeles for a while."

Noting a seriousness in his uncle's tone, Ted cautiously responded, "Are things really that bad, Uncle Pete?"

The elder Anderson nodded. "I'm afraid they are, Ted. This is all on the hush, but never have I seen our country so close to a nuclear war before. Why, just yesterday, our strategic forces went to a state of Defcon 2, which is only one step away from an actual launch order.

"It all started earlier in the day, when one of our U-2's overflew the North Pole and headed toward Soviet airspace. The pilot was on a routine mission, sampling the atmosphere for radiation. Yet to Soviet radar, the lost plane appeared to be the first of a wave of strategic bombers and their interceptors were immediately scrambled. We sent up a squadron of fighters ourselves, yet by the grace of God, our man realized his mistake and was able to turn back for Alaska before the Soviets could reach him. Needless to say, both sides are extremely jumpy, and next time we just might not be so lucky."

The jeep roared over a narrow asphalt road that was lined with stately coconut palms. The colorful town of Key West beckoned in the distance. Yet Ted Anderson hardly noticed the passing scenery.

"How are things on Cuba?" he asked. "Have the Soviets reacted to Kennedy's ultimatum as yet?"

His uncle downshifted the jeep and guided it smoothly around a slow-moving bus before answering. "The latest reconnaissance photos show business as usual. If anything, the Russian technicians seem to be in a greater hurry than ever to complete the installation of their missiles. The Air Force is pressuring the President to order an immediate airstrike to take out the sites, while the Army and Marines are preparing for a full-scale invasion. What really scares the dickens out of me is this naval quarantine we're currently in the midst of. The first Soviet ships have yet to penetrate this zone, and I'm afraid that the real danger of nuclear confrontation will be upon us when the first of their ships is intercepted."

"Perhaps Mom and Susie should get out of the city," said Ted. "But will it really make a difference?"

"As keepers of the peace, it's our job to ensure that they'll never learn the answer to that question."

A hushed quiet followed as the jeep sped through the outskirts of the town and approached the naval base's main gate. A group of no-nonsense, rifle-toting sentries inspected their I.D. cards, and only then were they allowed entry. The sea was visible in the distance as they headed for the nearby docks.

"Some reception committee I turned out to be. Filling your head with gloom and doom on the eve of your first real cruise. We'll work our way out of this mess like we always manage to do and mankind will persevere. Now aren't you in the least bit anxious to know more about your new skipper?"

Noting the way his nephew's eyes lit up with the mention of his new superior officer, Peter Anderson said, "Commander William Abbott is his name. He was born in San Diego in 1917, and is not only a decorated World War II veteran, but a fellow Annapolis grad himself. As such he'll be pushing you all that much harder, Ted."

"You mentioned that he was a stickler for details, Uncle Pete. What made you say that?"

The elder Anderson hesitated a moment before responding, "When I heard that you drew the *Swordfish*, I did a bit of checking, and found out that the crew had received an unusually high number of disciplinary reprimands. Most of these concerned basic rules infractions such as tardiness, and correspond to Abbott's arrival on the sub eight months ago. Though he might be known as something of a despot to his men, the *Swordfish* was the first sub in

17

Abbott's group to fly both the gold and silver dolphin flags, signifying a hundred percent officer and enlisted submarine qualification. So, however hard-nosed the commander might be, he certainly gets results."

"I'll be able to handle him," offered Ted, who sat forward expectantly when the tender he had spotted from the air loomed large as life before them.

Yet another pair of armed sentries guarded the docksite. As the jeep roared to a stop before them, Peter Anderson turned his head to address his nephew. "You're on your own now, kiddo. I can't tell you how proud you've made me. If your father was still alive, he'd feel likewise. So go and carry on his tradition, and we'll talk more when you return."

Ted grasped his uncle's hand and noted just the hint of a tear forming in Peter's eyes. His own rising emotions were making it difficult for him to swallow, and he quickly climbed out of the jeep and headed straight for the tender.

An alert Marine led him through the immense ship, which acted as both a floating repair shop and supply depot. After passing through a cavernous compartment crammed with electronics equipment, he reached that portion of the vessel where the *Swordfish* was berthed. Tied to the tender by thick mooring lines, with her sleek hull protected by a series of circular, rubberized fenders, the sub appeared even larger than it had looked from the air. Two figures could just be seen on top of its elongated sail, in the midst of an animated conversation. Several officers were gathered on the sub's deck, and it was this group of individuals that the young ensign was soon introducing himself to.

"Ensign Theodore Anderson reporting for duty."

It proved to be the tallest of these figures who responded. "Welcome aboard the *Swordfish*, Mr. Anderson. We've been expecting you. I'm Lieutenant Webster, the ship's supply officer. The way it looks, you got here just in time. We received our sailing orders only minutes ago. We'll be leaving with the next tide, so you should have just enough time to get settled. Ensign Avila here will take you below deck and show you your quarters."

A thin, bright-eyed Hispanic stepped forward and alertly nodded. "Ensign Adrian Avila at your service. I'm the ship's communications officer, and I'd like to also welcome you aboard the *Swordfish*. Let's hurry and get your gear properly stowed away so that I'll have some time to run you through the ship before we get under way."

Ted Anderson took an immediate liking to Avila, who exuded a sincere warmth. He followed him around the sail and down through the aft access trunk. The scent of machine oil met his nostrils as he stepped off the ladder's last rung. This put him in a cramped passageway lined with imitation wood-grain paneling.

"Welcome to officers' country," observed Avila. "Your berth is aft. We share the same stateroom. I hope you don't mind the top bunk."

Ted Anderson was relieved to have the likeable communications officer for a roommate, and followed him to their shared quarters. After stowing his gear in the locker located beneath his mattress, they proceeded to the officers' wardroom.

Seated at the large table, which had a semi-circular, blue leather booth set into the wall on its far side, were two individuals. Lieutenant Webster, the sub's supply officer, was standing rigidly in the passageway, his complete attention riveted on the brown-headed figure seated at the table's head.

"I don't give a damn about your lame excuses, Mr. Webster!" shouted the seated officer, who Anderson took at once to be the captain. "But the one thing you can be certain of is that I'm not going to hold up our mission for a lousy load of fresh produce. We're just going to have to do without."

"I understand, sir," replied the supply officer nervously. "I'll inform Cooky of our situation and have him begin planning an alternative menu."

The captain was already refocusing his attention on a series of navigational charts that lay on the table before him as he responded, "You do that, Mr. Webster. And I want a full report on this mix-up on the XO's desk by mid-rats."

There was a pained look in the supply officer's eyes as he briefly caught Ted Anderson's curious glance, then pivoted and exited the wardroom by way of the forward hatchway. With the captain still absorbed in his charts, Anderson turned his attention to the other seated figure. Calmly sipping a mug of coffee was a middle-aged black officer, with a pair of inquisitive eyes staring forth from his wire-rimmed glasses. Quick to return the junior ensign's stare, the seated officer raised his deep voice in greeting.

"Mr. Anderson, I presume. I'm Lieutenant Wilkins, the ship's executive officer. Welcome aboard."

Ted instinctively stiffened and replied after initiating a crisp salute, "Thank you, sir. I'm proud to be here."

The XO grinned. "At ease, Ensign. And you can belay that saluting. Around here, we like it more informal."

With this, the figure seated opposite the XO looked up briefly to examine the newcomer. His stare was intense, and though he was balding, his eyebrows were thick and he sported a full mustache.

"So you're our new weapons officer," commented the senior officer matter-of-factly. "I'm certain that you've gathered by this time that I'm Captain Abbott. I'm going to be blunt with you, Ensign. If I had my way you wouldn't be making this cruise. Because of our current crisis situation, I'd like to have a man with more experience at your station. But for some damn reason, Command disagrees, and that means that I'm stuck with you. So until you qualify and further prove yourself, Lieutenant Wilkins here will be responsible for supervising you."

The captain's attention was distracted when a short, wiry officer with bright red hair entered the wardroom from the forward hatch. The newcomer's presence prompted a passionate response.

"It's about time that you got down here, Lieutenant Keller!" barked the captain. "Now what in the hell kind of navigator do you call yourself, mister? Here we're about to embark on the most important mission of our lifetimes and you can't even present me with an accurate intercept point."

The freckle-faced navigator seemed to ignore the captain's sour mood as he efficiently bent over the wardroom table to examine the charts that were displayed there. After pulling out a map of the Caribbean, he pointed toward a line that was drawn in pencil to the northeast of the Bahamas. He then

21

cleared his throat and calmly expressed himself.

"I'm sorry about the misunderstanding, Captain, but I can only chart the data that Intelligence relays to me. Right now, our target lies somewhere in the waters just north of San Salvador, near the Tropic of Cancer. We're still awaiting the results of the latest sonobuoy drop to get its exact coordinates."

"And may I ask the exact nature of this target?" dared Ted Anderson.

Impressed with the youngster's bravado, the XO answered, "Why, of course you can, Mr. Anderson. The *Swordfish* has been ordered to tag a Soviet attack submarine that supposedly lies somewhere between our quarantine zone and an approaching Cuban-bound Russian trawler, loaded with nuclear warheads. Since there's no telling how the Reds will react if this trawler continues on its present course and is subsequently stopped and boarded by the U.S. Navy, Command wants this submerged Russian bogey under constant surveillance. Unfortunately, one of our Skipjack class subs that had been on the scene developed a reactor problem and was forced to return to Norfolk. We've just been called in to replace them."

"Damn nukes!" muttered Captain Abbott angrily. "They're so frigging complicated, no wonder they're always breaking down at the wrong time. I'll put my money on a good old reliable diesel-electric any day of the year."

There was a moment of constrained silence as all those assembled in the wardroom stared down at the chart of the Caribbean. It proved to be the captain who broke the spell by looking down at his watch and commenting, "Well now, gentlemen, the tide will be with us in another forty-five minutes, and we've got a ship to prepare for possible combat. To your stations, men, and may God be with us."

It was only then that Ted Anderson noticed the framed picture hung on the partition immediately behind the captain. It showed the open ocean and a huge silver swordfish that was in the process of lifting its razor-sharp bill high up into the air in an act of fearless defiance. The young ensign couldn't help but be inspired by this expert rendering, which hopefully caught the spirit of the vessel that fate had chosen for him to serve upon.

Less than twenty-four hours after the USS *Swordfish* set sail from the Key West naval station, its senior sonar technician picked up the sounds of an unidentified submerged contact in the waters north of San Salvador. It was this same alert sonar operator who was able to analyze the sound tapes of this contact and positively identify it as a Soviet November class attack sub.

Once the captain was informed of this fact, the crew was sent scurrying to their battle stations. Ted Anderson had been in the midst of an intensive inspection of the forward torpedo room when this alert was triggered. It was the XO who ordered him up to the sub's attack center.

The newest member of the crew arrived in the control room just as a top-priority dispatch from COMSUBLANT (Commander Submarines Atlantic) was delivered to the captain. It was as the officers gathered around the plotting table that Abbott explained their unique situation.

"The latest reconnaissance photos show the Russian trawler still headed straight for the quarantine zone. If their speed and course remains constant, they will be crossing into the zone in approximately two hours. Our surface ships are in position to intercept the trawler should it be necessary. Yet the presence of the November class vessel nearby is making Command extremely nervous, and rightfully so.

"I've just been ordered by the President to make audio contact with the Soviet submarine by utilizing our sonar system. In this transmission, we're to instruct the Russians to ascend to the surface with all due haste."

This revelation caused a wave of nervous chatter to rise among those gathered around the plotting table. It was the XO who proceeded to voice himself.

"Oh, come now, Skipper. Command really doesn't think that the Russians are going to fall for such a stunt. Why, it's ridiculous!"

Captain Abbott looked up and answered directly. "I agree one hundred percent, Lieutenant. That's why I'm taking the second half of the directive more seriously. It says here that if the Soviets fail to respond to our sonar hail, we're free to use any means at our disposal to convince the Reds that we mean business. And yes, gentlemen, that includes an attack with torpedoes."

"But that could very possibly be the opening shot of World War III!" observed the startled navigator.

The other officers seemed equally concerned and the captain forcefully responded, "You sound like a

24

bunch of scared old ladies! Do you think that we're merely out here to play war games? Don't forget whose bright idea it was to attempt sneaking those nuclear missiles onto Cuban soil in the first place. Our Commander-in-Chief has drawn the line, and it's our responsibility to enforce his will without question. So before that November gets between their trawler and our surface ships, we had better get to work negating its threat. Lieutenant Wilkins, what can you tell us about our adversary?"

"The November class represents the first nuclear-powered submarine in the Soviet Fleet," the black officer efficiently replied. "They're extremely large vessels, over three hundred fifty feet long and displacing some five thousand tons. Though they're formidably armed with eight torpedo tubes in the bow, and two stern tubes, the November class has one major design flaw that could be to our advantage. Unlike our own rounded, teardrop-style hull, the Novembers have a long, conventionally shaped hull with a preponderance of free-flood holes and other protrusions. So not only can we outmaneuver them, but they're also noisy as all hell."

The captain seemed to like what he was hearing, for a broad grin suddenly painted the corners of his full mouth. "Well said, Lieutenant. Have engineering prepare for flank battle speed. If we do get in a scrap with the Reds, we're going to need every available knot of speed to outrun them. Then you'd better get down to Sonar and explain our situation to Smitty. He's going to have to work out a method of communicating with the Russians once we close in on them.

"Lieutenant Anderson, do you think that you can handle loading tubes one, three, and six with conventional warheads?"

"Yes, sir!" snapped the new weapons officer, who was proud of the captain's newfound confidence in him.

"Then let's get on with it, gentlemen," added the captain. "For the destiny of the planet is now in the capable hands of the USS *Swordfish*."

Anderson was on his way to the deck below to carry out the captain's request when he was intercepted by the XO.

"It appears that you really stepped into the fire, Ensign. Are you going to be able to handle everything all right?"

Anderson sensed the XO's sincerity and answered accordingly. "I'll be fine, sir. I'm familiar with the equipment from sub school, and the men are most cooperative."

"Don't let that bunch of scalawags fool you," returned the XO with a sarcastic wink. "If you do have any questions, though, don't be afraid to ask the Chief. He's a war-tested sub vet, with just as many hours spent under the sea as the captain. Meanwhile, I'll be nearby in the sonar shack if you should need me."

Nodding that he understood, Anderson said, "Sir, I'm confident that I'll be able to handle the equipment and all, but I'm not really certain how I'll act if we're forced to take action."

"Join the crowd," offered the XO. "In fact, there's only a small handful of battle-scarred veterans on board who know what it's really like to go in harm's way. The rest of us can only hope that if the time comes, we'll do our sworn duty without flinching. So lighten up, and know that you're not alone with your anxieties. And remember, we've still yet to cross into the threshold of an actual war. Our adversaries are the greatest chess players in the world, and there's a damn good chance that all this is mere bluff and posturing.''

"I sure hope that you're right, sir," returned Anderson.

"We'll all know soon enough," said the XO, who was conscious it was time to get on with his duty. There was a distant look in his eyes as he turned to continue on down the passageway.

Ted Anderson was absorbed in thought himself as he proceeded in the opposite direction. He silently passed by the crew's quarters and ducked into the torpedo room. The familiar scent of machine oil permeated the air, and even though the young ensign was but a newcomer here, he already felt at home. Without hesitating, he addressed his men, who were gathered around the pneumatic pump mechanism.

"Okay gang, seal up that pump, and get to work loading tubes one, three, and six with wire-guided Mk-37's. And snap to it, because this is no drill!''

This last statement had its desired effect, and the men went scrambling over to the weapons rack to ready the torpedoes. This left Anderson alone with his Master Chief, who expertly reassembled the pump that they had been working on.

"Did you get her working?" quizzed the ensign.

The Chief grunted. "It should hold through this cruise. The incompetents who did our recent overhaul really botched the system up but good."

Looking up to see how the men were doing over at the weapons rack, the Chief added, "Are you really serious that this isn't a drill?"

"I'm afraid I am, Chief. It appears that our orders come right from the White House."

"If it's Mk-37's that we're loading, then we must be up against a Russkie submarine. May I ask what this has to do about enforcing that quarantine zone, sir?"

"Actually, Chief, it's pretty basic. The Soviets have a trawler loaded with Cuban-bound missile components headed toward the Zone even as we speak. We've got surface vessels up there ready to intercept them. Yet lurking beneath the adjoining waters is a Russian November class attack sub. To ensure that this platform doesn't interfere with our surface combatants, we're going to track down the submarine and order them to ascend. We've been authorized to utilize our Mk-37's only if they fail to respond to our directive."

The Chief scratched his forehead. "Ivan isn't the type who takes orders well from U.S. warships. The only way that we're going to be able to get them out of these waters is to blow them out of here."

"Can our torpedoes do the job?" queried Anderson.

Walking over to the nearby hydraulics loading ramp, the Chief delicately patted the nose of the torpedo currently being loaded into tube number one. "Just as long as the skipper gives us a clear shot, these little babies will run straight and true."

As the Chief supervised the actual loading of the torpedo into its tube, Anderson went over to the aft bulkhead to double-check the integrity of the Mk-113 fire control system. He was well into this complex process when he was once again called to the attack center by the XO.

This time as he entered the control room, the mood was noticeably tense. Perched behind the two seated planesmen, the captain silently stared at the instruments showing their depth and bearing, his face a grim mask of concern and worry. Behind him, the diving officer anxiously waited beside the console that controlled their buoyancy, while the navigator stood at the nearby plotting table intently immersed in his charts. Beckoning Anderson to join him at the weapons console was the XO.

"How did the loading of those torpedoes go, Ensign?"

Anderson made certain that the top portion of the console was lit by three green lights, indicating that the Mk-37's were ready to fire, before responding, "All went smoothly, sir. Did you have any luck in Sonar?"

The XO shook his head. "Negative, Mr. Anderson. We hit them with an active ping that could be heard all the way back to Murmansk, yet they didn't show the least bit of recognition. We even rigged up an underwater telephone, and transmitted our instructions for them to ascend in Morse code. Their only reaction was to hit us with active themselves, and our sonar operators are still in pain from the intensity of the deliberate sonic lashing."

"So I guess that leaves us with only one alternative," observed Anderson gloomily.

The XO looked down at his watch. "I'm afraid so, Mr. Anderson. At last report, that Russian trawler was less than fifteen minutes away from crossing into our quarantine zone. We've got a carrier task force up there ready to intercept them. But they'd be like sitting ducks if the November decided to offer some resistance. That leaves us no choice but to take some immediate action. The captain's hoping to hit them with a glancing shot off their stern that will force them to ascend with a minimum amount of damage and loss of life."

Anderson was well aware that though the captain's intentions might have been good, such an attack would be extremely difficult to carry out. If one of their torpedoes was to hit the November class vessel, there was no telling what kind of damage it would cause.

Of course, of equal concern would be the manner in which the Soviet sub would react once it realized that it was being fired upon. Surely they'd launch an attack themselves. Certain that the XO was considering this very same scenario himself, Anderson looked up when a deep voice broke in from the other side of the control room. "Lieutenant Wilkins, based on the last sonar readout, what kind of target solution can you give me?"

The XO efficiently checked the target data computer and replied, "The solution is excellent, Captain. We're ready to fire upon command."

Anderson watched as the captain turned to address the communications officer. "Mr. Avila, are you absolutely certain that all hailing frequencies are open, and that Command has a free channel to reach us should they so desire?"

The communications officer was quick with his

answer. "Our comm buoy is functioning perfectly, sir. Our direct channel with COMSUBLANT remains open, yet there's been no traffic since their last transmission a quarter of an hour ago."

With this, Anderson looked down to his own watch, and saw that in less than ten minutes time the Russian trawler was due to penetrate the U.S. quarantine zone. He thus wasn't surprised when he heared the captain bark, "Mr. Anderson, prepare to fire tubes one and six!"

Hardly aware of the XO's protective presence beside him, Ted turned to face the fire control panel.

"Open torpedo doors!" ordered the captain.

"Opening torpedo doors," repeated the weapons officer, who noticed a slight trembling in his right hand as he reached out to activate the switches that would accomplish this task.

Still finding it hard to comprehend the harsh reality of his current circumstances, Anderson did a double take when the row of green lights that would indicate that the torpedo bay doors had successfully opened failed to activate. Beside him, the XO also noted this disturbing fact, and he immediately reached over to trigger the toggle switches himself. When this failed to show results, he quickly turned to the captain and said, "Skipper, we show a continued red light on torpedo door activation!"

A look of total disbelief crossed the captain's face as he cried out passionately, "You've got to be kidding me, Mr. Wilkins! Reset that trigger mechanism and try it again!"

Though Ted Anderson was quite capable of handling this procedure, he didn't dare interfere with the XO as he tore open the console to carry out the captain's instructions. The sickening scent of burning electrical wiring filled the air as Wilkins removed the cover plate and peered inside.

"Christ, the entire circuit is frying!" exclaimed the XO. "Hand me that fire extinguisher, Ensign, before this mess gets totally out of control."

Anderson's pulse was beating madly as he vainly searched for the extinguisher, which he eventually found mounted at the base of the console. His hands were shaking badly as he pulled the pin out of its nozzle and directed it toward the smoking circuit box. A geyser of bubbling white dry chemical retardant soon had the fire under control, yet the captain seemed far from satisfied.

"This fiasco is inexcusable!" cried Abbott, who was quick to join them at the weapons console.

The XO's face was blank with disbelief. "It must have happened during our refit."

"I don't give a damn about your excuses, Mr. Wilkins! I'm not about to let this all-important mission fail because of a damn technical blunder. Get your keister down into the torpedo room and open those doors manually if you have to. Whatever it takes, I want results, and I want them now!"

The captain's face was red with rage and Anderson was genuinely relieved when the XO briefly caught his glance and glibly commented, "Come on, son, we've got some work to do."

The two were in the process of leaving the attack center when the excited voice of the communications officer cried out behind them.

"They've turned back, Captain! The Soviet trawler

is acknowledging the quarantine zone, and Command is ordering us to break off our engagement and return to Key West at once!"

A sigh of relief was shared by all as this news was ingested. This included the captain, who caught the intense stare of his XO and coolly commented, "Lieutenant Wilkins, I would like to see you in my quarters."

Then, without another word spoken, Captain Abbott lowered his head and strode quickly out of the control room.

The XO shook his head and spoke softly so that only Anderson could hear him. "It's times such as these that I really believe in that divine man upstairs. We came so close to the brink, so damn close."

Still shaking his head, he took off in the same direction as the captain. With the two senior officers now absent, the control room filled with anxious chatter as the men took a moment to vent their tensions.

Ted Anderson put the event into its proper perspective as he briefly surveyed the fire-control console. Most of the panel was still coated with the white fire-retardant chemical and appeared oddly out of place. Still contemplating the XO's parting words, he dared to think what the world would be like if the torpedo launch hadn't failed. If their attack had been a successful one, mankind might have tumbled over a precipice it could never hope to return from.

Chapter Two

The Present

Twelve nautical miles due north of Norway's Nordkapp Peninsula, the Elint ship USS *Turner* wallowed in the icy Barents Sea. Since arriving in the region six days ago, the handpicked crew had fought a constant battle with the harsh elements. Plagued by seasickness and frostbite, the one-hundred-and-sixty-man complement went about their daily duties with a minimum of complaints. This included those hardy seamen whose responsibility it was to keep the 455-foot long vessel's superstructure free of ice, for such an accumulation not only interfered with the dozens of sophisticated antennas specially fitted to the *Turner*, but could readily capsize the ship as well.

Seaman First Class Judd Shannon was born and raised outside of Duluth, Minnesota, and had always prided himself in his adaptability to cold weather, yet until the *Turner* arrived at its current position, he realized he never really knew the true meaning of the word cold before. As a junior communications specialist, it was up to him to keep the ship's sixteen-foot-wide dish antenna clear of icy debris.

He was about to begin his second trip topside in the last three hours. Bundled in a double-thick fur-lined parka, with drawn hood and thermal gloves, he looked like a creature from another planet as he turned to face his khaki-clad shipmates, seated comfortably at their consoles.

"Well, good buddies, it's icicle time once again. Are you sure that none of you want to join me? You don't know what you're missing."

"We'll take your word for it, Judd," replied one of the technicians.

"Don't forget to use your lifeline," added a petty officer. "Because if you go overboard out here, we'll be picking you up with a pair of ice tongs."

Though this remark was meant to be facetious, Judd knew that his shipmate was right. One slip and he'd be dead from exposure before he knew what hit him. Sobered by the thought, he took one last breath of warm air before unlatching the forward hatchway and slipping outside.

He walked down the unheated interior passageway with quick, full strides. The way he figured it, the quicker he completed the job at hand, the quicker he'd be able to return inside. Just knowing that it was Sunday and that the mess would be serving fried chicken and mashed potatoes shortly put a new spring into his twenty-one-year-old step.

He reached the exterior hatchway just as the ship was engulfed by a massive swell. The force of the breaker sent the *Turner* canting hard on its side, and

Judd blindly grabbed out for a nearby handrail to keep from tumbling over. The deck beneath him quivered, and the entire ship seemed to tremble as the vessel struggled to right itself. It seemed to take forever before it did so. Only when the deck beneath him had completely stabilized did he unlatch the hatch he stood beside and duck outside.

The cold hit him like a hard slap across his cheek. Having originated in the nearby Arctic icefields, the winds gusted with a constant intensity, and wind chills up to fifty degrees below zero were a common, everyday occurrence. His specially designed clothing barely countered this chill, and it was an effort just for him to breathe.

Back home in Minnesota, he was constantly outdoors. Even the harshest of blizzards never seemed to stop him. Yet this cold was different. It stung his skin and permeated his very bones.

After pulling down his woolen face mask, Judd checked his lifeline. The sturdy canvas tether was wrapped tightly around his waist, and he clipped its buckle onto the ice-encrusted handrail that was mounted beside the passageway he desired to traverse. Only after making absolutely certain that the connection was secure did he begin his way forward.

He tried to adjust to the roll of the ship beneath him, but the swells were arriving in irregular sets and slowed his progress. One particular wave hit the *Turner* with an unusual amount of force and its spray soon had him soaked. Within seconds the seawater turned into a solid sheet of ice.

As Judd carefully inched his way forward, he found himself questioning his rash decision to volunteer for this mission in the first place. For the last six months, he had been comfortably stationed in the Mediterranean, where the weather was warm and the scenery magnificent. Why anyone in his right mind would choose his current billet was unfathomable.

Yet Judd knew very well that it was the dynamic personality of the CIA recruiter who had interviewed him back in Naples that had convinced him to sign up. He had always been a lover of espionage stories, and when the opportunity to participate in such an operation presented itself, he was unable to resist.

A vicious gust of wind hit him full in the back, and because of the icy footing, it took a supreme effort to remain standing. Cursing his circumstances, he looked up at the gray Arctic twilight.

Unlike the spy novels that he had read as a teenager, during his brief tenure with naval Intelligence he had made no exotic ports nor met any gorgeous women. If anything, intelligence gathering was downright boring. Most of their time was spent huddled in the radio room monitoring the Soviet air waves. Since he spoke little Russian, most of these transmissions were completely unintelligible. He seriously doubted this was the case for the intelligence operatives back home, for shortly after these signals were intercepted by the *Turner*, they were beamed back to Washington for expert analysis.

Judd was currently headed toward the satellite dish where these captured signals were being projected homeward. Located on the deck above, he had to utilize a ladder to reach it. This portion of his precarious journey was extremely dangerous. As he reached the base of this ladder, he clipped his tether securely onto the handrail and took a deep breath to concentrate his thoughts. The icy air stung his lungs, but with a vision of a platter of steaming-hot fried chicken and mashed potatoes in his mind's eye, he began his climb.

Judd was halfway up the ladder when the *Turner* encountered yet another series of massive swells. Hanging on to the rungs of the ladder for his very life, he felt the ship suddenly surge upward. This was followed by a sickening downward plunge as the ship tumbled into the bottom of the trough that had previously lifted it toward the icy gray heavens. A tremor of energy coursed through the protesting hull, and for one frightening moment, Judd's grasp faltered. Only his canvas tether kept him from falling altogether.

Like a pendulum, he hung from the waist, swinging to and fro while the ship tried to stabilize itself beneath him. Strangely, the possibility of death never really crossed his mind as he struggled to right himself. Filled with the will to live, Seaman First Class Judd Shannon instead focused his thoughts solely on his continued survival. In such a way, he was able to hook the ladder with one of his feet. This eventually allowed his gloved hands to make solid contact also, and seconds later he was upright once again. Ignoring his pounding heart, he quickly scrambled up the rest of the ladder.

It felt good to have some solid footing beneath him, even if the passageway was completely covered with ice. Grateful to have his immediate goal within sight, he climbed yet another small ladder that gave him access to the satellite dish he was risking his life to attend to.

Three hours ago, when he had last visited this portion of the ship, he had left the dish totally clear of ice. The way it looked now, he could barely recognize it.

Judd used a fire axe to free the ice from the antenna's base. He welcomed the hard physical labor, for it allowed him not only to get his mind off his recent brush with death but to get his blood circulating as well. Thus, by the time he completed clearing the base, he was hardly aware of the extreme cold.

Because of the delicate nature of the dish itself, he returned the axe to its storage mount, removed a two-and-a-half-foot-long steel pick, and chipped the rest of the ice away from the rest of the sixteen-foot-wide circular structure.

He completed this task quickly, and turned from the antenna only after spraying its surface with de-icer. Hopefully this process would keep the system operable for at least another couple of hours, when the process would have to be repeated. Fortunately for Judd, he would most likely be snugly tucked away in his berth cutting z's by then.

The trip back below deck proved to be uneventful. The largest of the swells seemed to have passed, and he gratefully climbed into the interior passageway with a minimum of bumps and bruises. Even though this portion of the ship was not heated, the walls served to block out the incessant gusts of Arctic air, and the temperature was more comfortable. When he eventually did reach a heated passageway, it almost felt sweltering.

Sweat lined his forehead by the time he returned to the radio room. Manned by at least a dozen operators at all times, the compartment was usually bristling with activity. Yet this time as he sauntered inside, the place was as hushed as a church. Lit by the red lights of the consoles, the technicians were hunched over their receivers, as a mournful, somber symphony blared forth from the elevated speakers. Wondering if the guys weren't trying to pull some kind of scam on him, Judd cleared his throat and greeted them boisterously. "Shit, do you mean to say that I've been out there freezin' my balls off to clear that damn satellite dish, while you guys sit in here, snug as a bug in a rug, listening to the symphony? Now I ask you, is that fair play?"

Little was he expecting the tense response that flowed out of the mouth of the chief petty officer. "Cool it, Shannon! And, by the way, this isn't any ordinary symphony. It's a funeral dirge, and it's being broadcast simultaneously over every radio and television station in this portion of the Soviet Union."

"A funeral dirge, you say?" quizzed the puzzled seaman. "Who in the hell died?"

Seemingly in answer to this question, the voice of a commentator could suddenly be heard over the somber music. It was apparent that his shipmates had been anxiously awaiting this speaker, for all gave him their full attention until he finished speaking. Judd could only translate a small portion of this rapid discourse and had to rely on the Chief to explain just what was going on.

"My God, Premier Ivanov's been assassinated! And just wait until Washington learns they're blaming his death directly on us!"

A sigh of concern spread among the men, and only then was Judd certain that this wasn't just a bizarre hoax formulated for his behalf. Still clothed in his parka, he listened as the dirge continued to blare forth from the speakers and could only wonder what the Soviet Union's next course of action would be.

Approximately fifteen hundred miles to the southwest of the Nordkapp Peninsula lay the Ural Mountains. Stretching in a vast chain from north to south, the Urals were the symbolic dividing line between the European and Asian influences that comprised the unique Soviet character. Beyond their strategic importance, the ancient mountain range abounded with minerals, lumber, and a variety of wildlife. Fat trout spawned in the crystal clear streams, while bear, elk, deer, and bighorn sheep roamed its slopes. It was this last species of animal that called Alexander Gnutov back to the woods of his childhood.

The forty-nine-year-old career naval officer grew up outside the city of Sverdlovsk, where his father was a game warden. It was on his thirteenth birthday that Alexander's father gave him his first rifle and then took him into the same section of forest that he was currently traversing for his first hunt.

Even though that outing seemed to have occurred in another lifetime, merely walking the wilderness trails once again reawoke long-lost memories. Fortunately civilization had yet to take its toll here, and the solid stands of pine and oak were still intact. Yet, as he drove down to the village of Beloreck, where he had begun his journey on foot two days ago, he had seen the encroaching logging camps and knew that it was only a matter of time before they reached these woods.

He was presently following a narrow dirt trail through a particularly ancient stand of massive evergreen pines. The Belaja River surged nearby, and Alexander could clearly hear its current smashing its way downstream. A raven cried in the distance, and when a warm gust of wind, sweet with the scent of the forest hit him full in the nostrils, the veteran submariner found his thoughts far away from those of his professional duty. He was on the trail of the elusive bighorn sheep and would need to focus his entire attention solely on this quarry if his hunt was to be successful. An expert stalker learned to block out all outside stimuli and mentally become the animal that he wished to pursue. This was a secret his father had taught him thirty-six years ago, and was one he had never forgotten.

Alexander readjusted his backpack when the footpath began to steepen. A series of switchbacks took him out of the forest of pines and through a zone of twisted oaks. The air was noticeably warmer here, and for the first time since leaving his campsite, he began feeling the effects of his hike in his back and legs. He was certainly no child anymore, and decided it was time to take a break.

A fallen oak trunk served as his picnic bench as he removed his pack and pulled out his lunch. He had purchased his provisions in Beloreck. His simple repast consisted of half a loaf of pumpernickel rye bread, a wheel of tangy yellow cheese, and a ripe green apple. He washed the peasant's feast down with a long cool drink of spring water.

No sooner did he reshoulder his pack when a covey of quail strolled out from beneath a nearby blueberry bush. Several of the birds were plump adults, and would make a tasty dinner. Alexander momentarily grasped the padded case in which his rifle was stored before remembering that it was an altogether different quarry that had called him here. Watching as the birds waddled off into the protective confines of the surrounding underbrush, he rose to continue his hunt.

The trail climbed quickly now, and soon the oaks were replaced by thick clumps of brush and various rocky outcroppings. The temperature continued to rise, for there were no more tree limbs to block the blistering sun that shone from a glorious, cloud-free blue sky.

He was well up onto the slopes of Mount Beloreck, and as such was approaching the habitat of the bighorn. To acclimatize himself to the altitude, he momentarily halted, and after carefully scanning that portion of the rocky summit that still lay above him, turned to reexamine the valley that he had just emerged from.

A glorious landscape met his eyes. As far as he could see, a sea of green growth stretched to the horizon. The ancient forest seemed to be a single entity as the gusting wind caused its branches and leaves to sway in unison. The Belaja River was just visible, cutting its way through the floor of the valley itself. Its blue current rippled a frothing white where its meander was interrupted by a fallen boulder.

Feeling remarkably relaxed and at peace with himself, Alexander let his thoughts wander. With his gaze still locked on the wilderness valley, he pondered what had taken place in his life since his last visit to this overlook over three decades ago. At that time he had been a child, escorted into the forest on the hand of his father. Who would have dreamed that only two years later his father would be lying dead in his coffin, the tragic victim of a logging accident? Utterly stunned by his first real encounter with mortality, Alexander soon found himself being whisked off to Moscow to be raised by his uncle Dmitri. The move proved to be a wise one, for the capital city was truly a wondrous place that helped divert his thoughts away from those of grieving.

Dmitri was his father's older brother, and a university professor by trade. He had little practical knowledge of the woods, so he had introduced Alexander to the fascinating world of academics instead. Only an average student to that point, Alex learned how to use a library, and as his reading skills improved, so did his marks.

Science and mathematics were his favorite subjects. With his uncle's prompting, he enrolled in the Frunze Higher Naval School in Leningrad, where his interests expanded to physics, chemistry, and engineering. Graduating number one in his class, his next stop was the prestigious Grechko Naval Academy. His expertise in nuclear physics brought him to the attention of the academy's director. This former submarine captain recognized his potential and was primarily responsible for directing Alex into the Soviet sub force.

A long, gratifying career had followed. Starting off as a junior officer aboard a November class vessel, he gradually worked his way up through the ranks. All his efforts were rewarded three years ago, when he was finally given his own command. His ship, the *Kirov*, was presently docked near Murmansk, where it was being refitted. One of the Motherland's most sophisticated attack submarines, *Kirov* was a technological marvel, and it was a supreme compliment that the authorities had chosen him to command it.

Sincerely sorry that his father had not lived to see how he had turned out, Alex sighed, and angled his line of sight upward into the blue noon sky. Gusting on the thermals was a huge golden eagle. Easily one of the largest birds of prey that he had ever viewed, Alex wondered what the valley looked like from this perpetual hunter's lofty vantage point. Suddenly aware again of his own purpose here, Alex took one last appreciative look at the eagle before turning to reinitiate his climb.

An hour later, he came across evidence of a most exciting nature. The sheep droppings lay on the side of the trail, appearing to have been recently deposited. Though he still failed to actually spot the animal responsible for these feces, he nevertheless removed his rifle from its case and prepared it for firing. He was using a German-made Heckler and Koch 7.62mm hunting rifle that had a Zeiss 2.5-10 x 52 scope mounted upon its barrel. The weapon was purchased in East Germany, while Alex's sub was making a rare Baltic Sea port stop. Until this occasion, he had only used it on the firing range. Certain that it could do the job on live game as well as it had done on targets, Alex rammed a bullet into the firing chamber and removed the scope cover.

The trail curved upward and he cautiously pushed his way forward. As he slowly rounded a broad, bush-covered bend, he sighted a thick copse of oaks in the distance. The trail seemed to be headed toward this thicket, and Alex instinctively halted and fell to one knee. He put the stock of his rifle to his cheek and utilized the scope to thoroughly survey the tree line. He excitedly froze halfway through his scan, for perched beside a gnarled oak trunk was a magnificent white-fleeced ram. The curl of its horn was surely trophy size and Alex licked his lips in anticipation of a relatively easy kill.

To get within range he had to crawl on his belly. Luckily the trail was mostly free of obstacles, and he was able to progress with a minimum of rock bruises and thorn cuts.

The bighorn's attention seemed occupied on a disturbance taking place on the other side of the woods. When Alex reached the position he had originally sought to attain, he flicked off the rifle's safety, took a deep breath, and put the stock to his cheek. Similar to the view from a submarine's periscope, he aligned the cross hairs of the powerful Zeiss lens on an area of the sheep just below its neck. Then he ever so delicately pulled the trigger.

There was a thundering explosion, and as Alex rammed another round into the chamber, he realized that he could save this second bullet, for the ram had fallen dead in its tracks. The report of his shot was still echoing in the distance as he rose to claim his hard-earned prize.

It was at the exact moment Alex sprang to his feet that he spotted a mammoth brown object lumbering out of the distant tree line. Understanding now what had been most likely distracting the bighorn while he made good his approach, Alex identified this beast as a full-grown brown bear. Oblivious to Alex's presence, the shaggy, nine-foot-tall carnivore headed straight for the slain bighorn.

This was the Navy officer's first encounter with such a legendary beast in the wild and he couldn't help but be impressed. Yet if he wanted to claim the ram as his own, he would have to intervene quickly before the bear beat him to it.

With his rifle cocked at his side, Alex stepped forward and screamed out at the top of his lungs, "Get out of here, Pasha!"

Suddenly aware that it was not alone, the bear halted in its tracks and rose on its haunches. Its immense size was now clearly displayed as it peered down at Alex and menacingly pawed the air with its razor-sharp claws.

The Ural brown bear was no animal to take lightly. Alex remembered that his own father had had several encounters with such beasts, one of which he had to hunt down and shoot after it had killed a young camper. Today it was officially an endangered species, and, as such, intentionally shooting one of the creatures was against the law. Yet here on the slopes of Mount Beloreck there were no wardens to arrest him as he raised his rifle and centered its scope on the bear's forehead.

Alex hesitated a moment before pulling the trigger. Taking in the bear's enraged red eyes and snarling muzzle, he took a second to ponder the classic stand-off in which he was involved. For here were two predators, fighting over the spoils of the hunt, like creatures had done for millions of years. In a way it was a bit pitiful to have to eliminate such a magnificent beast, yet the same laws of nature that had guided their species' different evolutions also ensured the bear's eventual demise. Man was the dominant species of the planet now, and creatures such as the brown bear were doomed to extinction.

Not about to be denied his prize, Alex breathed in a deep breath and fingered the trigger. A millisecond away from finishing off the beast, an alien, hollow chopping sound suddenly distracted his attention. Searching the skies for its source, he soon picked out a tiny green object approaching the ridge on which he stood from the north. He knew in an instant that it was a helicopter and that it had come for him.

Alex turned back to the tree line in time to see the brown bear disappear into the forest with his bighorn clamped securely in its muzzle. Tempted to go into the woods after it, he reluctantly returned his gaze to the sky when the roar of the helicopter's engines intensified.

The vehicle was a Mil Mi-8 utility craft. It sported an elongated fuselage and a chin-mounted radome. The grind of its five-bladed rotors was almost deafening as it hovered over the ridge and slowly descended.

The rugged ground was too sloped for it to land,

yet it was able to hover some fifty meters above the ground while a harness was lowered from the main cabin. Though Alex was forced to strip off his backpack, he made certain to take along his rifle as he slipped on the shoulder-mounted harness device and soon found himself being abruptly yanked skyward.

Much like the golden eagle he had encountered earlier, he was able to briefly observe the earth from this unique vantage point. But the downdraft increased to a torrential velocity as he neared the helicopter's fuselage, and he was forced to close his eyes to shield them from the stinging gusts.

A pair of strong hands grabbed him by the shoulders and he was thus transferred inside. The interior of the helicopter was completely stripped, except for a single bulkhead-mounted bench. The pilot's cabin was separated by a partition, and Alex turned to face the fellow who had pulled him in.

"Captain Alexander Gnutov, I presume," greeted a helmeted figure in a green jumpsuit. "Welcome aboard."

"How in the hell did you ever find me?" said Alex, who had to practically scream to be heard over the rumbling engines.

The attendant pointed to a bulky, telescopelike device set beside the fuselage door. "Infrared scanners. From the reading I was getting, it seems you had some company down there. Whatever it was, it sure put out a hell of a lot of radiant energy."

"You don't know the half of it," replied Alex as he carefully laid his rifle on the floor next to the bulkhead. "Where are we off to anyway?"

"Sverdlovsk," answered the attendant. "From

there you'll be catching a shuttle jet bound for Moscow along with the other bigwigs."

Puzzled by this reply, Alex probed. "What's the occasion?"

A look of sudden awareness dawned in the young soldier's eyes. "That's right, Comrade. You've been out camping these last couple of days and haven't heard the news. General Secretary Ivanov was assassinated yesterday morning while he was on his way to the Kremlin. If we can get you back to Sverdlovsk in time to make that shuttle, you should be arriving in the capital in just enough time to catch his funeral."

Alex was clearly staggered by this revelation. "Why that's horrible news, Comrade! Have they caught the bastard responsible?"

The attendant shook his head. "At last report, he's still on the run. But the KGB is almost certain that he was sent by the CIA."

"I should have known the Americans would be involved!" spat Alexander disgustedly. "Premier Ivanov was a great man, and his death must not go unavenged!"

Pure anger flavored these last words as the veteran naval officer peered out the open hatchway, barely noticing the thick canopy of forest that stretched out to the horizon beneath them.

The Ilyushin jet carrying Captain Alexander Gnutov and several hundred other high-ranking military officers and governmental bureaucrats touched down at Moscow's Seremetjevo Airport a little after 6:30 P.M. The two-hour flight was a somber one, and the late spring sky was tinged with dusk when Alex exited the giant airliner and entered a specially reserved terminal. Waiting for him was a familiar, white-haired figure, smartly dressed in the distinctive blue uniform of a Soviet admiral.

"Good evening, Alexsi," greeted the old-timer discreetly. "I'm sincerely sorry to have had to call you back from your well-deserved leave, but I had no choice."

"I understand, Admiral," replied Alex as he followed the elder man over to the observation window.

The huge, four-engined jet that Gnutov had arrived on was clearly visible before them, as seventy-seven-year-old Viktor Chimki, former director of the Grechko Naval Academy, continued, "It's all like a nightmare come true, Alexsi. And to think that I was actually in the premier's office, waiting for him to arrive so that we could begin our daily intelligence update session, when the news arrived of his death. Needless to say, I was shocked into speechlessness!"

Well aware of the sincerity of this remark, Alex patted his mentor on the shoulder. "I felt likewise when I heard the news only a few hours ago. Is it true they've yet to capture the assassin?"

Staring blankly out the window, the admiral nodded. "At last report, he was still loose on the streets of the capital. The militia's been called out to help with the search, while the KGB has sealed off all the exits out of town. We'll find him eventually, even if we have to search every single building in Moscow."

"The rumors say that it was a CIA operation," continued Alex. "Has that fact been substantiated?"

"Who else could have dreamed up such a dastardly plot?" the white-haired veteran observed bitterly. "It's all too obvious the Americans were behind it. And we'll prove it for certain once we have their man in custody. Meanwhile, we have the all-important task of choosing a new leader to concentrate on. The politburo will be meeting this evening, immediately after the memorial service that will take place inside Lenin's mausoleum. In fact, I have a limousine waiting for us outside to convey us to Red Square so that we can participate in this grievous ceremony."

"Thank you for including me," said the junior officer.

"I wouldn't have it any other way," replied Chimki. "Besides, I must admit that I have ulterior motives for having you here. With Ivanov's passing, the moderates within our government have vastly strengthened their position. As you well know, our premier had been a great friend of the military. He understood and supported our position. When the deceptive Americans presented their infamous comprehensive nuclear weapons ban last month in Geneva, he saw it for the sham it was and wisely turned it down. The moderates were furious at the time, and swore to do their best to override Ivanov's decision. I shudder to think what may occur if they're able to elect one of their own as our new leader."

"Surely they're in no position to do so," countered Alex.

Chimki turned to meet the junior officer's gaze. "I sincerely wish I could agree with you, but I'm afraid I

52

know differently. Naval intelligence has just relayed a shocking report that I'm sure you'll find most sobering. Two days ago, Yakov Rosenstein, the leader of the moderates, rendezvoused with a senior CIA agent in Moscow's Sokolniki Park. It's believed the purpose of this clandestine meeting was to finalize the details of a daring plan, whose ultimate goal was the removal of Premier Ivanov from office. In such a way Rosenstein and his traitorous cohorts would steal the reins of government and place a CIA-picked lackey in our great leader's place.

"Unbelievable as it may seem, the first portion of this dastardly scheme has been carried out. By the grace of fate, our agents learned of the plot, giving us a single chance to intercede before the rest of the conspiracy is finalized. If the CIA is successful, they will have won World War III by firing just a single shot!"

The elder man's voice was trembling with emotion as he looked up to make certain they were still alone. Satisfied that the empty terminal guaranteed their privacy, he continued. "It is my belief Premier Ivanov's untimely death was nothing short of an act of war by the spineless Americans. The members of the defense council agree with this supposition, and have instructed me to implement the following plan to guarantee the Soviet Union's continued autonomy.

"Since it's only a matter of time before the assassin is rooted out and captured, and the whole world knows of America's treachery, the council wants our strategic forces in a position to take advantage of the public outcry that will inevitably follow.

"As commander of the Soviet Union's most

sophisticated attack submarine, we are counting on you, Alexsi, to be an integral part of our response. You will do so by returning to Murmansk immediately after the memorial service is concluded. There you will join your shipmates, who have also been called back from their leaves. The *Kirov* will then put to sea with a single purpose—to escort the ultimate revenge platform into America's very backyard."

"Are you referring to the Caspian, Comrade?" asked Alex, who was surprised by his mentor's emotional discourse.

"That I am, my friend," beamed the admiral triumphantly. "The Motherland's newest Typhoon class submarine is more than ready for its first patrol. It's currently being loaded with twenty SS-N-20 Sturgeon ballistic missiles. Each of these solid-fueled rockets will be carrying nine MIRVed nuclear warheads, with a range of over eight thousand kilometers. By positioning it off the southern coast of Cuba, near our secret base at Cienfuegos, we will be able to take out targets all over the western hemisphere in a matter of mere minutes. And total revenge will finally be ours to savor!"

Genuinely astounded by the scope of this plan, Alex said, "I thought the *Caspian* had been designed to exclusively patrol beneath the Arctic? Why even bother sneaking it into the Caribbean when it can take out these same targets from the Barents Sea?"

The old admiral's eyes lit up as he answered, "Your observations are most astute, Alexsi. But you fail to comprehend the all-important point that we're trying to convey with this unprecedented mission. Sure, we could merely send the *Caspian* into the waters beneath the Arctic ice pack and threaten the imperialists thus. But just think how much more dramatically we'll prove our point when the *Caspian* suddenly ascends from the silent depths only a few hundred miles from the American coastline. Their population will be horrified, just as they were when they learned of our halfhearted attempt to station nuclear missiles in Cuba in 1962. You should remember those black days particularly well, Alexsi, for if I'm not mistaken, you were in the midst of your first submarine patrol at the time, aboard the November class vessel, *Kalinin*.

"Didn't we swear afterward we'd never put ourselves in such an embarrassing position again? For Krushchev was attempting to posture the Motherland while we were in a position of military weakness. The Americans knew this very well, and their daring quarantine succeeded.

"Today the tables have turned. After decades of selfless sacrifice, it's the Soviet Union that holds the upper hand militarily. Yet with one idiotic treaty, the moderates are willing to negate our efforts. No matter the risks, we must not allow this to happen! So you will escort the *Caspian* into the Caribbean, and once the true identity of the assassin is revealed to the world, we will be able to revenge not only Premier Ivanov's death, but the Cuban missile fiasco as well!"

Though Alex still did not fully comprehend the admiral's logic, he nodded in agreement. "Very well, Comrade. I will do as ordered."

"That's what I wanted to hear," replied Chimki, who next looked at his watch. "I'll be able to rest more easily just knowing you're out there to ensure that the *Caspian* gets to its patrol station undetected. Now, it's time we got going. The service begins in an hour.''

Taking a final look at the massive airplane he had just arrived on, Alex turned from the window as his elderly host beckoned him onward. There was a spring to the old admiral's step that didn't coincide with his advanced age, and the forty-nine-year-old naval captain was forced to lengthen his own stride to keep up with him.

They rapidly crossed the empty terminal, and Alex was aware of a slight tightness in his legs. Having completely forgotten about the strenuous hike he had been in the midst of when he received this abrupt call to duty, he momentarily visualized his last view of the giant brown bear as it victoriously dragged his prized ram off into the tree line. Wondering if the beast had yet consumed the entire carcass, he ducked out a doorway and spotted the admiral's shiny black Zil limo parked beside the curb.

Chapter Three

Since intercepting the radio transmission informing them of the premier's death, the men of the USS *Turner* had been in a state of constant alert. Breaks were cut to a minimum, and even their mealtimes were shortened, as every piece of listening equipment stored within the 455-foot-long Elint ship's hull was turned toward the Soviet Union, in an effort to determine exactly how the Russians were reacting to the tragedy.

For Seaman First Class Judd Shannon, this alert couldn't have come at a worse time. He had been promised more hands-on training on the various encrypting devices. The chance of being qualified on such sophisticated equipment was one of the reasons he had signed up on the *Turner*, yet because of current circumstances, his services were needed elsewhere. As the junior rating currently on duty in the radio room, he was being utilized as a messenger. Because of the top-secret nature of much of the information they were handling, the *Turner*'s sound-powered telephones couldn't be trusted to relay this data securely and Judd was personally sent to the desired party, with a locked brief holding the coded message. His availability depended upon whether or not he was on de-icing duty topside. This uncomfortable task was still his top priority.

Judd was well into his shift, and had just returned from his second visit above deck in the last four hours. Because of the unstable situation inside the Soviet Union, it was extremely important to keep a clear channel open at all times between the *Turner* and Washington and thus Judd was ordered to make absolutely certain that the satellite dish was completely free of debris before stowing the pick and returning below deck.

Since his near brush with death earlier, the sea conditions had improved markedly. The swells had died down, and, as the winds lessened, even the outside temperature seemed more accommodating. Yet Judd still welcomed the steaming mug of hot chocolate that was awaiting him as he ducked into the radio compartment and stripped off his thermal jacket.

"Why, it's almost hospitable up there," observed the Minnesota native between sips of his drink. "As long as that wind is absent, it's not that much different than home."

"Yeah, but do you pick up this kind of crap on your radio back there?" returned the seated technician. "You should just hear this incessant Commie babbling. Their commentators barely stop to catch their breath."

"Sounds like an ex-girlfriend of mine," jested Judd

as he sat down beside the technician to observe his console more closely.

The receiver was a massive piece of equipment, extending all the way up to the compartment's ceiling. It was loaded with various digital readouts and filtering mechanisms, and had a single, large black-plastic frequency knob set in its center, within easy arm's length of the operator. A reel-to-reel tape recorder was constantly running above this dial, with a headphone jack located close by.

"What are you listening to?" quizzed the curious seaman.

"It's the voice of Murmansk," replied the technician, picking up an auxiliary set of headphones and handing them to Judd. As he put them quickly to his ear, he winced as a loud burst of static emanated from the phones. This was followed by an alien electronic tone that was delivered in choppy, staccatolike bursts.

"Don't sound like any radio station that I ever heard," observed the puzzled seaman. "In fact, to me it almost sounds like Morse code."

Surprised by this observation, the technician reached forward and clipped on his own headphones. He intently listened for a second before pivoting and calling out loudly, "Hey, Chief, we're picking up that weird signal once again!"

Quick to his side was a burly black petty officer. Without asking, he ripped off Judd's headphones and put one of the padded speakers up to his ear.

"Shit, that's the same one all right," he reflected. "I could have sworn that I've heard a similar racket once before. That one precluded the appearance of one of their strategic missile-carrying submarines."

"Then that noise is coming from a Russkie boomer loaded with nuclear warheads?" assumed Judd.

Ignoring the startled seaman, the petty officer scratched his forehead. "Though I'm still not certain that this transmission means that a boomer has just set sail, I'd better share it with the captain. Seaman Shannon, if you've still got control of yourself, I want you to take this message up to the skipper at once."

Embarrassed by his unintentional outburst, Judd alertly stood. "I'll do so at once, sir!"

The petty officer scribbled out a dispatch, and not bothering to stow it in a brief, folded it and handed the note to Judd. "Whatever the captain's doing, make certain that he reads this immediately!"

Judd saluted and stormed out of the radio room with this single mission in mind. Just knowing that the strange signal he had heard with his own two ears could be coming from a nearby Soviet submarine, and a boomer at that, put extra spirit in his step. He sprinted down the covered passageway, climbed an interior ladder, and proceeded straight to the bridge.

The *Turner*'s blond commanding officer was seated in his leather upholstered swivel command chair sipping a cup of black coffee and staring out an ice-encrusted porthole to the muted Arctic twilight beyond when Seaman Shannon approached him from behind.

"Excuse me, Captain, but Chief Blakely wanted you to see this at once, sir."

The eager seaman handed the dispatch to his

60

commanding officer and politely stepped back to await a response. It seemed to Judd that the captain took forever to put down his coffee cup, unfold the note, and then read its contents. For some reason Judd was relieved when the *Turner*'s senior officer anxiously sat forward and called out forcefully, "Mr. Goodson, what do you make of this?"

Judd looked on as the ship's executive officer strode over to read the dispatch that he had just delivered.

"I think the Chief could be on to something, Skipper," observed the XO. "Blakely's been at this game long enough, and his instincts are good."

"I agree," said the captain. "If it's that new Typhoon they've been preparing for patrol, it's probably headed due north, for the cover of the Arctic ice pack. Yet just to be certain that they don't try to sneak it into the North Atlantic, let's drop our towed variable depth sonar array. If this signal means they've just set sail, and they just happen to be heading for the GIUK gap, then we'll be right on top of them."

As the XO turned to relay this order, Judd contemplated the captain's words. He knew very well that, because of the Soviet Union's serious lack of warm water ports, their main naval units were forced to transit several well-known choke points when wanting to reach the open ocean. For their Northern Fleet based outside Murmansk this meant penetrating the strait of water separating Greenland, Iceland, and the United Kingdom, or, as it was known in the trade, the GIUK gap.

"Sailor, inform Chief Blakely that he has my

permission to transmit the data he mentioned back to base," instructed the captain.

Judd alertly nodded. "Aye, aye, sir. I'll tell the Chief that he has your permission to transmit."

Pivoting smartly, Judd left the bridge to deliver the captain's response. He always felt extra special when visiting this portion of the ship. Though he doubted that the captain even knew his name, it was invigorating just to be close to him. His say was gospel on the *Turner*, his power all inclusive.

Proud to be part of his team, Judd headed straight for the exterior passageway that would offer him the most direct route to the radio room. He ducked through a hatch, and was in the process of turning to his left when a man roughly grabbed him from behind. Shocked by the abruptness of this move, Judd struggled to free himself, yet found his arms pinned tightly behind his back.

"Hey, what's the idea?" cried the seaman, who assumed that he was once again the victim of a perverted prank. "Ease up, man, that hurts!"

"Shut up!" ordered a deep, gravelly voice from his rear. "Take us to your captain at once or we will kill you."

These words were pronounced with a heavily accented Slavic flavor, and Judd sensed trouble. Again fighting to free his arms, he vainly protested, "What the hell are you talking about? If this is your idea of a joke, then you must really be sick."

"This is no joke, Comrade. That I can guarantee you."

The man responsible for these icy words stepped before him, and Judd took in a muscularly built figure dressed in a black wet suit who had a lightweight machine gun draped over his shoulder. The stranger's ruggedly handsome face sported a thick black mustache, and Judd was certain he wasn't a member of the *Turner*'s crew.

"Do you understand me, Comrade? I said to take me to your captain!"

Whoever was pinning back Judd's arms increased the pressure of his hold as if to emphasize this command, and pain shot through the junior radio technician's body.

"Who are you, and why do you want to see the captain?" managed Judd defiantly.

"Vladimir, dispatch this fool," instructed the stranger.

Almost instantaneously, another wet-suited figure showed himself in front of Judd. This one had cruel blue eyes and a long scar extending all the way from his wide forehead to his square jaw. Pure ecstasy seemed to flavor his evil expression as he pulled a long, serrated commando knife from his waistband and held it menacingly against the hollow of Judd's throat. Sensing that the man meant business, Judd's nerve faltered.

"Easy now, mister, I hear you. The captain's on the bridge. Put away that knife and I'll take you to him."

A satisfied gleam sparkled in the mustached commando's eyes. "That's more like it, Comrade. But I'm warning you now, no tricks! Vladimir here takes to surprises very badly."

Nodding that he understood, Judd attempted to turn back toward the hatchway he had just stepped through before being accosted. He was able to do so only after the individual holding him from behind let go of one arm. Keeping the other in a tight hammerlock, Judd heard him whisper something in what sounded like Russian.

"He said go on!" translated the mustached commando, who appeared to be the leader.

Hesitantly, Judd did so, all the while softly whimpering, "I don't know what the hell is going on here, but I sure hope that the captain can make some sense out of it."

His captors remained silent as Judd led them onward. Conscious of the squeaking sound their wet, rubberized boots made on the metal deck, he crossed into the passageway that led to the *Turner*'s command center. His pulse was madly beating away in his chest by the time he reached the bridge's hatch.

"The captain's in there," revealed Judd shamefully.

He heard the men behind him snicker as their leader stepped forward. "Well done, Comrade. Now just act natural, and no one will get hurt. Open up the hatch and enter as you normally would. And no foolish heroics!"

Judd swallowed heavily and did as he was told. Pushing open the watertight door with his free hand, he stepped over the threshold and proceeded to the *Turner*'s bridge. He would never forget the scene that followed.

First to spot him was Lieutenant Commander Goodson, the ship's executive officer. By the initial look on his face, the XO seemed to be questioning what Judd was doing back on the bridge so quickly. Then the wet-suited commandos stormed into the room. There appeared to be five altogether. Four of them grasped lightweight machine guns, while the fifth still held on to Judd's arm.

The captain was still seated in his command chair when he spotted the intruders. He seemed to have been caught completely off guard by their sudden appearance, and as he swung around to question them he knocked over his half-filled mug of coffee. Cursing as the hot brew spilled onto his lap, the *Turner*'s senior officer ignored his own physical discomfort as the mustached leader of the commandos stepped forward and introduced himself.

"Good afternoon, Captain. I am Lieutenant Kazan of the Fifth Spetsnaz special forces detachment, and it is my solemn duty to place both you and your crew under arrest for the crime of violating the territorial waters of the Union of Soviet Socialist Republics."

"Nonsense!" retorted the enraged captain, who stood to plead his case. "We're a good two miles from your waters, so get the hell off my bridge, and put an end to this act of piracy at once!"

A smirk painted Lieutenant Kazan's face as he held his right hand out and snapped his fingers a single time. Without a second's hesitation, one of his associates sprinted over to the helm where he pushed away the American who had control of the ship's wheel. Then with one eye on the compass, the Russian began swiftly turning the brass steering mechanism until their bow pointed due south.

"I beg to differ with you, Captain," reflected Lieutenant Kazan sarcastically. Pausing a moment to look down at his watch, he continued. "As I see it, these are Russian waters that you're currently trespassing on."

"Cut this crap, Lieutenant!" shouted the red-faced American captain. "I don't know what the fuck you hope to gain by this lunacy, but if it's war you want, it's war you'll get. Lieutenant Commander Goodson, get these intruders off my bridge immediately!"

The XO seemed to have been waiting for this order, and as he stepped forward to carry it out, the commando who had been holding Judd suddenly let go of the enlisted man's arm. The relief was instantaneous, and Shannon decided that he could best redeem himself by trying to help the XO out. Yet no sooner did he make a move to join Goodson when the deep voice of the commando leader boomed out forcefully, "Halt this second, you fools, or you'll force me to bloody the deck!"

The XO seemed to ignore the command as he made an awkward attempt to rush the commando who stood nearest him. Sensing that the XO would never succeed with this valiant attempt, Judd looked on in horror as the scar-faced commando called Valdimir raised the short barrel of his machine gun upward and pointed it toward the XO.

"No!" screamed the Minnesota native as he rushed forward to disrupt the Russian's aim just as the commando squeezed the trigger. A deafening blast followed, and the bullets that had been intended for the XO sliced into Judd Shannon's midsection. As the gunsmoke cleared, the young sailor's blood-soaked body could be seen lying on the deck, his limbs madly twitching in the last throes of a horrible painful death.

"See what your foolishness has caused!" observed Lieutenant Kazan bitterly. "It was never our intention to harm your men, Captain. But you gave us no choice. So surrender this ship at once, or others will needlessly die also."

In no position to argue otherwise, the *Turner's* commanding officer relented. "You may stand back, Lieutenant Commander Goodson. I'll have no more of my men share Seaman Shannon's fate."

Turning to face Lieutenant Kazan, the captain added, "Now that you've added cold-blooded murder to your list of crimes, what do you intend to do to us next?"

The mustached commando rapidly replied, "You will immediately cut the power source to your radio receivers and transmitters. Then you will raise your variable depth sonar array and inform your crew that this ship has been impounded by the peoples of the Union of Soviet Socialist Republics. And you must emphasize that they offer us no resistance or I swear to you that they'll die like miserable flies."

There was a pained look on the captain's face as he momentarily met his XO's grim stare and hesitantly nodded. "If it will keep my men alive, I'll do what you ask. But as the Lord is my witness, you're going to pay for this in the end! Why in the hell are you even attempting such a foolhardy stunt?"

Oblivious to the American's question, the Spetsnaz leader stepped aside and pulled a portable walkie-talkie from the waterproof pouch slung over his shoulder. Placing the recessed microphone to his lips, he hit the transmitter and spoke out in rapid Russian. "Commander Gnutov, this is Kazan. You are free to proceed. Good hunting!"

*   *   *

It was the shrill ringing of his bedside telephone that awoke Secretary of the Navy Peter Anderson out of a dead sleep. His hand reached the receiver halfway through its second ring. With his eyes still closed, he put the phone to his ear and mumbled groggily into its transmitter. "Anderson here."

"Pete, it's Red Sutton," returned a familiar male voice. "Sorry about the early wake-up call, but we've got a black-flag alert on the *Turner*."

With this revelation, Anderson's eyes popped wide open and he could see from the soft yellow glow of the digital clock that it was 3:07 in the morning. "Hang on, Red. Are you at home? . . . Good. Let me get right back to you over the secure line in my study."

With this he hung up the receiver and sat up. Beside him, Betty barely stirred. As a veteran Navy wife, she was used to such calls and had long ago learned to pay them little attention.

Without putting on his slippers or robe, Anderson stood and padded noiselessly out of the bedroom. He made a quick stop in the bathroom to relieve himself and pour some cold water on his face before continuing on to his study.

The book-lined room had a most comfortable feel to it as he flicked on the lights, shut its paneled doors, and switched on the electric coffee percolator that Betty had filled the night before. Then he went straight to his desk, where he picked up the red plastic telephone handset and hit the second button of its automatic dialer. Seconds later, a voice on the other line answered, "Sutton."

"Red, it's Pete. Now what's this about the *Turner*?"

The chief of naval intelligence efficiently answered, "It all started late last night, when they failed to transmit their prescheduled position report. Such delays happen occasionally, and are mostly attributed to the adverse atmospheric conditions up there. Yet when they neglected to contact us on the back-up frequencies, we began to get worried. Because of the sensitive nature of their current mission, a Key-Hole was nudged out of orbit to see if it could locate the ship from space. It did so on its second pass, and showed the *Turner* being escorted into Murmansk by two Soviet Krivak class frigates."

"You've got to be kidding me!" observed Peter Anderson. "Are you certain that this ship was the *Turner*?"

"Absolutely, Pete. I just saw the pictures myself. The weather was clear and there can be no denying that she's ours."

Anderson hesitated a moment before continuing. "Maybe they've had a mechanical breakdown of some sort. Both of us know that the seas up there can be brutal."

"Then why no SOS?" retorted Red Sutton. "With all that radio gear they're carrying, surely they would have had the opportunity to inform us of any difficulties long before the Soviets arrived to help out."

"Speaking of the devil, Red, what's Ivan got to say about all this?"

The intelligence chief nervously cleared his throat. "This is the really strange part, Pete. When we queried the commander of their naval forces on the matter, the Soviets disavowed any knowledge of the matter. I bounced this off State, and they had a bit more luck. As you very well know, things are a bit of a mess in the Kremlin right now, yet a high-ranking member of the Soviet Defense Ministry was eventually contacted. Though he wouldn't outwardly admit they had the *Turner*, he did imply that they had some knowledge of the vessel. He promised to release an official communiqué at 6:00 A.M. our time.''

"That's one Soviet bulletin I sure don't want to miss," returned Anderson, who was already considering a worst-case scenario. "I sure hope that we don't have another *Pueblo*-type incident on our hands, Red."

"My thoughts exactly, Pete. I was stationed at Sasebo in '68, and was one of the first to hear Bucher's SOS. All of us are still trying to live down that fiasco.''

"I hear you, Red. Pull out all you can on the *Turner*'s current commanding officer. I realize that the CIA was involved in their mission as well, so I'm also going to need to know more about the ship's purpose and exactly what kind of extra gear they were carrying. If the Reds manage to get hold of one of our Q-35 decoders, we're really going to be in a hell of a jam. Meanwhile, I'd better get on the horn with the Joint Chiefs, and then the President's national security adviser. I think that it's best to prepare them for the worst, before that Soviet communiqué is released in a couple of hours.''

"Aye, aye, Pete. Talk to you shortly.''

Disconnecting the line, Anderson momentarily stared off into space, pondering the disturbing news he had just received. Though he prayed that it was only a serious mechanical breakdown that caused the

Turner to be on its way to a Soviet naval facility, his instincts warned otherwise.

As a thirty-year veteran of naval intelligence, Peter had learned long ago to trust his intuition. Now he was serving his country in another capacity as the secretary of the Navy. Though his current position on the President's cabinet had primarily bureaucratic responsibilities, his years of firsthand naval experience had given him an excellent overview of operational matters as well. Besides, he still had loyal friends in the service, such as Red Sutton, who kept him informed of the latest-breaking worldwide developments often before even the President was briefed.

Lately, he had been particularly fascinated by the events going on inside the Soviet Union. Premier Ivanov's untimely death had come as a complete surprise, as had the allegations that soon surfaced implicating the CIA with his assassination. Peter was positive that such suspicions were totally without substance. Yet since the killer had still not been caught and interrogated, the wild rumors still persisted.

This gave the military hardliners within the Soviet politburo just the type of excuse they needed to try to wrest the reins of government away from more moderate elements. And if such individuals had been successful in their attempt to gain control, perhaps the forced capture of the *Turner* was their way of getting even with the United States.

Anderson shuddered to think what would happen if this was indeed the case. If it was learned that the *Turner* had been taken in international waters, the

Joint Chiefs would be crying to move in and recapture it, and rightfully so.

One thing that he had learned in his years of military service was that, more than anything else, the Soviets respected strength. If the United States didn't react quickly to the *Turner*'s capture, the Russians would attempt such acts of piracy elsewhere, until America finally woke up and stood up for itself.

Of course, the President would still be hesitant to immediately play the military option if it was learned that the Elint ship had been illegally seized. Conscious of the political turmoil that was rampant in the Kremlin as a result of Ivanov's death, he would proceed most cautiously. Most likely he would follow Kennedy's example in 1962, when the dynamic young President first learned of the Soviet missile installations on Cuban soil. At that time, his military advisers had practically begged Kennedy to react with both a massive saturation bombing of the sites and a full-scale invasion of Cuba. Cautiously determining his options, the President chose the less confrontational approach of a quarantine. Since Peter Anderson had personally been in Key West at the time, and saw for himself the full extent of the military preparations there, he knew very well that a major war had been averted. But would the United States be so lucky this time?

Anderson anxiously stirred with this thought, and turned his attention to his cluttered desk, where a framed photograph sat behind the stacks of file folders and books. Clearly visible there, standing on the bridge of a submarine, was a handsome, blond naval officer, dressed in the khaki uniform of a captain. Though this middle-aged figure could easily have been his own twin in much earlier days, it instead belonged to his nephew Ted. Peter had never had a son of his own, and when his brother died in a tragic accident, the elder Anderson had adopted Ted and practically raised him.

Like his father, Ted chose to serve his country in submarines. He had only recently made full captain, and not only had a secure career before him but an attack sub of his own to command as well. Though this vessel was soon to be retired, Ted was talented and bright, and would all too soon have another ship to skipper.

As a proud uncle, who only just happened to be the secretary of the Navy, Peter fought the natural temptation to get involved with his nephew's work. But fortunately Ted was able to take care of himself, and Peter could stay clear of having to interfere on his behalf.

The one thing that he couldn't control, though, was the fragile state of the world's political climate. If this was indeed to be a time of increased tension between the United States and the Soviet Union, then as a submariner, Ted would all too soon be directly involved in the resulting conflict, for it was beneath the world's seas that the two superpowers flexed their political muscles, in a constant, perilous game of cat and mouse at fifty fathoms deep.

It proved to be the rich scent of perking coffee that diverted Peter's attention away from the photograph of his nephew. Quickly checking his watch, he turned to pour himself a cup of the hot brew and then got on with the series of all-important phone calls that awaited him.

Dawn was just breaking over the nation's capital when the USS *Swordfish* cast off from its tender and plunged into the cold black waters of San Diego Bay. From the top of the sub's sail, two officers scanned the fog-enshrouded sea, anxiously searching for any surface objects that might have escaped their radar.

The taller of these two figures was a twenty-six-year sub veteran, who had a close-cropped mop of thick blond hair and a tight, muscular physique. For Captain Theodore Anderson this patrol had special significance, for with its conclusion the USS *Swordfish* would be stricken from the ranks of the U.S. fleet, to be converted into a nautical museum in Galveston, Texas, which was their final destination. Anderson had many fond memories of the sub he presently guided past the muted lights of Point Loma, for not only had he been its skipper for the last one and a half years, but he had also made his very first patrol on the *Swordfish* twenty-six years ago. He had been but a raw ensign at that time, much like the recent sub school graduate who stood on the bridge beside him.

"Are you feeling any better now?" quizzed the captain, who still noted a greenish tint to the ensign's skin.

"I'm still a bit queasy, but I can handle it, sir," returned the neophyte submariner.

The two-hundred-and-ten-foot keelless vessel rolled in a heavy swell as the captain added, "That puss pad that the XO put behind your ear will do the trick soon enough. But don't worry, it's only like this when we're on the surface, and I can guarantee you that we won't be up here much longer."

"I can hang on until we go under, sir. But I still can't understand why this came about. In all my life, I never got seasick before."

Anderson stifled a chuckle. "Believe me, Ensign, it happens to the best of us."

Staring back into the fog, Anderson remembered well his first encounter with the sailors' nemesis called seasickness. He had also been on his very first patrol, and had come down with the uncomfortable ailment shortly after they received the orders sending them back to Key West. Unfortunately for him, those were the days before such medicinal wonders as puss pads were introduced, and he had learned to control his nausea the old-fashioned way—by puking his guts out.

The fog momentarily cleared, and the captain was able to get a clear view of his ship's rounded, teardrop-shaped hull as it bit into the surging Pacific waters. From his current vantage point, the *Swordfish* looked sleek and deadly. Not a single patch of rust showed on its blackened deck, and the captain found it hard to believe that the vessel was almost three decades old. Surely she still had some punch left. Yet it was a new era of high technology and nuclear power, and the diesel-electric propulsion system of the *Swordfish* didn't fit in with the modern Navy's future plans.

Evidence of the rapidly passing years of a radically different nature suddenly showed itself when a white-headed figure abruptly emerged from the sail's floor-mounted hatchway.

"Permission to join you on the bridge, Captain?" quizzed this veteran newcomer gruffly.

"Why of course you can join us, Admiral Abbott. Though I hope you're wearing a jacket. It's a bit nippy up here."

"You're starting to sound just like my wife, Ted," returned Rear Admiral William Abbott as he climbed up into the sail. "If that woman's not nagging about dressing warm enough, it's something else. You know, sometimes I wonder if it was such a good thing to retire when I did. At least when I was on patrol, I got to do all the complaining."

Anderson grinned. As one of the first captains of the *Swordfish* in 1961, William Abbott had been invited along to share in this final cruise. Though it meant giving up his stateroom, Anderson genuinely welcomed the old-timer's presence. As his own first commanding officer, Abbott had taught Anderson many an invaluable lesson in the true meaning of leadership. He applied much of this knowledge today, and would be forever grateful to the veteran submariner, who at one time in his early career Ted had actually despised.

"Now, son, that's no way to hold your binoculars. Raise your elbows out away from your body and you won't cut off the circulation to your hands."

While the white-haired veteran shared his expertise with the sub's newest member, Theodore Anderson once again grinned. Abbott seemed no different today than he had twenty-six years ago. Still able to fit into the same size uniform that he had worn at that time, the only noticeable difference in his physical makeup were the lines that creased his neck and eyelids and the fact that his thick brown mustache and eyebrows were now pure white.

"One thing that hasn't changed through the years is this damned southern California weather," reflected Abbott. "I still can't figure it out. A couple of blocks inland from the base it was as clear as can be. Why, I could even see the stars. Yet now, just look at it."

"We won't have to be dealing with this fog much longer," returned the captain. "I'll be taking us down as soon as we reach the two hundred fathom line."

Fondly patting the side of the sail, Abbott sighed. "You know, I sure missed this old tub. The moment I climbed aboard her, it was just like I had never left. I was even half expecting to see my old crew waiting for me below deck.

"I still think that the Navy is making a big mistake by forcing the *Swordfish* to retire. Her hull and engines are sound, and she's got at least another decade worth of life left in her. And who in the hell are they going to get to play the role of the enemy in those fleet exercises? The Reds have several hundred diesel-electric boats in service, and someday we might just have to take them on."

"It's certainly the end of an era," reflected Anderson.

"It's more than that," retorted the admiral. "This cruise signals the final victory of the nukes. For better or for worse, the Department has made its choice, and now we're just going to have to pray that it's the right one. If you ask me, we're putting too much trust in

77

technology. It's still going to be cunning and basic seamanship that our men are going to have to resort to when it comes down to winning naval battles. I haven't met a computer yet that can defeat a solid hull and a crew of well-trained, gutsy men."

Nodding in agreement, Anderson's response was cut short by the activation of the intercom.

"Captain, it's the XO," broke in a deep voice from the mounted, waterproof speaker. "I think you had better join me on the double in the radio room."

Surprised at the brevity of this request, Anderson responded, "I'm on my way, Lieutenant."

Before turning for the hatch, Anderson briefly addressed his esteemed guest. "I'll leave the lookout team in your capable hands, Admiral."

"Don't worry, Captain. These old eyes are still in pretty decent shape, and, besides, it's too damn penetrating up here to fall asleep on duty."

Laughing at this remark, the captain climbed down the ladder and entered the control room. Here almost every system on the fifteen-hundred-ton vessel could be controlled and monitored. He passed by the periscope well, and briefly glanced at the two planesmen, who were perched before their aircraft-style steering wheels. Behind them was the sub's Master Chief, whose current station was at the diving console. The current officer of the deck was standing halfway between the navigator's plotting table and the ship's radar unit.

"How's it look, Lieutenant Ridgeway?" questioned the captain rapidly.

"The fog looks solid all the way past San Clemente Island, Captain. So far the only surface units that we have to contend with are a bunch of tuna boats, located a good seven miles southwest of us."

"We should reach our diving point long before they become a hazard," replied Anderson. "Notify me the moment we have two hundred fathoms beneath us. Meanwhile, I'll be aft in radio."

"Aye, aye, sir," shot back the present OOD, who was also the vessel's weapons officer.

Satisfied that his crack crew could handle the ship, the captain crossed through the rest of the attack center and began walking down a cramped, cable-lined passageway. The sub's gyroscope passed on his right, with the tiny cubicle reserved for the vessel's office directly opposite it. The supply officer could be heard inside, busily typing out a memo.

Just before the passageway led to the curtained wardroom, it brought him to his desired destination. This all-important portion of the *Swordfish* was protected by a vaultlike door that was kept locked at all times. Only the senior radio technicians, the XO, and the captain had the lock's combination and could gain entry. An aftereffect of the John Walker spy incident, Anderson deftly dialed the proper series of numbers into the tumbler, pulled the heavy door open, and stepped inside.

The compartment was filled from floor to ceiling with banks of sophisticated equipment. Seated before a large digital console, completely absorbed in listening to his earphones, was the boat's communications officer. Behind him, studying a dispatch, stood the XO, Lieutenant Commander Stan Pukalani. The likable Hawaiian had been with Anderson for half a dozen patrols. He was extremely efficient,

79

could handle the men, and could be relied upon when the going got tough.

"Wait until you get a load of this, Skipper," greeted the Maui native. "We received it seconds before I called you down."

He handed the dispatch to the captain, who quickly skimmed it. Originating from COMSUBPAC, it was a Defcon 2 alert, indicating that Soviet-U.S. relations were extremely tense and that an actual shooting war could break out at any possible moment. Since serving in the Navy, Anderson had only experienced one other similar alert, and that was during the Cuban missile crisis. So he was well aware of the seriousness of their current situation.

"I wonder if this has anything to do with Ivanov's assassination," reflected the captain.

Before his XO could express his own opinion, the seated communications officer pushed back his headphones and spoke out excitedly. "I've got it, sir! The CBS morning news from San Diego."

Suddenly aware that the captain had joined them, he sat up straight in his chair and reached forward to depress a toggle switch. Almost instantaneously, a distant, static-filled voice broke from the room's elevated speakers.

"Again, to repeat our top story of the morning, the Pentagon reports that a U.S. Navy intelligence ship, the USS *Turner*, with two hundred and ten officers and enlisted men on board, was infiltrated by elements of the Soviet Armed Forces and subsequently forced to make port at the Russian naval facility at Murmansk. The Soviets are insisting that the *Turner* was engaged in espionage activities and was illegally violating Russian territorial waters. The Pentagon denies these allegations, and is insisting that the *Turner* and its crew be immediately released. An emergency session of the National Security Council is currently under way at the White House.

"General Roland Vessey, chairman of the Joint Chiefs of Staff, has already called this incident one of the greatest threats to world peace in the last three decades. General Vessey is on the record as urging the Soviets to free the *Turner* before the U.S. military is forced to take the initiative.

"America's NATO allies are reacting to the *Turner* incident with equal alarm . . ."

Signaling that he had heard enough, the captain looked on as the senior radio operator switched off the receiver. Catching the serious stare of his XO, Anderson curtly commented, "Maybe this last patrol of the *Swordfish* won't be so routine after all!"

Chapter Four

St. John, U.S. Virgin Islands

The trade winds blew in stiff hot southerly gusts as Delbert Hall, his younger brother Egbert, and their friend Stanley Wilkes climbed up the steep mountain trail. Thick stands of native manchineel, cordia, and sea grape surrounded the three teenagers, who were on their way from the nearby Hall residence to their self-proclaimed, private clubhouse on the hillside above. The trio had been gathering at this isolated spot since they were youngsters. It provided a secluded location, far removed from the nearest adult. Here they could listen to their music, smoke ganja, and rap to their heart's content without the fear of being disturbed.

An enormous bush of bright scarlet bougainvillea indicated that their goal was close, and Delbert increased his long fluid stride. In the pouch that he carried at his side was a fresh ounce of marijuana, or ganja as it was more commonly called in the

Caribbean. One of his Rastafarian friends in Cruz Bay had just brought it back from Kingston, and he couldn't wait to try out the legendary Jamaican pot.

Leading the way up the narrow trail that was little more than a goat path, Delbert passed by a stand of bird of paradise and spotted a single hummingbird sipping the nectar from one of the blossoming orange flowers. Yet he didn't dare stop to study the tiny, yellow-winged bird more closely, even though it was one of his favorite species of wildlife on the island. For he could only think of the magical golden herb that awaited his ingestion. Seconds later, he spotted the familiar trunk of the bearded fig tree at whose base their camp was located.

The site that he was soon entering was once a bustling sugar mill factory complex. Reminiscent of an ancient European castle, the thick-walled buildings had been constructed out of cleverly fitted stone, native coral, and yellow Danish ballast brick over two hundred years ago. Today only the bases of these structures remained intact.

Three plastic beach chairs, appropriated from one of the island's luxury resorts, were set up against the clearing's southernmost wall. Here, beneath the shade of the multi-branched fig tree, they gathered.

Egbert had been delegated to carry their bulky ghetto-blaster. The Japanese-made cassette player was one of their most cherished possessions, and Egbert carefully placed it on a shaded shelf of smooth coral and popped in a tape.

As the melodious reggae sounds of Bob Marley and the Wailers' "Legend" wafted through the air, Delbert got down to work. Seating himself on one of

83

the deck chairs, he reached into his pouch and pulled out a plastic baggie filled with marijuana, and a well-broken-in corncob pipe.

A satisfied gleam sparkled in Delbert's black eyes as he opened up the baggie and took an appreciative sniff. "Ah, my friends, it's pure nectar."

"I sure hope that this so-called Jamaican gold is as good as it's cut out to be. It certainly cost us enough," observed Stanley, who lay down in the deck chair located next to Delbert's lounger.

"Just you wait, Stanley Wilkes, this stuff is going to put you in Rastafar heaven," returned Delbert, whose light brown coloring, long braided dreadnoughts, and black mustache gave him a striking resemblance to the man whose voice emanated from the cassette player.

As Delbert proceeded to load the bowl of the pipe, his brother walked over to the three-foot-high rock wall that their chairs faced and looked out to inspect the southern horizon. It was a clear, cloudless morning, and the crystalline-blue waters of Coral Bay beckoned in the distance, with the Caribbean Sea stretching endlessly beyond. A mammoth, sleek cruise liner could be just seen steaming out of the Sir Francis Drake Passage from the northeast. Most likely bound for Charlotte Amalie, capital of the nearby island of St. Thomas, the white-hulled vessel seemed to cut effortlessly through the surging seas.

The distinctive, pungent scent of burning ganja met Egbert's nostrils, and he turned around in time to see his brother take a deep draw from the pipe. A broad grin etched Delbert's face as he held the smoke down in his lungs and passed the pipe over to

Stanley. By the time Egbert got a hit, his brother was exhaling a long ribbon of smoke out of his flared nostrils.

"I tell you, my friends, it's heaven on this earth!" observed Delbert ecstatically. "I told you that it would be worth the price."

Egbert remained standing and handed the pipe back to his brother. Meanwhile, Stanley emptied his lungs of smoke and broke out in a fit of coughing.

"Shit, that stuff's potent!" he managed between gasps of air.

"Shut up and smoke, Stanley Wilkes," directed Delbert, who repacked the pipe, lit its bowl, and took yet another massive hit before passing it on to his seated friend.

Egbert could already feel the effects of the ganja as he sat himself down on the edge of the wall and stared out to sea.

"Maybe I should reconsider Father's offer and become more involved with the business," dreamily reflected the youngest of the Hall boys. "He's worked hard to develop it, and with all the tourists pouring in, the rental car agency might finally start to pay off."

"Bullshit!" retorted his brother. "Pop's been toiling like a slave for five long years already, and what does he have to show for it? We all know that he doesn't stand a chance now that the big agencies like Avis and Hertz have moved into Cruz Bay. If he had any sense, he'd sell out now, before he gets even deeper in debt."

"But what about Pop's plan to contact the stateside travel agencies and put together package tours of the island?" countered Egbert.

"They're more of his pipe dreams, little brother. When are you going to wise up and see our old man like he really is? Have you forgotten already about the sandwich shop, and then his failed T-shirt venture? Why, I'll guarantee you that he's lost more money than he's ever earned."

Egbert took another hit on the pipe and handed it back to his brother. "At least Pop's trying," he offered after exhaling the pungent smoke. "The way I look at it, the only way to make some money around here is off the tourists. And since most of them are going to need a car if they really want to see St. John properly, the agency is bound to make a profit eventually."

"I agree with you that tourism is the only way to make the really big bucks around here," returned Delbert. "But it's never going to happen renting cars."

"Do you know of a better way?" questioned Egbert defiantly.

"I say move to the mainland," dreamily slurred Stanley, who held the pipe firmly in his lap. "In Miami or New York, a guy can make a real fortune in a matter of days. And I hear the chicks there are real stone foxes!"

"Shut up, Stanley, and quit hoggin' the dope," replied Delbert. "Have you already forgotten about Lionell Thomas? He had that same fool idea, and where did it get him? Why, the last I heard of him, he was rotting away in some prison in Florida. No, we're island people and we belong down here. So, since it's agreed that we're staying on St. John, let's look at this tourist situation from a different perspective."

"Oh, no, I hear that devilish tone in your voice again, Del," observed Stanley as he lazily reached forward and transferred the pipe to Egbert. "What's it going to be this time? Your last scheme to sell admission tickets to the tourists who wanted to visit Salt Pond Beach almost got us all thrown into jail. I hope you've come up with something better than that one."

Gazing out to sea, Delbert's line of sight focused in on the sleek white cruise ship that was almost directly opposite them now. "I certainly do, my friends. Although why I ever bother sharing my genius with you two ungratefuls, I'll never understand. What does the name Sam Lord mean to you?"

Stanley looked on dumbly as Egbert set the pipe down on the stone ledge that he had been perched on and replied, "Do you mean Sam Lord the pirate?"

"One and the same, little brother." Then, turning to face Stanley Wilkes, Delbert continued. "To you illiterates, Captain Sam Lord was an infamous eighteenth-century Caribbean swashbuckler who was based out of Barbados."

"What's a swashbuckler?" interrupted Stanley.

A look of disbelief crossed Delbert's face as he answered his stoned friend, "That's a pirate to you, Stanley. But regardless, Sam Lord terrorized shipping in this region. His band of cutthroats were responsible for plundering dozens of European-bound ships that were loaded with New World gold and silver.

"One of the tricks Lord pulled to lure these

treasure-laden ships into his trap was to move the signal beacons placed to mark dangerous reefs. Many an unwary captain fell for this ruse, and Lord was said to have amassed a great fortune."

"Are we going to go treasure hunting?" guessed Stanley.

"In a manner of speaking," shot back Delbert, who pointed out to sea. "In today's world, cruise vessels such as that one are the modern equivalent of the treasure ships of old. Their holds are filled with hundreds of rich tourists, loaded with cash and jewelry. So what if we were to follow Sam Lord's example and cause one of those vessels to run aground? Then we'd merely have to board it, and untold treasures would soon be ours for the taking."

Though Stanley seemed to be seriously considering this thought, Egbert didn't appear to want anything to do with it. "You've got to be joking, brother. This isn't the eighteenth century! How do you propose to dupe an experienced crew with an assortment of high-tech navigational gear at their disposal?"

Turning to face the straits that the ocean liner had just penetrated, Delbert responded, "Easy, little brother. Don't let all of that high-tech crap fool you. Benjamin Smith spent a whole summer working on one of those ships, and from what he says, half the time the captain and his first officers don't even have anything to do with the actual running of the boat. Why, one time they actually let ole' Ben steer the ship while the entire deck crew went out to get coffee!

"Now you all know the location of that reef that lies right alongside the Anegada Passage, where all those St. Thomas-bound cruise ships pass at least once a week."

"Do you mean Lucifer's Seat?" Egbert quizzed.

"That's the one, little brother. Pop used to take us up there fishing, where all those old wrecks are rumored to be.

"Well, if I remember correctly, there's a large floating beacon moored to the seabed there, to keep the sea traffic clear of the reef. All we'd have to do is relocate it a couple of hundred yards away, and then just pray that some green-horned deckhand is at the helm next time a liner passes. We'll be on and off before they know what hit them, with a fortune that will last a whole lifetime!"

An expectant smile turned the mouth of Stanley Wilkes, while Egbert shook his head cautiously. "I still don't know, Del. It sounds awfully dangerous to me. And what if the ship actually sinks?"

"No way, little brother. Those hulls are as thick as battleships. The coral will only hold them up a little while, giving us just enough time to lighten their load, with nobody getting hurt in the meantime."

It was evident that Egbert was still no fan of this scheme, and his brother reached out for the pipe and relit it. Handing the smoking ganja back to Egbert, Delbert pleaded, "Well, at least keep your mind open to my plan while I work out the details."

Egbert ingested a full lungful of smoke and stared out to the blue Caribbean, where the cruise ship was just initiating a broad turn that would take it to St. Thomas. While pondering the assortment of wealthy passengers that currently plied the decks of this vessel, a high-pitched female voice suddenly sounded in the near distance.

"Delbert! Egbert! Are you two lazy good-for-nothings up there?"

"Oh, shit, it's Mama!" observed Delbert as he reached out to pocket the pipe and his bag of ganja.

Seconds later, a plump black woman wearing a loose-fitting, one-piece cotton smock appeared on the clearing. She was sweating profusely and vainly attempting to stop the flow of perspiration streaming off her forehead with a soaked red bandanna.

"I thought that I'd find you shirkers up here!" she greeted between gasps of breath. "And there's no use for you to try hiding that reefer. I can smell that crap practically all the way back at the house. Now why aren't you two down at the lot helping your father with his cars like you promised? After all, as long as you still take shelter under his roof and eat at his table, it's your duty to give the poor, hardworking man a hand once in a while."

"We were going to stop down at the garage right after we left here," lied Delbert.

"Like hell you were," shot back his mother, who suddenly spotted the prone figure of Stanley Wilkes, lying on the lounge chair that was positoned beside her eldest son. Staring wide-eyed up into the sky, oblivious to the commotion going on around him, Stanley appeared to be in a world all of his own.

Mrs. Euphemia Hall disgustedly shook her head. "Oh, good Lord, just look what you've managed to do to poor Stanley! And to think that I just came from church, where his mother and the reverend were talking about how they hoped Stanley would take that summer counseling job. The way he looks now, he won't be sober till fall comes."

Bob Marley could be heard in the background wailing on about the plight of the Buffalo Soldier as Mrs. Hall scanned the ruins of the sugar mill. "Well, at least you didn't drag your sister in on this. Have either of you seen Myrtle?"

It was Egbert who answered her. "Myrtle left the house long before we did, Mama. I'll bet you anything that she's up at her hounfour."

Hearing this, a pained expression crossed Mrs. Hall's face. "I should have expected as much. I still don't know what horrible sin I committed in my past life to warrant such worthless children, but Lord knows it must have been a despicable one. Here I have two boys who are reefer addicts, and a daughter who thinks she's a voodoo priestess."

Looking high up into the heavens as if to console herself, Euphemia grasped the golden crucifix that hung around her sweat-stained neck. Mumbling a brief, silent prayer, she looked down and caught the eye of her youngest son.

"Be a good boy and go and get Myrtle for me, Egbert. Tell her that I need her to help me with the food for tonight's church social."

Then, turning to her oldest boy, her tone sharpened. "And you, Delbert Hall, will make certain to get Stanley out of this blazing sun and down to his house. Then if you know what's good for you, you'll be off to Father's lot. That poor man's going to kill himself working that place by himself. And to think that he's got two strong boys who couldn't even care if he dropped dead right in his tracks. Oh Lord, give me strength!"

91

Turning in a huff, Euphemia Hall moved her dripping bulk back toward the trail she had just emerged from. Daring not to incur any more of her wrath, her sons reluctantly stood and briefly faced each other.

"Don't forget to at least think about that gem of a plan I came up with, little brother. Because I for one can't take much more of this crap!"

Egbert thoughtfully nodded and took off for the trail that would hopefully lead him to his sister. It felt good to be off on his own after the unpleasant confrontation. He knew that his mother had every reason to behave as she did. As long as he lived at home, he would have to be more sensitive to the needs of his parents.

At seventeen years of age he was aching for a life of his own. His brother was a lordly two years his senior, and had actually lived on his own for six months last year. Egbert had visited the apartment that Delbert shared with a friend in Charlotte Amalie. It had been truly wonderful to do his own thing without worrying about reporting in to his parents. Egbert hated to return to Cruz Bay, but soon even his brother was on the Red Hook ferry homeward bound, when the marine maintenance company that he had been working for went out of business.

The only thing stopping him from moving out was money. But jobs on St. John were practically nonexistent, and thus the future looked dim, unless he wanted to surrender himself to his father's business.

Cars had never really appealed to Egbert. He was

far from being mechanically inclined and despised getting grease and oil on his hands. The Suzuki Samurais that his father rented were in need of constant work, and most of his efforts at the rental lot would be under the hood. Not looking forward to a lifetime of such menial drudgery, he just knew that he had to find another career.

The one thing in life he really enjoyed was the tropical forest he was presently walking through. The trees and flowering shrubs were like old friends to him. His keen eye spotted a full-grown calabash up ahead and he took in the long, thin branches and the tight, spiraling leaves of this thirty-foot-tall giant. He knew from school that its yellow bell-shaped flowers were pollinated each night by nectar-sipping bats, which found the floral structures by echolocation. The globular fruits that resulted grew to more than twelve inches in diameter, its hard, woody shell making an excellent watertight gourd for holding liquids.

Because of his sincere interest in such things of nature, one of his junior high teachers had recommended that he take up forestry. For an entire semester he followed this dream, even volunteering to sweep out the National Park offices in Cruz Bay every evening, just to be near the rangers. Yet grim reality set in when he flunked his first course in chemistry. Soon afterward, he dropped out of school altogether and had been just hanging out ever since.

The trail began sloping upward and Egbert started to feel the effects of the climb in his thighs and the backs of his calves. His sister Myrtle made this same climb almost every day of her life. Like her brothers, she too had a special place where she liked to get off to be alone. This clearing was located on the summit of the ridge he was ascending and offered a particularly spectacular view of the bay known as Hurricane Hole.

Several of the elders said that this spot was once a holy place, where the ancestors of old used to perform their secret religious ceremonies. Knowing Myrtle and her weird beliefs, that was probably why she had chosen it in the first place.

Myrtle had been born a year after Egbert, and was peculiar even as a child. She never had any close friends her own age. Instead, she preferred the company of the elders. She particularly liked to visit Miss Sarah, a strange old lady, who lived alone in a small shack not far from this very spot.

It was said that Miss Sarah was a self-proclaimed mambo, or voodoo priestess. A teacher of the old ways, many of the locals came to her for help. She was not only an expert Dokte feuilles, or herbal healer, but also adept at calling up Erzulie, the spirit of love, and Esprit, the spirit of the dead.

Both Egbert and his brother had sneaked up to her hounfour on the night of the full moon. Her voodoo temple was located in a small clearing behind her shack, and the boys had a chance to witness her in action. At least six other adults had joined her, and they heard the pounding drums long before they spotted them. All appeared to be naked as they danced wildly around the fire-circle, madly shaking their limbs and calling upon the spirit of Legba, the so-called Lord of the Crossroads. For an old lady, Miss Sarah had seemed unusually limber, and they could have sworn that they saw her naked body dance several times through the burning embers.

It was when the drums and chanting abruptly halted that they witnessed a mystifying event that the brothers still talked about to this very day. While hidden behind a fallen tree trunk, they had watched as the celebrants fell to their knees. No sooner did they hit the ground when a ghostly figure suddenly walked out of the opposite tree line. Dressed in what looked to be a tattered white shroud, this individual slowly approached the fireside. It was only then that the boys got a clear view of his face. Both had to struggle to keep from screaming out in terror upon viewing the glowing white eyes and emaciated face of Dr. Samuel Emmaus, an elder who had died and been buried over nine months earlier!

After that horrifying evening, they kept as far away from the old lady's shack as possible. They did so even when they heard that she had died. This was not the case with their sister Myrtle, who visited Miss Sarah's former residence with each full moon, to leave a tribute of fresh-cut flowers at her gravesite.

Some subjects were best left undiscussed, and voodoo was one of them. Their mother was a devoutly religious person and felt that the old ways were pure paganism and a sure path to hell. Myrtle, of course, felt otherwise, continuing with her stubborn beliefs regardless of her mother's emotional warnings. As for Egbert, religion wasn't really that important in his life. Not a lover of stuffy churches, he felt the presence of the Creator most strongly when smoking ganja and walking through the forests of St. John.

The Jamaican reefer he had just consumed had been extremely potent. His thoughts were deep and seemed to flow forth effortlessly. Feeling at one with the woods around him, he passed through a stand of yellow elder, whose golden, trumpet-shaped buds were the national flower of the U.S. Virgin Islands, and viewed his destination beyond on the summit of a rapidly advancing ridge.

The sun was high overhead as he climbed up onto this plateau. Positioned on its southern lip was a semi-circle of stunted frangipani trees. It was in the center of this circle of pink flowering trees that he found his sister.

At first Egbert thought she was merely asleep. Myrtle lay in a tight fetal ball before what looked to be a primitive altar. He made this assumption upon spotting the flickering white candle that glowed from a protected alcove and the assortment of artifacts deposited nearby, which included a human skull, a machete with a red bandanna tied around its hilt, and various colored bottles holding herbs and viscous oils.

He cautiously approached her, and it was as he did so that he saw her eyes were wide open and that she was trembling with fear. Egbert quickly made it to her side and delicately reached down to comfort her.

"Myrtle, what in the world has happened to you? Are you all right?"

These concerned words seemed to snap her out of her trance. Her eyes adjusted their focus, and taking in the figure of her kneeling brother beside her, she weakly managed to sit up. Reaching out to hug him, she spoke to him.

"Oh, Egbert, I'm so glad that it's you! I just had an unforgettable experience. I was in the midst of my morning prayers as usual when I was mounted by the spirit of Baron Samedi himself. The guardian of the cemetery took me to the crossroads, where Miss Sarah was waiting for me. It was Sarah who explained the reason that I had been called to the realm of the undead."

Shivering in recollection of this encounter, Myrtle turned from her brother and stared vacantly out toward the southern horizon. Egbert followed her line of sight that afforded him a magnificent view of the glistening waters of Hurricane Hole. He had just spotted a single boat, floating in the center of the bay, when Myrtle began excitedly talking once again.

"Miss Sarah's eyes were formed of fire, and she floated in the air before me speaking with the deep, hoarse voice of Damballah, the serpent. She warned me that a time of great evil was about to descend upon the earth sphere. The lords of light would have a single chance to counter this black tide. A terrible struggle would ensue, and if the blackness was victorious, the earth would be burnt to a crisp in a fireball of smoke and flame.

"It will be from the sea that our savior shall come. And if mankind passes judgment, He shall triumph, and the blackness will be sent back to the cold abyss from which it crawled!"

This last statement was delivered with particularly great emotional force, and Egbert contemplated his sister's disturbing presentiment while abandoning his gaze to the crystal-clear blue waters visible before

97

him. He couldn't help but wonder when this struggle that she spoke of would take place, and what physical form this so-called savior would take, as the midday sun rose high above the surging Caribbean.

Dr. Susan Patton was heartbroken. Only minutes ago, they had come across the body of Bubbles, floating lifelessly in the calm waters of Hurricane Hole. She had been working with the likable bottlenose dolphin for over a month now, and her death caught Susan completely by surprise.

Even in death, the corners of Bubbles's mouth turned upward in a smile as Susan's research assistant, Owen, jumped off the boat's transom and began the somber task of wrapping the sleek corpse in a net. They would then drag the body back to the nearby lab, where a complete autopsy would be performed.

Susan assumed that the dolphin had either succumbed to a viral infection or had passed away from sheer loneliness. Only last week, Bubbles's mate Max had died, after smashing his head repeatedly into the walls of his capture tank. Having worked exclusively with such marine mammals since graduating from college fourteen years ago, the blond marine biologist was no stranger to the great need of captive dolphins for companionship of their own species. Even though Max was from a different herd, he had gotten along with Bubbles as if they were long-lost friends, and in no time at all they were lovers.

After he had died, Bubbles moped around the

lagoon, unresponsive to commands and unwilling to feed. In fact, she had only begun eating again just yesterday. Susan fed her the live mullets herself and took this appetite as an excellent sign. And now to find Bubbles like this was simply shocking.

"Do you want to drag her on board, Doctor?" screamed Owen from the water.

"Just hook the net up to the tow line," replied Susan. "It should hold until we get to shore."

As her research assistant nodded and got started with this task, Susan reflected on what this death meant to her current project. She was currently under contract with the U.S. Navy to develop a super lightweight dolphin-borne harness. Such a device would be used to carry a specially designed fiber optic video camera, or any number of different objects. So far, after much trial and error, they had succeeded in producing a workable prototype. Yet now that they were just about to test the harness in the open seas, tragedy had struck twice. Another animal would have to be quickly found or all their hard effort would go for naught.

The sound of lapping water diverted her attention to the rear of the small, fiberglass runabout, where her research assistant could be seen pulling himself back into the boat.

"It sure is a sad sight to see," reflected Owen, who was a twenty-six-year-old graduate student at the University of Miami. "Yet it looks like she died peacefully enough. I'll drive us in."

Susan merely nodded and continued looking toward the boat's stern as Owen walked forward to the helm. She barely noticed it when the engine rumbled alive and they began slowly moving back to shore. Instead, her somber thoughts were centered on the lifeless gray corpse that they were towing behind them.

In her years of working with dolphins, she had witnessed many a death, and none of them could be taken easily. Each time it was like losing a good friend. After graduating from the same college that Owen presently attended, Susan went to work at Miami's Sea World complex, on Virginia Key. She was employed there as the head dolphin trainer, and for the first couple of months really enjoyed her work. The amusement park had excellent facilities, and there were always an abundant number of healthy, intelligent animals to build a relationship with.

It was right after they moved a half dozen of the dolphins into a new training tank that three of them were found dead the next morniing. An autopsy showed that a flulike infection was the cause, and the survivors were inoculated with antibiotics just as a precaution.

Susan brought up the idea of holding a memorial service for the dead dolphins. Yet management balked at this idea, and instead merely dumped the dead bodies out at sea. Upset with her employer's callous nature, her whole attitude toward her job started to change. Instead of appreciating the ultra-modern facility, she started looking at it as a concentration camp, with the dolphins as its unfortunate inmates. Held in the holding tanks against their wills, the highly intelligent, independent marine mammals eventually learned to adjust to their new confines, yet not after becoming little more than trained monkeys. Forced to perform for dozens of hours each and every week, they became totally dependent upon man, and all too soon lost both the will and the ability to survive in the wild.

She quit her job soon afterward, and returned to the university as a graduate student. It was while studying there at the Institute of Marine Sciences that she made her first contact with the United States Navy.

The Pentagon was interested to know if dolphins could be used as a protective buffer to keep sharks away from either a downed pilot or a group of its underwater operatives. Susan got the funding for this project, which was completed a year later. Though the initial tests showed negative results, another Navy contract followed, and soon she was able to afford to lease her own research facility here on St. John in the Virgin Islands.

The compact, shore-line installation was only minutes away from their current location. It was built in the late sixties, by one of the first serious twentieth-century dolphin researchers, a psychiatrist who wanted to teach the marine mammals to talk. In addition to a complete laboratory, the facility had a large holding tank and its own private lagoon. It was abandoned over a decade ago, when the psychiatrist lost interest in the project upon realizing that the great breakthrough in inter-species communication that he had prematurely announced to the world's scientific community was only the sound of the dolphins mimicking the voices of their human captors.

Susan hoped to do more practical work at the facility. She was able to lease it extremely cheaply, and so far it had fit her needs perfectly. Located on the balmy southeastern shore of St. John, it was isolated enough to guarantee their privacy, but close enough to civilization to get supplies and other research materials. Yet the one item she really needed now couldn't be purchased in town. It would have to be captured somewhere out there in the Caribbean Sea.

Taking a last long look at the net carrying the corpse of Bubbles, Susan turned in time to see Owen steer the boat around the rocky point that led to their lagoon. The blue water was as smooth as glass here, and her practiced eye picked out the outline of a sea turtle chomping away on a clump of underwater vegetation. A stingray gracefully swam beneath the boat, while a pair of feisty seagulls noisily announced their arrival in the lagoon from above. Bubbles used to be particularly fascinated with these birds, watching them soar on the gusting thermals as if she were up there in the sky herself. Suddenly depressed by this memory, she moved forward to prepare the boat for mooring.

Owen expertly guided them up to the simple dock and cut the engines just as Susan jumped ashore to tie the boat to the wooden pilings.

"Can you handle getting Bubbles into the lab yourself, Owen?" quizzed the marine biologist. "I've got a headache and want to get out of this sun for a while."

"No trouble," returned her bright-eyed assistant. I'll use the winch to get her out of the water and then carry her up to the lab on the gurney."

Confident that he could handle the job on his own, Susan pivoted and began crossing the wooden-slatted dock. She headed straight for the nearby A-frame structure that doubled as her office/living quarters. It was situated on the beach beside a grove of lofty coconut palms.

Once inside the building, the relief from the broiling sun was instantaneous. Though cooled by only a single, window-mounted air conditioner, a ceiling fan helped distribute the chilled currents throughout the room.

Though Susan had been headed for the medicine cabinet to get a couple of aspirins, she briefly halted at her desk upon noting the blinking red light of her telephone answering machine and reached forward to hit the recorder's play button. The tape rewound itself, and then the scratchy voice of a man broke from the machine's single speaker.

"Good morning, Susan, it's Commander Walker. I hope things are going well down there. I just wanted to let you know that I'll be coming down to Hurricane Hole five days from now. I know it's sudden and all, but I'll be bringing along a group of congressmen. They're with the budget committee and, as such, are responsible for your funding. So I'd appreciate it if you could put together a little show for their benefit. It doesn't have to be anything fancy. Just show off your dolphin and that harness you've been working so hard on. Maybe do something with the fiber-optic camera. I don't know, just use your imagination. My aide will call with all the details, so until Wednesday, take care of yourself."

The voice abruptly clicked off, and Susan looked down at the machine, her eyes wide in total disbelief. She rewound the tape and replayed it, this time praying that what she had heard had been a figment of her imagination. Unfortunately, it wasn't.

Her liaison with the Navy Department couldn't have picked a more inopportune moment to schedule this surprise visit if he had intentionally tried. And to even think that a group of congressmen would be accompanying him only made the situation that much worse!

It could take weeks for her to find another suitable dolphin to test the harness on. Of course, she could always close down the facility and return to the mainland, where she'd have no trouble finding a captive animal to try out the device. Yet the Navy had specified that it wanted the tests done on a wild bottlenose in open sea conditions. That was what had attracted Susan to the project in the first place, and she hated to have to sell out her ideals for convenience sake.

Supposing that her first step would have to be to call back Commander Walker at the Pentagon and explain her predicament, Susan was in the process of reaching down for the telephone when Owen came bursting into the room.

"Dr. Patton, you'll never believe what just swam into the lagoon!" he exclaimed.

Before Susan could attempt a response, the excited assistant continued. "I had just pulled the net holding Bubbles out of the water when something made me look out to the point. I did a double take at first, but there, clear as day, headed right for me, was a magnificent, full-grown specimen of *Tursiops truncatus*. The dolphin came right up to the docks, stuck his head out of the water, and seemed to look me right in the eye before turning and swimming off to play. Needless to say, I stopped what I was doing and ran over to seal off the lagoon.

"Come on out and have a look for yourself. Can you believe it? Our prayers have been answered!"

Susan's first impulse was that Owen was either telling a whopper of a lie or hallucinating. The one thing she could be absolutely certain of was the sincerity of his excitement. Tempted to share with him the contents of the telephone message, Susan held her tongue as she allowed Owen to lead her back outside.

Sure enough, the rippling wake of frothing water visible on the surface of the mirror-smooth lagoon belonged to a mature, seemingly healthy and intelligent male dolphin. As they gathered on the dock, the animal immediately swam over to check them out. He must have been trained by man and subsequently released, for he emerged out of the water on his tail fluke and let loose a barrage of rapid clicks, whistles, and moans. He then submerged, only to leap high in the air, slamming into the water with such force that Susan and Owen got completely soaked by the flying spray. It was at that moment that she decided to name him Sammy after her younger brother, who had the same mischievous look in his eyes and was a perpetual prankster.

Chapter Five

The undersea voyage from the Barents Sea to the deep waters of the Atlantic went remarkably smoothly. It was the Alfa class submarine *Kirov*, under the command of Captain Alexander Gnutov, that led the way southward. Following in the titanium-hulled *Kirov*'s wake was a vessel well over twice its size and ten times its displacement. This sub was the ballistic-missile-carrying ship the *Caspian*, one of the largest submersible warships ever to sail the seas.

They were just passing the island of Bermuda, and were well on their way to their final patrol station in the Caribbean Sea when Captain Gnutov excused himself to his cabin. Here he surrendered to a sound five-hour sleep. Such a continuous rest was out of character for him, since he usually got by with brief one-to-two-hour catnaps. Yet the great pressures of his current mission were finally taking their toll, and he collapsed onto his bunk completely exhausted.

He had been dreaming that he was deep in the

Urals hunting bighorns with his father. The dream had been so realistic that it took him several confused seconds to reorient himself when he finally awakened. The cramped, stark confines of the stateroom were a far cry from the thick woods he had dreamed about as harsh reality all too soon took over.

His sleep-filled eyes went straight to the bulkhead that lay at his feet. Only after he quickly checked the shiny brass compass and fathometer that were mounted there did he glance down at his watch. Genuinely surprised to find that five hours had passed since he had laid his head down on the pillow, Alexander yawned and stiffly sat up.

He had his duty to attend to, of course, yet he was hesitant to let go of the dream. His father had looked real as life, and was filled with energy and enthusiasm. He didn't seem to question why Alex was dressed in his Navy uniform as he led his full-grown son out of the zone of twisted oaks and up into the lofty realm of the bighorn.

"An expert stalker learns to block out all outside stimuli and to mentally become the animal that he wishes to pursue," his father had wisely observed as they spotted the first sheep droppings.

Now awake, Alex could still remember vividly the excitement that coursed through his body when he had spotted a magnificent ram, perched on a rock outcropping only a few hundred meters away. His father had spotted this animal also, and handed Alex his rifle. Yet when he brought the scope up to his eye, the prized ram turned into a snarling Ural brown bear. The ferocious beast rose onto its haunches, extending its monstrous body and viciously pawed the air before him with his massive claws. Alex delicately fingered the trigger and was just about to squeeze off a shot when he awoke.

Dreams painted strange pictures, Alex thought as he stood to make his way over to the toilet. His recent hunting trip must have stirred up powerful subconscious memories that were only now coming to the surface. Though the ram and the bear he had envisioned had been very real, his father had never lived long enough to see Alex reach manhood. Returning to the Urals last week must have triggered childhood memories of his father, and for one magical moment they had been reunited once again.

After relieving himself, Alex strode over to the washbasin, where he bathed his face in cold water and looked up at the small, wall-mounted mirror. The beard-stubbled face that stared back at him certainly didn't belong to that of a child anymore. In fact, it looked uncannily like his father's recently encountered image! He had the same brilliant blue eyes, broad forehead, and square, dimpled chin. Even his full head of spiky brown hair was similar.

Feeling as if he were seeing a ghostly apparition from another time and place, Alex turned on the other tap and soaked his face in a torrent of steaming water. This awakened him completely.

His thoughts were abruptly brought back to more mundane matters when the tart scent of boiled cabbage met his nostrils. Most likely emanating from the officers' wardroom located right outside his cabin, the smell of food made him conscious of a ravenous appetite. Deciding not to shave, he quickly dressed in his customary one-piece, navy blue jumpsuit and white canvas shoes. Attired identically to the other members of the crew now, he wasted no time ducking outside.

Seated alone at the wardroom table before a voluminous platter of food was the *Kirov*'s zampolit, Ivan Pavlodar. The balding political officer was in the process of stuffing his fat cheeks with a heel of black bread as he spied the ship's senior officer.

"Come join me, Captain," offered Pavlodar between bites of bread. "Igor has really outdone himself with this meal!"

Alexander merely nodded to an alert orderly and sat down at the head of the table. He watched as the zampolit took a gulp of tea and heavily swallowed before continuing. "I hope that your rest was a sound one, Captain. You were out for a good portion of the afternoon watch. Are you feeling okay?"

"Actually, I never felt better, Comrade Zampolit. I guess I was more tired than I realized. But now I'm properly rested and ready to get back to work. Has everyone been behaving?"

The political officer responded as the orderly arrived and placed a plate of food before the captain. "The crew have been applying themselves most diligently, Comrade. Though I must admit that for a time there, I was afraid that we might experience a serious morale problem. After all, the men were promised a full two weeks' leave."

"The defense of the Motherland does have its inconveniences, Comrade Zampolit," responded Alex, seeming to be distracted by his food. "Now let's see what culinary magic Igor has managed to come up with.''

Alex picked up his fork and moved aside the hunk of steamed cabbage that filled most of the plate, revealing several thick slices of boiled ox tongue and some cooked carrots.

"Ah, beef tongue and cabbage, the lifeblood of the Motherland. Now if I only had something to give this tea a bit more kick.''

The zampolit took this as the hint it was meant to be and removed a hand-sized pewter flask from his pocket. He unstopped it and reached for the captain's tea cup.

"Be my guest, Comrade. It's apricot brandy, distilled by my very own mother.''

Beckoning him to pour on, the captain cut into the cabbage and consumed a hearty mouthful. He followed this with a bite of tongue and some carrots, and only then did he pick up his tea cup. He took a sip and beamed appreciatively. "My heavens, that's tasty, Comrade Zampolit! You say that your mother was responsible for brewing this nectar?''

Ivan proudly nodded. "That she was, Captain. And she grew those apricots as well. That woman is surely something. Ever since my father died, she's been taking care of herself just like a youngster. Why, she'll be seventy-three next week, and she still manages to do her share of work on the commune.''

"Then our abrupt call to duty caused you to miss her birthday party,'' the captain reflected as he dug into his cabbage. "Where is this commune?''

"It's located outside of the town of Kamenets-Podolsk, in the Ukraine. It's hard to believe that I was there only last week. They were in the midst of spring planting at the time, and even I joined in to lend them a hand."

An introspective smile etched the political officer's plump face, and Alexander grunted. "Our land and its people are the real sources of the Motherland's greatness, Comrade. It is for their benefit alone that we risk our lives."

"Well said, Captain," returned the zampolit, picking up his tea cup to make a toast. "To the Motherland, and the gloriouis socialist experiment that allows all workers to share equally in its bounties!"

Lifting up his own cup, Alexander added, "To the Motherland!"

Both of the officers drained their glasses, and while Ivan Pavlodar refilled them, Alexander returned to his food.

"I hope things are going as smoothly aboard the *Caspian*," offered the zampolit. "I understand that the ship was rushed out of port just for this mission."

"The last time I spoke to Captain Sobrinka on the underwater telephone, he certainly didn't have any complaints to pass on," observed Alexander.

"Captain Mikhail Sobrinka wouldn't voluntarily pass on a complaint even if his nuclear reactors were going critical. That one's a man of few words, and from what I hear, a perfectionist as well. He's not the type to admit that any type of fault could possibly exist on one of his commands."

Alexander sensed a touch of bitterness in the zampolit's remark. "Comrade Sobrinka has a spotless service record. He was the captain of his own submarine when we were but pampered upper-

111

school students. He's demonstrated his ability to command on literally hundreds of successful patrols and as such is the perfect man to have at the helm of the *Caspian*, especially on a mission this important."

"Easy now, Comrade Gnutov. I wasn't putting the man down. It's just at sixty-three years of age, Sobrinka is at the twilight of his operational career. If all of us live to see this glorious mission completed, then Sobrinka should gracefully retire and allow younger, more capable officers like yourself to take his place."

This compliment hit home, and Alexander was momentarily placated. Yet he still responded guardedly, for as far as he was concerned, Soviet naval line captains were beyond reproach, especially by mere political officers. Stationed aboard every single ship of the Russian Navy, the zampolit was somebody every captain had to learn to live with. Having limited nautical skills, he was assigned by the Party to guarantee that the Navy remained completely subordinate. His responsibilities were thus to direct the ideological indoctrination of the men and to monitor their political reliability. In a lesser sense, the zampolit acted as a social worker for the crew to promote morale.

To Alexander, individuals such as Ivan Pavlodar were anachronisms who had to be tolerated until they were eventually eliminated completely. Yet until that time came about, he would have to make certain not to cross him.

"I should be getting back to the attack center now," commented Alexander as he took his last bite of the beef tongue.

"Before you go, at least help me finish off this bottle," offered the zampolit. "It's the last of my mother's tonic, and I'd hate to have to drink it down all alone."

"Very well, Comrade Pavlodar, for the memory of your dear mother you've convinced me to stay for one last drink."

The political officer grinned and refilled their cups with the final drops of brandy. "To the brave officers of the Soviet Navy, long may they live!" he toasted.

Alex raised his glass and listened as the zampolit continued. "And to our esteemed leaders in the politburo. May their vision be clear in these times of sorrow and destiny."

"I wonder if they've chosen a new premier as yet?" quizzed Alexander.

"From what I understand, it could take some time," answered the political officer. "They say the scene at the memorial service was quite tense, with the moderates and those promulgating a more conservative doctrine hardly speaking to one another. Since they are evenly divided, selecting a new leader will most probably be an exhausting task."

Alexander nodded. "I had the honor of attending the service and it was indeed as you say, Comrade."

The zampolit seemed to be surprised by what he was hearing. "You were at Lenin's tomb, Captain? I'm impressed. You must have very important friends."

Though Alexander had already said enough, the brandy spurred him on. "Admiral Chimki invited me. He was my adviser at the Academy, and was responsible for my choosing to serve the Motherland

113

on its undersea fleet."

The zampolit's eyes glistened. "The admiral is a great hero. My own contacts in the Kremlin share his vision. So it appears that I can speak frankly with you, Captain. In your opinion is it true that the moderates are in league with the CIA and directly responsible for Premier Ivanov's death? If this is the case, the Motherland could be in great peril if they should wrest the reins of power."

Since the political officer seemed to be sincere with his convictions, Alexander guardedly answered, "From my own firsthand observation, such a power struggle is indeed occurring. The atmosphere inside Lenin's mausoleum was so thick that you could cut it with the proverbial knife. Yakov Rosenstein and his misdirected cohorts turned what was supposed to be a solemn memorial service into a showcase for their own twisted political preferences. With the fresh corpse of General Secretary Ivanov lying in state before us, they had the audacity to get in a shouting match with the defense minister, calling him an elitist, who along with the military was leading the country to certain destruction."

"Why, the nerve of those traitorous cowards!" exclaimed the zampolit. "It's the result of too much reform, too quickly. In the old days, such blasphemy would not be permitted."

"And that's not all of it," added the captain. "Because when we were leaving the mausoleum, I personally saw Rosenstein conversing with one of the American television anchormen. He was saying such things as now is the time for the United States and the Soviet Union to disband their armies and mutually destroy their nuclear arsenals. And the American seemed to be swallowing every word of it."

"These are grim times, Captain. Yet one thing still puzzles me. How is it that the politburo sanctioned our current mission and the taking out of the Yankee Elint ship that was blocking our way?"

"Who says that they even knew anything about it?" retorted Alexander.

Shocked by this answer, the zampolit was about to respond when the *Kirov*'s senior lieutenant entered the wardroom. Ganady Arbatov was a relative newcomer aboard the attack sub. A recent graduate of the same academy that Gnutov had attended, the senior lieutenant had already proven himself as a hard-working, intelligent individual who could be counted on to carry out any number of complicated tasks. Yet his political allegiances were still suspect, and the two veterans wisely held their brandy-loosened tongues until they got to know him better.

"Good evening, Comrade Arbatov," the captain greeted. "How are things on the *Kirov*?"

The senior lieutenant remained standing and stiffly replied, "We are proceeding right as scheduled, Captain, with all systems giving us one hundred percent performance."

"Good," replied the captain. "But may I ask who's the senior officer of the watch now that all three of us are back here chatting away?"

"Lieutenant Kasimov is standing in for me until I return, sir. I was only on my way back to my quarters to pull out some charts of the waters that we'll soon be entering."

"At ease, Comrade," returned the captain, who

enjoyed teasing the high-strung neophyte. "I imagine that the *Kirov* can get along without us for a little while longer. So why don't you get those charts that you were after and join us here in the wardroom. I'd like to have a closer look at these new waters myself."

"Very well, sir," replied the senior lieutenant, continuing on down the passageway.

Without having to ask for him, the orderly suddenly appeared at the table, where he set down another cup, a pot of fresh tea, and a platter of oatmeal cookies.

"Igor takes better care of me than my own wife," observed the zampolit as he reached out for a handful of cookies.

Alexander took but a single cookie, which he found hot and freshly baked. The tea was a bit less tasty without the zampolit's homemade brandy in it, yet it was satisfying nonetheless. Alex was halfway done with his cup when the senior lieutenant returned.

Ganady Arbatov laid down a series of detailed charts on the table before the captain. The zampolit had to scoot over to another seat to properly see these maps, the first of which showed a polar view of the North American continent.

"We are approximately here, with the *Caspian* trailing ten kilometers behind us," stated the senior lieutenant as he pointed to a position just east of the island of Bermuda.

"And just how would you recommend that we reach our patrol station off the southern coast of Cuba?" quizzed the captain.

The alert senior lieutenant pulled out a small, clear plastic ruler and laid one end on their current position and angled the other end down to their destination, which lay to the southwest some thousand kilometers distant. Taking a second to study the chart, he replied, "It's obvious that the quickest route would take us through the Straits of Florida and around the western tip of Cuba via the Yucatán Channel. That would put us practically right smack in the black depths of the Cayman Trench and only a short distance from our naval base at Cienfuegos."

"Do you see any alternative routes?" continued Alexander.

Ganady pointed to the strait of water separating Cuba and Haiti. "We could enter the Caribbean by way of the Windward Passage."

Alexander paused a moment to take a sip of tea before responding. "Both of these routes would indeed get us to our destination in the least amount of time. But time isn't our only enemy on this mission, Comrade Arbatov. Both the routes you mention would lead us through some of the most closely monitored waters on this entire planet. We successfully dodged the imperialist SOSUS arrays in the GIUK gap only with the diversionary assistance of our surface battle fleet, which happened to be headed into the Norwegian Sea at the time. Yet in this instance, we won't be so fortunate. So how do you intend to fool the thousands of sea floor-mounted listening devices that litter these waters and would give the Americans instant notice of our arrival?"

"By superior equipment, stealth, and cunning, sir!" shot back Ganady. "The *Kirov* and the *Caspian* represent the most sophisticated undersea platforms that have ever gone to sea. Our ultra-quiet propellors and anechoic-tiled hulls will safely see us past the imperialist SOSUS arrays that you speak of."

Alexander stifled a chuckle. "If that were only the case, Comrade. Back at the Academy, our tacticians often saw things as they would like to, and not as they are in reality. Though our equipment is of the finest caliber, I seriously doubt if we'd be able to transit the choke points you speak of undetected. The American listening devices are just too sensitive, and not even the veil of a dense and well-defined thermal layer could mask us."

"Then how are we to successfully complete our mission?" quizzed the confused senior lieutenant.

"Think, Comrade!" retorted the captain. "Don't any other alternative routes come to you?"

"I believe that I see one!" answered the eager zampolit.

Genuinely surprised by the source of this response, Alexander signaled his political officer to continue. Ivan Pavlodar courteously nodded and did so.

"It seems to me that there are other straits of water that one could utilize by which to enter the Caribbean Sea. Though the route may be a bit more indirect, perhaps these secondary passages will be less littered with sensors."

The zampolit followed up this remark by pointing to the straits separating the Dominican Republic and Puerto Rico, and the Virgin Islands and Anguilla.

"Well, Senior Lieutenant, what do you say to this plan?" questioned Alexander thoughtfully.

Before answering, Ganady Arbatov pulled out yet

another chart. This one was of the Caribbean region exclusively, and showed the passages that the zampolit had mentioned in much greater detail.

"It appears that the water is deep enough to allow a transit in such spots," observed the senior lieutenant. "Though it would put us well out of our way."

Alexander beamed. "But what a small price to pay for our anonymity, my friend! Comrade Pavlodar, your insights impress me. Perhaps there are the makings of a brilliant naval tactician in that political brain of yours."

Pointing to the fairly wide straits of water lying to the immediate east of the Virgin Islands, Alexander added, "Naval intelligence reports that the Anegada Passage is totally devoid of American sensors. The waters are deep and quiet, with only an occasional cruise ship or sailboat plying its surface. We can thus gain access to the Caribbean Sea there and speed off to our patrol station near Cuba, with the enemy completely unaware of our presence!"

A satisfied smirk painted the zampolit's chubby face as he listened to this plan. The senior lieutenant was in the process of studiously examining this unorthodox route more closely when the wardroom's intercom loudly chimed. It was Alexander Gnutov who answered it.

"Captain here."

"Sir, it's Lieutenant Kasimov. Sonar has just reported an unidentified underwater contact. Maximum range, bearing two-eight-zero."

Alexander met the serious glance of his zampolit as he replied, "Run this signature through the sound analysis computer and see if you can determine its origin. I'll join you in the attack center at once."

"Should I sound general quarters, Captain?" questioned the alert OOD.

"Under our current circumstances, that's an excellent idea, Lieutenant Kasimov. You may open up a direct hailing channel with the *Caspian* as well."

With this said, Alexander replaced the intercom handset and stood. "I had a feeling that this cruise was going a bit too smoothly. Let's be off to the control room to determine if this visitor is indeed a threat or not."

"And if it is?" quizzed the zampolit, who stood, revealing his plump, pot-bellied figure.

The captain answered as he turned for the forward hatchway. "Then we'll soon see what kind of stuff the *Kirov* is truly made of, Comrade."

Absorbing this comment, Ivan Pavlodar fell in behind the senior lieutenant as the men scrambled out of the wardroom. They passed through that cramped portion of the sub where the enlisted men were berthed and traversed a narrow passageway lined with snaking cables. Seconds later, they entered the attack center.

Bathed in red light, this portion of the *Kirov* had an almost sinister appearance to it. Because of the compact size of the Alfa class vessels, computers automatically ran most of the sub's functions. In fact, its liquid metal-cooled nuclear reactor room was entirely unmanned. It was from the digital consoles of the attack center that the technicians monitored the engines and also directed the vessel's course, buoyancy, sensor readings, communications, and weapons systems.

There was a tense quiet in the air as the trio of newcomers headed straight for the sonar console. One of the seated figures sported a familiar mop of curly red hair and was lost in intense concentration, with a pair of headphones covering his ears. The captain gained his attention by touching his shoulder.

"Have you identified it as yet, Lieutenant Kasimov?"

Peeling off his headphones, the *Kirov*'s senior sonar technician answered, "The computer shows a sixty-three percent probability that it's a British Trafalgar class attack submarine, sir."

"A Trafalgar, you say?" repeated Alexander. "Then it's outfitted with one of the new pump-jet propulsion systems instead of a conventional seven-bladed propellor. Is it continuing to close in?"

Kasimov hastily scanned his console's green-tinted cathode-ray screen. "Yes it is, Captain, though it's doubtful that they're on to us as yet."

"Good," returned Alexander, whose brow creased in thought. "Has that hailing channel that I requested been opened?"

"It's ready when you are," retorted the seated technician.

The captain nodded. "Very good, Lieutenant. Let me know the second that they either change their course or show any hostile intent."

As the captain turned for the communications console, the sweating zampolit hurried to his side. "Why don't we change course ourselves and run from them, Comrade? As it stands now, they're bound to realize that we're out here sooner or later, and it's

121

imperative that the *Caspian*'s presence in these waters remains a secret."

Barely paying his political officer any serious attention, Alexander reached the station that he had been headed for. "Your concerns are noted, Comrade Pavlodar. But please leave the actual operational strategy to those more qualified. Both Captain Sobrinka and I have planned for this contingency, and we're well prepared to meet the British threat."

"The Trafalgar has suddenly slowed its forward speed, Captain!" exclaimed Lieutenant Kasimov from his nearby console. "I believe they've heard us!"

Alexander seemed to have complete command of the situation as he coolly reached out to grasp the red plastic handset belonging to their short-range, underwater telephone.

"Target bearing two-eight-zero," he barked into the transmitter. "Prepare to link up and wipe off."

A distant, muted voice repeated the message, and Alexander knew that the *Caspian* had definitely received his transmission. Continuing on to maneuvering now, the captain was once again queried by his anxious political officer.

"What in Lenin's name was that all about, Comrade?"

Though the curious zampolit's persistence was beginning to aggravate him, Alexander replied anyway. "To guarantee that the *Caspian* is not tagged by the Trafalgar, we will rendezvous. The *Caspian* will then scram its reactor, while we intentionally keep our power unit running. The enemy can only follow what it hears, and thinking that we're alone, will concentrate on our signature exclusively. Only as they continue to close in to investigate, will I order flank speed, and off we'll go on a wild-goose chase in the waters north of here. And once the English take the bait and order a pursuit of their own, the *Caspian* need only to start up its reactor once again and proceed on its way southward, with the enemy none the wiser."

An understanding gleam sparkled in the zampolit's eyes as he watched Alexander convey this plan to the engineering officer and the seated planesmen.

"Prepare to rendezvous with the *Caspian*!" shouted the captain, loud enough so that all present in the attack center could hear him. "And ready the *Kirov* for flank speed and steep maneuvering. We're going to give those Englishmen a chase that they'll never forget!"

Meanwhile, on the opposite coast of the North American continent, the USS *Swordfish* continued on its own voyage, totally unaware of the perilous chase that was about to take place beneath the waters off Bermuda. The last diesel-electric-powered submarine in the U.S. fleet had just finished passing down the coast of Baja California, and was in the process of entering the black depths of water belonging to that geological feature known as the Middle America Trench. This put them directly opposite the Mexican resort city of Acapulco, and half the distance to their immediate destination, the Panama Canal.

It had been almost forty-eight hours since the *Swordfish* had left its berth in San Diego. Soon afterward, the vessel submerged. The ride was smoother beneath the Pacific's depths, and the *Swordfish* cruised southward without fear of detection from above.

The only times the submarine was forced to ascend were to engage its snorkel device. And even then it wasn't necessary to break the surface of the ocean with the tip of their sail. Such an operation was necessary for the *Swordfish* to recharge its batteries. It did so by ascending toward the surface and raising its snorkel so that air was able to enter the ship through the induction piping. As this process was initiated, the engine exhaust gasses were subsequently discharged through a pipe in the after end of the sail, and the batteries could be vented and charged while presenting only a small, difficult-to-detect target from the air.

Deep in the interior of the vessel, the crew went about their duties oblivious to this all-important process, especially in the enlisted men's berthing area. Here those sailors not presently on duty caught up on their sleep, or in a variety of other ways passed the time until they were required to go back to their stations.

For Senor Sonarman Brad Bodzin, free time gave him a chance not only to catch up with his reading, but to enjoy one of the dozens of cassette tapes that he always made certain to bring along. He did so on his portable Sony Walkman, whose headphones ensured that he wouldn't disturb his fellow shipmates. They also produced excellent sound, considering their limited size and power source.

Bodzin had been in the Navy a little over four years.

The bright-eyed Houston, Texas, native had enlisted right after graduating from high school. His plan was to stay in long enough to qualify for one of the low-cost college loans the Navy offered after five years of duty. Then he would enroll at the University of Texas, where he hoped to major in music.

He was drawn to submarines completely by accident. Having gone through basic in San Diego, it was soon learned that he had abnormally sensitive hearing. Brad was quite aware of this gift, which had helped him become a master of the concert violin by his sixteenth year. To put his hearing ability to best work in his current environment, it was decided by the powers that be that he would go to sonar school.

An exhausting course of study followed. His favorite instructor at that time was a crusty submarine veteran of World War II whose stories of undersea combat in the Pacific had inflamed Brad's imagination. And after graduating number three in a class of fifty, Brad found himself with his pick of open assignments. Without a doubt in his mind, he chose submarines.

Sheer luck of the draw sent him to the *Swordfish*. Though most of his classmates downplayed service aboard a diesel-electric-powered vessel, favoring the modern nukes instead, Brad grabbed at the chance to serve on the last of her kind in the U.S. fleet. And ever since joining the handpicked crew, he hadn't been the least bit disappointed for doing so.

The nuclear tradition in the Navy was only but a few decades old, whereas the history of the fossil-fueled fleet went back over a century and included two major world wars. Being the last of her kind, the

Swordfish was a special boat, manned by a special crew. They understood their great responsibility as the keepers of a tradition that had practically won the war in the Pacific singlehandedly.

Brad was genuinely upset when he learned that their current patrol would be the *Swordfish*'s last. They had more than proved themselves in exercise after exercise, yet Command seemed convinced that a diesel-electric-powered submarine had no place in the modern Navy. The general feeling was that such ships were obsolete. Though Brad and his shipmates begged to differ with this rash opinion, they were powerless to argue otherwise.

There was a somber feeling shared by all those on board when they had left Point Loma two days ago. Yet they were to all too soon forget about their selfish concerns when word arrived of their current strategic alert. The world was once more at the brink of war, and as long as the *Swordfish* was still in service, they would defend their country until the very end.

The tape that Brad had been listening to abruptly clicked off, and he realized with a start that he had listened to both sides already. It was a newly purchased imported version of Prokofiev's *Alexander Nevsky Suite*. It appeared to be extremely well produced, yet for the most part he had been so immersed in thought that he hadn't paid the actual recording all that much attention. He knew, though, that he would have many more opportunities to study it more carefully and reached up to pull off his headphones.

Brad's narrow berth was situated above two others. He lay on his back with his curtain drawn, and could just hear the subdued voices of his bunkmates arguing down below him.

"I don't care what you say, Deke, but I still think that our present alert is a consequence of the *Turner* incident. The Pentagon's not about to just sit back idly and watch as one of our Elint ships is merely plucked from the open sea. Though I still can't understand why the *Turner* didn't at least try to defend itself."

These words came from the lips of Petty Officer Second Class Carl Harper, one of the sub's communications specialists. Harper had been in the radio room when the news of the *Turner*'s capture was first received, and as such helped to spread news of the incident throughout the ship.

Quick to argue his own opinion was Senior Seaman Deke Thompson, one of their machinists. "If you ask me, this whole alert can be blamed totally on the assassination of the Russkie premier. Washington understands the power struggle going on inside the Kremlin and wants us to be on our toes should the wrong element ascend to power. The *Turner*'s capture at this time was only coincidental."

"How can you even think such a ridiculous thing?" retorted Harper. "The *Turner*'s capture is an act of war, pure and simple!"

Brad could tell that Carl Harper's volatile temper was about to reach its breaking point. Pushing open his curtain, Bodzin leaned over to intercede.

"Hey, guys, cool it!" he whispered forcefully. "If you keep this up, you're going to awaken this whole damn compartment."

Carl Harper looked up and managed to lower his

voice. "I hear you, Bodzin, yet what do you feel is the real reason for our present alert status?"

"I think it's a combination of things," offered the sonar expert. "Sure, the capture of the *Turner* is part of it, as well as Premier Ivanov's assassination. And I'm sure there are a lot of things contributing to the fragile state of world relations that we don't even know about. Arguing about it will get us nowhere fast. So what do you say to concluding this discussion before it gets further out of hand?"

"I'm with you, Brad," returned Deke Thompson, who apparently had more important things on his mind. "How about joining us in the galley for lunch?"

Bodzin checked his watch. "Christ, I didn't realize it was this late already. I've got to be back in the sound shack in another thirty minutes. So unless I can convince the skipper to send me room service, I'll take you up on that invitation."

"Good, I'm starving," responded the machinist.

"You're always hungry, Thompson," observed Carl Harper sarcastically. "In fact, that may be your trouble. You think with your stomach and not your brains."

The brawny machinist tightly rolled up a wet terry-cloth towel and snapped one of its ends toward his bunkmate. Harper deflected this assault with his forearm, and was in the midst of preparing his own weapon out of a towel when Brad Bodzin once again came between them. Bounding off his bunk in his skivvies, the senior sonar technician held up his arms.

"You guys are worse than the Russians and the

Americans. So if you have to fight, do it out in the passageway, and at least let me get dressed in peace."

The two sailors, who were really the best of friends, made some halfhearted feints at each other before turning for the hatchway. Before exiting altogether, the machinist turned and briefly commented, "You're wasting yourself in the Navy, Bodzin. You should be in the United Nations. See you in the galley." Grinning, he then pivoted and moved his muscular torso out of the stateroom. Bodzin efficiently slipped into his blue coveralls and securely stowed away his Walkman before joining them in the mess hall. To get to this portion of the ship, he had to passs by the shut doors of the sonar room. Most familiar with the assortment of transducers, amplifiers, and other various high-tech digital equipment stored here, he continued on to the adjoining compartment.

The mood in this portion of the *Swordfish* was most definitely upbeat. The mess hall was a combination dining room, lounge, and conference room for the ship's enlisted personnel. It was brightly lit and kept spotlessly clean, with its dozen or so individual four-man tables and booths covered with plastic and edged with steel to keep the plates from slipping. The food itself was served cafeteria-style, and Brad could personally attest to the fact that it was among the best in the entire Navy.

Because of the confined, rote nature of sub duty, mealtime was often the focal point of the entire day. It was an event to be looked forward to, and the cooks did their best to not disappoint their shipmates by serving a variety of imaginative, well-prepared dishes.

This afternoon's meal was one of Brad's very favorites, for it was malt shop day. Juicy cheeseburgers, onion rings, french fries, and malted milks were the standard repast. To provide additional mood, the cooks had even loaded the juke box with sixties music, and *Leave it to Beaver* video tapes could be seen playing from the various partition-mounted television monitors.

Brad was hardly aware that they were presently several hundred feet beneath the Pacific as he loaded up his tray with food. Except for the noticeable lack of women and windows, he could be back home at his favorite high school hangout.

The chief cook was loading up the malt machine as Brad passed on the serving line. Since he was a fellow Texan from Brownsville, the two were already friends, and Brad was sincere with his compliments.

"You outdid yourself this afternoon, Cooky. Yet when are you going to pass out those lobster tails? I know you've been hoarding them away in the deep freeze these last couple of months, and there's no use saving them after this patrol is completed."

"I read you loud and clear, Bodzin," returned the head of the galley. "I'm saving the clam bake until we get into the Gulf of Mexico. Now what's it going to be, chocolate or strawberry?"

Though Brad would have liked one of each, his clothes were already fitting him tight enough as it was, and he chose an extra-thin strawberry milkshake.

"Thanks, Cooky. Are you going to be able to join us?"

The cook shook his head. "I'm afraid I'm going to

130

have to take a rain check, Brad. Two of my men are taking their qualifying tests today. and I'm a bit shorthanded."

"Well, don't work too hard," advised the sonar technician as he picked up his loaded tray and headed for the mess area.

He found his bunkmates in a corner booth, stuffing their faces with food and engrossed in the video monitor placed above them. They were hardly aware of his presence as he sat down, took a sip from his shake, and questioned, "What's old Beaver gotten himself into this time?"

Deke Thompson answered between bites of his cheeseburger, "The Beaver just broke his brother's baseball trophy after Wally warned him not to touch it. The poor kid is trying to glue it together before Wally gets home, and he's having a heck of a time getting the parts to fit properly."

Brad quickly got into the storyline as he went to work on his own meal. The chow was as good as it looked, and before he knew it he had polished off his two burgers and rings, and was putting the finishing touches on his shake. He took his last sip just as Ward Cleever was presenting the moral of the story to his youngest son, instructing him that honesty was always the best policy.

"If life were only that clearcut," reflected Brad, who contentedly patted his stomach and pushed away his tray. "Now I think a nice long stroll on the beach is in order."

Carl Harper looked up from his malted as if he was hearing things. Brad grinned and looked at his watch.

"Duty calls, gentlemen. The Chief asked me to relieve him early so that he could get his hair cut."

"What in the hell does he have to cut?" quizzed Harper incredulously.

Brad winked. "Ours is not to reason why, my friend."

He stood and turned for the forward hatch. He didn't have far to go until he reached his intended destination and ducked inside its cork-lined entranceway. The smell of sweat and coffee immediately met his nostrils.

The narrow, L-shaped compartment was packed from floor to ceiling with equipment. Three men were currently on duty here. Each of these individuals sat at a separate console, with headphones secured, their eyes riveted on their instruments. The figure seated farthest from the hatch sported black skin and a balding scalp, and it was toward him that Brad headed.

Without breaking the constrained silence, Bodzin gently tapped the Chief on his shoulder. Having been completely absorbed in his work, Chief Roy Small looked up with an annoyed scowl on his face, yet it only took one look at the figure that was disturbing him to cause his face to break out in a broad grin.

"It's about time that you got here, Bodzin," whispered the ten-year Navy veteran. "Doc's only cuttin' hair for another half hour, and then I want to check out that burger den I hear we got set up in the mess hall."

"What's it like out there?" quizzed Brad as he watched the Chief peel off his headphones and push away from the console.

"The humpbacks have returned," observed Small bitterly. "We've apparently got a hell of a school of squid beneath us, and the whales are feeding like there's no tomorrow, and really singing up a storm."

Standing to reveal a tall, thin body, the Chief winked. "Why, it almost sounds like one of those fancy French operas that you're into, Bodzin. So enjoy it, brother, because you couldn't hear Ivan sneaking up on us if you tried."

Prompted to argue otherwise, Brad held his tongue and turned to pour himself a mug of coffee before taking the now-vacant seat. He settled himself into the still-warm, leather-upholstered cushion and reached out to don the padded headphones. No sooner were they clamped over his ears when he heard a pulsating, mournful cry that sounded almost unearthly in its origin. The senior sonar technician was most familiar with their source as he looked up to scan the instruments.

The *Swordfish* was presently running at periscope depth, sixty-five feet beneath the Pacific's surface. They were traveling in a southeasterly course at a brisk twenty-seven knots.

The passive hydrophone array that he was responsible for monitoring was set into the sub's bow. The series of ultra-sensitive microphones were attuned to the seas lying directly in front of the *Swordfish*. Because of their alert status, they would be relying on the passive system almost exclusively, for an active "ping" would quickly reveal their presence should the enemy be lurking in the nearby depths.

It was clearly evident that the whales were all around them. The vociferous marine mammals were active brutes that could dive well beneath three thousand feet. That was almost three times the depth that the *Swordfish* could safely attain, and Brad respected them for this awesome physical capability.

Science was still not certain if such animals had a language or not, but Bodzin had no doubt in his mind that they did. He had listened to their persistent bellowing for hundreds of hours on end, and just knew that this was their way of communicating with one another.

If the songs of the whales did indeed turn out to be a recognized language, it was certainly one of the most beautiful ones ever to grace the planet. In a way it reminded Brad of an ethereal symphony. Sometimes, when he was on watch and the whales were in the vicinity, he would close his eyes and surrender himself to the strange, pulsating cries. He even got to the point where he could distinguish individual animals, and he swore he could pick out the sounds of another whale replying.

Someday he hoped to make a recording of such whale songs. Then he planned to sit down with his violin and compose a score, with his instrument linking the various cries in a single, integrated piece. Hopefully he'd get a chance to work on such a project—which he would call "Cry of the Deep"— once he was enrolled in the university's music program.

Being a trained musician gave Brad what he believed to be a genuine advantage over his fellow shipmates. For not only was his hearing more sensitive, but he was able all that much more easily to pick out discordant sounds from the vast mixture of noises fed into their headphones.

The oceans themselves were filled with a variety of natural sound, whether they were the boisterous clicks of a school of shrimp or the high-pitched whistles of a pod of passing dolphins. Like an adept conductor, the successful sonar operator learned to recognize and then filter out these naturally produced sounds and concentrate on the distinctive sonic vibrations that could be attributed solely to man.

Concentration was the key to this process. One had to learn to focus his senses and not let his thoughts drift elsewhere. The majority of time this rote effort was tedious and downright boring. Being an individual effort by its very nature, sonar work could also be extremely lonely, and it was at such times that Brad welcomed the approach of the whales, who became like long-lost friends to him.

With one hand on the filter gain, he carefully scanned the surrounding waters. Much like a blind person compensated for his lack of eyesight, it was nothing but pure sound that painted his mental picture of what lay in the waters before them. A humpback cow could be heard gently calling to its newborn, who answered in a tentative, high-pitched squeal, while in the distance, an elder cried out in long, penetrating bass-filled blasts that bespoke a loneliness that man could never hope to fully comprehend.

Brad absorbed these sounds and mentally plotted the musical notes that would unite these cries in an organized symphony. A haunting, mournful melody suddenly came to him, and, wishing that he had brought along some proper scoring paper, he mentally jotted down the individual notes out of which this movement would be comprised.

The only work that he could compare it to was Camille Saint-Saëns's, *Danse Macabre*. Yet unlike this piece, composed to evoke the horrible plague that had decimated Europe in the so-called Dark Ages, Brad's score would be dedicated to the wondrous glory of life.

Excited with this concept, he was in the process of redirecting the bow hydrophones to focus on that portion of the ocean that lay beneath their hull when an alien, surging sound suddenly caught his attention. Startled by this unexpected noise that originated from no living sea creature he had ever heard before, Brad turned up the volume gain. The unnatural sound became even more distinctive, and his gut instinctively tightened.

Only last month he had heard a tape of a Soviet Victor class submarine that had been tagged off the coast of Nicaragua. Its nuclear reactor's coolant pump had a characteristic surging hiss to it that was particularly audible whenever the vessel was under way at high speeds. The sound that he was currently hearing in his headphones was almost an exact duplicate of this prerecorded tape, and Brad Bodzin gambled that this was no mere coincidence. Sitting forward alertly in his seat, the brown-haired Texan reached for the intercom and initiated a single call.

Rear Admiral William Abbott was not used to

having to hold back his tongue and merely be an observer. But he was a guest aboard the *Swordfish*, and as such had to respect the authority of his former subordinate and let Theodore Anderson have the spotlight.

There were several occasions, though, when he just had to speak up. One of these incidents took place only minutes before, when he noted that the navigator had no knowledge of the sea conditions around them.

"There's more to navigation than just picking out points on a chart!" lectured the retired veteran. "A well-defined thermal can save your life, just as effectively as a sheltered port."

The young navigator was a scholarly, sensitive lad, who openly admitted that he had been lax in following the latest underwater sensor data. He was last seen buried in a plethora of thermal gradient figures and surrounding water temperatures.

"There's nothing like knowing the exact location of the nearest thermal layer," observed Abbott to his host as they continued their rounds of the control room. "You never know when you might need it."

"I agree," returned Ted Anderson, who guided them past the vacant fire-control station.

Abbott momentarily halted beside the console holding the torpedo-firing panel and grinned. "You know, it seems like only yesterday that you were as green as that young navigator back there. I'll never forget the look on your face when you and Wilkins discovered that short in the fire-control wiring system. Then, when the XO called for the fire extinguisher, I thought you'd drop from a stroke before you finally found it right at your feet."

"I almost did," revealed Anderson. "You know, to tell you the truth, at the time I didn't think much of how you read us the riot act afterward. After all, as the spanking new weapons officer, I didn't feel it was my fault that the refit boys screwed up their job. But now I realize that it was my responsibility to make certain that the system was completely operational. Excuses don't mean much in wartime."

"Amen," sighed the admiral. "And don't think that it was easy having to chew you out like I did in front of the others either. It's no joy being everyone's number one pain in the keister, but that's the only way I knew to get your attentions. Believe me, Ted, I was only teaching you how to survive the best I could."

This sincere statement was punctuated by the forceful voice of Lieutenant Pukalani, the current OOD. "Captain, Sonar reports a possible unidentified underwater contact, bearing one-zero-zero, relative rough range thirty thousand yards."

Quickly turning to face the XO, Anderson shouted, "Who called this sighting in, Lieutenant?"

"It was Petty Officer Bodzin, sir."

Well aware that the crewman whom the XO had just mentioned was one of the best sonar operators that he had ever worked with, Anderson strode over to pick up a nearby intercom handset.

"Mr. Bodzin, it's the captain. What have you got out there?"

The cool voice on the other end of the line answered most efficiently. "Sir, I believe I'm picking up the sound of a reactor coolant pump. It's still at maximum range, and we've got some noisy humpbacks to contend with as well, but I think I can also hear two tandem, corotating propellors, which leads me to presume that we could have a Soviet Victor III headed our way."

"Good work, Mr. Bodzin. Let me know the second that you can get a positive signature on the contact."

"Aye, aye, sir!" returned the alert sonar operator.

Disconnecting the intercom, Anderson turned to face his XO. "Lieutenant, rig the ship for a possible deep submergence. Also inform maneuvering that we might be needing flank speed shortly."

Briefly catching his esteemed guest's wizened glance, he continued his flurry, this time addressing his remarks to their navigator. "Mr. Delano, I believe you've got the latest data on the availability of any usable thermal layers. Is there anything nearby that we might be able to utilize to our advantage?"

"I believe there is, Captain," shakily responded the navigator. "Our sensors show a well-defined thermocline at the seven-hundred-and-fifty-foot level."

"Excellent!" said Anderson as he turned back to his respected guest. "For the last several weeks, Intelligence has reported picking up the signature of a Victor III in the area. It's here as a show of support for the Kremlin's proxies in the region. This same vessel is also said to have one hell of a noisy reactor coolant pump, and that's what apparently gave them away."

Admiral Abbott grunted. "The Victor III is a formidable warship. It's designed exclusively for antisubmarine warfare, and is fitted with the latest in sensors and armaments."

"I see that you've been keeping up with your homework," observed Anderson lightly.

"Some habits are hard to break," returned the retired veteran, whose brow tightened. "With this damn alert and all, you're going to be wanting to know as much about this Red bastard as possible. That is, if you intend to share the same seas with him."

Anderson didn't have to hear any more to know what his former commanding officer was thinking, for it had crossed his mind as well. "Hell, no!" exclaimed Ted. "Ivan's just going to have to find himself another playmate, because the *Swordfish* has plans of its own."

This emotional remark was met by a dreaded pinging sound that reverberated through the control room with a nerve-shattering intensity.

"We've been tagged!" cried the XO, who turned to the captain for guidance.

"Sound battle stations and take her down to nine hundred feet!" ordered Anderson. "And have maneuvering give us full power! I want to be but a knuckle in the water that Ivan will never be able to follow in a thousand years!"

It was the diving officer who instructed the bow planesmen to put on the dive, and as they pushed forward on their steering mechanisms, the *Swordfish* lunged downward. Those standing had to brace themselves as the angle of this descent increased to the point when objects not properly battened down clattered down to the deck and shifted toward the forward bulkhead.

William Abbott held himself upright by grasping

onto the brass railing that encircled the periscope well. A feeling of excitement filled him, and for the first time in years he felt totally alive and invigorated.

Peering out at the seated planesmen, whose upper torsos were straining hard against their protective harnesses, the old-timer watched as the depth gauge continued its mad spin downward. They had just passed beneath the three-hundred-foot level, and already the vessel's hull was beginning to groan and creak in protest. He knew that the *Swordfish* would be subject to a variety of minor leaks at this point and could visualize the engineers as they struggled to halt the trickles of seawater before they became an unmanageable torrent.

Deeper and deeper they went, and Abbott briefly caught the resolute expression locked on Theodore Anderson's ruggedly handsome face. Grasping on to the same rail that Abbott held, the blond captain watched the spiraling depth gauge with total absorption. His mere presence spoke command, and Abbott felt proud to have been an instrumental part of his early operational development.

Sure he had been hard on the lad. Yet he was this way with all of his subordinates, and especially tough with those few he sensed had the true ability to be real leaders.

In the months after Anderson first joined the *Swordfish*, he had proved himself time after time an individual who could handle himself under the worst type of pressures. He was superintelligent and a quick learner, who wasn't above taking the responsibility when those beneath him failed. The enlisted men had sensed this quality, and gave him their one hundred percent loyalty. With this support, his future was all but assured.

Abbott's attention was diverted by the sickening sound of dripping water. A sudden cool mist hit him full in the face, and he turned in time to view a fine current of seawater spraying forth from the hatch that led to the sail. Before he could shout in warning, an alert chief perched beside the diving console cried out forcefully, "Leak in the main trunk! Ensign, man this station while I stop it."

As the vessel's navigator replaced the chief, he stood and struggled to reach the leaking hatch without losing his balance. The pot-bellied non-commissioned officer proved to be the hero of the moment as he inched his way forward, oblivious to any personal peril. Twice he slipped and almost went down, but he persevered and eventually made it to the bottom of the trunk. The falling spray seemed to be steadily increasing, and, soaked to the skin, the chief began the difficult job of climbing up the ladder to check the leak's source firsthand.

The *Swordfish* had just broken the six-hundred-foot level when the leak abruptly stopped. Seconds later, the chief appeared in the bottom of the trunk, dripping wet yet apparently none the worse for wear.

There was no time for celebration as the hull continued ominously groaning around them. All eyes seemed glued on the depth gauge, which was rapidly approaching the sub's crush threshold.

Abbott momentarily caught the captain's concerned gaze as they broke seven hundred feet.

"We should be reaching that thermocline soon," observed the XO leadenly.

"At seven hundred and twenty-five feet," the Hawaiian added. "The outside water temperature should begin dropping rapidly about now. Ivan's sonar will really start to give him fits."

Almost to emphasize this statement, the hull reverberated with a rapid succession of sharp, tapping sounds. This mysterious patter was reminiscent of the sound raindrops made on a tin roof, and the XO responded with pure puzzlement flavoring his tone, "What the hell?"

William Abbott had heard this same alien racket once before, while on a patrol on the closing days of World War II. To ease the control room crew's anxieties, he spoke out boldly. "That was no thermocline that the navigator found beneath us at this depth. Those are squid! And they'll serve our purpose just as well."

Astounded by this revelation, the captain managed the barest of relieved grins. If his esteemed white-haired guest's observation indeed proved to be a correct one, the immense school of jet-propelled marine organisms that they were passing through would veil them from the enemies' sonar just as effectively as the thermocline would. Confident that William Abbott knew what he was talking about, Anderson relished the moment when they would have these waters to themselves once again. For then he could begin initiating the directives that would put them back on course for the Panama Canal, and the crystal-blue Caribbean that lay beyond.

Chapter Six

The oars bit into the warm waters of the Caribbean Sea with a bare splash. There was a muted squeal as Egbert pulled the rough wooden handles up toward his chest, before lifting up the oar heads and extending his long arms to repeat once again the monotonous process. There was an alien tightness in his upper arms and shoulders, and the palms of his hands had long since callused over. Yet, because their skiff's engine had conked out soon after they reached Norman Island, he knew he would have to put up with this physical discomfort if they intended to reach their goal as planned.

The blinking red strobe light of the channel buoy that they were headed toward was just visible on the distant horizon. Behind them, the lights of St. John had long since faded.

A gentle swell rocked the battered wooden vessel, and Egbert heard the voice of his brother bark out behind him. "For God's sake, Stanley! You'd better give me a hand bailing, or we'll have to swim the rest of the way."

"Jesus, Delbert! You're a real slave driver," protested Stanley Wilkes. "Can't a guy take a second's rest without you getting on his case?"

"A second's rest?" retorted Delbert. "Why, you've just been sittin' there pickin' your nose ever since we left Norman Island over a quarter of an hour ago. So if you want your fair share of loot, you'd better give me a hand."

This threat seemed to do the trick as Stanley reluctantly responded, "All right, Delbert, you've made your point. So quit your harping and hand me that coffee tin."

Egbert could hear the sound of water being scooped out of the bottom of the boat and emptied over its side. They had borrowed the skiff from a friend of their father, with the premise that they were going to use it to do a little night fishing. As they were soon to learn, not only was its engine unreliable, but it leaked like a sieve as well.

Inwardly cursing his rash decision to go along with his brother's plan, Egbert quickened the pace of his rowing, as if the resulting pain would be just penance. The boat groaned with this increased effort, yet its forward progress remained barely affected.

The channel buoy beckoned teasingly in the distance, seemingly just as far away as it had appeared fifteen minutes ago when the engines died. Though Egbert wanted to postpone the mission at that time, Delbert would hear no part of it. It was obvious that his brother was in a hurry to implement his plan, and not even the threat of sinking could convince him to return to St. John and try again after the engine was repaired.

Egbert was beginning to wonder if this entire screwball plan was such a good idea in the first place. It was fraught with too many unknowns, the worst of which, to drown before they were even able to reach the damned marker buoy. Yet unfortunately he had no other alternatives. He was totally broke, and, as it turned out, didn't even have a real home anymore.

His current predicament came about shortly after Delbert first presented the plan at the site of the abandoned sugar mill. It was immediately afterward that Egbert had had that weird confrontation with his sister. Myrtle's mad babblings had certainly given him a fright, and were most likely the reason for his hasty decision to go back to work at the rental car agency. He did so that very afternoon.

No sooner did he arrive at the lot when a call arrived from a frantic tourist who had driven his Suzuki off a cliff. It was Egbert's first task to extricate the smashed vehicle.

The car was wedged precariously on a cliffside, between two massive manchineel trees. It was a good fifty feet from the pavement, and when it was all over, had taken some six hours to free. It was a backbreaking, frustrating job that took the combined efforts of half a dozen men and all three of the island's tow trucks.

The next morning, his father instructed him to lubricate and change the oil of several of the most frequently traveled rental vehicles. Never a lover of mechanical labor, Egbert grudgingly accepted this task. By lunchtime his hands were so covered with grease that he found himself totally without an appetite. Even after stringently washing his hands, he still felt dirty. When a pan of filthy oil accidentally overturned and spilled all over his favorite blue jeans and sneakers, his disgust turned to pure loathing. He angrily stormed off the job to change and didn't return until the next morning.

His father seemed to be taking it for granted that Egbert had made his final decision, and that he would be dedicating the rest of his life to the agency. This was far from the case, and it all came to a head late one afternoon, when both of them were inside the cramped office counting the week's paltry receipts.

His father had been making an effort to share with Egbert his future plans for increasing their business. Egbert had heard these grandiose ideas many times before and didn't have the nerve to expose them as the pipe dreams that they were. Unable to express his true feelings, Egbert decided then that he had but one course open to him. Since it was cruel to build up his father's hopes, he would run away from home and build a life of his own.

With his few possessions stuffed in a knapsack, he left home that same night and took off for the abandoned sugar mill. Here he spent a sleepless night, plagued by mosquitoes and his own anxieties about the future. Delbert joined him soon after sunrise, and the pipeful of ganja that he brought along did much to ease Egbert's fears. When Stanley Wilkes joined them with the cassette player, it was almost like old times again. With Bob Marley and the Wailers blaring in the background, Delbert once again presented his daring get-rich plan, this time with not a single detail left out. Having nothing to lose, Egbert and Stanley gave the scheme their blessings, and they sealed their agreement with a blood pact.

The rest of the day was spent accumulating the equipment that they would need to carry out the operation. Since it was agreed that cutting and transplanting the huge channel marker would be physically impossible, they planned to blacken out its reflector light and erect a substitute beacon on the nearby shoals at Lucifer's Seat.

Lady Fortune was with them when they found a secondhand buoy for sale in a marine surplus store in Charlotte Amalie. Though it cost them their entire savings, they were also able to purchase a battery-powered strobe light, which fit perfectly into the buoy's upper chamber. Then all they needed to complete their shopping list was a can of waterproof black paint and a brush.

Finding the proper boat to get them to the shoals was their biggest worry. Since renting one was out of the question, they could either resort to stealing a suitable vessel or borrowing one. They decided upon pursuing this latter course, and after a bit of persuasion, convinced a family friend to lend them his fishing skiff for a share of their catch.

With the weather's cooperation, they put to sea soon after sunset. Propelled by the craft's small outboard engine, they cruised out of Coral Bay and crossed the Flannigan Passage. The last vestiges of twilight had faded from the night sky as they approached Norman Island. Egbert had been in the process of marveling at the myriad of twinkling stars visible in the black heavens when the engine suddenly sputtered and stalled. After a bit of effort, Delbert got it going again. Yet, minutes later, it conked out once more, and this time, no matter how hard they pulled on its starter cord, the engine refused to turn over.

Though Egbert suggested that they return to St. John at this point, Delbert argued passionately otherwise. His appeal won them over only when the flashing red strobe of their intended goal was suddenly visible around the far southern shores of Norman Island.

For some reason, Egbert had volunteered to do the rowing. Though it was a physically demanding task, at least it kept him occupied and allowed him time alone to mentally sort out his various problems.

The creak of the oars had an almost hypnotic effect on him. He had finally learned to use them with a smooth, even rhythm, and his previously pained palms, arms, and shoulders were at long last numbing. Deciding to make the best of the situation, he allowed his mind to fill with visions of wealth, and a life beyond material worry.

It proved to be the voice of his brother that snapped him out of his brief reverie. "Damn it, Stanley! I thought that you agreed to do your fair share?"

"Oh, come off it, Delbert," returned Stanley. "Can't a guy at least take a leak in peace?"

The boat rocked hard aport, and Egbert was forced to quickly scoot to his right to keep the fragile craft upright. "Hey, what's going on up there?" he questioned forcefully.

"Keep your cool, little brother," answered Delbert.

149

"Our good buddy Stanley here almost made us shark meat when he stumbled while zipping up his trousers. As if there's anything to stuff back into his shorts anyway."

"Hey, what's that supposed to mean?" retorted Stanley.

Egbert interceded before things got further out of hand. "Stop your foolish bickering, both of you! Now since I'm up here doin' all the work, the least you guys can do is give me some peace and quiet. Or maybe I should turn us around, and we can properly sort this thing out back in St. John."

"Not after we've come this far," observed Delbert. "I can see the channel marker as clear as day, less than a mile up ahead of us."

Turning to look over his shoulder, Egbert confirmed this fact. The buoy was clearly visible now, its beacon shining with a blinding intensity. Aware that his efforts were finally paying off, he returned to his rowing with a feverish intensity. The skiff seemed to surge through the calm water, and before Egbert realized his progress, his brother's voice boomed out behind him.

"Easy, little brother! Swing on upwind, and I'll try to catch it with the boat hook."

Egbert was shocked by the proximity of the bobbing buoy, which lay only a few feet away from their bow. Using one of the oars as a rudder, he followed Delbert's advice, and turned the boat upwind. He then pulled the oars in as the skiff floated practically right up to their objective.

Delbert had no trouble hooking the channel marker, which turned out to be quite a bit larger than any one of them had expected. Once they were securely tied up beside it, the three got to work blocking out its blinking strobe.

As Egbert used a flat wooden stick to stir up the paint can, Stanley surveyed the bobbing buoy, which loomed well over seven feet tall beside them. "Our marker's not even half this size," he reflected. "Won't somebody spot the difference?"

"Not at night," answered Delbert. "And definitely not once we black out its light. Why, from the open waters of the Anegada Passage, you'll never even know that this baby ever existed. Besides, with our beacon flashing away on Lucifer's Seat, they'll have absolutely no reason to suspect that anything out of the ordinary has even occurred."

"If you say so, Del," returned Stanley, who firmly grasped the wire paintbrush that Delbert next handed him.

By this time the paint was properly mixed and Egbert handed the can to his brother commenting, "Since I did all the rowin', you dudes can do the paintin'."

Delbert looked to Stanley and nodded. "That sounds fair enough, little brother. As long as you agree to row us back as well."

Expecting just such a reply, Egbert shook his head disgustedly. "You're one in a million, Del. I don't know why I put up with you."

Delbert grinned and shrugged his broad shoulders. "Some of us got it, and some of us don't. And speakin' of those that don't, what do you say that we get on and complete this project, Stanley Wilkes?"

Stanley looked up at the flashing beacon and

questioned. "But how are we going to reach it? I never dreamed that it would be so damn big!"

Delbert massaged his wide forehead as if he were in the midst of a great pain. "Stanley, my man, if you'd only open those brilliant eyes of yours, you'd see that there's a ladder built into the other side of the buoy. How else do you think that the Coast Guard can service it?"

A look of wonder creased Stanley's face as he walked up to the bow of the skiff and spotted this feature. "Why, I'll be damned," he said with a sigh.

Behind him, the two brothers exchanged the briefest of amused chuckles before Delbert barked out loudly, "Okay, let's get this show on the road. Stanley, you'll do the actual painting, so you go up the ladder first. I'll be right behind you with the can. So watch your step, and please hold onto that brush. It's the only one we've got."

Stanley nodded that he understood, and after securing the handle of the brush in his waistband, reached up to grasp the ladder's lowest rung. Since the skiff was so low in the water, he was able to make contact with the ladder only after timing the arrival of the next swell and stretching his arms upward just as the boat was lifted by the surging sea. He then awkwardly began his climb, with Delbert following close on his heels.

Egbert breathlessly watched as they reached the top of the buoy. Bobbing away in the open ocean as they were, this was an accomplishment in itself. The bright intensity of the strobe caused him to have to turn his eyes away from the beacon, so he could only imagine the scene that was taking place above him as

152

Stanley went to work blacking out the light's smooth glass cover.

Egbert took this opportunity to turn around and peer out in the direction from which they had originally come. The lights of St. John had long since faded, though he could just make out the gray outline of Norman Island. It was on the southern shoals of this uninhabited, rock-strewn archipelago that they would next plant their own buoy. Called Lucifer's Seat by the unfortunate ancients who made an unexpected landfall here, the razor-sharp coral reef directly adjoined the main channel. This feature was of particular interest to scuba divers, who described it as a sheer wall that fell off abruptly to a trench over a thousand feet deep.

Rumor had it that several of the galleys which were unlucky enough to strike the reef, subsequently plunged into this trench. It was said that their cargoes of gold, silver, and gems still littered the ocean floor here, just waiting to be plucked from the deep. Surprised that his brother hadn't thought up a scheme to salvage this treasure by now, Egbert turned back to the buoy when there was a loud shout, followed by the resounding sound of something large crashing into the nearby waters.

With the assistance of a flashlight, Egbert scanned the sea and soon picked out the wide white eyes and soaked black head of Stanley Wilkes floating beside the channel marker. Strangely enough, he was waving the paintbrush high overhead, all the while madly treading water just to stay afloat.

*   *   *

Dr. Susan Patton wasn't a bit surprised how splendidly her work was going. She could tell from the very beginning that Sammy would be a joy to work with. The dolphin was not only extremely intelligent, but he also had a sincere desire to please his human instructors. It was this last quality that allowed her to teach him in three days what would take other dolphins three weeks or longer to learn.

As she sat in her office watching the video tapes Owen had taken of this training period, Susan realized how very fortunate she had been. If all went as planned, they'd be fitting Sammy into the harness tomorrow morning. Then they'd give him several hours to get used to the device before attaching the miniature fiber-optic camera to it and sending him out into the lagoon for some basic retrieval exercises. Several retrievals in the open sea would follow. And by that time he'd hopefully be ready for the arrival of Commander Walker and the congressional committee, who would be arriving late Wednesday morning.

Thus, with no time to waste, Susan reviewed the video tapes to make certain that she had not missed any weaknesses in Sammy's behavioral makeup. The earliest frames showed her making the first tentative steps toward building their relationship. She did so by touch and voice. Sammy loved to be petted. He particularly liked it when she gently stroked his sides with a stiffly bristled brush.

Unlike most newly captured bottlenose dolphins, Sammy started feeding almost immediately. His appetite was a voracious one, and her assistant was full-pressed to supply the dozens of pounds of live mullet that he swallowed whole, headfirst.

As Sammy became increasingly comfortable with her, Susan began utilizing a high-pitched whistle as a conditional reinforcer. She would put this device into play, accompanied by various hand signals, whenever she demanded a task from him. He soon learned to associate the whistle with feeding time, and would do his best to please Susan so that she'd get on with serving the meal. In no time at all he was retrieving balls and hoops on command, and even diving to the bottom of the lagoon to bring back specially designed, weighted lead rings.

On the second day of full training, Sammy was transferred to the beachside capture tank. Though he was a bit skittish at first, he soon adjusted to his new confines and even wolfed down a couple of mullet as certain proof of this fact.

It was at this point that Susan got into the water with him. The tapes of this exciting encounter flashed on the monitor, and the blond marine biologist would never forget the moment when their bodies first touched. Sammy's skin was smooth and supple. As she stroked the area beside his pectoral fins, he gently nudged the sides of her thighs with his snout. There was an almost sexual quality to this caress, and Susan flashed back on one particular portion of a diary segment that she had recently read, written by the psychiatrist who had originally built this tank twenty years ago.

In his ongoing effort to further teach a dolphin human language, an experiment was initiated in which one of his female lab assistants would live with a bottlenose, day and night, for a period of over two months. A bed was erected on a platform at the center of the tank, and it was here the assistant slept, with her student resting close at her side.

Several weeks into the experiment, the dolphin began showing unmistakable signs of sexual attraction. He would nip at the assistant's legs whenever he got the chance and would attempt to jam himself up against her and knock her over.

The diary segment included several passages of a most fascinating nature, in which the assistant described the moment when the dolphin first allowed her to take his sexual organ in hand. The organ, which was positioned inside a sheathlike enclosure, was described as being flat and triangular in shape. As she grasped it, the animal would start shaking its body, and with his mouth open and eyes closed, would attain an orgasm in approximately thirty seconds.

Though Susan certainly didn't have this kind of encounter in mind as she swam beside Sammy in the tank, she couldn't help but feel sensually attuned to him. His sleek body was smooth and powerful, and there could be no doubting that he was consciously aware of her as well.

A tight new bond existed between them as Susan reluctantly left the tank and Sammy was transferred back to the lagoon once more. With their relationship now firmly established, Susan began teaching him a very special retrieval process that would be an important part of Wednesday's demonstration.

One of the weighted rings was fitted with a battery-powered, waterproof beacon. This light not only blinked, but also let out an ultrasonic signal. It was then tossed out far into the lagoon, where it sank to the bottom. By raising her balled fist high over her head and blowing the whistle, Susan indicated to Sammy that she wanted him to retrieve this object. He did so without a moment's hesitation.

Once Sammy became accustomed to the harness, they would board the skiff and guide him out into the open sea. At this time they would train him to follow the boat, and to accomplish several of the retrieval procedures outside the sheltered waters of the lagoon. If all went well, he'd be ready for the actual demonstration right as scheduled.

To best show off the harness's varied capabilities, Susan planned an unofficial treasure hunt. This event would take place Wednesday afternoon. After taking her esteemed guests on a quick tour of the facilities, she'd guide them onto a forty-eight-foot dive boat that she had already rented for the day. A picnic lunch would be served, and with a local steel band providing the necessary atmosphere, they'd leave the sheltered waters of Hurricane Hole and cross Coral Bay. Sammy would be swimming at their side as they initiated a quick trip over Flannagan's Passage, with their final anchorage being off Norman Island beside the shoal known as Lucifer's Seat.

She'd picked this particular spot for two reasons. First off, it provided the open ocean setting that the Navy had requested from the very beginning. Her second reason was a bit more theatrical. Lucifer's Seat was formed by a magnificent coral reef that directly adjoined a thousand-foot-deep trench. Several of the local divers had told her about the dozens of ancient wrecks that supposedly lined the sea bottom here. Unfortunately, their great depth kept them out of the reach of the average scuba diver. This was not the case for Sammy.

A dolphin did not have to worry about decompression sickness, or the bends, as it was more commonly known. Linked to the surface by the fiber-optic camera he would be carrying, Sammy would be sent after the weighted ring that Susan would throw out into the blue waters. Then she merely had to raise her balled fist high overhead and blow the whistle in order to send him plummeting into the depths to retrieve it.

It would take Sammy approximately four minutes to reach the bottom of the trench. If fortune was with them, hopefully, as Sammy located the ring and proceeded to return it to the surface, the specially designed camera he'd be carrying along would catch a glimpse of some of the wreckage accumulated there.

Surely such a demonstration would not only show off the capabilities of the harness device itself, but also showcase the exciting possibilities that awaited its application. Heretofore unexplored areas of the planet's ocean bottom could thus be explored, and for the first time ever, man could share in the vast wonders of the deep. If all went well, an entirely new project of a much greater scope could possibly await her. She envisioned hundreds of dolphins such as Sammy scanning the depths with their harness-borne cameras. There was no telling what they'd come upon. Even the legendary lost continent of Atlantis could possibly await them!

Inspired by such a grandiose thought, Susan switched off the video recorder and issued a wide yawn. She had been working over fourteen consecutive hours, and an equally demanding day awaited her tomorrow. Yet before surrendering to the call of her mattress, she decided to walk down to the lagoon to check on the condition of her all-so-special prodigy.

Outside, the night was hot and humid. The moon had yet to rise, and the stars shone forth in abundance in the clear black heavens. It was ghostly still, and the only sound audible was the persistent slapping surge of the surf.

Susan needed to use a flashlight to follow the meander of the narrow earthen footpath that led down to the beach. Once on the soft white sand, she kicked off her sandals and watched as the crabs scurried for shelter, her torch's narrow beam illuminating these nocturnal creatures like the light of a newly arisen sun.

As she stood on the edge of the lagoon, her feet cool in the wet sand, her gaze wandered off to the sea beyond. The Caribbean looked menacingly black and all-encompassing, its waters ever flowing like a single entity. And a peace descended upon her, her thoughts soaring far away from everyday worries and responsibilities. She was suddenly at one with the night, and as such became one of its protected creatures.

Susan stood in this trancelike rapture that was interrupted only when a loud slapping sound broke the surface of the nearby waters. Suddenly aware again of her purpose here, she was in the process of reaching into her pocket to remove the whistle with which she had hoped to call forth Sammy when she

159

realized that she wasn't alone. Lying in the still waters of the lagoon, only a few feet away, was the familiar sleek body of a dolphin. Yet it was this creature's mischievous black eyes that immediately captivated her, and without having to see any more of the animal, she knew that it was Sammy.

Had it been a psychic force that enabled her to call the dolphin without having to use her whistle? Or perhaps it was the other way around, and it had been Sammy's extrasensory abilities that had summoned her to the side of the lagoon. Such a thought stirred the roots of her imagination, and it was only then that she heard the distant, monotonous beat of a single drum, emanating from somewhere in the hills far behind her.

High above the cove of water known as Hurricane Hole, on a volcanic promontory formed over a million years ago, the mortal female known as Myrtle Hall initiated her summons of the ancient ones. Her altar was a handmade, crude affair, set in a semi-circle of stunted frangipani trees. So intense was her concentration as she beat away on the gourd, the human-skin drum, that she didn't notice the massive bats swooping down over her to drink the sweet nectar from the fragrant pink frangipani flowers.

A single red candle flickered alive before her from a protected alcove in the altar, beside which was placed a human skull and a machete, whose hilt was covered by a red bandanna. Various colored bottles of herbs and viscous oils completed this macabre setting.

Her adoration was an especially effective one, for she had been taught the age-old secrets of voodoo by a mambo of the first degree. Though Miss Sarah was long dead in her grave, her spirit still walked the crossroads, just waiting to be called back to do service.

Thus it was to Baron Samedi, the guardian of the cemetery and the lord of the crossroads, that her initial prayers were directed. Timing her petition to the constant beating of the drum, Myrtle lost her gaze in the flickering red candlelight. As she repeated the ancient words, her pulse quickened, and she suddenly found herself magically whisked off to the carrefour, the place where the four roads met. Waiting for her here was a familiar white-haired old lady who hovered several inches above the foggy ground, her eyes formed of pure fire.

When the ancient elder finally greeted her, it was with the deep, hoarse voice of Damballah, the serpent. "Greetings, chosen one. The time of darkness is almost upon us. The evil approaches and the savior has arrived to do battle. Know this, and raise your prayers in support of he who dares challenge the black tide of death.

"And if the vodoun gods find your petitions worthy, then perhaps they shall intercede, and the blackness will be sent to the cold black depths from which they once crawled. As a mortal who has been buried alive screams in utter terror to be freed from his coffin, so shall the zombielike sleep be upon the evil ones. For it shall be the final struggle that will decide their destinies. So return to the world of man, child, and keep your heart clean. And perhaps

Erzulie shall be merciful and the world that you know will be spared a fiery end.''

With the conclusion of these puzzling words, the apparition of Miss Sarah faded into the fog, and Myrtle once again found herself back before the flickering flame of her altar. The air was ghostly still, and except for the cries of the night creatures, all was deathly silent. Certain that her vision had been a very real one, Myrtle pondered the great responsibility that had been placed upon her shoulders. For it would be her prayers alone that would decide the destiny of an entire planet!

Chapter Seven

Captain Mikhail Sobrinka couldn't be more satisfied with his ship's progress. After all, this was the *Caspian*'s maiden voyage and they had already transited waters that no Typhoon class sub had ever visited before. This in itself was a major accomplishment, and a tribute to the hardworking men and women who had made the unprecedented patrol possible.

As he continued his inspection of the huge vessel, with his trusty senior lieutenant at his side, Sobrinka marveled at the *Caspian*'s novel design. Unlike any other class of submarine that had ever put to sea, the Typhoons were comprised of two parallel, one-hundred-and-thirty-meter-long pressure cylinders, wrapped in a broad outer casing. Yet another third pressure cylinder lay directly beneath the sail and housed the attack center and command spaces. Such an arrangement provided additional protection from torpedo attack by creating a two-meter shock buffer between the inner and outer hulls.

The captain was currently crossing into the aft portion of the ship where the *Caspian*'s dual propulsion units were located. Another unusual feature of the Typhoon class was that each of the pressure cylinders contained its own nuclear reactor and steam turbine plant, each of which drove a separate seven-bladed propellor. The two units were capable of independent operation and thus acted as an additional fail-safe measure should an attack or a mechanical breakdown render one of the reactors inoperable.

At sixty-three years of age, Mikhail Sobrinka had been in the Navy when the Soviet Union's very first nuclear-powered submarine became operational in 1958. The reactors that powered these November class vessels were crude in comparison to the units aboard the *Caspian*. Of course in three decades practically every other mechanical feature had changed as well, from the high-tech, state-of-the-art electro-optical sensors that they carried, to the *Caspian*'s awesome offensive capabilities.

As they approached the port propulsion unit, the waxlike smell of warm polyethylene met his nostrils. The spacious passageway they traveled down filled with the muted hum of heavy machinery, and the captain anxiously anticipated the equipment-packed compartment that lay beyond the next hatchway.

"Let me get your radiation badge for you, Captain," offered the alert senior lieutenant as he stepped forward and reached into a recessed shelf set beside the reactor room access trunk.

"Why, thank you, Comrade Jarensk," replied Mikhail Sobrinka, who accepted the badge and pinned it to his chest.

As the senior lieutenant did likewise, Sobrinka gestured toward the hatchway that faced them. "Shall we go and see how Chief Litvak and his men are doing? I still say it's a wonder that they were able to get the system on line when they did."

The *Caspian*'s second-in-command answered while feeding an electronic keycard into a recessed slot set into the adjoining bulkhead. "They certainly deserve a medal for their efforts, Captain. After all, their initial orders were to prepare for a departure from Murmansk two weeks later than we actually set sail."

The hatch slid open with a loud hiss and the captain grunted. "Let's just keep our fingers crossed that all remains operational."

Stepping through the double-wide trunk, the white-haired veteran officer entered a cavernous compartment completely painted in red, its deck covered by a thick green rubber matting. An eerie, tomblike silence prevailed, except for the hollow whine of the ventilation blowers and the muffled surge of the powerful pumps that constantly circulated a high-pressure stream of coolant water through the reactor grid.

Taking in the complex mass of snaking pipes and cables that lined the walls and ceiling, Sobrinka grinned upon spotting the familiar, pot-bellied figure of Master Chief Yuri Litvak perched before the maneuvering console. The ever-vigilant chief hovered above the seated attendants like a mother hen, his eyes darting from the panel of dials that monitored the volume, temperature, and pressure of the coolant as it passed in and out of the reactor. Every so often he'd reach forward and trigger one of the small pistol switches that controlled the rods and altered the reactor's power level. So intense was his concentration that the captain had to clear his throat loudly to catch the chief's attention.

"Good evening, Comrade Litvak," greeted Mikhail Sobrinka. "How goes it?"

A smile lit the chief's lined face as he took in the source of this salutation. "Why, Captain, this is a surprise! You honor us with your esteemed presence."

"Nonsense," retorted the captain, who stepped forward to join the chief beside the console. "I'm sorry I didn't have a chance to personally visit you much earlier in our voyage, but my attentions were needed elsewhere. Besides, I knew that the *Caspian*'s propulsion system was in good hands with you and your men at the controls. Have you encountered any major problems so far?"

The chief shook his head. "Absolutely none, Captain. Both units have been purring away like a newborn kitten."

"That's incredible considering the haste with which this entire mission was conceived and implemented," returned the captain.

"That it is, Captain. Would you like to take a look at the heart of our little system here?"

"Why, of course, Chief. Lead on!"

After giving a series of last-minute instructions to one of the seated technicians, the chief led the *Caspian*'s two senior officers to the center of the spacious compartment. Here there were two inspection windows cut into the deck itself. Without a moment's hesitation, both the captain and his senior lieutenant went to their knees and bent over. They examined the fully visible, self-contained space holding the reactor machinery, which was approximately seven meters below. This included the rods that controlled the fission process and the glowing, fist-sized ball of uranium, from whose core the vessel's power source was derived.

"It's truly wondrous how such a seemingly insignificant amount of material can be responsible for such incredible amounts of energy," reflected the captain as he stiffly sat upright.

"I've been working with nuclear reactors for the last two decades, and they still amaze me as well, Captain,' returned the chief, who offered one of his giant hands to help Mikhail Sobrinka stand once again.

Touching the radiation badge pinned to his chest, the captain added, "Though nuclear power might have its dangers, it's certainly a far cry better than having to rely upon fossil fuel and batteries. Without our reactors to power us, missions such as the one we're presently on would be impossible to complete successfully."

The mere mention of their current duty caused a frown to crease the chief's forehead. "If my calculations are correct, we should be entering the Caribbean Sea shortly. Is it still the waters off Cienfuegos that we're bound to?"

The captain appeared equally concerned as he answered, "That they are, Chief. We will be completing our transit of the Atlantic sometime this evening within the next few hours. The route we've

167

chosen is a bit out of the way, but it should allow us to remain clear of the American SOSUS sensors that litter the sea floor of the more standard passages."

"I know it's none of my business, sir, but what are we doing here in the first place? I always thought we were designed exclusively for service beneath the ice pack."

The captain listened to the chief's words and heavily sighed. "So did I, Comrade. Yet as a first-line ship of the fleet, the *Caspian* is well prepared to go wherever Command sends her. As far as I know, this is the first time that a Typhoon class vessel has been sent on such a mission."

"And exactly what mission is that, Captain?" dared the chief.

Sobrinka returned the veteran sailor's gaze and winked. "You just take care of our propulsion system and give me anything that I might ask of it, and when the time comes you'll be among the first whom I'll share the details of our mission with. First we have to transit that passage, cross the breadth of the Caribbean Sea, and attain our patrol sector off the southern coast of Cuba. So, can you wait for an answer to your question until then, Comrade?"

The chief wisely grinned. "Do I have any other choice in the matter?"

Mikhail lightly patted Litvak on the back and turned to address his senior lieutenant. "Come, Comrade Jarensk, we still have the missile magazine to inspect before dinner. And since the chef is cooking up a mess of his infamous Ukrainian borscht this evening, we mustn't tarry a second longer."

"Don't be such a stranger," offered the chief,

watching as the two senior officers exited the compartment from its forward access hatch. Taking a moment to thoughtfully stroke his square jaw, he then turned back toward the main propulsion console to continue his duty.

Meanwhile, the captain led the way quickly down the tunnellike passageway that connected the aft section of the *Caspian* with the rest of the ship. As they passed by the hatch leading to the control room, Mikhail briefly halted and addressed the lieutenant. "Lieutenant Jarensk, I want you to go into navigation and pull all charts we have of the Anegada Passage. Make certain to include the specially prepared series that Intelligence was supposed to have transferred to us back in Murmansk. I'll be waiting for them in the taiga."

"At once, sir!" returned the senior lieutenant.

Watching as he smartly clicked his heels and turned to duck through the adjoining hatch to get on with this task, Mikhail continued on down the passageway. The ship's missile magazine, or taiga as it was fondly called, was located forward of the sail. This was unlike all other classes of ballistic-missile-carrying submarines that stored their rockets in the stern half of the ship.

The captain had to admit that he was far more at home in the massive, silo-lined compartment than he had been back in engineering. The nuclear reactors would always be alien to him, yet ballistic missiles were something he could readily understand. For here were the deadly objects that the *Caspian* had been designed around.

The twenty SS-N-20's were each stored in individual launch capsules, in side-by-side rows of ten apiece. The silos themselves were painted brown and green, and indeed resembled the forest from which the magazine got its nickname. Like the taiga, the missile capsules appeared like the trunks of a stand of mighty trees. Yet this was as far as the similarities went.

The SS-N-20 was the mightiest weapon in the Soviet's underwater arsenal. Powered by solid-fuel propellants, each missile carried nine MIRVed warheads with a maximum range of over 8,300 kilometers. Even from their current position, they could hit targets all over North America, excluding portions of northwestern Canada and Alaska. With a yield of one megaton, or the equivalent of one million tons of TNT each, the *Caspian*'s 180 separate warheads could alone wipe out every single major metropolitan area on the U.S. mainland and still have a missile or two remaining in reserve. Mikhail thus had an awesome responsibility, one which he did not take lightly.

Command of the *Caspian* was the pinnacle of a long naval career that spanned over four decades. The son of an itinerant Siberian coal miner, Mikhail was living proof that the socialist system offered every citizen of the Motherland an equal chance to follow his dream.

As a lad he used to sit on the shores of Lake Baikal and dream of the day he'd be able to put to sea himself. The opportunity came to him several years later, when his above-average school marks and natural leadership abilities had caught the eye of the leader of his Young Pioneers group. It was on his recommendation alone that Mikhail gained entrance to the Makarov Pacific Ocean Higher School in Vladivostok.

The Great War had only just ended, with the American atomic attack on the cities of Hiroshima and Nagasaki signaling the beginning of a new age of international relations. To compete in this new world, the Motherland was forced to radically redesign and revamp its fighting forces. Scarred badly by massive losses on the western front, the military had little time to taste the sweet fruits of their hard-earned victory. In only a few years, Soviet scientists were also to unlock the secrets of the atom. And it was now up to the military to find a way of effectively delivering these awesome weapons of destruction.

The Soviet Navy took this challenge very seriously, and by 1958 had a fleet of submarines at sea that could actually launch nuclear-tipped ballistic missiles from their holds. It was on such a Golf class vessel that Mikhail had qualified. Though such ships were dependent upon diesel-electric power and had to surface first before releasing their load of limited-range nuclear missiles, these warships were a forerunner of things to come.

By 1967, a new generation of sophisticated, nuclear-powered ballistic-missile-carrying submarines joined the Soviet fleet. As a fully trained weapons specialist, Mikhail was transferred to one of these Yankee class ships on which he served with distinction for five years until the first Delta class vessel was ready for its premier patrol. It was on one of these potent, reliable platforms that he attained the rank of senior lieutenant and eventually became a full captain.

In 1980, when the first Typhoon class vessel was already well on its way to completion at the Severodvinsk Shipyards, Mikhail was sent to the General Staff Academy at Moscow as an instructor. Though this transfer was a major promotion and included a luxurious apartment and even a car of his own, he genuinely missed duty at sea. Mikhail expressed himself to his immediate superior officer, Admiral Viktor Chimki. A submariner himself at one time, Chimki understood his problem and began doing some delicate probing on Mikhail's behalf at the General Staff of the Defense Ministry. When the construction of the fifth Typhoon class boat was authorized in 1986, it was unanimously decided that Mikhail Sobrinka would be its commanding officer.

Needless to say, Mikhail was thrilled with this assignment. After an extensive training period, he was sent to the Severodvinsk shipyards to help coordinate the *Caspian*'s launching. Sea trials followed, and as the boat was in the process of undergoing its final refit, his present orders were received.

It was ironic that it was Admiral Viktor Chimki who personally delivered these sailing orders. Though a good fourteen years Mikhail's senior, Chimki seemed to look no different from the first time they had met in 1974. He did seem a bit more somber, though, as he took Mikhail aside and explained what Command wanted from the *Caspian*.

Premier Ivanov's untimely death was the reason

for their hurried departure from Murmansk. Fearful that American CIA agents had played a direct part in this assassination, the Defense Ministry had ordered the *Caspian* to deploy in the waters immediately south of the Cuban city of Cienfuegos. Once this CIA link was established for certain, it would be the *Caspian* that would act as the ultimate revenge force.

They would do so by launching a single missile with nine MIRVed warheads. As a just price for America's gross wrongdoing, the cities of Miami, Key West, Tampa, Jacksonville, Pensacola, Mobile, New Orleans, Shreveport, and Houston would disappear forever in an atomic firestorm. And before the strategic forces of imperialism could answer with a strike of their own, a final ultimatum would be delivered to the American President, warning him that much greater devastation awaited his country if he dared convey the orders releasing the U.S. triad. And of course it would be the *Caspian*'s continued presence that would keep him from doing so!

As Mikhail began walking down the padded passageway that lay between the two rows of SS-N-20 missile silos, the reality of his current mission finally hit home. They were on a cruise that would change the very hand of destiny. And as far as Mikhail was concerned, it was about time!

Ever since the closing days of World War II, he believed, the United States had played the part of an aggressor as dangerous as Hitler's crazed hordes. The byproducts of capitalism were deceptive evils that subtly worked their way into a people's moral fabric and corrupted their social outlook. Greed of possessions was their poison, with imperialism being the vehicle that spread these so-called democratic values to the peoples of the world.

For four decades Mikhail had watched this cancer grow. In countries such as Korea and Vietnam, the people dared to stand up to Uncle Sam, and, as a result, were spared the ravages of capitalist ideology. Unfortunately, they were exceptions to the rule, as imperialism was spread to the far corners of the globe, contaminating even Mao's China and the Motherland herself!

Beneath the world's oceans, the Americans were fighting an unofficial war of their own. It had all started during the Cuban missile crisis, when the U.S. Navy had the nerve to tag every single Soviet submarine in the open seas. This battle took the form of American submarines maneuvering their attack platforms dangerously close to similar Soviet boats. To keep from colliding, Russian crews were often forced to take drastic measures, with all of this occurring in international waters.

Mikhail was no starnger to such skirmishes. Once when he was at the helm of a Delta class boat that was innocently cruising beneath the Barents Sea, an American Sturgeon class attack sub was located following close in their baffles. Not only did the U.S. ship attempt to run them aground, but they released a powerful sonic lashing that had permanently deafened one of Mikhail's sonar officers.

This was not an isolated incident, and Mikhail and his fellow sub captains found themselves frustrated with Command's continued reluctance to order some sort of retaliatory efforts of their own. Unfortunately, it took the sudden death of a great leader to finally awaken them from their cowardly stupor.

Proud that Command had chosen him to set the record straight, Mikhail carefully checked the integrity of each of the sealed missile launch tubes. He had gotten as far as silo number seven when he was aware of another's presence behind him. He turned in time to see his senior lieutenant briskly stroll down the walkway with a tubular chart rolled beneath his arm.

"Captain, the only chart of the passage that you spoke of is from the *Caspian*'s regular library. Are you absolutely certain that others were supposed to be delivered to us?"

"Why, of course I'm certain!" retorted Mikhail forcefully. "The Defense Ministry itself was supposed to be sending them to us by special messenger. Surely you overlooked them, or perhaps they've been misfiled."

The senior lieutenant shook his head. "Though I've got the navigator sorting through the files now to check that very possibility, he remembers nothing about any such special delivery."

A disbelieving look crossed the captain's face. "Surely he's mistaken. Perhaps in the excitement of our early departure he mislaid them."

"With all due respect, sir, that's extremely unlikely. Lieutenant Tura is a most efficient, tidy officer. He's not the type to overlook such an important thing."

In no mood to argue otherwise, the captain shrugged his shoulders. "Well, what more can I say? If they're not there, they're not there. It's as simple as that. So let me see the chart you're carrying."

The senior lieutenant handed Mikhail the map, a

standard projection of the Leeward Islands. It showed the eastern edge of Puerto Rico, the Virgin Islands, and the strait of water lying to their immediate east.

"The ship's library does have several more detailed renderings of the normal transit points into the Caribbean Sea, via the Florida Straits or the Windward Passage," observed the *Caspian*'s second-in-command. "Perhaps we should divert our course to one of these locations."

"Absolutely not!" retorted the captain. "There's a most definite reason why we picked the Anegada Passage, Comrade. It's lightly monitored, and isn't even covered by a sensor array. And now that we're traveling on our own, it's even more important than ever before that we enter the Caribbean as stealthily as possible."

"Perhaps we should wait for Captain Gnutov and the *Kirov* to join us before continuing," offered the senior lieutenant.

Studying the chart he was holding, Mikhail grunted. "And who knows when that might be, my friend. The English are skillful sailors, and though their equipment might not be as advanced as ours, they're more than capable of giving the *Kirov* a good chase. Don't forget that Gnutov's job was to keep the Trafalgar class vessel as far from us as possible. Thus there's no telling how distant the *Kirov* had to travel to lose them.

"No, Comrade, I'm afraid my orders are absolutely clear in this matter. We must get to our patrol station with all due haste, with or without those special charts or the *Kirov*'s protection."

176

With this said, Mikhail Sobrinka did his best to make the best of their situation. "Cheer up, Comrade Jarensk, and don't look so glum. This chart has plenty of bathymetric detail for us to follow. And besides, don't forget that the Anegada Passage is a regularly traveled route. That means that the U.S. Coast Guard maintains channel markers in the area. Why, even without a map, we'd be able to trace the transit channel merely by ascending to periscope depth and following the blinking buoys all the way to the open seas of the Caribbean."

Suddenly looking down at his watch, Mikhail added, "We will be approaching the passage shortly. Topside it should just about be twilight. That means by the time we reach the straits it will be pitch black up there. Can you think of a better time to ascend to periscope depth? Of course you can't, Comrade! So trust this old veteran, and let's go and feed our bellies. I can practically smell that Ukrainian borscht from here, and there will be plenty of time for worrying once we've eaten our fair share of it."

The senior lieutenant's expression softened. "You're right, Captain. This transit is no different than any other. I guess I've just become a bit of a worrywart in my old age."

"Old, you say?" repeated Mikhail. "Why, you don't know what that word really means yet, lad. And don't think that you hold the monopoly on worrying either. I've got a hole in my gut to prove it. So I'd better plug it up with some of the chef's borscht and then get on with the job at hand."

Beckoning his second-in-command to lead the way to the wardroom, Mikhail Sobrinka wisely winked.

And in that second, the tension of the moment was completely dissipated.

The *Caspian*'s officers' mess was located amidships, on the deck directly beneath the attack center. It was of considerable size, and had a large circular table set in its center. A deep blue carpet and wood-paneled walls gave the wardroom a clublike atmosphere. This feeling was enhanced by the series of framed photographs that encircled the room, showing various pictures of the world's largest inland body of water for which the vessel was named.

Mikhail Sobrinka and his senior lieutenant entered and found several of the ship's officers gathered around the table in the middle of their meals. Upon noting the two newcomers, these officers stopped their conversations and put down their knives and forks.

The captain reached his customary seat and briefly greeted them. "At ease, Comrades. I hope it tastes as good as it smells, and that you've left me and the senior lieutenant here some leftovers."

This remark served to break the ice, yet the officers only returned to their meals and conversations when the orderly placed several bowls of food before the captain and his second-in-command. Mikhail wasted no time digging into this anticipated feast.

As expected, the main course was Ukrainian borscht. Their chef was a native of Kiev, and this dish was his homeland's specialty. Immersed in the rich beet broth were chunks of potatoes, carrots, onions, celery, and tangy sausage. Served alongside the borscht was a bowl of steaming cabbage, a basket of flavorful onion rolls, and a tall glass of *kvass*.

178

Mikhail had a particular fondness for this lightly fermented beverage that was brewed from malt and flavored with hops.

Picking up his glass, the captain raised it in the air and toasted. "To the Motherland, Comrades! Long may she live in peace and equality."

The others present at the table lifted their own glasses upward to return the toast. As each of them took a sip of their beverages, they watched as their captain lowered his glass and began eating in earnest.

Between bites of sausage, Mikhail addressed the *Caspian*'s supply officer, who was seated on his left. "The chef has outdone himself, Comrade. This bowl is filled with all types of surprises. Now tell me, how did your inventory of the ship's stores go?"

The supply officer answered after taking a long sip of *kvass*. "The results are still being tallied, sir, but it looks like we're going to be at least a metric ton short on basic foodstuffs. Because of the sudden nature of our departure, most of these shortages concern our fresh-frozen stocks of meat, chicken, fish, and produce. Is there a chance that we'll be able to restock in Cienfuegos, Captain?"

Mikhail took a moment to completely chew up a mouthful of cabbage before answering, "I still can't say for certain, Lieutenant. Right now, it all depends on Command. That means we'll just have to make do with the dehydrated and canned goods until orders sending us to port are received. So I guess we'd better enjoy meals such as this one while the fresh food lasts."

The supply officer meekly nodded and the captain

returned to his food with renewed gusto. After polishing off his cabbage, he went to work on the borscht, which he consumed without a word wasted. Only after mopping up the remaining juice with a roll did he drain his glass of *kvass* and issue a satisfied belch.

This was the sign for the orderly to serve dessert. After completing a bowl of chilled fruit compote that had a dollop of *smetana*, or sour cream, on top of it, the captain decided it was time to properly address those assembled around him. Lightly striking the bottom of his spoon up against the rim of his glass, Mikhail stood and cleared his throat.

"As most of you very well know, the *Caspian* will be entering the waters of the Caribbean Sea shortly. This will put us less than forty-eight hours away from our final destination in the black depths off the Cuban port city of Cienfuegos. I'm certain that many of you are wondering why we've been called to sea on such short notice and would like to know the reason a Typhoon class vessel has been chosen to undergo such a mission. For we are far away from the ice fields beneath which we were originally designed to operate.

"Unfortunately, I am not yet at liberty to divulge the answers to these puzzling questions. I have been authorized to brief you on the details of our mission once we've attained our final patrol station. Until that time, be satisfied with the knowledge that the *Caspian* is embarked on an assignment of the utmost importance, one which will directly affect the destiny of not only the Motherland, but the world itself."

This comment immediately caught his audience's attention. Looking down at his watch, the captain observed, "The passage that will lead us into the Caribbean rapidly approaches, and it's time to prepare the ship for this transit. Senior Lieutenant, send the crew to general quarters and assemble the senior command staff in the control room."

"At once, sir," returned the *Caspian*'s second-in-command, who alertly stood to carry out these orders.

As the others also stood, the captain patted his stomach and added, "We've been fed well, and now it's time to properly work off this meal. To your stations, men, for the glory of the Motherland!"

After a quick visit to his cabin, Mikhail proceeded straight to the *Caspian*'s control room. Set immediately beneath the sail, in an individual pressure cylinder of its own, this compartment was the nerve center of the giant warship. Bathed in red light to protect the crew's night vision, the control room was spaciously designed, with the latest in high-tech digital consoles lining its walls.

"Lighten the ship and take us up to periscope depth," ordered the captain, beckoning the senior lieutenant to join him at the periscope well.

A muted chime sounded, and Mikhail reached forward to flick a series of toggle switches. There was the loud swish of hydraulic oil as the scope rose upward from below. It was the captain, who grasped the device's arms and bent over to gaze through its protective rubberized coupling. With the assistance of a night-vision unit, he was able to scan the rippling horizon, even though the sun had long since set. The bare outline of an island lay off their starboard bow, and Mikhail stood back and grunted. "I believe that land mass to our starboard is called Norman Island. St. John is obscured behind it."

To verify the captain's observations, Senior Lieu-tenant Jarensk leaned over and peered out the scope himself. He sharpened the focus mechanism and initiated a complete three-hundred-and-sixty-degree circle of the waters around them.

"It appears that you're correct, Captain," returned Jarensk. "The channel cuts abruptly to the right up ahead, and we must be extra cautious not to hit the reef that borders the island there. Yet where are those Coast Guard channel markers that you mentioned would be found here?"

Replacing Jarensk at the scope, Mikhail took another long look at the strait of water before them. He had taken it for granted that the United States Coast Guard would have some sort of directional buoys in the passage. But try as he might, he was unable to spot them.

"That's odd," mumbled Mikhail, still draped over the perisocope, oblivious to the pain that had begun throbbing in the small of his back. "I guess that I was mistaken in my assumption."

To be certain, he doubled the magnification of the viewing lens. Still finding no blinking channel beacon, he increased the viewing magnification fivefold, then ten. This was the scope's maximum power, and allowed him to just view a dim red strobe light, cutting through the darkness in the waters adjoining the nearby island.

"I've got it!" he exclaimed. "Though it's certainly not as powerful as I expected, that's one of their marker buoys, all right. Though I'm positive we could have transited the passage without its assis-tance, it's still nevertheless comforting to know the true extent of the channel."

Quick to replace Mikhail at the scope was his senior lieutenant.

"I see it, Captain. But are you sure it's the channel marker? It seems awfully close to the shoreline."

"Of course I'm sure," retorted the white-haired veteran. "The Americans are meticulous in these matters. So don't tarry, and plot a course that will take us just to the left of it."

In no position to argue otherwise, the senior lieutenant determined the proper course coordinates and relayed them to the seated helmsman.

"All ahead one-third!" added the captain, who was already mentally visualizing the vast, deep waters of the Caribbean Sea which lay immediately beyond.

The *Caspian* ever so gradually began picking up forward speed, as its dual seven-bladed propellors bit into the calm waters of the Anegada Passage. This increase in velocity was barely noticeable inside the vessel's control room, where the command staff was engrossed in their instruments.

It was the ship's senior lieutenant who was able to best gauge their continued progress. Draped over the perisocope, he watched as the red flashing beacon continued to get closer and closer. He was able to view the buoy under normal magnification now, gently bobbing in the waters before them.

"How much depth do we have beneath us?" boomed the authoritative voice of the captain behind him.

"Three hundred and twenty-five fathoms, sir," returned the ensign assigned to monitoring the fathometer. "The channel seems well defined, yet I am starting to pick up a bit of bottom irregularity."

"That's only normal in these waters," replied the

captain. "Don't be afraid to call out if the depth changes radically."

"Yes, sir!" shot back the sensor operator.

Satisfied that all appeared to be going smoothly, the senior lieutenant dared to back away momentarily from the periscope. He caught the captain's contented gaze and was just about to comment on their excellent progress, when the high-pitched voice of the sensor operator cried out frantically. "My instruments show a solid shelf dead ahead of us, sir!"

"Emergency stop!" forcefully ordered Mikhail Sobrinka. Yet before he could follow up this directive, there was a violent concussion accompanied by the deafening sound of rending metal. Pitched forward by the sheer force of this unexpected collision, Mikhail found himself flung to the deck, with his senior lieutenant crashing down close beside him. The vessel rolled hard on its side, and the two senior officers uncontrollably tumbled into each other, all the while madly reaching out for something solid to stabilize them. As the interior lights blinked off, and on, then off once again, they smashed into the forward partition, along with an assortment of loose equipment that was also jarred loose by the impact.

The deck quivered and shook. There was the acrid smell of smoke in the air as the mighty underwater warship's electrical systems overloaded and shorted out. Still bathed in a tomblike blackness, Mikhail struggled to sit upright. He found himself gasping for breath, for the wind had been knocked out of him by the force of his fall. In the time it took him to regain his breath, he listened to the sickening sound of the sub's groaning hull and the moans of his

184

fellow shipmates scattered somewhere in the darkness around him.

"Get those emergency lights on!" he managed between painful gasps.

It seemed to take an eternity before this directive was finally carried out. The dim red light of the battle lanterns cast a ghostly shadow as he surveyed the compartment's disheveled interior. Prone men and gear lay everywhere, and it was obvious that their situation was a most serious one.

Only the two seated planesmen remained in their padded chairs, held in place by their safety harnesses. Yet they seemed totally unresponsive, merely staring out with shocked eyes at their instruments.

There was a loud, bubbling burst of venting ballast audible, and the *Caspian*'s trim seemed to shift backwards on its stern. The captain reacted instinctively.

"Good heavens, Comrades, get control of yourselves! Planesmen, initiate an immediate emergency ascent. And get someone on that diving console to blow those ballast tanks!"

Mikhail was prepared to cross the compartment to undertake this task himself, when the boat's chief of the watch righted himself and went to work on triggering the ballast release that would hopefully send them surging to the surface. Expertly addressing his commands into the keyboard, the chief looked out to the instruments on the console and cried out in alarm. "She's not responding, Captain! We seem to be taking on water, and sinking stern first!"

"Hit those ballast controls manually if you have to, Chief, but get us to the surface at once! Our very lives are at stake here!"

The *Caspian* shifted hard on its side and once again Mikhail was thrown violently into the forward bulkhead. He was momentarily knocked unconscious by this blow, but when he eventually came to, he was aware of the blackness around him. Yet he had little time to dwell on their lack of interior lighting, for the cant of the deck had shifted in the opposite direction. He only kept from sliding back across the control room's deck and smashing into the aft bulkhead by grasping the brass handrail that lay beside the periscope well. It was obvious that they were experiencing the imbalance of trim that the chief had mentioned, and were presently sinking into the depths stern first.

The *Caspian*'s double-thick hull once again groaned in protest, and the captain sensed that they were in the midst of an uncontrollable dive. This was confirmed by a warbling electronic tone that indicated the vessel was rapidly approaching its maximum depth. Beyond this threshold, the *Caspian*'s hull could be cracked open at any moment, and one by one the sealed bulkheads would begin smashing, cracked open by a monumental pressure that they were never designed to hold up against.

Somewhere in the darkness a young sailor screamed out in terror. The palms of Mikhail's hands bit into the brass handrail, and he fought the urge to surrender to his own horror and merely let go of his grasp. But the captain's will to live was strong, and he spat in the face of temptation by crying out with all his might, "Chief, if there's any way that you can possibly reach that manual trim switch, blow those aft tanks now! It's our only chance!"

Unbeknown to Mikhail was the fact that the very sailor whom he was so desperately addressing had managed to wedge himself up against the diving console, where he was in the process of blindly groping for this same trigger mechanism. Fighting against his own inner urge merely to give up to the beckoning void, the chief won his struggle against panic by mentally visualizing his newborn son and wife of only ten months. Not wishing to leave them alone in this hard world to fend for themselves, he applied himself with a superhuman effort. With the dexterity of a blind man, he touched each of the instruments until he finally located the switch that he had been desperately searching for. Issuing the briefest of prayers, he then depressed it.

The darkened control room filled with the raucous sound of venting ballast. And ever so gradually the level of their descent evened itself out.

Mikhail Sobrinka no longer had to grasp the handrail to keep from sliding off into the blackness. Able to sit up now, he listened as the incessant warbling tone of the depth-warning device continued its nerve-wracking symphony. And beyond, the hull itself could be heard creaking under a pressure of immense proportions.

It was soon afterward that the *Caspian* struck bottom. This impact was accompanied by a bone-shaking concussion that caused the captain's nose to start bleeding. Yet the vessel's hull miraculously remained intact, and as long as it did so, the shaken survivors inside still had a chance, no matter how slim it might be, to keep on living.

Chapter Eight

From the exposed sail of the USS *Swordfish*, the coast of Panama beckoned in the distance like a twisting green and brown snake. This would be Ted Anderson's first transit of the legendary canal, and he listened with sincere interest as Admiral Abbott reminisced about his past visits here.

"That's Taboga Island over there," observed the retired veteran while pointing to a small land mass lying off their port bow. "During the war, the Germans had an informant living there, whose job it was to monitor all of our traffic bound for the Caribbean. It seems they were especially interested in cargo and troop vessels. The word was passed on to their Atlantic command, and like clockwork, they'd have one of their U-boats waiting on the other side to greet us."

"Did we ever catch this informant?" quizzed the blond-haired captain.

Abbott nodded. "We certainly did. Our intelligence boys were able to pinpoint his radio transmitter, and after landing a boatful of Rangers on Taboga, we caught the bastard red-handed. The only trouble was that he blew his own brains out with a Luger before we could properly interrogate him."

Anderson grimaced with this revelation and then looked down to the detailed chart of the Canal Zone, that he had folded before him.

"Things were so different back then," he reflected. "Today the Soviets merely have to position one of their satellites above the canal to see precisely what we're up to. Why, I wouldn't be surprised if they're filming us from space even as we speak."

Looking up into the blue heavens, Anderson raised the middle finger of his right hand up into the sky and mockingly commented, "That's for the USS *Turner*, Ivan!"

His elderly guest facetiously grinned. "Now is that any way for an officer and a gentleman to behave, Captain?"

"Sometimes this Cold War gets awfully damn frustrating," returned Anderson.

"If relations between the United States and the Soviet Union remain on their current course, I'm afraid that you'll get the chance to vent your frustrations sooner than you think, Ted. And that's one war I hope to God I'm not around to witness. Although I still think that we'll kick Ivan's butt all the way back to Moscow!"

"But Lord only knows the great price we'll have to pay to do it," responded Anderson stoically.

The loud metallic buzz of the intercom interrupted them, and a deep male voice broke from the waterproof speaker. "Captain, it's the XO. Senior

Sonarman Bodzin requests permission to join you on the bridge, sir."

"Permission granted," replied the captain without hesitating.

Looking back out to the rapidly approaching coast of Panama, Anderson remarked, "Bodzin's our sonar whiz. He's the one who smelled out that Victor III back off of Acapulco. Believe it or not, he's also a concert violinist, and, from what I hear, a damn good one at that."

"The many faces of today's Navy," jested Abbott, watching as a bright-eyed, brown-haired figure crawled out of the floor-mounted hatch.

"Thank you, sir, for allowing me to join you up here," greeted the petty officer second class.

"It's good to have you," returned the captain. "I don't believe you've had a chance to meet our distinguished guest as yet. Mr. Bodzin, may I present Rear Admiral William Abbott."

The senior sonarman instinctively stiffened, yet it was the white-haired veteran who held out a warm hand in greeting. "I'm proud to make your acquaintance, son. The captain here tells me that you're the one who first heard that Victor. May I ask what it was that gave them away?"

Brad liked the veteran's no-nonsense tone and quickly answered him. "It was his coolant pump, sir."

"Yet wasn't the bogey at maximum range when you tagged 'em?" continued Abbott. "That's a hell of a long ways off to hear a pump!"

Brad shrugged his shoulders. "I guess it is, sir, but that's the way it was."

"I'm not doubting your word, sailor," explained the retired veteran. "But it sounds to me like you just might have the gift."

"The gift, sir?" repeated the puzzled sonar technician.

The admiral looked over at the captain before going on. "What I'm referring to is the almost uncanny ability that a rare few have for detecting the enemy's presence long before they show up on normal channels. I've seen a handful of sonarmen with your talent, and each one who served with me was responsible for saving the day in more than one instance. It's almost as if they had psychic powers of some sort."

Brad grinned. "I doubt if I could be included in that group, Admiral. Because the only gift that I'm aware that I have is above-average hearing."

"Don't sell yourself short, son. Some of us just have a special feeling for the sea and its inhabitants, and my gut tells me that you're one of them. Now the captain tells me that you're a fiddle player as well. The missus is quite a symphony buff herself, and never fails to drag me along to the concert hall whenever she gets the chance. Do you have a favorite piece?"

Surprised at the new direction of their conversation, Bodzin responded. "That I do, sir. I guess my favorite is Beethoven's Violin Concert in D, Opus 61."

"I heard that very piece played live by the Los Angeles Philharmonic just last week," returned the admiral. "It was magnificent!"

With this remark, Abbott noted an astonished look

etch Anderson's face, and he commented, "What's the matter, Captain, didn't you think that old admirals went to the symphony? You'd be surprised to find out what I've learned about life since I retired."

Brad Bodzin listened to this discussion and found himself sincerely fond of the white-haired, outspoken veteran. Yet he still found it hard to believe that he was actually up on the sail conversing with his captain and a retired rear admiral. Surely his bunkmates would never believe it!

A gust of warm, humid air hit the Texan full in the face, and he turned to study the approaching coastline. The *Swordfish* rocked in a gentle swell, and he spotted what appeared to be the entrance to the canal, cut into a low-lying promontory beside a broad sand beach. A small patrol boat was also visible leaving this inlet, and it looked to be headed their way.

"Captain, it looks like we could be having some visitors shortly."

Anderson followed the sonar technician's line of sight and picked out the small vessel that he had referred to. To view it in more detail, the captain used a pair of binoculars. He was somewhat surprised to find it flying the American flag.

"It's one of ours," he thoughtfully announced. "And it appears that it's manned by a squad of Marines."

The intercom crackled alive with the voice of the XO. "Captain, we've just been contacted by a U.S. Marine launch that's headed our way from Fort Amador. There's a Lieutenant Lawrence Sykes on

192

board, who's requesting permission to board along with three of his men."

"What's his business with us, Lieutenant?"

"He says that he's been sent by his brigade commander, to act as our escort while we transit the canal, Captain. I took the liberty of contacting brigade headquarters in Balboa, and he checks out, sir."

The launch was less than three hundred yards away from the *Swordfish* by now. Anderson looked at the four helmeted and armed Marines standing near the boat's transom and replied, "Very good, Lieutenant. Issue an all stop, and send the boarding party topside on the double."

"Aye, aye, sir."

Less than thirty seconds later, the main propulsion shaft ground to a halt and the sub's forward momentum lessened considerably. Soon afterward, the deck party climbed through the forward hatch. The three occupants of the sail watched as they began attaching a collapsible set of boarding steps to the hull, near the forward access trunk. No sooner did they complete this process when the launch pulled up beside them.

The sea was fairly calm, and the pilot of the small launch had no problem guiding his vessel up against the hull of the *Swordfish*. Protected by a set of rubber bumpers, the launch maneuvered until it was immediately beside the temporary stairway, and one by one the Marines began boarding. The leathernecks wore green fatigues, flak jackets, and each soldier had an M16 rifle slung over his shoulder. The actual transfer took less than a minute, and all too soon the

193

pilot of the launch was able to cast off and return to port.

As the new arrivals began crawling down into the hatchway, the captain barked into the intercom, "Mr. Pukalani, have the senior Marine officer join me on the bridge at once. Also, inform Maneuvering to give us all ahead a third."

"Aye, aye, sir."

By the time the *Swordfish* was under way once again, yet another figure was emerging through the trunk that was cut into the floor of the sub's sail. This black-skinned, stockily built newcomer wore a pair of aviator's sunglasses, and quickly scanned the three sailors who stood before him, then addressed his greeting toward William Abbott.

"Captain Anderson?"

"I'm Anderson," broke in the captain, who was standing at the retired veteran's side.

Quick to adjust to his mistake, the Marine saluted. "I'm sorry, sir. I'm Lieutenant Lawrence Sykes. On behalf of Brigadier General Jeremiah Prescott of the First Marine division, I'd like to welcome you to the Canal Zone."

"I appreciate the welcoming committee, Lieutenant," returned Anderson. "But isn't such a thing a bit unusual here? I was just expecting a local Canal Zone pilot."

"It's true that we don't do this for just everyone, Captain," responded the Marine. "But I'm afraid we've had a little trouble with the local Communists here lately. Just yesterday, they shot up a Spruance class destroyer as it was passing through the Miraflores locks. Fortunately, there were no casualties on our side, though several sailors did get wounded. Thus, until we're able to get the zone completely secured, General Prescott felt it best to put additional armed parties on all transiting warships."

Admiral Abbott couldn't help but interrupt at this point. "So the Commies are at it even here in Panama. I should have expected as much with this continued alert and all. Speaking of the devil, what's the latest news on the USS *Turner*, Lieutenant?"

The black Marine hesitated a moment before responding. "As of the last news broadcast, the situation in Murmansk remains the same. The Reds are still crying that they caught us spying in their territorial waters, yet there's still no word from the *Turner*'s captain or any other member of its crew."

"I hope to God we're planning some sort of rescue mission to get them out of there," reflected William Abbott emotionally. "Even if it means sending in the Sixth Fleet, we can't afford to let those Red bastards get away with such a clear-cut act of piracy. And here I thought we learned our lesson back in '68 during the *Pueblo* incident."

The Marine nodded in agreement. "It's certainly time for the United States to walk tall, sir. From what I understand, the situation is really beginning to sour here in Central America. During the last couple of days, left-wing insurgents have initiated what appears to be a series of coordinated attacks in El Salvador, Honduras, Guatemala, and of course here in Panama. They're well armed and trained, with Soviet-bloc weapons and know-how. And they don't appear to be pulling any punches, as that attack on our Spruance indicates."

Looking out to the advancing coastline, the Marine added, "We'll be crossing beneath the Thatcher Ferry Bridge shortly. The hot zone begins after we pass Balboa and approach Miraflores. So if it's okay with you, Captain, I'd advise that all bridge personnel be outfitted with helmets and flak jackets."

Anderson briefly met the concerned glances of his co-workers and responded, "Whatever you say, Lieutenant."

"I'd also like my men to join me up here, Captain," added the Marine. "You'll be picking up your pilot in Balboa, so I'm afraid it could get a little cramped up here."

"We'll try not to get in your way, Lieutenant. My executive officer will be standing the first topside watch as we enter the causeway. And since that will be any minute now, my associates here and I had better start heading below deck ourselves."

The entrance to the canal could be clearly seen in the distance. Several freighters were visible, moored to a modern dock facility that jutted out into the Pacific on a thin peninsula of land. A set of railroad tracks linked this facility with the mainland. The skyline of Panama City beckoned to its right, with a solid ribbon of jungled coastline stretching in the opposite direction.

Confident that their transit would be a successful one, Ted Anderson instructed his XO to join him on the bridge. Lieutenant Pukalani arrived topside with a helmet and a flak jacket in tow. The watch was transferred, and the captain was now free to escort both William Abbott and Brad Bodzin back below deck.

It wasn't until they safely arrived in Balboa and picked up their pilot that the captain excused himself from the control room to return to his quarters. His usual stateroom was being lent to Admiral Abbott, and he was currently sharing a cabin with his second-in-command. After a quick shower, he lay down in the bunk with every intention of taking a brief catnap. He was exhausted after personally supervising the transit down the coast of Central America, yet, strangely enough, sleep would not come to him. Instead, his weary eyes drifted off to the wall-mounted desk, where a virtual pile of paperwork awaited his attention.

He had hoped to get to this pile of work much earlier in the cruise, but the unscheduled meeting with the Soviet Victor III class submarine off Mexico had diverted his attentions elsewhere. Now that they had just entered the canal's largest lock, and were well on their way to the Caribbean, Ted decided that if he couldn't sleep, at least he could get some of this paperwork out of the way. For if all continued smoothly, they'd be pulling into Galveston before he knew it.

Still dressed in only his skivvies, he crossed over to the cramped desk and seated himself heavily behind it. After switching on the lamp, he picked up the topmost manila folder. Inside this heavy portfolio were numerous documents relating to the decommission of the *Swordfish*. Once they arrived in Galveston, there were a long list of tasks that he would have to attend to. The contents of this folder detailed each and every one of them. They ranged from the removal of the weapons systems to the transfer of personnel, and included such menial concerns as ensuring that the food lockers were fully emptied and sanitized. Altogether, this tedious process would take him over three months to complete.

Anderson had to admit that he wasn't looking forward to delving into the folder's contents since it finalized his command's termination. For eighteen months the *Swordfish* had been his home, with its crew his virtual family. Of course his relationship with the sub went back much longer, to the earliest days of his active naval career. Having William Abbott aboard helped him put this span of almost three decades in its proper perspective.

Their recent run-in with the Russian Victor proved that the *Swordfish* still had some fight left in her. With the aid of a tremendous school of squid, and the turbulent knuckle of water left in their baffles as a result of a perfectly executed escape maneuver, they had managed to lose the enemy. This was quite an accomplishment considering that the Victor was one of the newest warships in the Soviet fleet, while the *Swordfish* represented an era long past. But perhaps it was true what Admiral Abbott had said, that technological advances would always play second fiddle to basic seamanship and cunning. For those were the qualities that were an instrumental part of their escape.

Peering down at the manila portfolio beneath the one he presently held, Ted realized that he had still not taken a look at his mail. Inside this second folder was a collection of over two weeks' worth of unread correspondence. Deciding that the documents relating to the sub's decommissioning could wait, he reached down to see what the postman had brought him.

On top of this stack was a pink envelope, whose neat printed script was most familiar. It was a letter from his ex, Rachel. He tore it open, and first to fall out was a photograph. His pulse quickened as he took in a picture of his daughter. Six-year-old Laura was dressed in a Brownie outfit. Her freckled face was most compatible with her mop of thick blond hair, shaped in her favorite pixie cut. She seemed to have grown an inch or two since he had seen her last, and Ted warmly grinned upon spotting her just legible signature in crayon on the back of the photo.

Putting this picture aside, he reached into the envelope and removed the letter. It was several pages thick. Rachel's handprinted scrawl was easy to read, and in no time at all he was able to work his way through it.

Though it was mostly trivial in nature, the news brought back a long flood of memories, some joyous, the others quite painful.

They had originally met at a USO dance in Charleston ten years ago. Ted had been the consummate Navy bachelor until this time, yet fell instantly under Rachel's exotic spell. She was certainly the most beautiful woman he had ever laid eyes on, with long red hair and a perfect figure. A Navy brat herself, she knew just what she was looking for as she first caught Ted's eyes from the other side of the dance floor.

A whirlwind romance followed, and three months later, they were man and wife. Those had been innocent, exciting days. Still infatuated with each other, the months passed quickly, setting up a household and adjusting to married naval life. But the handwriting was already on the wall when Rachel began complaining about his all-too-frequent trips away from home, many of which had lasted over three months.

Hoping that a family would help fill in those lonely hours when he was away, they began working on making a baby. After a series of tragic miscarriages, Laura was finally brought into the world, and joy filled the Anderson household.

Their new daughter proved to be the center of their lives, and for the first few years everything seemed to be going so well. This included Ted's career, as he was at long last named a full captain and given command of his own attack sub. Yet this new assignment demanded that he spend even more time away from home, and soon Rachel began complaining once again.

It was two years ago that she made him an ultimatum, demanding that he either got a more normal job or the marriage was over. This had been a truly trying time in Ted's life. He sincerely loved his wife and daughter, but he loved his career as well. And now Rachel was asking him to give it all up just as he had attained his lifelong dream, the command of his own submarine.

This had been something that he had worked for long before he met Rachel. In fact, for as long as he could remember, such duty was all he had asked for in life. The demand that he give it all up like this seemed unfair to Ted, and thus had he expressed himself. Rachel was unmoving, and after a variety of marriage counselors failed to solve their differences, a divorce was reluctantly agreed upon.

They made an amiable settlement, with Ted having visiting rights whenever he desired. Rachel and he were still good friends, and after two years apart, were finally putting their lives back together again.

In the letter that he had just read, Rachel mentioned that she was still seeing a divorced doctor whom she had met at Laura's clinic. Ted had even met this man at his daughter's last birthday party and trusted him implicitly. He would be an excellent provider, and a good substitute father to Laura. Assuming that they would announce their marriage plans in the near future, Ted neatly folded up the letter and placed it back in the envelope. He sighed and took in the framed photograph that was above the desk before him.

The picture showed his XO and his wife, who was also a native Hawaiian. They were standing before a tropical waterfall, with their five children gathered at their feet. From the flowered leis that graced their necks, this was obviously a holiday outing and there could be no doubting the love and joy all of them shared for one another. This was the kind of tight, understanding family that Ted had always dreamed of having, and he couldn't help but wonder where he had gone wrong.

Looking back to the photograph of his daughter that he had just received, Anderson knew that he was fortunate to at least have Laura. She was still the joy of his life, and he could only pray that they would remain close, even if her mother should marry once again.

As for his own future marriage plans, Anderson

just couldn't say. He supposed that if the right woman ever came along, he'd be open to the possibility of some kind of permanent commitment.

For the last year and a half, the *Swordfish* had taken up the good majority of his time. He had had little time for social functions, which made the opportunities for meeting that special someone all the more slim.

Several months from now he'd be in a much better position to reevaluate his personal life. By that time the *Swordfish* would be decommissioned, and he'd be on his way to a new assignment. Most likely he'd be headed to Washington, D.C., at that time. Though he'd much rather be at sea, a staff position would mean that he would attend more social gatherings, and once the word got out that he was single, he was certain that he'd have his fair share of women to pick from.

Chuckling at this thought, Anderson began sorting through the rest of the mail. There were the usual bills and junk mail, and he spotted a letter from an ex-shipmate. There was also the latest quarterly edition of the *Naval Submarine League's Review* to peruse, as well as this month's *Proceedings* magazine. Anderson was in the midst of flipping through this last publication when a sudden, raucous clanging noise filled the cabin with an alien sound. This twangy, metallic staccato noise repeated itself several more times, and the captain's first impression was that someone was beating on the outer hull of the *Swordfish* with a hammer. He was soon to learn otherwise when the intercom activated and the excited voice of the XO barked out forcefully, "Captain, we're being shot at up here!"

Anderson's initial reaction was disbelief. But

remembering the marine lieutenant's warning, he quickly responded. "Clear the bridge at once, Lieutenant! And get those Marines below deck as well. I'll meet you in the control room."

The explosive whine of gunfire provided the background noise as the XO answered, "Will do, Skipper."

As the clanging sound of several more bullets ricocheting off their hull and upper deck met his ears, Anderson hurriedly dressed himself. He ducked into the passageway, and found himself facing several puzzled junior officers, who had been gathered around the wardroom table eating.

"What's going on up there, Captain?" quizzed the sub's weapons officer.

"Believe it or not, it seems that we're under attack from leftist guerrilla forces who are working the canal's banks. I'll know our exact status once I reach the control room."

Shocked by this surprising turn of events, the officers pushed away their plates and stood to join the captain as he rushed out of the wardroom. They arrived in the vessel's attack center in time to see the last of the Marines climb down off the sail's access ladder. The leatherneck was followed by Lieutenant Pukalani.

"Christ, it's unbelievable up there!" observed the out-of-breath XO. "One minute we were peacefully being pulled into the Pedro Miguel locks, and before we knew what hit us, all hell was breaking loose!"

"There appears to be at least two dozen of them," added the black Marine lieutenant. "They're hidden in the jungle on the south shore, yet appear to be lightly armed."

"Thank God for that," returned Ted Anderson, looking up as the white-haired figure of William Abbott rushed into the control room.

"Is it true that we're under attack?" he breathlessly questioned.

Anderson nodded. "It appears so, Admiral."

"Then may I ask what the hell we're going to do about it?" continued Abbott passionately.

Ted Anderson took in a deep breath and responded, "Though Lieutenant Sykes here thinks that they're only armed with light caliber weapons, we can't rule out that they're not going to hit us with either a mortar or an armor-piercing round of some sort. Is there enough water beneath us to allow a descent?"

The XO shook his head. "Negative, Skipper. We're in a lock holding area, and there's barely enough water around us to keep us afloat."

"I'd like permission to return topside with my men, Captain," requested the Marine. "At least we can fire back at the bastards."

"Has anyone thought of calling in an airstrike?" quizzed William Abbott. "You do have air cover here, don't you, Lieutenant Sykes?"

The Marine officer grinned. "We sure do, sir. In all the excitement, I completely forgot about the new Harrier squadron that pulled in here last week. They'll make quick work out of those Red bandits soon enough. Is there a radio transmitter around here that I could borrow?"

The captain was quick with an answer. "Mr. Pukalani, escort Lieutenant Sykes back to the radio room. Make certain that Harper and his crew give the lieutenant their full cooperation."

"You got it, Skipper," returned the XO, who quickly pivoted and led the anxious Marine out of the control room.

A series of sharp concussions echoed off the outer hull, and Ted Anderson balled his fists in frustrated rage. "It's like being a sitting duck in a shooting gallery up here. Damn, if we only had some more water beneath us!"

William Abbott ambled up to the captain's side and softly commented, "You should be counting your blessings, son. If they were to hit us with a mortar round, or even an incendiary grenade for that matter, things could be looking a lot worse. The Marines will get them off our necks soon enough. Yet I'd hate to miss the show. Do you think we could watch it through the periscope, Captain?"

Anderson found himself unable to turn down the retired veteran. "I imagine it could be arranged. And since you came up with the idea of calling in an airstrike, you get the box seat on the attack scope."

"And to think that there are some on board the *Swordfish* who say you're cold-hearted," mocked Abbott as he followed the captain over to the periscope well.

"Raise both scopes!" ordered Anderson firmly.

With a loud hydraulic hiss, both the normal scope and the attack version rose from the well. As Abbott followed him onto the elevated platform, the captain grasped the normal periscope's handles and peered through the hard rubber viewing coupling. He needed to turn in a half circle until he got the angle he desired.

Lit by the bright sun was the southern shore of this

portion of the canal. Though a section of the concrete lock could just be seen, a thick grove of coconut palms predominated. Carefully scanning this tree line, Anderson halted when the muzzle flash of a firing rifle spit from the grove with a tongue of fire. Several other muzzle flashes followed, and assuming that the majority of the insurgents were gathered in this section, he increased the scope's magnification twofold. The tree line seemed to jump forward, and soon he could actually make out the individual barrels of the rifles. Each of these weapons was pointed directly at the *Swordfish*, and judging from the numerous flashes of fire that could be seen, the leftists had plenty of ammunition to use.

There was a sudden flurry of activity inside the grove, and Anderson gasped upon viewing a half dozen fatigue-wearing rebels in the process of setting up what appeared to be a mortar.

"Jesus, they've got a mortar out there!" exclaimed the captain.

"I see it!" retorted Abbott, who was perched beside the attack scope. "Let's just pray that Fidel forgot to send them any ammo."

There was a heavy feeling in Anderson's gut as he watched one of the soldiers pry open a wooden crate and carefully remove an elongated shell. Last-minute adjustments were made on the mortar itself, and two of the soldiers prepared to drop the round into the hollow launch tube. Seeing this, the captain cried out passionately, "Secure all stations, incoming mortar round!"

He breathlessly watched as a puff of white smoke veiled the mortar, indicating a successful launch.

Seconds later, a geyser of white water formed in the channel, one hundred yards in front of the *Swordfish*. This was followed by the arrival of a moderate shock wave that rocked the deck beneath them.

Looking back to the grove, the captain winced as he watched another round go skyward. This one seemed to miss them altogether. Yet when the boat shook in the grasp of another shock wave, it was William Abbott who excitedly cried out, "I'll bet my pension that it went long. This means that they've got the range now. Next time they've got us for sure!"

Anderson's pulse quickened as he returned his line of sight back to the grove. With the admiral's apocalyptic observation still ringing in his ears, he watched as the soldiers prepared to fire another round. The captain couldn't help but feel as if he was in the midst of a horribly realistic nightmare as the commandos prepared to drop in the next shell.

Frustrated and filled with rage, Anderson was in the midst of whispering a desperate prayer when a sudden disturbance in the tree line caught his attention. He blinked in disbelief when the ghostly head-on profile of a single jet aircraft seemed to float straight up over the palm fronds. Hovering in the air like a prehistoric beast from another time, was a McDonnell Douglas AV-8B Harrier. Appearing lethal in its camouflaged paint scheme, the Marine attack jet vectored its wings slightly downward and let loose a furious barrage of 25mm cannon fire. At the same time, the Harrier emptied its swept-back, stubby wings of the cluster bombs it had been carrying. Almost instantaneously, the entire palm grove erupted in a solid, blistering wall of flame and smoke. Still shocked into speechlessness, Ted Anderson watched as the Harrier ascended straight upward, dipped its wings in greeting, and shot off overhead with its afterburner wide open.

"Holy Mother Mary!" cried William Abbott. "Did you just see what I saw?"

Stepping back from the scope, Anderson met the retired veteran's shocked stare and curtly commented, "Thank you, United States Marine Corps. Next stop, the Caribbean Sea!"

Chapter Nine

It was well past noon by the time the open air jitney carrying Commander Richard Walker and the congressional delegation pulled off Centerline Road and reached Hurricane Hole. The heavy rains of the morning had long since dissipated, and the sun beat down with a vengeance from the clear blue sky. The high humidity and unmerciful heat had prompted the four male members of the group to shed their jackets soon after landing on St. Thomas. It was mere decorum and habit that kept them from pulling off their ties as well.

The small van pulled to a halt on the side of the narrow asphalt road, and its passengers were afforded a magnificent view of Coral Bay on their right.

"My, isn't that about the prettiest sight that you ever did lay your eyes on," observed Senator MacMillan Lewis, the portly, silver-haired statesman from Alabama.

"Right now, I'll settle for an air-conditioned room, and an ice-cold frosty beer," retorted Sam

Clay as he patted his soaked forehead dry with a wrinkled handkerchief. The ranking black member of the House of Representatives' Committee on Appropriations added, "And I always thought it was hot back in Philly!"

Their khaki-uniformed naval escort pointed to a pathway that cut through a dense clump of sea grapes and appeared to lead down to the water. "The facility isn't far now. Yet I'm afraid we have to go the rest of the way on foot."

"Thank goodness I wore flats," reflected the sole female member of the group, Congresswoman Beth Whitly of Colorado.

As Commander Walker exited the van and beckoned his distinguished guests to join him on the roadway, Senator Irv Waxman of New York loosened the tight knot of his tie and rolled up his long sleeves. "Damn, if I knew this was going to be a field trip, I would have dressed in shorts and sneakers."

"I'd have liked to see that," returned Senator Lewis. "If you ask me, you New Yorkers were born in suits and ties."

Not the least bit amused by this facetious remark, Waxman climbed out of the van and turned to help Congresswoman Whitly exit the vehicle. As he grasped her hand, he found it cool to the touch, and Waxman couldn't help but wonder why the heat didn't seem to affect her at all.

Commander Walker took the lead as he escorted the four politicians down the earthen trail.

"This compound that we're about to enter was first built in the sixties," he said, while continuing to set their moderate pace. "It was designed expressly for

210

dolphin research by Dr. Lewis Marvin, the famed psychiatrist."

"Isn't he the one who invented the biofeedback-monitoring technique that the NASA astronauts are going to be using for deep space flight?" questioned Beth Whitly.

"That's the guy," answered the commander. "Long before Dr. Marvin began his work with the space agency, he dreamed of the day when man could actually teach a marine mammal the intricacies of human language. He picked *Tursiops truncatus* because of their high intellect and ready ability to train."

"*Tursiops truncatus?*" repeated Congressman Clay.

Richard Walker was quick with a clarification. "I'm sorry, *Tursiops truncatus* is the scientific name for the Atlantic bottlenose dolphin. This is the same species you usually see performing at marine parks."

"Ah, you mean Flipper," observed Senator Lewis, whose blue-and-white pinstripe seersucker suit was matted heavily in sweat.

"Did Dr. Lewis ever succeed in his quest to teach a dolphin to talk?" continued Beth Whitly.

The commander answered while leading them out of a grove of purple-flowered crepe myrtle and onto a wide sandy clearing. "Unfortunately, after spending a great deal of time and effort, he failed to come up with the results he originally hoped for, though his work did provide reams of new and fascinating material on the behavior of the Atlantic bottlenose."

Shading his eyes from the fiery sun, Walker pointed toward the compound they now faced. "This

211

facility was lying vacant until Dr. Patton leased it for the project. It's comprised of the central building you see before you that houses the main office and living quarters, a small laboratory, tool shed, and a holding tank. She's also got the exclusive use of that lagoon."

A blond figure in khaki shorts and a short-sleeved top rounded the main structure and headed toward them. She also wore a white sun visor, and when she raised her hand in greeting, Commander Walker added, "There's Dr. Patton now. So come on, folks, I'm sure she's got some cool refreshments waiting for us somewhere down there."

This was all the incentive that was needed to get the foursome moving once again. As it turned out, they met their hostess halfway between the compound and the woods they had just emerged from.

"Good afternoon!" greeted Susan Patton. "Welcome to Hurricane Hole."

It was Richard Walker who met her with a warm handshake and initiated the introductions. "Hello, Susan, it's good to be back. May I introduce my distinguished traveling companions? First off, from the United States House of Representatives, I'd like you to meet Congresswoman Beth Whitly. Ms. Whitly is from Colorado, and is the chairwoman of the Committee on Merchant Marine and Fisheries."

Susan shook hands with a tall, slender, middle-aged brunette, who was dressed neatly in a light blue linen suit. The two women politely smiled and Walker continued. "Next, I'd like you to meet Congressman Samuel Clay, from the state of Pennsylvania. Representative Clay is the ranking Democrat on the House Appropriations Committee."

212

"In other words, I'm the guy you go to when you want the money," greeted the balding black politician with a warm grin.

Susan liked him immediately, and found his handshake friendly and firm as the commander went on. "From the Senate Committee on Commerce, Science, and Transportation is New York's Irv Waxman. The Senator is the co-author of the Marine mining bill recently signed into law by the President."

The sweating New Yorker's handshake was indifferent, and Susan was relieved when a portly, white-haired gentleman in a wrinkled seersucker suit stepped forward to introduce himself.

"Good afternoon, Dr. Patton. I'm MacMillan Lewis from the Senate's Armed Services Committee. But you can just call me Mac, like my constituents back home in Alabama do. This is really a lovely spot you have down here."

The portly senator reminded Susan of her grandfather, and she was instantly charmed by his thick southern accent and deep blue, caring eyes.

"Why, thank you, Senator," replied Susan a bit shyly, and proceeded to address the group as a whole. "Once again, I'd like to sincerely welcome all of you to the Virgin Islands. I realize you've had to fly many hours to get here, and hope you won't be disappointed with what you see. Shall we start off with a quick tour of the facility?"

"That sounds wonderful, Susan dear," returned Senator Lewis. "But would that tour happen to include a cool drink?"

Susan smiled. "Of course it does, Senator. And I've

213

even got lunch to go with it, if my assistant ever gets back here with the food.''

The white-haired statesman nodded and took Susan by the arm. "Did anyone ever tell you that you have a wonderful smile, darling? Now tell me, what's a beautiful girl like you doing in an isolated place like this with only a bunch of dolphins for company?''

Susan began sharing the story of her life with him while leading her distinguished guests to the office. She purposely had lowered the thermostat of the room's single air conditioner for their visit, and a collective sigh of relief sounded as they gratefully ducked inside. Cool drinks were passed out, and Susan stood before them to explain their itinerary.

"I've decided that the best place for you to see the harness at work is out on the open seas. So I hope you don't mind, but I've planned a little boat trip for us this afternoon. We won't be gone long, and I should have you back in Cruz Bay in plenty of time for dinner.''

"We can take it," commented Sam Clay. "Our last little outing took us to the desert at China Lake, California. We were there to see a demonstration of some of the so-called SMART munitions at work. Yet wouldn't you know that we'd arrive there right in the midst of a howling sandstorm! I'm still scraping the sand out of my dentures.''

"Do you go on such excursions often?" queried Susan.

Congresswoman Whitly put down the bottle of apple juice she was sipping from and answered, "Not as often as we'd like, Doctor. The Pentagon's budget has skyrocketed, and there are literally thousands of projects that are requesting new funding. Since there's not enough of the taxpayers' hard-earned money to support all of these requests, someone's got to weed out the wasteful projects from the worthy ones.''

"In other words, darling, we roam the country to smell out the dogs," added MacMillan Lewis.

Senator Waxman polished off his Diet Coke and addressed Susan directly. "From what we understand, a good deal of money has already been channeled into your project and that recently you've requested even more. How much longer is it going to take you to show some concrete results?''

Susan briefly met Commander Walker's sympathetic glance before responding. "Working with live dolphins in open water conditions isn't the easiest of tasks, yet I believe that the harness is finally ready to go beyond the prototype stage. As you'll soon see for yourselves, my initial experiments involve the use of a miniature fiber-optic video camera. The extra funding I requested is for design modifications for devices other than the camera.''

"Such as mines, or other such explosive devices?" queried Congresswoman Whitly.

Susan seemed a bit uncomfortable with this question and Commander Walker was quick to formulate an answer for her. "Actually, the Navy has a variety of uses for Dr. Patton's new harness, and ordinance delivery is only one of them.''

"So you do admit, Commander, that the Navy is utilizing innocent marine creatures as living torpedoes," continued the red-faced politician.

"I didn't say that!" retorted Walker. "Though we're dealing with heavily classified material in this matter, I can assure you, Representative Whitly, that the U.S. Navy has no plans to develop the kamikaze-type techniques you're referring to."

There was a threatening gleam in the politician's eyes as she responded, "That had better be the case, Commander. For if our constitutents were ever to learn otherwise, there'd be a cry of outrage that would be heard all the way to the Pentagon!"

The tense confrontation was momentarily defused by the arrival of Susan's assistant. Owen seemed embarrassed as he entered the office and took in the distinguished group assembled before him.

Susan was genuinely relieved by his sudden appearance, and after initiating a quick round of introductions, suggested that they get on with the demonstration outside. Cooled and refreshed, her guests concurred.

They made a brief stop at the capture tank. Upset to find it empty, Congressman Clay lightly questioned. "Where's Flipper?"

There was a devilish look in Susan's eyes as she merely grinned and beckoned them to follow her down to the lagoon. They assembled on the wooden pier, which had a good-sized dive boat moored to its far end.

Well aware that she had her audience's full attention, Susan reached into her pocket and removed a thin silver whistle. She then put this device to her lips and blew with all her might. This barely audible sonic blast resulted in two separate events happening almost simultaneously. From the interior cabin of the boat, a native steel band launched into a spirited rendition of "Matilda." And at the center of the lagoon itself, Sammy broke the surface of the water and burst into the air in a smooth, graceful leap. There was an astonished gasp from his audience, and he repeated the jump in the opposite direction for those who missed it the first time.

This leap resulted in a chorus of applause, and the dolphin headed straight toward the pier for a proper introduction.

"This is Sammy, folks," offered Susan. "He's a full grown bottlenose of unknown age, who voluntarily came into our lagoon from the open seas less than a week ago. Though we haven't had all that much time to work together, Sammy's one of the most intelligent dolphins I've ever met. Sometimes he's so smart that it's downright scary."

With his ever-smiling face held clear of the water, Sammy scanned the faces of the newcomers. He seemed particularly interested in Congresswoman Whitly and he carefully inspected her from head to toe.

"Looks like you got yourself an interested beau, Beth," jested Senator Waxman.

Whitly scowled at this remark, and almost as if defending her honor, Sammy angled his snout beneath the lagoon and proceeded to splash the senator from New York with a ribbon of water. Though Waxman didn't appear to take this soaking lightly, his colleagues responded with a round of hearty applause.

"Darn you, Sammy," reflected Senator Lewis. "If you only knew how many of us on the floor would

217

like to give old sourpuss Waxman here a soaking of our own but can't summon the nerve to do it. Why, I bet you're a Republican."

Sammy responded with a burst of high-pitched dolphin talk, and the politicians roared with laughter. Susan looked over and caught Richard Walker's eye. The naval officer seemed relieved that all was going well, and Susan could only pray that things would continue that way.

"Is everyone ready to see Sammy really do his thing?" she queried.

Hearing not a word otherwise, she led them onto the boat. As the band began playing their arrangement of "Islands in the Sun," the boat left the pier, crossed the lagoon, and began transiting the sparkling waters of Coral Bay. Sammy followed close beside them, finally settling in to ride their bow wake as the ship attained its cruising speed.

The island of St. John was beginning to grow smaller on their stern as Owen carried out the ice chests holding their lunch. Several of the local women had cooked up a mess of fried fish and potato salad, and all the politicians but one dug into it with a frenzy.

Congresswoman Whitly had been starved only minutes earlier. But as soon as the boat crossed into the bay, she began to get seasick. Susan cursed herself for forgetting to bring along some Dramamine, and could only treat her nauseous guest with a cool towel and some comforting words.

Meanwhile, back beside the transom, Owen was showing off the harness that they would soon be attaching to Sammy. It was made out of a lightweight, clear plastic material, and was designed to fit around the dolphin's upper body. Though the apparatus didn't appear to be intricately constructed, Commander Walker was quick to explain its uniqueness.

"What you're seeing before you is a result of years of hard work and frustrating experimentation. Since scientists first began seriously working with dolphins in the sixties, the development of an effective harness device has been a number one priority. Hundreds of various types were tested, yet all proved either too cumbersome or too confining. For the various tasks that man has in mind for our marine mammal friends such as Sammy, an effective harness is a vital necessity. Thus it was for the design of such a mechanism that Dr. Patton was approached.

"This particular harness was designed per Navy specs to hold a Krommer-type, fiber-optic video camera. Owen, could you show the congressmen what this device looks like?"

The alert research assistant reached into a nearby metal storage locker and held up a flashlight-sized silver cannister, that had a miniature lens on its tip. He then proceeded to clip it onto the top of the harness and connect its end with a thin plastic wire that he removed from a large, deck-mounted spool.

The commander continued. "This Krommer-type camera was originally designed for use on the space shuttle. It can operate on a bare minimum of light and is extremely sensitive to even the smallest detail. The resulting picture is subsequently relayed back to our monitor by means of this ultra-thin fiber-optic cable that can extend well over a thousand feet beneath the ocean's surface."

"Why, that's truly remarkable, Commander," reflected the red-cheeked senator from Alabama. "When we were flying over here from Puerto Rico, you pointed out to us our sea-mining ship, the *Global Explorer*, as it was drilling off Roosevelt Roads. Just think how much easier their work would be if we could outfit a whole bunch of Sammys with such cameras. Why, those dolphins could lead us right to those minerals. As our authority on marine mining, doesn't that make sense to you, Irv?"

Senator Waxman dully nodded. "It sounds like the possibilities are there, Mac. But before I get myself all hot and bothered, I want to see this camera in action."

"You'll have that opportunity soon enough, Senator," replied the commander, who looked up to check on Susan's status.

He spotted her chatting away with Congresswoman Whitly inside the main cabin, and in an effort not to disturb her, Walker quizzed Susan's young assistant. "Exactly where are we headed, Owen?"

The tanned grad student stepped back and turned toward the boat's bow, where he pointed out a large land mass approaching on their left. "That's Norman Island. We'll be anchoring off its southern coast, in an area called Lucifer's Seat."

"How in the hell did it ever come up with that moniker?" questioned Senator Lewis.

Quick to grab the spotlight, Owen answered. "I believe the Spanish were the first to name it. The passage that lies before us is one of the main entryways into the Atlantic from the Caribbean Sea.

Thus these waters have seen plenty of homebound European galleons, loaded to the gunwales with New World treasure. The southern coastline of Norman Island directly adjoins this main transit channel, which is several thousand feet deep in some places. Its shallows also contain a spectacular coral reef. Pity the poor ship that struck this formation, for it's said that the wrecks of over a half dozen treasure galleons lie untouched on the bottom."

"Maybe we should send Sammy down with the camera to see if he can find one of these vessels?" jested Congressman Clay.

Owen grinned. "That's exactly what we propose to do today, sir."

This was the first that Richard Walker had heard of such a plan, and he found himself warmly grinning. When he had initially called Susan to announce their visit, he had mentioned something about putting on some sort of show for the politicians. But never in his wildest dreams did he ever expect a real live treasure hunt! Inwardly praising her ingenuity, he hurriedly scanned the faces of the three congressmen and found them equally excited. Even the poker-faced senator from New York appeared enthusiastic.

"I hope our man of the hour hasn't deserted us," remarked Senator Lewis. "Where is Sammy, anyway?"

"We'll most likely find him riding the bow wake, sir," answered Owen. "He uses it like a surfer, and can keep up with us while only spending half the physical effort."

MacMillan Lewis leaned his portly hulk over the

deck rail and caught Sammy in just such a position. "That creature is truly incredible. I bet he's got an I.Q. higher than most congressmen I know."

"That's certainly not saying much," retorted Sam Clay with a wise wink.

There was a roar of laughter as this innocent joke was ingested. In the background, the band began playing "Mary Ann." Several seagulls lazily circled overhead, and the previously scorching air was cooled considerably by a combination of the gentle breeze and the spray of water that kicked up as the ship's bow bit into the surging waters of the Caribbean Sea.

They reached their destination soon after a dessert of tart pineapple spears was passed around. Checking the fathometer, Susan made certain that they were close enough to the reef but still had plenty of water beneath them as she signaled the ship's captain to cut the engines and drop anchor. Sammy sensed that something was going to happen now, and swam expectantly around the boat in tight spiraling circles.

As Susan assembled her guests on the stern, Owen changed into a short-sleeved wet suit. With mask, snorkel, and flippers in hand, he then jumped overboard and Sammy was quick to greet him with a gentle nudge of his snout.

The politicians looked on breathlessly as Susan proceeded to hand her assistant the harness. Owen prepared to attach the device onto Sammy's body, but the dolphin had other ideas, and playfully nipped at Owen's flippers in an effort to distract him.

It took Susan several blows on her whistle and a flurry of hand signals to finally calm the dolphin down. Like a chastised schoolboy, Sammy meekly swam up to Owen, and the grad student took this opportunity to slip the harness onto him in one deft movement.

The clear plastic apparatus fit Sammy's body like a glove. It molded him perfectly, with the camera mount just visible to the side of his right pectoral fin.

"In our initial tests, the harness was found to offer practically no water resistance whatsoever," lectured Susan. "The fit actually improves the longer it's worn, until it almost becomes part of the animal's skin surface. Thus it can be worn indefinitely, and with the addition of a homing device, will finally allow us to be able to track a school of dolphins in the open ocean."

"The Navy has quite a few other plans for it," added Richard Walker. "As we place more and more human aquanauts in undersea habitats, the harness will allow us to use the dolphins to deliver supplies from the surface. It will also be utilized for repairs to our SOSUS arrays and for ordinance pickup."

Susan carefully picked up the miniature camera and attached it to its fiber-optic umbilical cord. "But as it looks now, the most exciting application appears to be as a camera mount. Shall we see what awaits us on the floor of the sea here?"

There was a feeling of anticipation shared by all as Susan lowered the camera rig down to her assistant. As Owen clipped it securely into its mount on the top of Sammy's neck, Susan switched on the partition-mounted video monitor. The surging surface of the sea before them appeared on the screen, and Susan flashed Owen a thumbs-up.

She then proceeded to remove a heavy, circular hand-sized hoop. Set on the top of this weighted ring was a battery-powered strobe light and an ultrasonic homing beacon. Susan triggered these devices and held it up before her guests.

"To get Sammy to dive to the bottom of the trench beneath us, I'll be utilizing this lead hoop. Though Sammy's been trained to retrieve it, we've only had a single chance to try such a pickup at this great depth, so please bear with us, folks."

She then pivoted and held the ring high over the side of the boat. Only when she was certain that Sammy saw its flashing red beacon did she toss it into the water before him. She gave it several seconds to sink out of sight before putting the whistle to her lips and blowing it in three sharp blasts. Having received his go signal, Sammy immediately dove for the depths below.

From the stern of the dive boat, the only indication of Sammy's descent was the mad spinning whine of the spool holding the ultra-thin fiber-optic cable. All eyes went to the video monitor, which had a digital clock displayed in its lower right-hand corner. Like a scene from an underwater movie, the rest of the screen filled with a solid expanse of blue water. Every so often the rounded tip of Sammy's head could be seen as the dolphin streaked ever downward.

The digital clock indicated that he had been down for precisely two minutes when Susan finally commented, "He should be approximately halfway to the bottom of the trench now. Though very little direct light reaches these depths, there should be just enough to suit our purpose."

The cable continued to play out in a grinding whine, and when the digital clock passed three and a half minutes, a dim flashing red light suddenly was visible on the video screen in the veiled depths beyond. The massive scaly flanks of a startled grouper momentarily flashed on the monitor, and as the strobe intensified, the outline of yet another object began gradually forming in the background. It seemed to fill the entire screen and appeared to be manmade.

"Is that one of those treasure ships Owen was telling us about?" quizzed the excited congressman from Pennsylvania.

Susan couldn't really say what this mysterious object was, which had evidently gotten Sammy's attention as well. Ignoring the nearby retrieval ring, the dolphin approached the smooth-skinned, blackened mass and began swimming down its tubular-shaped length. It seemed to stretch on forever, and when Sammy passed a towerlike structure built into its midsection, Commander Walker gasped.

"Susan, do you know about any recent wrecks of modern warships in this area?" he questioned.

With her eyes still glued to the video monitor, the blond marine biologist shook her head and answered, "Not that I know of. The only wrecks that I'm aware of in these waters are those of the Spanish galleons that are rumored to have sunk here."

Sammy had been under for over four and a half minutes now, and as he continued down the mysterious object's rounded spine, a central, rudder-like device was suddenly visible. Richard Walker reacted only after viewing the bright red, five-pointed star etched on the metallic surface here.

"My God, it's a sunken Soviet submarine!"

From the surface of the Anegada Passage, the tip of the periscope cut a bare frothing swath in the surging blue Caribbean waters. Sixty-five feet below, Senior Lieutenant Ganady Arbatov gazed out the scope's viewing lens, and took in the small wooden surface craft bobbing in the nearby waters. Noting its bearing and range, he spoke out to share additional information regarding this sighting with his commanding officer.

"Captain Gnutov, it appears to be flying the American flag. I can see several individuals gathered on its stern deck, and a swimmer in the water beside them."

"I'll bet you it's one of their dive boats," reflected Alexander Gnutov, as he politely pushed the senior lieutenant away to look through the lens himself. "It's a dive boat all right. I can tell from its open cabin and wide transom. A hundred kopecks says that they're treasure hunting!"

"Treasure hunting?" quizzed Ganady Arbatov.

The captain backed away from the periscope and responded, "For gold doubloons and pieces of eight. Come now, Comrade Arbatov, didn't you ever read Robert Louis Stevenson's *Treasure Island* as a child?"

Shaking his head that he hadn't, the captain sighed. "Thank the heavens for my uncle Petyr's book collection. Back in the seventeenth and eighteenth centuries, while the imperialist armies were

226

busy wiping out the native inhabitants of these islands, hundreds of treasure-filled galleons set sail for Europe with tons of plunder. An active fleet of pirate ships existed in these very waters which were responsible for sending many a gold-laden ship to the bottom here.

"The waters of the Virgin Islands are clear and warm. And from what I understand, the capitalists flock here to vacation with their scuba tanks, masks, and flippers. Their greed for wealth even fills the hours of their leisure time!"

Taking a last look at the anchored dive ship quickly fading behind them, the captain stood. "They certainly won't be bothering us, Comrade Arbatov. But remain at this station with your eyes peeled. As long as we're in this channel, we can't be too cautious."

"Very good, sir!" returned the senior lieutenant, who wasted no time returning to the periscope.

Alexander Gnutov scanned the control room and spotted the *Kirov*'s zampolit beside the ship's navigator. Their attentions were riveted on the chart table, and the captain decided to see for himself just what it was that they were so absorbed with.

"What's so interesting, Comrades?" greeted the captain lightly.

It proved to be the political officer who responded. "I was just having Lieutenant Natya here plot the exact course of our chase with the Trafalgar class vessel, Captain. I'm certain that Command will find this detailed documentation most interesting."

"I'm certain that they will," returned Gnutov, who looked down to the surface of the chart table.

227

The bathymetric chart showed the island of Bermuda and the waters that surrounded it. Two parallel series of different colored lines crisscrossed the Atlantic here. It was the navigator who explained just what these lines corresponded to.

"The red line indicates the *Kirov*'s course, the blue corresponds to the Trafalgar. It was here, off the eastern coast of Bermuda, that the wipe-off maneuver was successfully accomplished. To allow the *Caspian* to escape southward undetected, the *Kirov* headed due north, at a flank speed of over forty-five knots. Using the various submerged seamounts of the Bermuda Rise to our best advantage, the *Kirov* then proceeded to willingly slow down to allow the slower English boat a chance to catch up. For the next twenty hours we then proceeded to lead the Trafalgar on a blind chase that ended here near the Muir Seamount."

"Finding that deep scattering layer was an act of brilliant seamanship, Captain," praised the zampolit.

Alexander Gnutov grunted. "I don't know if I'd go that far. Since the *Caspian* had had plenty of time to make good their escape, it was time for us to continue on our own mission as well. The *Kirov*'s superb sensors, and our ability to dive beneath nine hundred meters of seawater, allowed us to lose the English fox with a minimum of brilliance on my part, Comrade Pavlodar."

The political officer wiped his sweat-stained jowls with his handkerchief and chuckled. "I'd still like to see that English captain's face when he realized that he had lost us. After all that effort on his part, such a

228

thing had to be most frustrating."

"He should have known from the very beginning that they had no chance of ever catching us," observed the navigator proudly. "After all, as an Alfa class vessel, the *Kirov* is the fastest, deepest diving submarine in the entire world. Not even the latest American vessel can touch us."

The captain's gaze narrowed. "Don't be so sure of that, Lieutenant Natya. Always remember that there is no sure thing when it comes to underwater warfare. Like any hunt, there are a wide variety of outside forces that affect a successful outcome, and technological advantage is only one of these factors."

Pointing toward the two colored courses, Gnutov continued. "The British captain showed great daring in his pursuit of us. He pushed his vessel to the very limits of its endurance, and wasn't beyond a few surprises of his own, such as that time he suddenly scrammed their reactors, causing us to momentarily lose them on our hydrophones. So never forget to always respect your opposition, no matter how outdated and unsophisticated his hardware may seem."

With this point made, Gnutov abruptly changed the course of their conversation. "Now all this talk of tactics and strategy is most stimulating, Comrades, but we mustn't forget the *Kirov*'s current objective. The passage that we are presently transiting is extremely treacherous, with one wrong turn sending us all instantly to our watery graves."

Well aware of what the captain was referring to, the navigator reached out and replaced the chart they had been studying with one that lay directly beneath it. This chart was a detailed rendering of the Anegada Passage. It had a series of red X's marked on its surface, showing their course's progress. Picking up the red marker, Alexander Gnutov added several more X's to this line of plot marks, extending it just past the land mass labeled "Norman Island."

"So, our excellent progress continues," reflected the zampolit.

Seeming to ignore this comment, the captain expressed his remarks to the navigator. "Lieutenant Natya, I want you to constantly update this chart. The officer of the deck will give you the latest satellite location data. Plot this information without fail. I want to know our exact position to the nearest square centimeter, each and every second that we remain in this passage. Do I make myself absolutely clear, Comrade Natya?"

The rigid tone of Gnutov's voice clearly expressed his upset, and the navigator nervously nodded. "Of course I do, sir. I'll get on it at once!"

As he returned his vigilance back to the job at hand, the zampolit beckoned the captain to join him beside the vacant fire-control panel. "Please go easy on him, Captain. It's my fault that he strayed from his duty. I shouldn't have bothered him until we were well out of the transit channel."

"That's beside the matter," retorted Gnutov. "Lieutenant Natya is more than aware of his current responsibilities, and no outside force whatsoever should have distracted him away from them. Even with the aid of these specially detailed charts that Intelligence was able to forward to us as we were leaving Murmansk, this channel is an extremely

230

dangerous one. A coral reef can be most unforgiving, and I don't have to remind you that our mission is only yet half completed."

The zampolit nodded. "Perhaps we should have waited until cover of night to transit this channel, as the *Caspian* was ordered to do."

"Unfortunately, we have no more time to waste, Comrade Pavlodar! Our encounter with the English sub kept us away from our real duty for too long. Though Captain Sobrinka and the *Caspian* are quite capable of taking care of themselves, we have been ordered to escort them all the way to Cienfuegos. And since they have a good twenty-hour headstart on us, it's going to take everything we've got to reach them as directed."

"We'll catch up to them with plenty of time to spare, Captain. Cuba is still a good forty-eight hours away, and since we can travel at almost twice the velocity as the *Caspian*, we should have no trouble reaching them as ordered."

Alexander Gnutov seemed amused with the zampolit's calculations. "I still say you're wasting yourself with mere political concerns, my friend. There are the makings of a decent sailor inside that stubborn head of yours."

The political officer was sincerely flattered by this remark. "Why, thank you, Captain. But don't underrate the importance of the Party. It's the glue that keeps this crew together as a fighting entity."

"I'm certain that you're correct with your astute observation," Comrade Pavlodar. But more mundane matters call me back to the helm. Charts or no charts, my gut tells me that there's more to this damn passage we're transiting than meets the eye!''

Genuinely surprised by this unexpected revelation, the zampolit watched as the captain pivoted to return to the periscope well. Though he certainly didn't share Gnutov's paranoid concerns, Ivan Pavlodar nonetheless turned to make his own way back to the chart table to count the minutes left until the waters of the Anegada Passage were well behind them.

Chapter Ten

Secretary of the Navy Peter Anderson was homeward bound on the beltway, when he got the call requesting his immediate presence at the Pentagon's underground situation room. Since it was his old friend Red Sutton who had placed this call, Peter didn't even bother asking what it was all about. While preparing to use his cellular mobile phone to tell his wife Betty he would be late, he instructed his chauffeur to do whatever was necessary to cross the rush hour-filled highway, and make a U-turn at the next exit. Ignoring the honking horns, rude hand gestures, and threatening shouts this abrupt maneuver generated, his driver did as he was ordered, and soon they were headed back toward Arlington.

An immense, five-sided cement structure loomed ominously in the distance. Built on the banks of the Potomac River, immediately across from Washington, D.C., the Pentagon was constructed as the world's largest office building, housing over thirty thousand people. It contained the offices of the Joint

Chiefs of Staff and the other chiefs, as well as the secretaries of the Army, Air Force, and Peter's own office.

The Pentagon was in actuality not one single building but about fifty, all interconnected to form five complete pentagons, placed one inside another in a series of concentric, five-sided rings. Peter's office was located in the E-ring, the outermost and therefore largest of the rings. This portion of the building was dominated by marble columns, terrazzo floors, and had an abundance of private elevators. It also provided the only rooms with a view of the surrounding countryside.

They pulled back into the lot they had just left a quarter of an hour before, and Peter's chauffeur dropped him off at the private security entrance. A pair of alert Marines greeted him with a salute and unlocked the bulletproof glass door that took him to a marble-lined hallway. Halfway down this corridor, he halted before the sealed doors of an elevator. A plastic key card gained him entrance to this lift, which was soon whisking him downward.

The situation room was located several stories beneath the building's ground floor. Buried in tons of fortified concrete, the room was designed as a crisis management center and could survive all but a direct nuclear strike.

As it turned out, Peter had been called to this infrequently visited portion of the Pentagon only this morning, to be briefed on a serious incident that was taking place in the Panama Canal Zone. Much to his shock, he was to learn that a United States Navy submarine, in the process of transiting the canal, was under attack by a group of leftist insurgents. When he learned that this vessel was the USS *Swordfish*, his shock intensified to actual horror, for his nephew Ted was this boat's skipper.

By the grace of God, what had started out as a potentially disastrous surprise ambush had been defused by a single Marine Harrier attack jet. Without a single U.S. injury, except for a few ricochet marks on its hull, the *Swordfish* had survived the attack. And by the time Peter Anderson was ready to leave the office to go home, the sub was reported entering the protective depths of the Caribbean Sea.

Peter prayed that he was not being called back to the situation room to be briefed on yet another international incident involving the *Swordfish*. His nephew and his crack crew had certainly seen enough action for one day.

He assumed that this abrupt call back to duty most likely had something to do with the USS *Turner*. The captured Elint ship had yet to be heard from, and perhaps something had taken place in Murmansk to finally break the stalemate. Hoping that this was indeed the case, he looked up expectantly when the lift braked to a stop and its doors opened with a hushed hiss.

He needed to give a handprint to be allowed entry into yet another corridor. This one was lined in white tile and led to a cavernous room dominated by dozens of manned consoles all facing a huge Perspex screen. Peter's eyes went directly to this screen, on whose surface was displayed an immense map of the Caribbean basin. Lying to the immediate east of

235

Puerto Rico, a blinking red star was highlighting the general area of the U.S. Virgin Islands.

Peter's first fear was that his nephew was somehow yet again in trouble. But the *Swordfish* was over a thousand miles away, on the opposite corner of the basin, somewhere off the coast of Central America.

A gentle hand tapped him on the shoulder and Anderson turned and set his gaze on the bespectacled face of the current chief of naval intelligence, Admiral Red Sutton. Once a valued subordinate on Peter's own staff, Sutton was both a respected associate and a longtime friend, this last attribute being a rarity inside Washington's beltway.

"Sorry to have to call you back, Pete, but something's taking place off the island of St. John that I thought you should be aware of."

Walking over to a nearby console, Sutton addressed its seated occupant, who was dressed in the distinctive blue uniform of an Air Force sergeant. The soldier alertly addressed his keyboard, and seconds later the scene on the room's central screen abruptly changed. Displayed now was a detailed map showing the island of St. John and the strait of water lying directly to the east of it. It was in this waterway that yet another red star was blinking.

Returning to Peter's side, Red Sutton continued his briefing. "Approximately three and a half hours ago, my office was contacted by a certain Commander Richard Walker of Naval Research, Development, and Acquisitions. Walker was calling on an unsecured line from the island of St. John, where he's escorting a group of four congressional bigwigs who are investigating Defense Department procurement policies. The particular project in question had to do with the development of a dolphin-borne harness device.

"To properly show this apparatus in action, the researcher in charge of the project leased a dive boat and took Walker and his group out into the waters adjoining the Anegada Passage. Here a specially trained dolphin was fitted with the harness, which had a very unique adaptation to it—a miniature, fiber-optic camera. The dolphin was then sent to the bottom of the passage, supposedly to film some sort of ancient wreck that is rumored to litter the sea floor there. Yet the pictures that were relayed topside showed no such ancient remains. Instead, an object of a much more recent vintage soon filled the screen of their video monitor."

Halting with this enigmatic revelation, Sutton once again addressed the seated Air Force technician. Yet this time as the soldier addressed his keyboard, the picture on the Perspex screen split in two, with the map still displayed on the right half and a video tape presentation on its left portion.

Peter Anderson studied this video footage, which evidently had been filmed under water. Though it was poorly lit, he watched as what appeared to be the top portion of a dolphin flashed on the screen. Next, a large grouper swam in and out of the lens, which seemed to be focusing in on a distant blinking red beacon of some type. Yet this flashing light soon faded, to be replaced by an elongated, black cylindrical object that looked disturbingly familiar, though Peter still couldn't place it. Scratching his forehead in thought, Anderson listened as Red Sutton continued.

"This footage was relayed over a secured satellite transmission, broadcast from our naval station at Roosevelt Roads, Puerto Rico. Commander Walker was flown here with the tape from St. Thomas, in the jumpseat of an F-14 Tomcat."

The chief of naval intelligence momentarily hesitated as the screen filled with a towerlike structure built into the cylinder's midsection. It was at this point that Peter Anderson identified it. "Is that a submarine, Red?"

Sutton nodded. "It sure as hell looks that way, Pete. But just wait a second. The best is yet to come."

Anderson's eyes were glued to the elevated screen as the vessel's conning tower gave way to yet another portion of rounded deck. This section of the hull had a large rudder sticking up from its surface. And it was as the secretary of the Navy caught a glimpse of the five-pointed, bright red star that was etched on the rudder's metallic surface that he exclaimed, "Holy smokes, it's Russian!"

It was at this point that Red Sutton instructed the technician to freeze the frame. Pointing to the screen, he added, "It didn't take my boys long to analyze this tape and figure out exactly what we've got here, Pete. As unbelievable as it might sound, they're one hundred percent positive that the vessel displayed on the screen before us is a Soviet Typhoon class ballistic-missile-carrying submarine, and a recently built one at that!"

Peter Anderson's tone was tinged with both disbelief and rage. "What in God's name is a Typhoon doing off the coast of the U.S. Virgin Islands?"

"That's what we're currently trying to figure out," returned Sutton. "One thing that's apparent is that it appears to be disabled in some way. Most likely it was on its way to Cienfuegos, when either a catastrophic mechanical breakdown or a collision with the nearby reef sent it tumbling to the bottom. Evidently the Soviet authorities don't even know its status, for we've yet to pick up any unusual activity on their emergency search and rescue frequencies."

"This whole thing is simply incredible, Red. In the first place, what in the hell is a Typhoon doing down in the Caribbean? They're designed for use in the Arctic!"

Sutton removed his wire-rimmed eyeglasses and answered while rubbing the bridge of his nose. "I don't know, Pete, maybe this whole thing is a show of strength on the part of the Kremlin hardliners in response to their ridiculous allegations that the CIA was in on Ivanov's assassination. This sub's presence here could tie in with the capture of the *Turner* as well."

"How's that?" quizzed Anderson.

"It's been almost a week since the *Turner* was abducted. If the Typhoon has only been disabled for less than twenty-four hours as it appears, the Russians would have had plenty of time to move the sub out of Murmansk and down into the Atlantic."

"The Nordkapp choke point!" observed Peter Anderson excitedly. "With the *Turner* out of the way, the Typhoon would be free to transit the GIUK gap without our prior knowledge."

Sutton nodded. "If I remember correctly, the Soviet Northern Fleet was headed northward through the

239

gap at about this same time. That would produce just enough of a distraction to allow the Typhoon free passage into the Atlantic."

Rubbing his hands together expectantly, Anderson questioned, "Has the President been informed of this as yet?"

Sutton shook his head that he hadn't, and the secretary of the Navy continued. "Well, when he does, I expect that all hell is going to break loose. Having a Typhoon this close to our shoreline is a direct violation of the longrange ballistic missile treaty. It's a clearly provocative move on the part of the Soviet military, and will have to be answered accordingly. With this card in our hand, they'll have to release the *Turner* and her crew, and issue a complete apology as well."

A wry gleam emanated from Red Sutton's eyes as he responded. "But the trick is going to be when we're going to play it? Because if this sub has indeed been disabled in such a way that it's been unable to inform Moscow of its dilemma, then we can really play this one out in style."

After once again addressing the seated technician, Sutton pointed to the screen, whose left portion was filled with a snapshot of a single, immense surface ship. This vessel had a full-sized drilling derrick set into its equipment-packed deck, from whose stern flew the Stars and Stripes.

"She's the marine mining vessel the *Global Explorer*, fifty-one thousand awesome tons of state-of-the-art machinery. Over the length of two football fields, she's designed to excavate nodules of copper, nickel, and other minerals from the sea floor. The vessel does so with the assistance of a digging claw weighing over six million pounds. This device can be extended over eighteen thousand feet deep by sixty-foot-long segments of pipe, which are connected with threaded joints.

"I'm certain that you remember Project Bellatrix. The *Global Explorer* was the vessel that successfully exhumed that sunken Soviet Golf class submarine from the depths of the Pacific off Hawaii. Since she's working in the waters only two hundred miles west of St. John, I propose bringing her in for yet another salvage operation."

Peter Anderson's gaze remained locked on the picture of the ship occupying the left portion of the screen, and, noting his continued interest, Red Sutton continued. "I don't have to tell you what we learned from our examination of that Golf class submarine. Even though it was no technological marvel, the wreckage showed us the Soviets' strengths and weaknesses, and we could act accordingly. But can you imagine having one of their newest strategic platforms to pick apart and study? Why, it would be the intelligence coup of the century!

"At long last we could see for ourselves the true extent of modern Soviet marine engineering. And to even think that we will be able to examine an operational SS-N-20 warhead is simply mind boggling. It will set the Soviet strategic program back decades!"

Thoughtfully nodding in agreement, Peter queried, "Do you think that there could be some surviving crew members inside the Typhoon?"

Sutton caught his old friend's concerned glance

241

and responded, "Since its hull integrity appears intact, that possibility has to be dealt with. We can do so by flying in a deep submergence rescue vessel from Charleston. Then, once our boys board the Typhoon, they can not only check for survivors, but also determine the true extent of its damages and if we're going to have a radioactive contamination problem or not."

Looking back to the picture of the *Global Explorer*, Anderson sighed. "With all that equipment and personnel down there, I'd sure like to have a couple of our subs in the vicinity to ride shotgun."

"I'm afraid that could be a problem," returned Sutton. "All of our Sixth and Second Fleet attack vessels are either stationed in the Mediterranean or up in the North Atlantic, in response to the *Turner* incident."

Sutton stepped forward and once again addressed the seated Air Force technician. As the intelligence chief rejoined Peter Anderson, the Perspex screen filled with a map of the entire Caribbean basin. A tiny blue dot began flashing off the coast of Nicaragua, and Sutton added, "Though it does appear that we have one attack sub in the region, the USS *Swordfish*."

Well aware that Peter Anderson's nephew was at the helm of this warship, Red Sutton unnecessarily questioned, "Can they handle it, Pete?"

"I guess that they're just going to have to," remarked the secretary of the Navy, who realized that his nephew's beloved command had just gotten itself a reprieve.

*   *   *

"Captain Sobrinka, may I join you?" questioned the senior lieutenant cautiously.

"Of course you can, Comrade Jarensk," managed the captain, who sat alone in the *Caspian*'s vacant attack center, staring off into the room's dim red depths.

"I have that completed damage control report that you requested," offered the *Caspian*'s second-in-command as he limped over to join the captain on one of the narrow benches that lined the compartment.

With his weary eyes locked on the nearby fire-control console, from where the sub's ballistic missiles would be launched, Mikhail Sobrinka listened as his senior lieutenant continued. "I've completed roll call and must sadly report that we've lost twenty-three men. This includes our zampolit and Chief Engineer Litvak. Fifty-seven men remain seriously injured with various fractures and concussions. Incidentally, most of these casualties took place in the forward weapons room, when one of the Type 65 wake-homing torpedoes broke off from its rack and was loose for several terrifying minutes before it was finally restrained. Per your instructions, I've set up a temporary morgue in the aft storage compartment.

"As expected, both the ship's primary nuclear propulsion units have been damaged beyond repair. Our battery-powered auxiliary system has also taken a severe beating, but the chief electrician promises that he'll do his best to keep it running as long as humanly possible. Because of our critical power situation, the *Caspian* has no hydraulics pressure, and we remain unable to vent the emergency ballast tanks to attempt an ascent.

"The situation in communications is just as bleak. Seconds after we hit the reef, the main transmitter broke off its mounting and crushed to death three of the seated radio operators before they could get off an SOS. An electrical fire followed, and the system is completely inoperable.

"Fortunately, the taiga rode out the collision well. Although without hydraulics pressure, the outer missile hatch couldn't be opened even if we desired to attempt a launch."

As the senior lieutenant halted to catch his breath, the captain somberly voiced himself. "And how are the surviving crew members reacting to our dilemma, Comrade?"

"Morale is quite low, sir. Earlier, an unfounded rumor began spreading among the enlisted men that one of the reactors had split open and was spewing out deadly radiation all through the ship. The men began to panic, and I was forced to intervene with an armed contingent of officers. I believe I was able to calm their fears, yet there's no telling what's going to set them off next."

"You did well, Comrade Jarensk. Though we often talked about him in derogatory terms, it's times such as these that we are really going to miss the zampolit. Our political officer had a genuine feeling for the men, and would have been the perfect individual to keep them under control in these fearful times of stress and doubt. But we will just have to learn to get along without him, as we will have to do with so many other valuable members of the *Caspian*'s crew. So with that said, we must come

244

up with a plan that will ensure the continued survival of all those fortunate enough to be among the living."

The captain's voice seemed to strengthen as he sat forward and continued. "The way I see it, our primary concern is going to have to be air. With the carbon dioxide scrubbers inoperable, we will all too soon be in a critical situation. Thus to conserve oxygen, I think it's best if we limit the crew's activity to a bare minimum. Only those watches that are absolutely necessary for the *Caspian*'s continued well-being are to be manned. The rest of the time I want the men in their bunks, either resting or sleeping. After this meeting is adjourned, I also want you to calculate exactly how much breathable air remains in the ship. For this is the one all-important element on which our continued survival hinges.

"Next is the problem of food and water. Was there much damage in the galley, Comrade?"

The senior lieutenant alertly answered, "The fresh water tanks remained intact, Captain. As for our food situation, the mess chief is in the process of a complete inventory of surviving rations. Of course without power, the refrigeration and freezer compartments are completely useless. The rank smell of rotting meat was beginning to pervade the ship, and I ordered him to jettison all the spoiled stores out through the disposal hatch. As you know, our premature departure from Murmansk resulted in an incomplete larder to begin with. Yet the chief estimates that we still have at least three weeks' worth of canned goods that can be served with a minimum of preparation."

"Thank the fates for that," retorted the captain. "Forward this inventory to me as soon as it's completed and have the chief draw up some sort of rationed menu.

"Now that we've touched upon the basic problems such as food and water, it's time to consider that of morale. It's most important that the crew's spirits are kept at a level where they won't lose hope, for once that occurs, we will lose all discipline as well."

"But how are we to give them hope in what surely is a hopeless situation?" reflected the senior lieutenant.

This observation drew an immediate response from Mikhail Sobrinka. "Don't say that, Comrade! That is just the type of defeatist attitude I want banned from the *Caspian* at all cost."

Almost to emphasize this remark, the dim red emergency lights abruptly blinked off. The blackness quickly swallowed them, and the captain angrily cursed. "Damn it! Can't our electricians even keep a system as basic as our emergency battery-powered lights on line?"

In apparent answer to this question, the lights blinked back on once again, yet they seemed dimmer than ever before.

"That's more like it," said the captain, who stood and began nervously pacing the deck with his hands cocked behind his back. "Things aren't as disheartening as they seem, Comrade Jarensk. Never forget that we have been assigned an escort, whose task it is to rendezvous with us in our appointed patrol sector. Surely Captain Gnutov and the *Kirov* are well on their way to this very spot. And when they find it vacant, don't you think that they will convey this shocking discovery back to Command? Why, of course they will, my friend! And once this news hits the Defense Ministry, a comprehensive search will be immediately initiated. Our preplanned transit route will be traced to the nearest square centimeter, and our discovery will be all but assured. So cheer up, Comrade, and spread the ray of hope to your ship-mates. Our rescue is imminent, I just know it!"

Though he was far from enthusiastic, the senior lieutenant responded, "Of course it is, Captain. Please excuse my moment of weakness. It's just that so much has occurred in these last few hours that it seems that none of my thoughts are all that clear."

"No excuses are necessary, my friend," retorted Mikhail Sobrinka. "These are stressful times for all of us and you are a credit to your uniform."

"Thank you for your vote of confidence, Captain. I'll try not to let you down."

Standing, the senior lieutenant added, "If there's nothing else that you need from me, sir, I'll get on with my duty."

The captain merely nodded, and his subordinate smartly pivoted and ducked out the forward hatch-way. This left Sobrinka alone once again.

As he paced the entire length of the compartment, the captain contemplated the damage control report. Though the twenty-three deaths were a tragic loss of life, he knew that they were very fortunate. The *Caspian*'s hull had remained intact, and they had settled on the sea floor at a depth just within their crush threshold. This was a stroke of luck, for a difference of only a few dozen meters could have been disastrous for all of them.

His one real concern was breathable air. But as long as the senior lieutenant carried out his orders, there was the slimmest chance that they'd be able to hang on until they were located and rescued. It was while wondering if the *Kirov* would be the ship that would find them that the lights again failed.

Suddenly engulfed in total blackness, Sobrinka blindly reached out to grab on to something solid and cracked his elbow against a sharp metal ledge. The excruciating pain that resulted shot through his body and the captain angrily cursed. Unable to see where he was, Mikhail took the only prudent course that was available to him, and he carefully kneeled down to position himself on the deck below.

The pain soon passed, yet when the lights failed to return, he could but remain in this position until his night vision sharpened. Leaning against a partition, he covered his face with his hands and bemoaned his predicament.

In that black moment, it was all suddenly very clear to him. He had failed to exercise proper judgment, and as such would be the only one held at fault for the *Caspian*'s sinking. Over four decades of dedicated service would be wiped out in a single careless stroke, and he would be banished to the gulag in complete disgrace.

As captain, of course he was the one ultimately responsible for the *Caspian*. Regardless of the cause of their collision, the fact remained that one of the most powerful strategic platforms in the Motherland's fleet was for all effective purposes knocked abruptly out of service. So not only was his reputation ruined, but the country he had sworn to protect with his very life if necessary was weakened as a result of his incompetence.

Mikhail dared to think how the news would be received back in the Defense Ministry. Admiral Chimki and his cohorts would be stunned, for their daring plan would be dealt a fatal blow. Though there were always other ballistic-missile-carrying submarines that could replace them, the crucial timing that the attack was relying upon had no substitute. For such an opportunity might never again present itself.

Smacking the palm of his hand hard against his forehead, Mikhail Sobrinka decided that there were only two things he could do to rectify the situation. First would be to use all his resources to save as many of his shipmates as possible. Eventually, Command would locate them, and proper rationing of air, food, and water would ensure that the rescue that would follow would not be in vain.

And once he was positive that rescue was imminent, he would save his family's honor with a single pistol shot to his head. And perhaps his failure would then somehow be forgiven.

In another portion of the Caribbean, the men of the USS *Swordfish* were just sitting down for the first serving of dinner. In the sub's wardroom this meal consisted of baked ham, candied sweet potatoes, string beans, and corn bread, with a slice of blueberry pie for those with room for dessert.

At his usual place at the head of the wardroom

table was Ted Anderson, with Admiral William Abbott seated on his right and the vessel's XO perched in the booth directly opposite the captain. Also seated in the booth was Ensign Steve Delano, the ship's navigator.

"Well, Mr. Delano, what did you think of your first transit of the Panama Canal?" questioned William Abbott between bites of ham steak.

The young ensign completely chewed his food and swallowed before answering. "It was an incredible experience, sir. I never realized the great difference in the water levels between the Pacific and the Atlantic. Why, in the Gatun locks alone we were lowered over eighty-five feet. The engineers who designed it did a remarkable job."

"You can say that again," observed the admiral. "Not a bad piece of craftsmanship for a civilization which only mastered the art of flying some eleven years earlier."

Doing some quick mental calculations, the XO spoke out. "So the canal was completed in 1914?"

Abbott nodded. "Though I wasn't personally there to see the first ship go through myself, it was quite an achievement for the times."

"I certainly could have done without that terrorist attack, though," commented Ted Anderson.

"I don't know, as long as no one on our side got hurt, I thought it was kind of exciting," returned Abbott. "Watching that Harrier rise up over that stand of palms and then proceed to blow those Commies away was worth the price of admission alone."

"I must admit that it was quite a sight," concurred the captain. "Yet I hope that encounter wasn't an indication of things to come. If attacks like that continue, someone on our side is bound to get hurt sooner or later."

Putting down his fork, the admiral responded with great emotion, "It's our damn fault for giving them back the canal like we did. I don't care what you say, but those people just aren't politically stable enough to trust running such a strategically vital installation."

"That canal treaty meant absolutely nothing," offered Stan Pukalani. "The U.S. isn't about to lose such an important waterway just for the sake of a piece of paper. We'll find some way to weasel our way out of it, and the Marines will be there to secure our interests, just like they were there to save our butts."

"Well said, Lieutenant," replied Abbott. "But what sticks in my craw is that we had to go and give it away in the first place. And to a bunch of drug-running terrorists at that!"

Ted Anderson swallowed a bite of corn bread and voiced his own opinion. "There can be no doubting that sometimes our foreign policy is a bit naive. To the rest of the world the canal treaty was a noble exercise, in which a so-called imperialist power transferred sovereignty of an important land mass to its rightful owner. Yet, unfortunately, though our intentions were good, our timing was lousy."

"I don't think the time will ever be right," said Abbott. "Central America is a cauldron of poverty and instability. The Communists have already got a major foothold here, and things are going to get a lot worse before they get better. Do you really think that these people appreciate democracy and are willing to fight for it? All they care about is where their next platter of beans and rice is coming from.

"And before you accuse me of being a racist, can you imagine a time when we no longer have free access to the canal? Our already depleted merchant marine force will have to sail thousands of miles out of their way, and undertake a perilous cruise through the treacherous waters of South America's Drake Passage, just to go from the Atlantic to the Pacific. And all because some wide-eyed liberals want to show the world that Uncle Sam is not such a bad guy after all. Do you realize what losing the canal would mean to the U.S. Navy? The consequences are almost unfathomable!"

The admiral's passionate discourse was interrupted by the arrival of a young, redheaded seaman. Walking up to the head of the wardroom table a bit hesitantly, communications specialist Carl Harper handed the captain a folded sheet of paper.

"This just came in from COMSUBLANT, sir. It was labeled most urgent."

Ted Anderson scanned the communiqué, and before revealing its contents to the others, addressed the sailor who had delivered it. "Very good, Mr. Harper. You may return to your station."

"Aye, aye, sir," replied Harper, who turned and quickly exited.

Anderson looked back down to the message and reread it. Seemingly lost in thought, he only looked up again when William Abbott's gravelly voice addressed him. "Come on, Captain, the suspense is killing all of us, and you look like you just saw a ghost."

Anderson sighed. "In a way I have. Mr. Delano,

252

I want you to draw up an immediate course to St. John, in the U.S. Virgin Islands. Strangely enough, we've just been ordered there with all due haste."

Handing the communiqué to his right, the captain watched as Admiral Abbott carefully read it.

"Well, I'll be," reflected the wide-eyed veteran. "Looks like we're going to have to postpone this old rust bucket's retirement party after all!"

Chapter Eleven

The narrow earthern trail led eastward, away from the rocky coastline and into the foothills of the Sierra de Trinidad mountains. Alexander Gnutov had hiked it several times before. But that was almost three decades ago, and he was somewhat surprised to find the footpath much as it had been at that time. He couldn't say the same for the port complex that he had left a half hour ago. Twenty-seven years ago, Cienfuegos had been but a sleepy little fishing village. Today it was a modern city, with over one hundred thousand inhabitants.

Briefly halting to catch his breath, Alexander turned and focused his glance in the direction from which he had just come. Lit by the soft light of dawn, the Cuban city of Cienfuegos lay in the near distance. He had been constantly gaining altitude since leaving on this hike, and so he could also see much of the city's surrounding environs. The majority of these suburbs hugged the rugged, palm-tree-lined coast. Dozens of large, ocean-going ships of all kinds were moored at the pier complex, and Alexander could just make out the top portion of the hollowed-out cavern where his own command, the *Kirov*, was berthed.

Alexander yawned and briefly stretched his tight limbs before pivoting and continuing his climb. His goal, a wide ledge of volcanic rock projecting from the summit of the hill he was presently climbing, was clearly visible before him. It was a good five hundred meters distant, and since he wanted to reach it by sunrise, Alexander continued his brisk stride anew.

After the long underwater voyage from Murmansk, this excursion was most welcomed. The cramped confines of the *Kirov* were not conducive to the type of exercise that he most enjoyed. A good hike was like a health tonic to the veteran submariner. It refreshed his body as well as his mind.

Even as a young child, he had always craved the open spaces of the woods and hills of his birthplace. It was therefore ironic that most of his adult life had been spent submerged beneath the world's seas, in a tight, tubular cylinder of steel barely a hundred meters long.

The path began a series of steep switchbacks. Climbing this winding incline with a fluid ease, Alexander breathed in the hot, sultry air. Sweat matted his forehead, and he scanned the surrounding landscape that was dry and covered with rock, cactus, and scrub.

This was in vast contrast to the hills that he had last been hiking through, and Alexander was most conscious of his current alien environment. Momentarily startled when a large lizard scooted across the path, his thoughts went back to his first visit to these foothills, twenty-seven years ago. He had been but a junior officer aboard the November class submarine *Kalanin* at the time, and was introduced to this path by a very special guide.

He had met Maria in the port commander's office. Immediately captivated by her dark Latin eyes, long brown hair, and exquisite figure, Alexander dared to ask the teenage secretary if she knew of any good trails in the area. An avid hiker herself, Maria invited the blond Russian sailor from Sverdlovsk to join her on an excursion the very next day. Though Alexander had to rearrange his leave time to make this date, he instantly accepted and met her that same evening to finalize their plans.

Over powerful rum cocktails, they got to know each other better. Considering her young age, Maria's Russian was excellent. One of the benefits of Castro's revolution were the hundreds of Soviet teachers who were soon arriving in Cuba. Maria had the benefit of such an instructor during her formative junior high days, and could ramble on about Russian history and the intricacies of socialist theory for hours on end.

She chose a romantic seaside restaurant where Alexander had his first experience with that tasty delicacy called lobster. Though he was hesitant to try it at first, by the time dinner was over he had consumed a massive two-pounder all on his own.

Intoxicated by both the rum and his delightful company, Alexander could hardly believe it when Maria invited him over to her apartment near the seashore for a nightcap. It was a warm, tropical evening, and a brilliant full moon was just rising over Cienfuegos Bay as they reached her place.

Maria's apartment was a cramped, one-bedroom affair that she shared with her mother, who was off visiting an aunt in Havana. Alexander had had little experience with members of the oppposite sex, and really didn't know what to expect as she poured them rum and pineapple juice cocktails and sat down on the couch close beside him. Seconds later, she was in his arms.

Their lips hungrily merged as one, and he allowed himself to be completely possessed by his rising passions. He was in a strange new land, with a gorgeous, exotic woman, and even though he was a virgin, he would not be denied this chance to at long last taste the forbidden fruit of lust.

Maria seemed to be no stranger to the game and wasted no time removing Alexander's shirt. Her hungry lips went to his muscular chest, and he followed her lead and fondled her pert, heaving breasts with both his hands and his tongue. Her need seemed to rise at this point, and as her nipples hardened in dark, budlike buttons, she unzipped his trousers and grasped his swollen manhood. She seemed to like what she was feeling, and gasped at its pulsating length and width.

Her lips replaced her hands, and Alexander swooned in pure ecstasy. Instinctively, he found his way to her love channel. Parting the dark pubic bush with his fingers, he probed her inner recesses, his mere touch bringing forth a gush of hot, spurting fluids.

Maria passionately cried out, and lifting her head

from his crotch, turned her body around and mounted him. She cried out again when his erect shaft penetrated her tight, wet depths. Muttering away in rapid Spanish now, she moved her hips downward until his all was taken. Then she slowly pulled her hips back, until only the tip of his phallus was connected. And again she plunged herself downward, this time quickly repeating the process until a spirited rhythm was established.

They seemed to go on like this for an eternity when Maria's cries of passion suddenly increased to a point that she was almost screaming in pleasure. Alexander felt his own seed begin to rise at this point, and as her body quivered in an uncontrollable series of orgasms, he joined her in bliss.

Still joined as one, they lay in each other's arms, temporarily spent and satisfied. Not long afterward, they repeated this mad coupling, and Alexander's orgasm was just as intense. And only then did he surrender to a sound, dreamless sleep.

Alexander awoke to find it morning. The scent of perking coffee filled the air, and he found Maria in the kitchen, happily preparing a picnic lunch. Though Alexander would have liked to make love once again, she teasingly kissed him on the lips and reminded him of his original desire to do some hiking. Shrugging his shoulders, he went off to shower and dress before allowing himself to be led up the sloping trail that afforded him his first real look at the tropical homeland of the Soviet Union's newest ally.

Alexander found it hard to believe that almost three decades had passed since that fated night when he lost his innocence. Yet returning to the trail once again, he allowed memories long since forgotten to return to his consciousness just as if they had occurred only yesterday.

An introspective grin painted the veteran's face as he completed climbing the series of switchbacks and viewed his goal before him. The volcanic promontory was just as he had remembered it. Formed out of a smooth ledge of solid rock, it had a single massive boulder set in its center. Twenty-seven years ago, they had sat on top of this same rock to have their picnic and look out to the sights below. In fact, he could almost taste the tangy chicken and rice dish that Maria had prepared as he climbed onto the boulder and seated himself on its smooth, flat surface.

No sooner did he settle himself into this position when the dawn sun broke the eastern horizon in a blaze of golden light. A stiff, cool wind, full with the scent of the sea, hit him square in the face as he gazed out to the surging blue Caribbean. A single tanker could be seen following the transit route that would eventually take it to Cienfuegos. Alexander had followed this same route only yesterday, though they made the approach completely submerged. Only when the *Kirov* pulled into its specially designed underwater berth, located inside of a hollowed-out sea cave, did the vessel break the surface.

During his first visit to these waters on the *Kalinin*, they had no such covered berth to dock inside. Rather, they had to do so in the port itself, and were thus under the constant scrutiny of the American U-2 surveillance planes that were constantly overflying the island.

Those were tense, exciting days, and as Alexander looked on as the dawn continued to take shape, his thoughts returned to the afternoon the *Kalinin* almost fired the first salvo of World War III. They had been on picket duty at the time, cruising in the waters just north of San Salvador. The brash young American President John Kennedy had overreacted in typical imperialist fashion, and had issued his infamous Cuban quarantine. The same twisted Western logic that said it was okay to station U.S. ballistic rockets on the Soviet border in Turkey insisted that a reciprocal move by the Soviets to install missile sites in Cuba was nothing short of an act of war.

It was as a Soviet tanker filled with missile components approached this quarantine zone that the *Kalinin* was called in to ensure its safe passage. Yet at about this same time their sonar operator detected a U.S. Navy attack sub rapidly approaching on a direct intercept course. Since this was obviously an aggressive move on the part of the Americans, the Kremlin had no choice but to prepare to defend itself.

Alexander had been stationed in the torpedo room, and had personally supervised the loading of all eight of the *Kalinin*'s forward tubes. The captain had actually ordered them to open the torpedo doors and program a final attack angle when word came down from the control room for them to stand down. Only later did he learn the reason why the attack had been so abruptly canceled. Intimidated by the American's strong reaction, Premier Khrushchev had ordered the tanker to return to the Soviet Union so as not risk an armed confrontation with the U.S. Navy.

Alexander and the majority of his shipmates had been genuinely upset when they heard this news. To them it bespoke cowardice and military weakness on the part of the Motherland. Yet now almost three decades later, Alexander knew that Khrushchev had had no choice but to back down. Outnumbered when it came to nuclear warheads and reliable strategic delivery systems, the Soviet Union would have fared badly in an atomic exchange. So what Alexander and his co-workers had mistaken for a lack of nerve on Khrushchev's part was only circumspection.

And today the tables had finally turned, and it was the Motherland that was bargaining from a position of nuclear superiority. Through hard work and selfless devotion to the cause, the Soviet strategic arsenal was second to none other on this planet. This was particularly the case beneath the world's seas, where vessels such as the *Kirov* ran deeper and faster than any submarine that the West had in its inventory.

Just thinking about his present command again caused Alexander to look out to the blue Caribbean with a new sense of intensity guiding his stare. For, somewhere out there, beneath the surging depths, yet another example of Soviet naval superiority patroled the deep seas. Larger than any submarine that had ever sailed the seven seas, the *Caspian* was the pride of the Soviet Fleet. Locked within the Typhoon class vessel's missile magazine was enough nuclear destruction to wipe from the map almost every single major population center on the entire North American continent!

Alexander's eyes proudly gleamed with this

thought. Yet he still couldn't help but wonder in what portion of the Caribbean the *Caspian* was patrolling. One thing that he was certain of was that Captain Sobrinka and his crew were not to be found in the preplanned sector the Defense Ministry had informed them of. The *Kirov* had only just completed an intensive sweep of these waters, and not a hint of the *Caspian* was ever chanced upon.

To Alexander this could mean but two things. Either Sobrinka had received a patrol station other than the one Alexander was originally informed of, or during the time that the two subs were apart, the *Caspian* had experienced some sort of mechanical difficulty that had kept them from attaining the final rendezvous. It was with this hope in mind that Alexander decided to make this unplanned stop in Cienfuegos.

Much to his dismay, the *Caspian* wasn't waiting for them in port as he had presumed. The commander of the Soviet naval facility at Cienfuegos seemed equally puzzled, and immediately queried the Defense Ministry in Moscow. An obscure answer to this query arrived back in Cuba only a few hours ago. Without offering any type of explanation as to where the *Caspian* could be found, Alexander was ordered to remain in port until directed elsewhere. Though this was not exactly the type of response he had expected to receive, Alexander took advantage of this unexpected port stop and initiated his current hike.

The sun was rapidly climbing into the heavens now, and the new day was well upon them. Far in the distance a rooster crowed, and the hot wind gusted with a new fury.

From the top of the volcanic boulder, Alexander breathed in the sultry air and found himself suddenly homesick. Though his current vantage point offered him a spectacular view of the surrounding landscape, it was still blood alien to him. Palm trees and tropical flowers might be beautiful to some, but he would rather be in the cool green hills of his birthplace, where the ancient oak and the mighty pine prevailed in a world of tumbling mountain streams and woods filled with bountiful wildlife.

Wiping the sweat from his forehead, Alexander knew that he could never be happy living in the tropics. Snow and ice were in his veins. And how could one possibly live without the miraculous change of seasons?

Back in the Urals, the day that was just dawning before him had already long passed. The woods would be pitch black now, with the roar of the crashing brook and the incessant cries of the night creatures filling the sweet air like a symphony. And somewhere in their depths, the great Ural brown bear he had encountered in the foothills slumbered, dreaming of the fat ram that had been so wondrously delivered practically straight into his massive, razor-sharp paws.

Stirred by this thought, Alexander wondered when he'd have another chance to return to such a wilderness paradise. He was currently a world away, and there was no telling how many lonely months this vigil would demand of him.

With the dim hope that the orders sending them homeward would be awaiting him at the port facility below, the submariner took one last look at the glistening waters of the Caribbean before standing and initiating the long hike back to town.

The helicopter flight from Puerto Rico's Roosevelt Roads naval station to the waters of the Anegada Passage took the secretary of the Navy a little less than two hours to complete. He had been whisked down to the Caribbean from Andrews Air Force Base on a Boeing C-135 Stratolifter. Once at Roosevelt Roads, a Sikorsky SH-60B Seahawk helicopter was waiting to transfer him the rest of the way to the seas off St. John.

Peter Anderson looked out of the chopper's central fuselage viewing port to the crystal blue waters visible ten thousand feet below. The roar of the vehicle's twin turboshaft engines whined incessantly in the background, and the chop of the Seahawk's four rotors rose with almost a hypnotic quality.

Actual operational deployments out of Washington were rare for Peter, and he couldn't help but be excited when the President asked him to personally supervise the all-important salvage operation that would soon be taking place off the Virgin Islands. As of his last phone conversation with Red Sutton a little over an hour and a half ago, the Soviet Defense Ministry had yet to show any signs that one of its Typhoons was missing in the Caribbean. This was excellent news, which the United States planned to make the most of.

Outside, the island of St. Thomas could be just seen passing on their left. Anderson had visited this

264

same island on his honeymoon, and could make out the profiles of three large cruise ships anchored in the main port of Charlotte Amalie. A series of mountainous hills surrounded this bustling facility that twenty-five years ago was but a tiny, tropical outpost.

Soon they were speeding over the waters of Pillsbury Sound, and Anderson was afforded his first view of St. John. They were gradually losing altitude now, and the island's luxurious tropical terrain beckoned invitingly. Since most of its mountainous landmass was a national park, it had been mostly spared the development that had scarred its sister islands. White sand beaches were bordered by waters so clear that he could actually pick out the adjoining submerged reefs.

They were passing over a particularly rugged mountainous ridge when a soft electronic tone chimed from his helmet's intercom speakers. This was followed by the voice of the Seahawk's pilot, who in this instance was female.

"Mr. Secretary, those are St. John's Bordeaux mountains that we're currently passing over. Coral Bay lies directly before us."

"How much longer until we get to our final destination, Lieutenant?" quizzed Peter into the miniature chin-mounted transmitter.

"Actually, we've got the *Global Explorer* in sight now, sir," responded the pilot. "We should be down on her deck in another five minutes."

Satisfied with this answer, Anderson watched as the bay of water the pilot had just mentioned passed below them. It seemed to be just as large as the harbor facility at Charlotte Amalie, but this was where the similarity ended. For only a single sailing vessel was anchored in the sparkling clear waters, with the shrub- and beach-covered coastline all but unpopulated.

He knew that somewhere on this coastline was located the research laboratory where the scientist directly responsible for their exciting discovery was working. He had read more about her project during the flight down from Andrews.

Dolpins had always fascinated him, but it wasn't until he had read the comprehensive briefing package his aides had gathered for him that he realized how little he really knew about these highly intelligent marine mammals.

While working in the Office of Naval Intelligence, he once utilized a group of dolphins to help locate an F-14 Tomcat that had crashed off the coast of Catalina Island in California. It was a destroyer's towed array sonar sled that eventually found the downed aircraft itself, yet one of the dolphins did spot a Phoenix air-to-air missile that was being carried beneath the Tomcat's fuselage and had been jarred loose during the ditching. Though this was an important find, no one in the Pentagon really gave the dolphins' efforts much second thought. They considered them more of a sideshow than anything else, and continued dolphin research was delegated to the back burner.

Somehow Dr. Susan Patton had been able to squeeze out the funding to begin her work on St. John's Hurricane Hole. And lucky thing for the country that she had been able to do so! For the money spent on the development of the lightweight, dolphin-borne harness had already paid off a millionfold.

The incredible pictures that had been relayed topside because of this harness were fresh in Anderson's mind as the helicopter continued losing altitude. The east end of St. John passed beneath them, and after transiting a relatively narrow watery passage, yet another mountainous island became visible. This one was significantly smaller than St. John, and was bordered on its southeastern coast by a good-sized, elongated reef that was clearly visible from the air above. It was in the deep blue waters directly beside this submerged reef that a conglomeration of surface ships were anchored.

The largest of these vessels was over six hundred feet long, with its equipment-packed deck dominated by an immense derrick. Anderson had seen pictures of this ship before, and knew it to be the *Global Explorer*. And it was to the flat pad built onto its stern that he was ultimately headed.

As they circled to prepare their final descent, he identified the two other ships anchored nearby. The smallest of these vessels was a Pegasus class gunship, that had sprinted down from Key West at an awesome forty-five knots. It did so by utilizing its eighteen-thousand-shaft horsepower, waterjet propulsion, gas turbine engine, and its unique hullborne hydrofoils.

As an early advocate of producing more of these lightning-fast ships, Anderson was well aware of their history. They were originally conceived as a NATO project, to be built jointly by Germany, Italy, and the United States for service in the Baltic and Mediterranean areas. Only a single six-ship squadron

267

was authorized and funded by Congress, when the European countries subsequently withdrew from the project.

Since being deployed in the early eighties, they had more than proved themselves as the Navy's fastest ships with excellent range, superb seakeeping qualities, and a potent punch. Mostly used to intercept suspected drug runners, they were armed with a single 76mm gun and two quad harpoon missile launchers that were mounted on the fantail.

The vessel anchored beside the gunship was almost twice its length. It sported a characteristic catamaran-style hull, and was designed solely for transporting, servicing, and lowering a deep submergence rescue vessel, or DSRV as they were more commonly called.

The DSRV itself was not visible in the bay of this ship. This meant that it was presently being deployed beneath the water's surface. Looking much like a fifty-foot-long, elongated air cylinder with a tilting shroud on the stern protecting its single propellor, the DSRV was developed to rescue the crew of a submarine accidentally immobilized on the sea floor. It did so by locating and mating with the distressed sub, and then transferring the crew inside its pressure capsule.

Anxiously awaiting the report that its three-man crew would be bringing to the surface shortly, Peter Anderson turned from the window and rebuckled his safety harness. The mad clatter of the spinning rotors roared with an almost deafening intensity as the Seahawk slowly settled downward.

They landed with a bare jolt, and as the engines

were disengaged, the relief from the grinding noise was almost instantaneous. It was the airborne tactical officer who opened the fuselage door for him, and Anderson wasted no time climbing out onto the deck of the ship upon which they had just landed.

Waiting for him beside the landing pad was a tall, handsome naval officer, who stepped forward with a spirited greeting. "Welcome aboard the *Global Explorer*, Mr. Secretary. I'm Commander Richard Walker."

As they exchanged handshakes, Anderson replied, "Thank you, Commander Walker, it's exciting to be here. If I remember correctly, you're the Navy's liaison with Dr. Patton and were one of the first to see our amazing find."

"That I was, sir," returned the commander, who was distracted by the sudden arrival of a freckle-faced seaman.

"Commander Walker," interrupted the eager enlisted man. "Captain Brown wanted you to know that the *San Clemente* is on its way up, sir."

"Thank you, son," replied the commander, who returned his attention to his distinguished guest. "That's our DSRV, Mr. Secretary. They initiated their first dive over an hour ago. Would you like to go down to the moonpool and watch them ascend?"

"I'd love that," answered Peter Anderson as he removed his suit jacket, loosened his tie, and rolled up his sleeves. "I'm afraid that I didn't have time to change and properly prepare for this heat, Commander. Is there somewhere we can stow this?"

He proceeded to hand the officer his suit coat, which Walker then handed to the freckle-faced enlisted man.

"Seaman, hang Secretary Anderson's coat in the wardroom."

Conscious now of the identity of their guest, the seaman stiffened. "Aye, aye, sir!"

As he turned to do his duty, the commander's hand went to wipe off his own forehead. "I'm still getting used to this heat myself, Mr. Secretary. Although I didn't think it possible, it's sultrier here than it is back in Washington."

Peter Anderson patted his own face with his handkerchief. "I agree, Commander. Now where's this moonpool that the seaman mentioned?"

Beckoning the bureaucrat to follow him, Richard Walker explained, "The moonpool is located amidships. It's actually a rectangular cutout opening to the sea, that's over a third of the ship's length. Its primary purpose is to hold the mineral extraction claw that's lowered to the bottom by the sixty-foot lengths of interconnected threaded pipe.

"When under way, the pool is kept sealed by two massive steel plates that slide together and are edged with a rubberized gasket. At that time the water is then pumped out, with the plates being able to hold over sixteen million pounds of additional weight."

"On the way down, I reread the file on the successful salvage job that the *Global Explorer* did on that Soviet Golf class sub that sank off Hawaii," remarked Anderson. "I guess the moonpool is where the remains were initially examined."

The commander was in the process of leading them down a covered stairway as he answered, "Yes, it was, Mr. Secretary. Though it's certainly been

270

totally decontaminated since then, of all the radiation that came on board along with those Russian nuclear-tipped torpedoes we discovered on the Golf.''

"That was quite an operation," reflected Peter. "Yet do you really think that it was worth the hundreds of millions of dollars it ended up costing the taxpayers?"

Commander Walker thought a moment before offering his opinion. "From what I understand, the Golf was in pretty bad shape even before we plucked her from the sea floor, eighteen thousand feet beneath the surface. So it's hard to believe that we were really hoping to find much of value when we decided to salvage her. I do think that the money was well spent merely for this ship's sake. Even beyond her ability to extract minerals from the ocean's depths, without the *Global Explorer*, what we're attempting to do today would be impossible."

Walker led them through a passageway lined with dozens of thick electrical cables. In an adjoining compartment, they passed by a cavernous room filled with an assortment of engineering machinery. There was a loud mechanical whine in this portion of the vessel, and the naval officer had to practically shout to be heard over it.

"That noise is coming from the engine room. Fitting out at fifty-one thousand tons, the ship has two normal engines and five thrusters, that together produce over twenty-two million horsepower. Such immense power is needed for stable positioning. Thus even with eighteen-foot swells and forty-knot winds, her thrusters could keep the ship within one hundred and fifty feet over a tiny computer-tracked

271

target more than eighteen thousand feet below. If you ask me, that ability alone was worth the millions spent to develop her."

Absorbing this comment, Peter followed his escort down a series of ladders. The drone of machinery faded, to be replaced by the more palpable sound of lapping water. The scent of the sea permeated the air, and he all too soon spotted for himself just where this scent was coming from.

The so-called moonpool was larger than he had been anticipating. As they walked along the latticed catwalk that completely encircled it, Peter found himself awed by the opening's sheer size. Over two hundred feet long and a hundred feet wide, it was like viewing a colossal swimming pool that had a steel-plate high-rise surrounding it.

They were headed toward a narrow platform that extended several feet out into the water when Peter saw that they were not alone. Barely visible in the choppy water were two wet-suited divers. Only as Peter continued his approach did he spot the object they were so feverishly working on, a sleek, full-grown dolphin.

"Ah, there's Dr. Patton and her assistant now," revealed his escort. "And, between them, you can just spot the star of this whole show, Sammy the bottlenose dolphin."

Peter found himself smiling as he climbed down onto the platform and got his first glance of the plastic harness that the researchers were in the process of removing. Once this device was free, they turned for the platform themselves and began climbing up the ladder that led from the water. As the dolphin proceeded to merrily swim around the pool's perimeter, Peter turned his attention to the two wet-suited figures who were soon standing before him.

It was Commander Walker who initiated the introductions. "Mr. Secretary, I'd like you to meet Dr. Susan Patton and her assistant Owen."

"It's an honor to meet you both," offered Peter Anderson, along with a handshake.

"The honor's ours," returned Susan as she shook the water from her mop of curly hair and continued. "When Commander Walker told us that the Secretary of the Navy would be joining us here, I had to admit that at first I didn't believe him."

Peter liked her directness, and her warm green eyes as well. "It's hard to believe that I'm down here myself, but so it is." Reaching out for the clear plastic harness that her assistant had been holding, he added, "So this is the device that made the discovery possible. You know, it's lighter than I had expected. Where's the video camera?"

"It's back in the lab," returned Susan. "We've just completed installing a new mount that allowed Sammy to place a magnetic directional finder on the Soviet sub's hull."

"We decided to install such a device to assist the DSRV," added Richard Walker. "All they have to do is home in on the sonic signal that the beacon constantly emits and they can find Ivan in even the murkiest of conditions."

Shaking his head and grinning, Peter returned his gaze to the still-swimming dolphin. "And how's our hero taking all this excitement?"

Susan followed the direction of his gaze and answered, "Sammy's a real ham, Mr. Secretary. He loves the extra attention, and is just as excited as we are."

Watching as Sammy leapt clear of the water and then crashed into the surface with a loud smack, Peter sincerely remarked, "Well, we're happy to have you aboard, Doctor. It was the President himself who cleared your presence here. I won't bother either one of you with a formal oath of secrecy, but please remember that everything you have seen so far, and will be experiencing in the days to come, must be kept in the strictest confidence. You are to share it with no one, no matter how close they may be to you. The security of our nation is directly at stake here, and the President wants to be absolutely certain that you realize this and act accordingly."

Briefly looking over to her wide-eyed assistant, Susan retorted, "We understand completely, Mr. Secretary. You have our sworn pledge of complete secrecy. And please don't hesitate to ask for our help if we can be of any future assistance."

"I'll remember that, Doctor," returned Peter Anderson.

A loud bubbling noise suddenly diverted their attention to the center of this moonpool. In the process of breaking the surface of the water there was a black, cigar-shaped object, filling nearly a quarter of the tank's two-hundred-foot length. It had a small humped enclosure on its top deck with the letters "DSRV—San Clemente" printed neatly on its side in white.

Sammy could be seen excitedly circling the

submersible as its hatch opened, and out popped the head of a single sailor wearing a cap. Moments later, the DSRV's thrusters activated, and the vessel gently inched its way over to the platform. With the help of two alert seamen, who arrived from the catwalk, the *San Clemente* was soon securely moored.

The sailor who was wearing the cap crawled out of the top hatch and jumped down onto the platform. He was dressed in blue coveralls, and not only had no rank insignia on his sleeves, but was shoeless as well. As he scanned the faces of those gathered before him, he seemed to cringe upon spotting the familiar figure of the Secretary of the Navy.

Noting his surprise, Richard Walker interceded. "Mr. Secretary, I'd like you to meet Lieutenant Bill Long, the *San Clemente*'s driver."

The lieutenant stiffened at attention and issued a crisp salute. "I'm sorry that I'm out of uniform, sir. The *San Clemente*'s kind of cramped, and this outfit seems to serve me the best."

"At ease, Lieutenant," offered Peter Anderson. "I'm not here for an inspection. So relax, sailor, and tell me, just what did you find down there?"

Bill Long issued a sigh of relief and only then answered. "We found the Typhoon at eight hundred and seventy-three feet, Mr. Secretary. That ultrasonic directional beacon that the dolphin placed on its hull called us right to it.

"She's lying upright on a base of solid sand. Except for several gashes in its bow, the hull appears intact. This was confirmed when we placed a unidirectional hydrophone up against the vessel's sail."

"What do you mean by that?" quizzed Peter.

"Our microphone picked up distinct machinery noise coming from inside the vessel, sir. We also believe we heard the muted sound of human voices, all of which proves that whatever took that monster down, must have just crippled her."

Noting how this revelation affected the secretary, the DSRV driver added, "I believe that our transfer skirt can fit onto the Typhoon's forward access trunk. Shall we initiate a rescue, sir?"

Peter Anderson seemed to be momentarily lost in thought before eventually answering. "I'm afraid that's going to have to be the President's decision, Lieutenant. Can the *San Clemente* handle the task if we get the go-ahead?"

"No problem, sir!" shot Bill Long directly. "Though it could take a few trips to remove the entire complement. Why, you should just see that sucker, it's enormous!"

Peter Anderson turned to address his uniformed escort. "Commander Walker, I'm going to need a secured line to Washington."

"You've got it, Mr. Secretary. I had the *Global Explorer*'s communications officer establish a secured frequency over an hour ago. I've arranged for you to be able to use the captain's stateroom to make your calls in. This same room will also be your living quarters while you're aboard, sir."

Already distracted in thought, Anderson muttered, "So we've got a crew of Ivan's finest trapped on the sea floor beneath us. And not only do we have the capability to save them, but also to salvage their sub as well. Damn if this doesn't take the cake!"

Glancing down at his watch, he knew that in a few more hours his nephew would be arriving in these waters along with the USS *Swordfish*. Their protection was absolutely necessary if they were to continue on with the rescue in earnest. For it was common practice that Soviet ballistic-missile-carrying submarines never went to sea without an attack vessel as an escort.

Doubting that they would take kindly to the U.S. Navy's intentions, the Soviets would most likely fire first and ask questions later. The *Swordfish* was needed to ensure that they wouldn't be able to take this belligerent course if they so desired.

The *Global Explorer* rolled in the grasp of a moderate swell, and Peter was abruptly brought back to reality when he found himself having to reach out to keep from tumbling over. It was the firm grasp of Lieutenant Bill Long that served to keep him upright. And it was only as he looked up to thank him for the helping hand that Peter noted the logo of the Miami Dolphins' football team emblazoning the rim of the DSRV driver's orange-and-turquoise cap.

Chapter Twelve

Admiral Viktor Chimki couldn't believe the contents of the telephone conversation that he had only seconds ago completed. He had been on the line with the deputy director of the KGB for well over ten minutes. During this time, the agent forwarded to Viktor a detailed description of their continued chase for the armed suspect whom they were absolutely certain was Premier Ivanov's assassin.

After a comprehensive dragnet of the city, they had actually cornered the suspect in the Universitat metro station on Moscow's south side. Yet just as police reinforcements arrived at the terminal, he ran out onto the crowded platform and let loose a volley of automatic weapons fire from a compact Uzi machine gun. Bodies of both innocent commuters and policemen alike littered the blood-splattered floor as the suspect darted off into the black depths of the nearby metro tunnel. At last count there were thirteen bodies being carted off to the morgue, with another twenty-seven seriously wounded. But just as tragic was the sobering fact that the assassin was continuing to evade their best efforts.

The deputy director swore on his parents' grave that they would have the killer under lock and key shortly. With the assistance of literally thousands of armed KGB and militia troops, the entire south side metro system was being scoured. And like a fox cornered by a pack of baying hounds, he was bound to be flushed out eventually.

After leaving the KGB agent with strict orders to notify him the moment the suspect was again sighted, Viktor hung up the phone. A dull ache throbbed beneath his forehead, and the veteran fought the temptation to go down to the south side and become involved in this manhunt himself. But as the stack of portfolios that littered his desk so aptly proved, he had his own work to keep him occupied.

Yet before returning to his duty, Viktor pushed his chair back from the desk and stiffly stood. He then proceeded to cross his bookcase-lined office, until he was positioned before one of the room's massive picture windows.

With his hands on his hips, Viktor angled his line of sight to the exterior courtyard clearly visible before him. Comprised of a copse of ancient elms, an ornate flowerbed, and several wooden benches, the clearing was currently vacant. Usually only occupied at lunchtime, and then only when the elements co-operated, this spot was one of Viktor's favorites to lose himself in contemplation when a particularly thorny problem presented itself.

Only this morning, he had spent over an hour perched on one of these benches, sipping his tea and attempting to put the nerve-racking events of the last few days into their proper perspective. The air had been brisk, and filled with just a hint of the summer that would soon be upon them. As the sun broke from the cloud cover, he viewed several other signs of the advancing season. In the process of breaking the surface of the rich soil of the flowerbed were the green tips of the tulips. Soon they would be out in all their glory, coloring this portion of the Kremlin grounds in a rainbow of bright color. The elm trees were also beginning to blossom, their branches filled with fat green buds. All of this was certain proof that they had survived yet another frigid Arctic winter, and the previously frozen earth would once again have a chance to participate in the great mystery of rebirth.

Spring had always been his beloved Lydia's favorite time of the year. No matter what pressing affairs of state filled his hours, he always managed to find some time to take his dear wife out into the countryside to enjoy the new season together. Yet it had been almost three years since he had last visited their dacha outside of the village of Nazajevo, on the banks of the Schodna River. Though he had often thought about driving out there to get away from the great pressures of the city, ever since his wife was paralyzed by her stroke, he just didn't have the heart to do so without her.

Lydia had been in a Moscow nursing home for the last two and a half years. Unable to speak, or even sit up in bed for that matter, she was gradually wasting away. During his last visit two days ago, she didn't even recognize him. This brought tears to Viktor's eyes, for he remembered his dearest as a robust, intelligent woman, who had a zest for life and a quick wit to match.

With the help of a cook/housekeeper, the seventy-seven-year-old veteran managed to make do. Thankful for his own health, at least he had his work to fill in those long, lonely hours. Without his duty to keep him occupied, he would have long ago given up.

A pair of fat ravens flew past the window, and Viktor watched them effortlessly soar over the thick stone wall that formed the courtyard's opposite perimeter. This portion of the Kremlin faced directly southward, and he could just see the trickling green expanse of the Moscow River flowing in the distance. Beyond, the great city of Moscow stretched to the horizon.

Illuminated by the late-afternoon sun, he could make out a skyline dominated by modern concrete-and-steel high-rises. Yet still visible between these soulless structures were the onion-shaped domes of an Orthodox church. Though Viktor was certainly no churchgoer, he could readily relate to the familiar gilded cupolas that reminded him of a past that today's younger generation could never hope to fathom.

In his six decades of service to the Motherland, he had been a firsthand witness to history in the making. Having enlisted in the Navy at the tender age of eighteen, he was a part of the first five-year plan under which the relatively new country was rearmed. He first got his hands bloodied on the decks of a Soviet destroyer during the short-lived Russo-Finnish war of 1939. A year later, he was transferred to a submarine and went to work preparing for the upcoming struggle with Nazi Germany.

The Great Patriotic War began officially in June 1941, when German troops first set foot on the Motherland's soil. Four years, and over twenty million casualties later, the Soviet Union emerged scarred but victorious.

Viktor was the first to admit that during the war the performance of the Navy was for the most part inefficient and ineffective. This was due in large part to the great numbers of experienced naval officers who were removed from duty during Stalin's earlier purges. Morale was low, and modern equipment such as sonar and radar, all but nonexistent.

With the rank of a senior lieutenant, Viktor emerged from those difficult years with a new understanding of the Soviet Navy's problems and potentials. Stalin also recognized the importance of a strong fleet, and initiated an intense, postwar build-up. Viktor became involved with the development of the successful Whiskey and Zulu class submarines that were equalled by very few Western boats. Then, in January 1956, Admiral Sergei Georgiyevich Gorshkov was appointed Commander-in-Chief of the Navy, and the fleet was even further strengthened.

Under Gorshkov, Viktor rose in rank to a full captain. His accomplishments included being in command of the Zulu class sub that test-launched a submarine-carried ballistic missile an entire two years before the United States laid down the keel of a similar vessel. Future duties included commanding one of the first November class nuclear-powered boats and initiating the premier deterrent patrol of one of the Yankee ballistic missile submarines that featured improved hull and reactor designs and extremely accurate weapons delivery systems.

Soon afterward, Viktor was named a rear admiral and transferred to Leningrad's prestigious Grechko Naval Academy as its headmaster. Though he sincerely missed sea duty, working at the Academy allowed him to be an instrumental part in shaping the direction of the Soviet Navy's future, for beyond hardware, a strong fleet relied upon its personnel.

With Admiral Gorshkov's retirement, Viktor moved over to the Defense Ministry. A native Muscovite, he enjoyed returning to the city of his birth, which was rapidly changing into one of the most cosmopolitan population centers in the entire world. The Kremlin had been his base of operations ever since.

Political intrigues and bureaucratic squabbling were far from duty on the open sea. But he was too old to command a warship, and, besides, his country needed him to promote the cause of military strength in this unprecedented era of moderation and subsequent weakness. The enemy they faced today was just as dangerous as Hitler's Nazi hordes. Imperialism was a deceptive enemy that softened one with promises of disarmament, yet at the same time poisoned the world with blind greed and want of material possessions. Gone unchecked, capitalism would spread like a cancer, and the Soviet Union's grand socialist experiment would be no more.

The only way to fight this disease was to never abandon the principles on which the Revolution was founded. A strong military was essential to not only counter worldwide imperialist aspirations, but to guarantee internal order as well. This was an all-important lesson that the moderates had all but forgotten.

Fooled into believing that the United States was actually sincere with their overtures of world peace, Yakov Rosenstein and his moderate cohorts were traitorous fools, for if they had their way, the military would be stripped of its power and nuclear weapons would be totally eliminated.

Little did the idiots realize that as soon as the Motherland was disarmed, the imperialists would make their move. Intoxicated by the accumulation of wealth and material possessions, the Soviet people would lose their identities, and the Western conquest would be complete.

What really scared Viktor was the realization that the moderates were as powerful as they actually were. Already holding six of the thirteen seats on the ruling politburo, all they needed to do was to elect one of their own as the new premier and the Motherland's doom would be sealed.

If the KGB would only successfully complete the manhunt that was currently taking place on the other side of the Kremlin wall, Viktor could show the entire world the West's true colors. That was why the assassin had to be apprehended alive, and done so quickly.

The Motherland's citizens were no fools. And once the CIA plot was unearthed, and the evidence linking them to Yakov Rosenstein presented in a public forum, the moderates would be finished. Yet until this time came to pass, he could only anxiously await that most anticipated moment.

Massaging the constant, dull ache that continued to throb in his temples, Viktor turned from the window when a sudden knock sounded on his door. Without waiting for an invitation, his secretary entered the office, pushing a silver tea cart before her. Katya had been with him since he had left the Grechko Academy and knew his needs and moods better than anyone on the planet. Acting as both a trusted confidante and a substitute wife, the forty-nine-year-old Ukrainian sported a shapely figure and long thick brown hair. Never having married, she was passionately dedicated to serving his every desire.

"I took the liberty of bringing some food along with your tea, Admiral. After all, you barely touched your lunch and only had but a single slice of toast for breakfast."

As she pushed the cart to a halt beside the two straight-backed chairs that sat beside the window, Viktor responded, "As usual, both my appetite and the rapidly passing hours have managed to escape me, Katya dear. If it wasn't for you, I'd probably just wither away."

"You're already too skinny as it is, Comrade," retorted Katya as she pulled off the large napkin that had been covering the cart's top surface.

Viktor glanced down at the appetizing tidbits displayed there. Tastefully laid out on an exquisite bone china set that had once belonged to the Romanovs was a delightful assortment of cold cuts that included sliced ham, smoked sturgeon, and a tasty concoction of herring fillets, chopped onions,

285

and sour cream. A basket containing several different varieties of thickly sliced bread lay in a silver basket, beside which was positioned a plate full of delicate pastries.

"My, this is a feast fit for a czar! Will you at least join me, Katya?"

"Though I already had my tea, I'll do so just to make certain that you eat something," returned the secretary efficiently. "So what can I serve you, Comrade?"

Not wishing to incur her wrath, Viktor sheepishly answered, "A helping of your delicious herring on a heel of black bread would be fine, my dear. And if it's all right with you, I'd like something a little stronger than sugar to sweeten my tea with. This day's been nothing but a nightmare of frustration and waiting, and maybe some brandy would help me relax."

"I think that can be arranged, Comrade," replied Katya, picking up a crystal decanter that had been set beside the teapot. As she poured some of its dark brown contents into the bottoms of two china cups, she added with a wink, "I thought you might be feeling a little tense this afternoon, so I brought you the last of the five-star Napoleon. I hope you don't mind if I share a bit with you?"

"Why, of course not, Katya! It will do my heart good not to have to drink such nectar alone. Yet, please, must you spoil it by having to add the tea?"

Katya chuckled and proceeded to half fill the cups solely with brandy. She handed one of these to her white-haired boss and kept one for herself.

Viktor appreciatively sniffed the golden liquor before raising his glass and toasting. "To the

Motherland! Long may she prosper in peace and equality."

Katya raised her drink upward and delicately clinked the edge of Viktor's cup. She then followed his lead and took a sip of the aromatic libation. The brandy was strong, and flowed down her throat like a mouthful of molten lava. Yet as soon as the shock of this initial drink wore off, her mouth filled with a delightful taste that had her craving for more.

Noting her pleasure, Viktor observed, "Pretty tasty stuff, isn't it, my dear? Remind me to invite the French naval attaché to dinner soon. He never fails to refill our larder."

"I already put a tentative date on your calendar," returned Katya. "Now let me make you that sandwich."

Astounded by both her efficiency and intuitiveness, Viktor shook his head in wonder. "What did I ever do to deserve an angel such as you, dearest Katya? You bring a ray of sunshine into this lonely old sailor's heart."

Katya tore off a heel of black bread and loaded it with a thick herring fillet. Making certain to top it with a dollop of sour cream and plenty of chopped onions, she then placed the sandwich on a plate and handed it to Viktor.

She watched as he voraciously consumed this taste treat, and as he chewed down the last biteful, leaned forward to prepare him yet another. Noting the way the old-timer's gaze wandered down to her ample cleavage visible from her loose-fitting blouse, Katya softly remarked, "And if you're a good boy and eat all your herring, maybe Katya will give you a massage

287

for dessert."

Viktor met her seductive gaze and contentedly smiled. "You know my mind better than I do, my dear. If only I would have met you when I was a young buck. You and I would have made quite a pair, Katya Morzovaya."

An alien tightness seized his loins. His advanced age kept him from completely fulfilling this desire, yet certainly didn't keep him from fantasizing what their relationship could have been like. With this delightful vision in mind, he consumed his second sandwich and leaned back in his chair to properly enjoy his drink.

"One thing has always puzzled me, my dear. Why is it that a woman with your intelligence and looks never got married? In all our years of working together, you never once mentioned having a boyfriend, or even going out on a date for that matter."

Katya took a long sip of her drink before answering him. "That side of life was never important to me, Viktor. My career has always been my number one priority. Though in all honesty, I must admit that I once did have a horrible crush on a certain dashing naval officer, whom I first began working with fifteen years ago."

Suddenly realizing that this naval officer was himself, Viktor put down his drink and stood up to take his secretary in his arms.

"Oh, my dearest, why didn't you ever share your feelings with me?" he emotionally questioned.

Secure in his warm, tight grasp, Katya tearfully replied, "Oh, stop it, Viktor. You were a happily married man, and what was I to do, play the role of the second woman?"

Her sweet scent was full in his nostrils, and the mere touch of her luscious body prompted a stiffness in his lower extremities that he hadn't experienced in years. Squeezing her even tighter, he was in the process of tracing the shapely curve of her buttocks with his right hand when the sound of a loud knock on his locked office door abruptly diverted his attention. The spell was broken, and as he backed away and began straightening out his uniform, he softly queried Katya. "Was I expecting anyone this afternoon?"

"You had no appointments that I know of," she answered. "Let me go and see who it is."

Though Viktor would have liked to tell her to ignore this interruption, he didn't and watched as she quickly walked over to the door and opened it. Standing on the other side was a familiar, gray-haired individual, smartly dressed in the uniform of a Soviet Air Force marshal.

"Am I disrupting anything?" greeted Konstantin Bucharin, the director of Air Force intelligence.

"Why of course not, Marshal," returned Katya as she stepped aside and beckoned the distinguished-looking officer to enter. "I was just serving the admiral his tea. Can I pour you a cup, Comrade? Or perhaps you'd like a sandwich?"

Bucharin shook his head. "No thank you, Katya. I'm running behind as always, and only stopped off here for a moment."

Well aware that it was very unusual for the officer to visit without calling first, Katya sensed that he was the bearer of important news. Thus she quietly exited the office herself without further comment.

Viktor watched as his old friend crossed the room toward him, and noticed that he was carrying a leather portfolio tightly in his grasp. They met with a brief hug and Bucharin wasted no time expressing himself.

"Sorry I didn't call first, Viktor. But I was down the hall in General Vnukovo's office when he received the latest Salyut satellite photos of the Caribbean basin. There was something in the series I was certain that you'd find most interesting."

Bucharin reached into the portfolio and handed Viktor a single glossy photograph showing a mountainous tropical island bordered by a large expanse of water. Clearly visible floating on the surface of this sea were three ships. First to catch Viktor's eye was the largest of these vessels, whose equipment-packed deck was dominated by what appeared to be a full-sized derrick. Anchored beside this ship was a small gunboat, while a larger vessel with a catamaran-style hull lay in the waters close by.

"Exactly what portion of the Caribbean is pictured here, Comrade?" questioned the admiral.

Konstantin Bucharin answered directly. "That's the Anegada Passage. The land mass is Norman Island, off the coast of St. John."

This revelation struck Viktor like a punch to his stomach. "The Anegada Passage, you say? Have these ships been positively identified as yet?"

"Preliminary analysis indicates that the larger of the three vessels is the *Global Explorer*, the U.S. Navy's infamous marine salvage vessel, while the gunboat is one of their Pegasus class hydrofoil combatants. It's the identity of the catamaran that's particularly upsetting, my friend, for it's believed this ship is exclusively designed to carry the DSRV."

This last term was unknown to Viktor and he immediately questioned. "And just what is a DSRV, Konstantin?"

"That's a deep submergence rescue vessel, Comrade. In other words, it's what the U.S. Navy uses to rescue the crew of a disabled submarine."

"By the grace of Lenin, the *Caspian*!" exclaimed Viktor breathlessly.

Konstantin Bucharin somberly nodded. "That's my thought precisely, Comrade. Even more frightening is the fact that only two days ago the *Global Explorer* was deployed off the coast of Puerto Rico, near America's Roosevelt Roads naval station. One of our operatives actually spoke with one of its civilian technicians and learned that the ship had just come upon an immense find of nickel nodules on the floor of the sea there. If this was indeed the case, why move the ship so abruptly to the waters off the Virgin Islands?"

"Can any of us ever forget the day over a decade ago that we first learned of the *Global Explorer*'s existence?" offered Viktor, whose unbelieving gaze remained locked on the photograph. "For this is the same ship that plucked the wreck of our sunken Golf class submarine off the floor of the Pacific."

"Could they be attempting to do the same thing with the *Caspian*?" dared Bucharin.

Looking up to catch his associate's dread-filled glance, Viktor responded. "No wonder Alexander

Gnutov and the *Kirov* weren't able to locate the *Caspian* earlier. Captain Sobrinka didn't get his patrol coordinates mixed up like we originally suspected. The Americans must have attacked and sunk them!"

"But that would be a direct act of war!" exclaimed Bucharin.

"No more so than helping to assassinate our premier," retorted the admiral.

"Then what's stopping us from answering with a full-scale nuclear strike?" quizzed the Air Force veteran.

Viktor's eyes gleamed as he answered, "Certain indisputable proof, Comrade. For you must never forget the ridiculous political climate we are currently forced to operate in."

Bucharin didn't seem to agree with this. "Surely this photo would be enough to convince the moderates that an act of war has been committed. The loss of a Typhoon class submarine is not something that even the likes of Yakov Rosenstein would take lightly."

Viktor shook his head. "If only I could concur with you, Konstantin. But unfortunately I can't. If I know Comrade Rosenstein, he'll be screaming for undeniable evidence before even considering what we know to be certain proof."

"But how can he explain why the *Kirov* failed to come upon the *Caspian* during its search of their patrol station?" countered Bucharin. "And why hasn't Captain Sobrinka answered the emergency messages we've been faithfully sending him for the last forty-eight hours? Why, it's clear as day that they've been sunk, and this photo is unquestionable evidence!"

Again Viktor played the part of the devil's advocate. "The moderates will merely say that the *Caspian* is patroling in the wrong portion of the Caribbean and can't hear our dispatches because of mechanical difficulties. And since a proper military response is impossible without their support, we must deliver to them this irrefutable proof."

"But how are we to do that?" quizzed Bucharin.

Viktor slowly turned and angled his gaze so that it took in the courtyard visible from his office's window before responding, "Don't forget that the *Caspian* isn't alone out there, my friend. We shall call in Alexander Gnutov and the *Kirov*!"

Sixty-five feet beneath the waters of the Caribbean Sea, the USS *Swordfish* continued on its new course to the northeast at flank speed. Oblivious to the new morning that had just dawned above them, the crew went about their duties in a perpetual state of darkness. The sub's cramped confines could only produce an artificial environment that knew no day or night.

Petty Officer Second Class Brad Bodzin had learned to regulate his time by consciously monitoring his digital watch and mentally visualizing the condition topside. The meals of the day helped give this vision added reality, as breakfast corresponded to morning and so forth.

He knew that he was very fortunate to be a sound sleeper. With only a thin curtain to provide privacy, the enlisted men's communal stateroom was not always the most quiet of places for one to catch up on his shuteye, especially if one had any shipmates who snored.

To help him relax when it was time to sleep, Brad liked to clip on the miniature headphones of his cassette recorder and listen to a piece of music. Beyond mere enjoyment, the music helped filter out the sounds of those around him and gave the illusion of having his own space.

The Texan was just coming to the end of a sound six-hour sleep and was in the midst of a fascinating dream. He was swimming in a warm, crystal clear sea, surrounded by hundreds of frolicking dolphins. The sleek marine mammals seemed to have adopted him as one of their own. They called to him with a variety of clicks, whistles and moans, and Brad answered with the melodious strains of an original violin composition, which he called "Cry of the Deep."

A feeling of great peace and happiness engulfed him. The dolphins were like old friends who were welcoming him home after many years of being away. One of the animals was particularly affectionate and swam close at his side, sporting a massive, streamlined body, an ever-smiling mouth, and a pair of inquisitive, mischievous eyes. He seemed to be trying to convey to Brad a deep, primeval secret that related to the days at the beginning of time when their species were like brothers.

The Texan was actually beginning to comprehend the dolphin's language when he became aware of yet another presence. Emanating from somewhere in the black depths below, it provoked a sudden feeling of fear and great anxiety. His dolphin seemed to sense this cold presence also, and the animal began darting through the water in quick, erratic movements.

Brad fought with his leaden limbs to keep up with the dolphins, who were slowly but surely drawing away from him. And soon he was alone in the rippling water, which seemed to have turned cold and murky. From below, he was once again aware of an alien malevolence whose mere presence filled him with utter dread.

The sonar technician was awakened from this disturbing vision by the muted tones of his digital wristwatch. His eyes popped open, yet it took several confused seconds for him to reorient himself. It proved to be the raucous snores of one of his shipmates that served to bring him all the way back to waking consciousness.

He lay on his back on the cramped bunk, covered by only a rumpled white sheet. His curtain was tightly closed, and he could see from the time displayed on his watch that it was 6:01 A.M. He yawned and scratched his beard-stubbled jaw and briefly closed his eyes in a vain effort to re-create the wild dream. But try as he might, all he could remember of this vision was a single scene showing the seas filled to the horizon with frolicking dolphins.

The sounds of his fellow shipmates stirring in their bunks diverted his ponderings, and he pulled back the curtain and slipped down from his mattress to the deck below in an effort to beat them to the head. Dressed in only his skivvies, Brad sleepily crossed the compartment, ducked out its sole hatchway, and entered the head. Here he relieved himself, and then ambled over to the washbasin to brush his teeth and shave. He was just coating his face with shaving cream when the first of his shipmates entered. Both Carl Harper and Deke Thompson shared the same watch periods as Brad, and thus had similar wakeup times. As usual, Thompson made his way over to the urinal as if he were sleepwalking, while Carl Harper went straight to the sink to begin washing up.

"Christ, Bodzin, you're certainly up with the chickens this morning," greeted the communications specialist as he scrubbed his face with soap and hot water. "Couldn't you sleep?"

Brad answered after removing the excess lather from his lips. "Actually, I conked right out as soon as I hit the sack. I didn't even get a chance to listen to the tape I wanted to hear."

"At least you saved some wear and tear on your batteries," returned Harper, who rubbed his pimply cheek and decided that he could skip having a shave and no one would know the difference.

By this time their bunkmate joined them at the washbasin. Deke Thompson's eyelids were still heavy with sleep as he turned on the tap, cupped his hands and soaked his face in cold water. This seemed to do the job and soon the brawny machinist was back in the world of the waking.

"Brother, did I have a wild dream," observed Thompson as he prepared to shave. "I was stranded on this desert island, with nothin' but the sea, sand, and palm trees for company, when all of a sudden

296

these damn drums start beating. And what walks out of the jungle but a procession of gorgeous Polynesian babes, dressed in nothin' but grass skirts and flowered leis. Man, were some of those dolls stacked!"

Brad caught Carl Harper's glance in the mirror and winked. "Sounds like someone on board the *Swordfish* is getting horny. Just stay in your own bunk tonight, Thompson."

The machinist's face turned in a disgusted expression. "Have no fear, Bodzin, you're not my type. I just hope that I can somehow find my way back to that dream island and get to know those natives a bit better."

Harper grinned. "Speaking of dream islands, we should be getting close to the Virgins. I still can't help but wonder what in the hell came down to divert us away from Galveston?"

"Maybe my dream was a sign of things to come, like that Nostradamus dude, and we're going to the islands for some R and R," offered the machinist. "This could be Command's way of recognizing the sub's excellent operational record."

"Dream on, Nostradamus," returned Carl Harper. "That's not like the U.S. Navy I know. I can't help but think that our new orders have something to do with the *Turner* crisis. As far as we know, the Russians still have our ship, and maybe we're going to even the score by snatching one of their vessels that just happens to be stationed in our backyard."

Brad Bodzin listened to these comments and held back his response until he scraped off the last of his whiskers. "I think we might be headed eastward to search for something that's located on the sea floor there, like a sunken ship. The XO was poking his nose around the sound shack yesterday afternoon, and was particularly interested in the state of our bottom-scanning sonar gear. He even had me warm the unit up and then give it a try."

"I still hope we're headed to the Virgin Islands for some R and R," commented Deke Thompson, who voiced himself while quickly gliding his razor down his upturned neck. "Yet whatever the reason turns out to be, I'm kind of glad that this old pig boat has got herself a reprieve. The *Swordfish* wasn't ready for retirement yet, especially after that overhaul we just completed on her engines. So if we do see some action, this old gal can certainly stand up against the best of them, as Ivan learned back off the coast of Mexico."

"At least we won't go hungry," offered Carl Harper after washing out his mouth. "Scuttlebutt has it that Cooky's got orders to empty out the larder, and that includes those filet mignons he's been saving."

"Right now, some pancakes, sausage, and a hot mug of joe will do just fine," returned the machinist. "Anybody want to join me?"

"That sounds awfully good to me. I'm starving!" remarked Brad Bodzin as he stashed away his toiletries and turned to pull on his blue coveralls and sneakers.

While the three seamen proceeded to the mess hall, their commanding officer perched before the sub's attack periscope, his gaze locked on the profile of a large surface ship that was just visible on the distant horizon. Taking in the unique, towerlike derrick that extended from this vessel's equipment-cluttered deck, Ted Anderson backed away from the lens and addressed the white-haired veteran who anxiously stood beside the periscope well.

"Take a look for yourself, Admiral. It's the *Global Explorer* all right. Make no mistake about it."

Quick to make his way over to the scope, William Abbott peered through the lens and responded, "Well, I'll be. I haven't seen that distinctive profile since the *Explorer* pulled into Long Beach after completing her initial assignment. I was one of the first outsiders to board her and see just what it was that they pulled out of the Pacific."

The admiral joined Ted Anderson beside the periscope well and continued. "I must admit that was one assignment that our intelligence people didn't botch. They did a hell of a job coordinating the design of the boat and then working with the Navy to get the damn thing built. If it wasn't for that hotshot reporter at the *Los Angeles Times* chancing upon that stolen memo like he did, the public would still never know that the salvage operation ever took place."

Ted Anderson was genuinely fascinated with Abbott's discourse and cautiously probed. "Although all I know about the matter is hearsay, I understand that most of the wreckage was in pretty bad shape."

Abbott nodded his head. "So it was, Ted. But don't forget that it was being pulled up from a depth of over eighteen thousand feet beneath the ocean's surface. It was an incredible engineering feat and resulted in more information than the public was led to believe.

"Why, just inspecting that Golf class sub's hull allowed our analysts to determine the state-of-the-art of Ivan's welding program. We pulled out an entire nuclear-tipped torpedo that told much about their weapons program. And one of the code books we chanced upon explained how the captain received clearance from the Kremlin to launch the two ballistic missiles they were equipped with. And then there were the bodies."

"Bodies?" quizzed Anderson.

Abbott instinctively softened his voice. "If I remember correctly, we came upon six complete skeletons and a variety of assorted body parts. Incidentally, these remains were subsequently buried at sea, in a videotaped service that was an exact duplicate of established Soviet naval practices. These same tapes came in handy when the story broke on the international wire services. At least we could say that we laid their dead to rest properly."

Astounded by this revelation, Anderson again queried. "I wonder what the *Global Explorer* is doing in these waters, and why we've been instructed to rendezvous with them?"

"The last I heard, the ship had been adapted to mine the sea floor for minerals," answered Abbott. "Who knows, perhaps someone's trying to jump their claim."

The captain grinned at this remark, surely meant to be facetious, and returned to the periscope. It was as he scanned the horizon that he spotted the Pegasus class gunboat that was just visible anchored behind the mammoth marine-salvage vessel. He had seen the

300

speedy hydrofoils at work off Key West, and couldn't help but wonder why such a warship had been called into these waters also. Hopefully he'd know the answer to this question shortly, he thought, stepping back and addressing the control room crew.

"Prepare the boat to surface! Lieutenant Pukalani, I'd like you to join me on the sail once we're topside, and bring along our signalman."

"Aye, aye, Captain," returned the XO, who watched as the diving officer prepared to lighten the *Swordfish*.

To a rumble of venting ballast, the submarine angled upward until its sail and the top portion of its deck were clear of the sea's surface. It was only then that Ted Anderson began his way up a steep ladder that took him to a sealed overhead hatchway. With a bit of effort he cracked this hatch, and to a spray of cool saltwater, the air pressure equalized with a loud whoosh.

The exposed bridge was still draining seawater as he climbed onto the sail and scanned the horizon. The morning sun was working its way up into the heavens, and with only a few milky white clouds to veil its radiance, the resulting heat was immediately noticeable. Yet even the tropical air was refreshing, after having run submerged for over forty-eight hours.

As the XO and the signalman joined him, Anderson raised his binoculars and examined the surface of that portion of the sea they were headed toward. He knew that the larger landmass located off their port bow was St. John, while the smaller mass immediately before them was called Norman Island.

The keelless *Swordfish* rocked in a gentle swell.

Reaching out to steady himself, Anderson listened as his XO matter-of-factly observed, "We're well within visual range of the *Global Explorer*, Skipper. Shall we go ahead and hail her?"

"You may proceed, Lieutenant. Let's keep the chatter to a minimum."

The XO instructed the signalman to initiate the task of contacting the marine salvage vessel. The senior seaman did so by utilizing a hand-held, battery-powered signal lamp. By expertly manipulating its powerful beam with a shutter mechanism, they were able to communicate with the surface vessel without having to resort to more traceable radio waves.

Barely a minute after the first hailing signal was sent, a corresponding beam blinked forth from the *Global Explorer*'s bridge. It was the signalman who translated it.

"They're requesting the presence of both Captain Anderson and Admiral Abbott on the *Global Explorer*, sir. They're in the process of sending a launch to initiate this transfer."

This compact motorboat was soon spotted and Ted Anderson curtly commented, "Looks like I'd better throw on some khakis, because it finally looks like I'm going to find out just what the hell it is that we're doing out here."

Forty-five minutes later, Ted Anderson and William Abbott were in the process of entering the *Global Explorer*'s spacious wardroom. Waiting for them there were two men, one of whom was smartly dressed in the uniform of a U.S. naval commander and the other attired in civilian garb. Looking like an older version of the newly arrived sub captain, the civilian rose from his chair and warmly greeted the men. "Good morning, Captain Anderson, Admiral Abbott, welcome aboard the *Global Explorer*."

As he stepped forward to offer his handshake, Secretary of the Navy Peter Anderson's face broke out in a broad smile. "I hope my colleagues here don't mind if I break with service decorum and call my favorite nephew by his first name. It's good to see you, Ted."

The commanding officer of the *Swordfish* was just as enthusiastic as he accepted his uncle's firm grasp and responded, "My heavens, this is a surprise! Do you mean to say that the President finally let you go south of the beltway?"

Peter grinned and turned his gaze to the white-haired individual standing at his nephew's side. "And it's good to see you again, Bill. Has it really been five years since we last saw each other?"

The retired veteran nodded. "If this senile memory of mine is correct, it certainly is. I believe the last time we talked was at that U.S. naval institute seminar in New London, right before the President named you to his cabinet. So I'll excuse you for not calling like you promised."

"I guess things did get a little hectic soon afterward," observed Peter. "How's retired life been treating you?"

Abbott patted his tight stomach. "I'm still managing to hold my own, though with three square meals a day and nothing to do but fish and play golf, I'll most likely be going to pot soon enough."

Suddenly aware that there was one other member

of their party who had yet to be introduced, Peter Anderson rectified this situation. "Gentlemen, I'd like you to meet Commander Richard Walker of the Naval Department's office of Research, Development, and Acquisition. I guess you could say that it's indirectly because of the commander that we're gathered here today."

After exchanging handshakes, Richard Walker voiced himself. "The secretary would like me to brief you on our situation. But before I get started, how about joining us for some coffee?"

This sounded fine to the two newcomers, who helped themselves to a steaming hot mug of strong Navy brew. Following Peter Anderson's lead, they seated themselves around the wardroom table as Commander Walker continued. "Four days ago, I arrived in these same waters along with a congressional delegation. The purpose of our visit was to view a demonstration of a newly developed harness that was designed to fit onto the body of a dolphin. The department planned to utilize such a device to hold an object such as a video camera, that could be subsequently conveyed into the ocean's depths with minimal human involvement and risk.

"As it turned out, the developer of the harness indeed utilized a miniature fiber-optic camera to display her invention's worthiness. This demonstration took place in the waters directly beneath this ship. Yet instead of the ancient wrecks that she intended for her dolphin to film, pictures of a much different sort were soon relayed back to us."

Richard Walker reached for a folder on the table before him and removed a series of eight-by-ten photographs. As he passed them to his guests, he added, "These photos you're viewing are sequential stills, cut from that same video tape. Though the quality is not the best because of poor lighting conditions, I'm certain you can make out the object our dolphin chanced upon. It doesn't take much imagination to see that what we have on the sea floor eight hundred and seventy-three feet beneath us is a submarine, and a damn big one at that. After an intense analysis at the Office of Naval Intelligence, and a subsequent eyeball examination by the DSRV *San Clemente*, we are one hundred percent positive that what you're viewing is a disabled Soviet Typhoon class submarine that evidently struck the adjoining reef during an attempted transit of the Anegada Passage."

This revelation caused an astounded gasp to escape the lips of both newcomers. Certain that he had their complete attention, it was the Secretary of the Navy who continued. "The best is yet to come, gentlemen, because, to our best knowledge, this vessel went down before it was able to notify Moscow of its unfortunate predicament."

"Do you mean to say that the Soviets don't yet know that this Typhoon has even sunk?" queried William Abbott incredulously.

"I certainly do, Bill," retorted Peter Anderson. "I know it sounds unbelievable, but Lady Fortune has finally come our way, and we're not about to turn our backs on her. For what you're about to become involved with will be the greatest intelligence coup of the century. Just think of it, one of the Soviets' most sophisticated warships practically served up to

305

us on a silver platter!"

With his astonished gaze still locked on the photograph that he had been studying, Ted Anderson questioned. "This hull looks intact. Is there anyone alive inside?"

Again it was his uncle who answered. "The *San Clemente* was able to place a hydrophone up against the Typhoon's sail. Not only did they hear machinery noises, but what they believed to be footsteps and human voices as well.

"Twenty-four hours from now, our DSRV will be descending to attempt a rescue. Only after the last Soviet crew member has been removed, will the salvage operation begin. Since the Kremlin's bound to hear about our find eventually, and since they won't be exactly thrilled when they do, we thought it best to call in some reinforcements. Yet most of the fleet has been scrambled into the North Atlantic in response to the *Turner* incident. When combined with the current NATO exercises in the Mediterranean, I'm afraid we found ourselves stretched a little thin. And that's when the *Swordfish* came into the picture. Like the old trouper she is, her country is asking for one more task from her before she sails off into the history books. So can you ride shotgun for us, Ted, at least until the heavy guns show up?"

Without a moment's hesitation, Ted Anderson forcefully replied, "Of course we can do the job! Just name the chore and it'll be done."

Expecting no less from his nephew, the secretary of the Navy continued. "As you very well know, it's extremely doubtful that the Soviets would send one of their Typhoons into these waters without an attack sub escort of some type. Because the Kremlin has yet to respond to this accident, it's apparent that the attack vessel and the Typhoon became parted sometime before the mother ship attempted running this passage So in the event that this escort should return, we're counting on the *Swordfish* to keep them off our backs until either more reinforcements arrive or the salvage job is completed."

"You can count on us," returned a very confident Ted Anderson. "Though the *Swordfish* might be old in years, she more than makes up for her age in sheer will and tenacity. Yet if a Soviet attack sub should show up, how are we supposed to handle it?"

Peter traded a long, concerned look with Richard Walker before responding. "Because of the uniqueness of this situation, and the crisis atmosphere generated by the seizure of the USS *Turner*, the normal peacetime rules of engagement are going to be stretched a little should such a scenario present itself. You are authorized to shoot back only if Ivan makes the first threatening move. We're relying on you to use your discretion on this one, Ted. We certainly don't want to have to go and sink one of their vessels, but as many a wise old soldier has said in the past, better them than us."

"It's about time this country started walking tall once again," observed William Abbott. "Why, possessing that Typhoon will more than make up for our loss of the *Turner*."

"Let's not write our boys off just yet," reflected the secretary of the Navy. "And, Bill, considering the dangerous new direction of the *Swordfish*'s mission, you're more than welcome to watch this thing play out from here."

"Hell no you don't, Peter Anderson! I weaned that old rust bucket, and I'm not going to abandon her now, just when the going gets tough. So if her skipper doesn't mind this old salt's company, I'd like to stick it out to the bitter end."

"Admiral Abbott is more than welcome to stay with us," offered Ted. "Hell, he already saved our ass a couple of times just on the cruise down from San Diego."

"Then I guess you're stuck with him, Theodore," retorted Peter Anderson, his eyes gleaming with pride. "Though I wish that I could join you also, somebody's got to stay up here and run this damn circus. So keep your feet dry, and good hunting!"

Chapter Thirteen

Ever since receiving the urgent orders that sent it
surging from its top-secret mooring at Cienfuegos,
the *Kirov* had been traveling at flank speed. Propelled
forward at a speed in excess of forty knots, the Alfa
class attack submarine attained this unprecedented
velocity by utilizing its unique, unmanned propulsion plant to its fullest extent. Unlike any other vessel
in the world, the *Kirov*'s nuclear reactor employed a
lead-bismuth mixture as its primary coolant. Such a
substance increased the temperature in the reactor's
steam generator, resulting in the engine's exception-
ally high horsepower.

From the *Kirov*'s attack center, Captain Alexander
Gnutov monitored the digital indicator that displayed the vessel's current speed. Satisfied that the
propulsion plant was operating as efficiently as
possible, he continued his rounds, next stopping
before that station reserved for navigation. Here, the
ship's navigator was in the process of updating their
course chart. Quietly positioning himself behind the

navigator so as not to disturb him, Alexander discreetly glanced over his broad shoulders.

The chart he was working on was an expanded view of the entire Caribbean basin. Their present course could be determined by following a line of red X's that began at Cienfuegos and took them to the southeast. After leaving the southern coast of Cuba behind them, they transited the channel separating Jamaica from the westernmost shore of Haiti. Here, their course turned due eastward, past the southern coasts of the Dominican Republic and Puerto Rico. Only recently, they had jogged to the northeast as the *Kirov* entered the waters of the U.S. Virgin Islands.

"It appears that we continue to make excellent progress," broke in the familiar voice of the zampolit from behind Alexander. "Twenty-four hours of continuous flank speed is a lot to ask from a vessel, and the *Kirov* has responded to the challenge and then some. Her designers should be proud."

Though Alexander was in no mood for idle chatter, he politely replied, "That they should, Comrade."

Aware now of the captain's presence behind him, the navigator looked up from his study of the chart and commented, "We're rapidly approaching those coordinates that Command forwarded to us, Captain. We should be within sensor range sometime during the next hour. But one thing still puzzles me, sir. Since this was the same route we used during our initial transit of the Anegada Passage, and since the *Caspian* preceded us into these waters, why didn't we chance upon them several days ago? At the very least, we should have been able to pick up an emergency

310

radio signal from them."

"That's a good question, Lieutenant Natya," replied Alexander. "I can only assume that the damage the *Caspian* suffered somehow affected its ability to use the radio systems."

"What else do you expect after an American torpedo attack?" offered the political officer. "Most likely the cowardly imperialists were waiting in ambush, and Captain Sobrinka and his brave crew never knew what hit them."

Alexander was perturbed by this groundless observation. "We still don't know that fact for certain, Comrade Pavlodar. For all we know, the vessel that Command suspects to be on the sea floor before us might not even be the *Caspian* at all. And even if it does turn out to be the Typhoon, who's to say that it wasn't a mechanical failure or for that matter a simple navigational error that took them to the bottom?"

"These waters are extremely treacherous," added the navigator. "Coral reefs and submerged shoals abound. And without those special charts that we received back in Murmansk, it would be quite easy to choose the wrong channel."

The zampolit would have no part of this. "But you're forgetting that Captain Sobrinka had the benefit of these very same charts, Comrade. Besides, their navigational systems are state-of-the-art, and any vessel that can successfully transit the Arctic icefields can surely handle a reef or two. No, my gut tells me that an American torpedo is to blame. I only hope that the bastard who took this shot is still in the vicinity, so that we can properly revenge our great

311

warship's loss."

Alexander Gnutov listened to these unsubstantiated allegations and fought back the impulse to respond. Yet challenging the ill-informed political officer would get him nothing but an argument, and this was certainly something he could do without. Ever since receiving their current orders, Alex had been in a sullen mood. This hadn't been the case when he began his unexpected Cuban shore leave. If anything, his day of hiking in the hills surrounding Cienfuegos left him refreshed and relaxed. With his mind filled with pleasant memories of his last visit to this tropical paradise over two decades ago, he returned to the sub base ready to get back to work. Little was he prepared for the tragic news that awaited him there.

The dispatch had originated with Admiral Chimki. Alexander had visited his Kremlin office several times in the past, and knew that its grandeur perfectly suited the visionary genius who worked there. Not prone to exaggeration, Alexander's naval mentor ordered the *Kirov* to return to sea with all due haste. For it was his fear that the *Caspian* had not attained the wrong patrol sector as they had presumed, but that the mammoth Typhoon class vessel was currently lying disabled on the bottom of the Anegada Passage.

Alexander took this disastrous news quite seriously. As he gathered together his crew and initiated their present journey, a persistent nagging doubt was constantly at the back of his mind. For, if the *Caspian* had indeed gone down in these waters, he couldn't help but feel personally responsible for its loss.

As the missile-carrying ship's delegated escort, it

was the *Kirov*'s duty to ensure that such a tragic accident never befell them. Alexander would be directly guilty of neglect of duty should the *Caspian* be placed inoperable by an outside force during the course of their joint patrol.

Though it could all be blamed on their encounter with that Trafalgar class attack sub off the coast of Bermuda, excuses were meaningless. What Command desired were results, and in this respect the *Kirov* had miserably failed.

Alexander knew that he should have spent a lot less time in losing the English vessel. Surely, considering the *Kirov*'s superior handling capabilities, they could have led the persistent Brits astray without having to waste an entire twenty-four hours doing so. That would have most likely allowed them to join the *Caspian* in transiting the treacherous waters of the Anegada Passage together. But fate had kept them apart, and now one hundred and fifty brave men and one of the most powerful warships that the world had ever known could very possibly be lost because of Alexander's incompetence.

It was not knowing the certainty of the situation that really got to him. From what he gathered from Admiral Chimki's dispatch, it was still only a suspicion that was sending them on their current mission. Thus, as far as Alex was concerned, they couldn't get to their current destination fast enough.

Looking up to check their speed and course, the captain sensed that the answer was close at hand. Any moment now, they'd be able to utilize their bottom-scanning sensors and determine if tragedy indeed awaited them on the floor of the cursed passage. Yet, until he learned this fact for certain, there was always that dim hope that Command's worst fears would prove to be groundless.

The *Kirov*'s senior lieutenant was seated at the engineering station as Alexander crossed the control room and addressed him. "Lieutenant Arbatov, cut our forward speed to loiter velocity. We are getting close to our goal, and we certainly don't want to announce our presence prematurely by steaming in under full power."

"Very good, Captain," replied the senior lieutenant, reaching forward and efficiently feeding a series of commands into the computer keyboard. Almost instantaneously, these instructions were relayed back to the *Kirov*'s propulsion plant. And thirty seconds later, the digital speed indicator began dropping.

"I also want the stealth systems on line, and a state of ultra-quiet to prevail," added the captain. "There's no telling what kind of reception awaits us, Comrade, and we must be ready to respond to all contingencies."

"Shall we load any weapons?" queried the *Kirov*'s second-in-command.

Alexander hesitated a moment before responding. "It's still too early for that, Lieutenant. Let's wait until we see exactly what it is we're up against."

"Captain," cried the voice of the sonar officer from the opposite side of the attack center. "I believe that we're close enough to attempt that scan of the sea floor. Shall I give it a try?"

"By all means, Lieutenant Kasimov!" returned Alexander as he hurriedly crossed the compartment.

All eyes were on the green-tinted CRT screen as the sonar officer addressed his keyboard. Several seconds later, a powerful burst of contained sound streamed forth from the *Kirov*'s bow sonar array. This blast was projected downward, into the black depths of the waters before them. As it bounced off the sea floor and returned to its source, a series of lines began forming on the technician's monitor screen. It showed a flat shelf of sand, holding a single massive, immobile object. It only took one look at this object's rounded hull and elongated sail for Alexander's worst fears to be realized.

"It's the *Caspian* all right," observed the somber sonar officer. "No other vessel on this planet has those distinctive lines."

The captain's gut tightened as he looked over to meet the condescending glance of his zampolit. Ivan Pavlodar seemed to be relishing Alexander's dismay as he subtly commented, "So Admiral Chimki's suspicions were correct ones after all, Comrade Gnutov. This is indeed a black moment for all of us."

"What are we to do now, Captain?" queried the redheaded sonar officer.

Alexander heavily sighed before responding, "We will do as ordered, what else, Comrade?"

"And just what is that?" dared the junior officer.

Again the captain's gaze met that of his political officer as he cautiously answered, "We have been instructed to notify Command as soon as the *Caspian* has been located. We will do so at once, and then get on with the next portion of our mission, which is to keep the Americans from attempting to salvage her. A suitable Soviet flotilla will be on its way from

315

Murmansk shortly, yet until it gets here, we have been elected to protect the *Caspian*'s integrity. We have been authorized to use torpedoes if needed, but whatever the cost, the U.S. Navy must not be allowed to examine the contents of that hull!"

Nodding in support of the captain's firm position, the zampolit added, "Since it was most likely an imperialist torpedo responsible for this tragedy, I'd say that the odds are good that the Americans have already begun this salvage effort. Take us to periscope depth, Captain, and let us see for ourselves if the vultures are already circling the carrion."

Alexander looked to the bulkhead-mounted clock before replying. "I'm just as anxious as you are, Comrade Zampolit, to see if such an effort has been initiated. But by ascending in broad daylight, we'd be risking almost certain discovery. Don't forget that these waters are unusually clear and one of their aircraft could easily spot us should we approach the surface. In only two more hours the sun will be setting. So to guarantee our anonymity, surely we can wait until then to ascend. Meanwhile, we can best serve the Motherland by silently loitering in the black depths, with our sensors ever on the alert and our lips buttoned. For it's absolute quiet that will serve as our best ally."

"Your observations are most wise, Captain," returned the zampolit in an unusually subdued tone of voice. "I'll help spread the word among the men. Because nothing must keep us from carrying out our sworn duty, and we're relying on you, Comrade Gnutov, to do just that."

Thankful for this vote of confidence, Alexander

316

nodded and then headed for the radio room to send the brief, high-burst VHF signal that would inform the Kremlin of their sobering find.

Two and a half hours later, the *Kirov* silently ascended to its periscope depth. There was a hushed tenseness in the attack center as the vessel's senior officers gathered at the periscope well. It was Alexander Gnutov who ordered the scope upward and anxiously peered out of its hard-rubber viewing coupling after it rose from the decks below with a soft hydraulic hiss. Efficiently scanning the encircling waters, his line of sight eventually focused itself in on the northern horizon, where the bobbing lights of an anchored surface ship invitingly beckoned. He didn't need to utilize the scope's unique night-viewing capabilities to see the great size of this vessel, whose equipment-cluttered deck was dominated by a single, massive derrick.

Stepping back to allow his associates a look at this ship, Alexander waited in silent introspection. As he expected, the only one to immediately voice himself was the zampolit.

"Will you take a look at that brute! Surely that's a Yankee salvage vessel."

The captain waited for the political officer to see his fill and step away from the scope before matter-of-factly commenting, "If I'm not mistaken, that ship's name is the *Global Explorer*. Though officially listed in the U.S. Navy roster as a marine-mining vessel, this same platform was originally designed with one purpose in mind—to gather from the icy depths of the Pacific the sunken Golf class submarine, *Baikal*."

317

A collective gasp passed the lips of his captivated audience, and the zampolit wasted no time adding his ruble's worth. "I also remember that incident, Comrades. It was a prime example of Yankee audacity at its wasteful best. For what could they have possibly hoped to find intact on a ship that had plummeted to the bottom, eighteen thousand feet beneath the ocean's surface?"

"Yet the crafty Americans indeed succeeded with their primary mission," added the captain. "And though they might have garnered few secrets from the already obsolete *Baikal*, they managed to perfect an incredible salvage technique that not even the Motherland has been able to match."

Frustrated by this revelation, the red-faced zampolit emotionally remarked, "Let's sink them now, while we've got the imperialistic pirates in our sights!"

Such a thought had also crossed Alexander's mind, but he remained cautious. "That's a very tempting proposition, Comrade Pavlodar, but we've yet to see evidence that would prove that they've actually begun a salvage operation here."

"What more proof do you need?" quizzed the zampolit as he pointed toward the empty periscope. "Isn't the mere presence of that ship up there evidence enough?"

The political officer's argument was given additional substance by the excited observations of their sonar operator. "I'm picking up submersible screw sounds, Captain! Bearing zero-four-zero."

"That would be in the waters almost directly beneath the Yankee salvage vessel," reflected the zampolit. "Destroy this target now, before it plucks from the depths secrets that no Westerner can ever be allowed to get his slimy hands on!"

Spurred into action by the political officer's urgent promptings, Alexander strode over to the sonar console to address directly its seated operator. "Lieutenant Kasimov, exactly what is the nature of this new contact?"

The redheaded technician answered only after closing his eyes and focusing his complete attention on the distinctive whirring sounds that were streaming in through his headphones. "It's a single propellor, Captain. And from the number and intensity of revolutions, I'd say that it belongs to one of their miniature, battery-powered submersibles."

"I tell you, it's an American rescue vessel!" whined Ivan Pavlodar, who had followed Alexander across the compartment. "You must destroy it now, before it compromises the great secrets locked within the *Caspian*'s hull!"

Alexander Gnutov found himself in the midst of a dilemma that every peacetime soldier most feared. By ordering a torpedo launch, he could very well be firing the first salvo of World War III. Yet by doing nothing, the Soviet Union's most sophisticated underwater platform was about to be violated.

Of course if the zampolit was correct, and the Americans were directly responsible for the *Caspian*'s sinking, he would not hesitate to order an attack. But he still didn't know this fact for certain, and thus his indecision.

"Sir, the miniature sub continues its approach toward the sea floor," monitored the sonar officer. "There's no doubt that its destination is the *Caspian*."

A new urgency flavored the zampolit's words as he

desperately pleaded, "Please, Captain, for the sake of the Motherland, destroy this submersible before it's too late! Have you already forgotten Admiral Chimki's latest orders?"

Two and a half hours ago, when they had sent the VHF radio message informing Command of their find, headquarters had ordered the *Kirov* to stand by for further instructions. The dispatch that followed was brief and direct. Once again originating in Admiral Viktor Chimki's Kremlin office, it gave Alexander full authority to use force if necessary to defend the *Caspian*'s integrity should the Typhoon class vessel be further threatened.

Since there could be no doubting the identity of the mother ship currently floating above on the calm waters of the passage, Alexander could only assume that this new contact they had just picked up was an American DSRV. Such a vessel was designed to rescue the crew of a submarine disabled on the bottom and could be readily adapted for salvage work. With this sobering thought in mind, Alexander made the only logical choice available to him.

"Lieutenant Arbatov, have the weapons officer load tubes one, three, and five with acoustic-homing antisubmarine torpedoes. Tubes two, four, and six are to be loaded with free-running anti-ship torpedoes."

"Very good, Captain," responded the senior officer, who immediately proceeded to relay this directive to the *Kirov*'s torpedo room.

A relieved grin etched the zampolit's face as he joined the captain at the fire control console. "I realize that this decision was a difficult one for you,

Comrade Gnutov, but you must rest assured that you are doing the right thing. The imperialists must not be allowed to get away with this act of piracy. And just as important, the crew of the *Caspian* call from their watery graves to be avenged. The Motherland's honor is at stake here, and no matter the consequences, we must not shirk our sworn duty, regardless of how unpleasant it may be."

While absorbing these sincere remarks, Alexander's eyes scanned the digital panel showing the progress of the orders he had just relayed to his senior lieutenant. He noted that the last of the anti-submarine torpedoes had just been loaded, and as the weapons crew began preparing the antiship projectiles, he turned his head to address sonar.

"Lieutenant Kasimov, interface the underwater contact's sound signature with the acoustic-homing computers in tubes one, three, and five."

"At once, sir!" replied the red-haired officer.

As Kasimov began efficiently addressing his keyboard, Alexander turned back to the fire-control console. He watched as two green lights lit up above the panel marked, Tube Number One. This indicated that not only was the torpedo stored in this tube ready to fire, but that the miniaturized computer positioned behind its warhead knew the exact acoustic identity of the target it would soon be ordered to home in on. As dual green lights followed above the panels reserved for tubes three and five, the captain unlocked the central triggering mechanism. Having only initiated this sequence in practice exercises, his pulse quickened as he depressed the toggle switch that subsequently armed the warhead stored in tube

321

number one. Almost instantaneously, a red light began ominously flashing above the two green ones.

"Lieutenant Kasimov, how do you read our submerged contact?" questioned Alexander.

"Loud and clear, Captain," answered the sonar officer. "They've just descended beneath the one-hundred-meter level, with another hundred and seventy meters to go before they reach the deck of the *Caspian*."

Alexander briefly hesitated, yet it was the zampolit who spoke up to urge him onward. "Do it now, Captain! Fire the torpedoes, and protect the secrets locked within the *Caspian*'s hull."

Having already made his decision, Alexander somberly replied, "We will launch the initial attack against the DSRV. Only if the Americans persist will we target their surface vessel."

Though the zampolit would have preferred to take out both vessels while the element of surprise was in their favor, he held his tongue and listened as the captain turned to address the senior lieutenant.

"Lieutenant Arbatov, open torpedo door number one."

Ivan Pavlodar's own pulse quickened as he breathlessly watched the *Kirov*'s commanding officer reach up and prepare to depress the switch that would send the first of their torpedoes surging out of its tube in a frothing hiss of compressed air.

Petty Officer Second Class Brad Bodzin was well into his second watch of the day. This additional duty was prompted by a personal request from the boat's skipper. In no position to even think about turning the captain down, Bodzin readily volunteered his services, and after a brief break for chow, returned to the sonar room for yet another six-hour stint.

As he sat at the console, headphones strapped over his ears, the good-natured Texan contemplated the briefing Theodore Anderson had shared with the entire crew less than an hour ago. Only having just returned himself from a brief excursion topside, the captain related to them a remarkable tale of a sunken Soviet submarine lying disabled on the sea floor beneath them. As U.S. surface vessels prepared to salvage this warship, the DSRV *San Clemente* was to be sent into the depths to remove any surviving Russian crew members.

For the last ten minutes, Bodzin could clearly hear the *San Clemente* as it began this rescue attempt. Its signature was the distinctive whirring whine of a single, battery-powered propellor. He had been able to readily follow the DSRV as it initiated its journey from the surface and knew it was currently well in the midst of its descent, just passing the four-hundred-foot level.

Brad's job was to not only continue monitoring the *San Clemente* but to scan the surrounding waters for any unwelcome visitors. Both the captain and Admiral Abbott had made it a point to corner Bodzin alone and express Command's fears that other unfriendlies could be in the area. These fears were truly grounded in reality since the disabled vessel was a ballistic-missile-carrying boat, or a boomer—the more common name. Such platforms rarely went on patrol without an escort of some type in the vicinity.

And since this escort was most likely another attack sub, Brad's duty was most clear.

The sonar technician couldn't help but feel honored at the captain's personal attention. It was evident that they were relying upon him to keep both the *Swordfish* and the various rescue vessels out of harm's way. And Bodzin wasn't about to let them down.

Quick to put his gift, as Admiral Abbott so aptly called it, to work, Brad settled himself into the upholstered chair and cleared his mind of all distracting thoughts. After committing the distinctive signature of the DSRV *San Clemente* to memory, he began the arduous task of sweeping the surrounding seas of all ambient sound. This job was facilitated by the current operational status of the *Swordfish*.

Since Captain Anderson's briefing, the sub had been hushed in a state of ultra-quiet. With their own near-silent, battery-powered propellor spinning with only the bare number of revolutions needed to keep them at depth, all unnecessary systems had been shut down. This included such basic devices as their galley's ice-making machine. Since such noise could not only give their presence away to the enemy but distract their own sensor operators as well, Brad welcomed the quiet, which made his difficult job all that much easier.

He was currently in the process of scanning the seas off their port bow. He did so by slowly turning the large black dial set into the console before him. In such a way he was able to isolate and direct the dozens of sensitive hydrophones set into the sub's hull.

With his other hand he controlled the volume and

the various filtering mechanisms. This last system was most useful in screening out unwanted noise, such as the natural clicking chatter of a large school of shrimp that had recently passed their way.

Only after Brad was completely satisfied that the seas before them were clear did he switch to the hydrophones that lined their stern. The usual rumbling whine of the *Swordfish*'s own engines was noticeably absent as he scanned their baffles, that hard-to-monitor pocket of water lying directly behind them.

It was at this point that pure instinct instructed the Texan to increase the volume gain. He did so to its maximum amplification, and as the sound of the surging sea filtered in through his headphones, Bodzin became aware of a distant, whirring sound that was somehow alien. His gut tightened as he sat forward and expertly manipulated the various sonic filters. In such a way he was able to isolate the noise that had drawn his attention.

The distant, muted whine was disturbingly familiar. Not appearing to be strong enough to be emanating from another submarine, he shuddered in sudden awareness only after flashing back to an ASW exercise they had participated in last summer. At that time he had heard a similar racket, as the *Swordfish* was attacked by an American 688 class vessel that was playing the role of the aggressor. Though it was only armed with a dummy warhead, he would never forget the sickening footprint left in the wake of the approaching torpedo that the *Swordfish* had just managed to escape at the very last moment. And now he was experiencing this terrifying sound again, and this time it was no mere exercise!

As he was in the process of reaching out for the intercom to contact the captain, he realized that this supposed torpedo didn't appear to be gaining on the loitering *Swordfish* at all. Instead, it seemed to be streaming off into the depths below them. Momentarily puzzled by this realization, Brad suddenly gasped in awareness. This weapon hadn't been aimed at the *Swordfish*, but was intended solely for the unwary, three-man crew of the unarmed DSRV!

Meanwhile, on the deck above, Ted Anderson and William Abbott were gathered around the chart table when the frantic call from Sonar arrived, informing them of the attack on the *San Clemente*.

"Damn it!" cursed the captain, who took little time inciting his crew into action. "Lieutenant Pukalani, keep someone on the horn with Sonar and find out where in the hell that shot came from. Lord only knows that we could very well be the next target. Then we're going to need to load some Mk-48's and an Mk-70 as well.

"Engineering, get those turbines on line! That DSRV's a sitting duck down there, and unless we can get between them and that torpedo, they're doomed."

Inspired by this observation, William Abbott hastily commented, "Captain, if that shot is coming from that Russkie attack sub we've been expecting, it will most likely be an acoustic-homing device. The only chance the *San Clemente* has is to cut its engines and then pray that the Red torpedo loses them in the process."

With little time to spare for deliberation, Anderson

326

nodded. "Sounds logical to me, Admiral. Lieutenant Pukalani, have communications hail the *San Clemente* at once. Inform them that they're under torpedo attack and to immediately cut their engines. If they can do so quick enough, we just might have enough time to launch that Mk-70."

Already picking up forward speed, the *Swordfish* initiated a tight-spiraling downward turn that put them on a direct intercept course with the doomed DSRV. Yet the Soviet torpedo still lay between them. Surging forward at a speed over four times faster than the *San Clemente* could attain, the weapon had managed to get a tight sonic lock on the DSRV's propulsion unit.

The torpedo was a mere ten thousand yards astern of its unwary target when the *Swordfish*'s urgent message finally reached the *San Clemente*. Lieutenant Bill Long was at the DSRV's helm, and without a second's hesitation, disengaged the submersible's propulsion unit.

Back on the *Swordfish*, Brad Bodzin heard the *San Clemente*'s engine grind to a halt. Unfortunately, the torpedo continued its mad pursuit, and Bodzin could only convey this somber fact back up to the control room.

Ted Anderson took this information all in stride and barked out to the weapons officer, "Fire that Mk-70, Lieutenant!"

Seconds later, a bubbling burst of compressed air surged out of the *Swordfish*'s bow. The entire hull momentarily quivered as the Mk-70 shot out of the torpedo tube and rocketed downward on a pre-programmed intercept course. Also known as a mobile submarine simulator, or MOSS for short, the Mk-70 was designed to simulate the sound signature of a fleeing submarine. In this case it was hoped that with the *San Clemente*'s engine shut down, the Soviet torpedo would be fooled into following the MOSS in the DSRV's place.

In the best position to monitor this desperate tactic was Brad Bodzin. Though he still had no idea where the submarine responsible for this attack was located, he was certain that if the *Swordfish* was to be the next subject of this mystery vessel's ire, they would have long since been fired upon. This left only the crew of the DSRV to be concerned with.

The Mk-70 continued cutting a distinctive path through the sea. Its course remained true, its engine strong and unyielding. Yet the enemy torpedo still showed no signs of wavering. Still locked on the coordinates where it last sensed its original target, the torpedo's muted drone undercut the higher-pitched whine of the MOSS decoy. Their only hope was that the Mk-70 would arrive in time to distract the torpedo. Yet the seconds were rapidly running out, with the Soviet weapon less than three thousand yards away from the *San Clemente* now.

Brad anxiously hunched over the console. With his eyes tightly shut, he pressed the headphones over his ears, all the while mentally visualizing the mad pursuit going on in the seas beneath them. Somewhere in these same depths, the doomed crew of the *San Clemente* waited in the blackness. Brad wasn't a religious person, but he nevertheless found himself mouthing a silent prayer for their protection.

What seemed to take a virtual eternity, in fact took less than a minute as the signatures of the decoy and the torpedo seemed to momentarily merge into one entity. Surely the weapon would strike the DSRV any second now, and Brad reached out to turn down the volume gain to protect his eardrums from the ensuing blast. Yet just as his hand made contact with the black plastic dial, the two signatures abruptly separated once again. The high-pitched whine of the MOSS decoy rose distinctly in the background, with the throaty, muted roar of the torpedo suddenly seeming to gain in volume. This hopefully meant that the torpedo was reacting to a new sonic source and was automatically increasing its speed to catch up with this new target.

Brad's suspicions seemed to be confirmed when the Mk-70 could be heard initiating a wide, preprogrammed turn. Straining to catch up with it, the torpedo adjusted its course and surged forward in a sudden burst of unexpected speed. Again the two signatures appeared to merge, and just as Brad ripped the headphones off his ears, the depths filled with a deafening explosion. A mild shock wave shook the deck beneath him, and Brad waited a full minute before cautiously replacing the headset.

A ghostly quiet met his ears, only to be replaced by a sudden muted whirring sound that brought him nothing but pure joy. This was the familiar signature of the *San Clemente*'s engines being started!

A wide, relieved grin turned the corners of the sonar technician's lips as he listened to the DSRV as it picked up speed. Soon it was well on its way on a new course straight to the safer waters topside.

Eight hundred and seventy-three feet below the

sea's surface, the explosion rumbled through the hull of the *Caspian* like a deep, bass boom of distant thunder. Jarred awake by the shock wave that followed, Captain Mikhail Sobrinka looked out into the pitch-black interior of his cabin. A cold sweat had formed on his forehead, and as the muted rumbling faded, the horrifying dream that he had been in the midst of rose in his consciousness.

This had been the second time in as many days that the macabre vision had recurred. In each instance, the nightmare seemed to have come to him moments before waking up. Never having experienced anything like this before, the naval veteran remained lying on his mattress, his inner vision focused on the dream's disturbing contents.

It had all started in an alien jungle setting. It was a hot, steamy night, and a single beating drum drew him down a narrow earthen pathway that was surrounded by creeping vines and thick tropical foliage. The cries of the night creatures throbbed incessantly, and every so often a rustling noise could be heard in the nearby undergrowth, indicating that he wasn't alone here.

As he continued down the trail, he passed a machete, stuck into the packed earth. Tied around the implement's hilt was a red bandanna, and it was at this point that his anxieties began to inexplicably grow. Mortal fear weighed his heavy limbs as he transited a steep switchback that led directly onto a wide volcanic plateau.

Waiting for him on this clearing was a single young black girl, perched before a crude stone altar. A flickering red candle was set before her, and as

Mikhail struggled to gather the words to address her, the sound of beating drums intensified to an almost deafening level. As the rhythm increasingly quickened, his heartbeat seemed to follow, and soon it was a struggle merely to breathe.

With his chest heaving for air, Mikhail looked back to the young girl to implore her assistance, yet she had mysteriously vanished. In her place was a swampy crossroads. A thick mist veiled the ground, and in the distance he could just make out a group of slow-moving figures, who were all so gradually approaching him.

Again he fought with his weighted limbs to flee. Yet the previously solid ground had turned to quicksand, and as he began sinking down into the sticky muck, he got his first clear view of the ghostly procession that was headed his way. And never would he forget what his startled eyes saw. For the creatures who now floated before him were dressed in tattered funeral shrouds and had faces formed from pure bone. It was the eyes that were particularly disturbing, for they were filled with flickering tongues of fire.

Crying out desperately to the black heavens for help, Mikhail found himself sinking farther into the quicksand until only his shoulders, arms, neck, and head were not buried. And the last earthly thing that he saw before being consumed altogether was the mocking grin of one of the skeletoned demons, who sported a long mane of scraggly gray hair.

Buried now in the rich black earth, Mikhail vainly fought to free himself. But his limbs were unmoving, and as the last of the air was consumed, he spent his final breath screaming out in mortal terror, begging even for death to end this terrifying torment.

It was always at this point that he awoke from his deep slumber. Gratefully staring out into the black confines of his stateroom, Sobrinka would ponder the horrid vision until his waking consciousness wiped the nightmare from his mind.

In this instance, it proved to be a sudden knocking on his cabin door that diverted his thoughts from the grisly dream. Struggling to clear his dry throat, the *Caspian*'s commanding officer responded in a hoarse voice, "You may enter!"

The door swung open and a shaft of dim red light met Sobrinka's eyes. Lit in the muted emergency lighting was the tall, thin figure of his senior lieutenant.

"Sorry to disturb you, Captain, but there's a serious disturbance going on in the crew's quarters. One of the men there has gone berserk, and has barricaded himself inside the head where he's threatening to kill himself."

Quickly brought back to full waking consciousness, Mikhail stiffly sat up. Still dressed in his wrinkled coveralls, he responded while hurriedly putting on his shoes.

"We discussed this very possibility, Comrade Jarensk, and now it appears that the men are starting to reach their breaking points. We must defuse this potentially dangerous situation before it spreads to the others, like fire through a dry forest."

The captain stood and followed his second-in-command out into the passageway. The air was noticeably chilled here, and Mikhail could gauge its poor oxygen content by the dull ache that began pounding beneath his temples. As they turned toward the ladder that would take them down to the crew's quarters, the senior lieutenant questioned, "Did you hear that explosion that sounded outside our hull several minutes ago, Captain? I wonder what on earth could have caused it."

Conscious now that this disturbance hadn't been a new part of his nightmare, Sobrinka answered, "Though I was asleep when it struck, it sounded much like the report of a torpedo. Who knows, perhaps our comrades have finally arrived to rescue us."

"I thought the very same thing," replied Jarensk as he ducked through a hatchway. "If it's indeed the *Kirov*, then Captain Gnutov will make quick work out of any Yankees who dares stand in his way."

Though Mikhail didn't share in his colleague's optimism, he knew such hopeful thinking was good for morale and responded with this in mind. "I told you that we'd be found soon enough. All they needed to do was retrace our transit route when we didn't show up at our patrol station. And once the *Kirov* positively locates us, all they have to do is keep the Americans at bay until Command sends in a suitable salvage vessel. Surely we can hold out until then."

Leading the way down a wide ladder, the senior lieutenant didn't respond until Sobrinka had joined him on the deck below. "I've reworked my calculations, Captain. If the men continue remaining as inactive as possible, it's just possible that we'll have enough air to hold on another seventy-two hours."

The captain was winded by their short climb, and

took a moment to catch his breath. As he massaged his pounding forehead, he replied as optimistically as possible. "That's plenty of time for Command to put a submersible rescue vessel on an IL-76 and fly it down to Cienfuegos. From there it's only a forty-eight hour cruise to this passage, giving them just enough time to remove the *Caspian*'s complement before our air supply fails us."

Signaling that he was ready to continue down the passageway, Mikhail listened as his senior lieutenant suddenly voiced himself.

"If what we heard was indeed a torpedo exploding, I can't help but wonder if it was one of ours, and what its target might have been."

"We can only hope that it was Alexander Gnutov's way of signaling any Americans in the area to back off," reflected the captain. "If only we could rig an underwater telephone. I'd give up my entire pension to know what's going on up there."

A muted cry sounded in the distance, and the two officers wasted no time increasing their pace. After passing through the empty recreation room, they entered a passageway lined with imitation wood-grain paneling. Illuminated by the dim red lighting was a group of anxious individuals perched before a shut hatchway. One of these figures was several centimeters taller than his shipmates, and it was toward this individual that Mikhail directed his inquiry.

"Chief Markova, what in Lenin's name is going on here?"

The big-boned Siberian engineer immediately answered, "It's Seaman Azov, Captain. Without any warning at all, he seems to have gone completely insane. I was in the berthing compartment myself when he unexpectedly shot up from his bunk and began madly shouting his head off about being buried alive. We tried to constrain him, but he seemed to have the strength of ten men as he knocked us away and went scrambling for the head. He's been locked inside ever since, and from that last scream, I'm afraid he just made good his threat to commit suicide."

Briefly reminded of his own recurring nightmare, Mikhail Sobrinka found himself with little time for selfish introspection and he responded, "If I remember correctly, Azov was a promising missile technician from the Ukraine. Perhaps I can talk some sense into him."

Making his way through the crowd gathered in the corridor, Sobrinka rapped on the shut hatch with his knuckles.

"Comrade Azov, it's Captain Sobrinka! Open this door like a good lad, and let's talk."

Breathlessly waiting for a reply, the captain tried once again. "Come on, Comrade, quit being so pigheaded and open up! Things aren't as bad as they seem."

Again his plea got no response, and just as Mikhail was wondering if they'd have to force the hatch open, a strained voice broke from the head's interior.

"It's useless, Captain! Don't you see, we're all going to die in the most horrible way imaginable, buried alive in this high-tech coffin!"

"Why, that's pure nonsense, Comrade Azov!" returned the captain. "Didn't you hear that explo-

335

sion outside our hull several minutes ago? Surely that means the *Kirov* has arrived in these waters, and that our rescue is imminent."

There was a brief pause as these optimistic words were absorbed. And when the frightened seaman next voiced himself, a tinge of hope flavored his tone.

"Do you really think that this is the case, Captain?"

"Of course I do, Comrade," answered Sobrinka. "Would I dare lie to you, my friend? After all, we share the same predicament, and the same fears as well. So open that hatch, lad, and we'll talk out this thing like gentlemen."

There was an anxious chorus of concerned chatter from the mouths of those gathered in the passageway. Finding themselves with their anxieties soothed by the captain's words, they waited for this plea to take effect on their disturbed shipmate. It apparently did so thirty seconds later, when the grating sound of the hatch being unlocked met their startled ears. Soon afterward Seaman Azov appeared, his brow bloodied, his limbs still trembling.

"That's more like it," greeted the captain softly. "Now why don't I have the chief take you into the wardroom. We can take a look at those nasty cuts on your forehead, and over a nice cool glass of water discuss these groundless fears of yours."

Angling up his dark eyes to directly meet the glance of Mikhail Sobrinka, the disturbed seaman pathetically pleaded, "Please don't let us die, Captain."

Delicately patting the skinny Ukrainian on his back, Mikhail responded. "Don't worry, lad, I'll get you safely topside if it's the last thing I do. So let's get you off to the wardroom, and your shipmates here can return to their bunks. We've wasted enough oxygen as it is. And since our rescuers are already most likely on their way, we must conserve each precious breath.''

There was a somber feeling in the passageway as the crew leadenly shuffled back to their bunks. Watching as the chief led the Ukrainian missile technician off to the wardroom, the captain sighed heavily. He knew that he had managed to win this one small battle. But how much longer would it be until the next serious crisis was upon them? And could he take the nerve-wracking pressure himself?

His recurring nightmare was surely a sign of his own mental deterioration, his personal fears of their impending deaths expressing itself in macabre visions of being buried alive. But as the *Caspian*'s commanding officer, it was imperative that he set the tone of the state of their morale. Hope was the essence that would keep the crew unified. Without it, discipline would be lost and their dooms sealed.

The dull, persistent pain continued throbbing beneath his temples, and the sixty-three-year-old veteran looked down at his watch. He had to hold himself together for at least another seventy-two hours. If their rescue wasn't effected by then, it wouldn't matter much how he handled himself, as the one hundred and seventeen surviving crew members of the *Caspian* shared the same fate of death by asphyxiation.

Chapter Fourteen

Secretary of the Navy Peter Anderson personally went down to the *Global Explorer*'s moonpool to greet the crew of the returning DSRV. He arrived at the rectangular opening, with Commander Richard Walker at his side, just as the *San Clemente* broke the water's surface. Though the sun had long since set, a bank of powerful spotlights adequately illuminated the scene as the cigar-shaped submersible's top access trunk popped open. A head appeared in the hatchway, topped by a familiar orange-and-turquoise cap. As the wearer of the cap spotted them and waved in greeting, the DSRV's side-mounted thrusters activated and the vessel angled its way over to the lattice steel platform.

Peter Anderson didn't even wait for the *San Clemente* to complete this short trip to voice his concern. "Is everyone okay in there, Lieutenant Long?"

The DSRV pilot flashed them an okay sign with his right hand. Yet he waited until his boat was safely moored before joining them on the platform and emotionally expressing himself. "Did you ever find out who in the hell it was who took that shot at us?"

Peter Anderson shook his head that they hadn't and added, "The *Swordfish* is still searching the seas for them, but so far they've come upon absolutely nothing."

"Have you ruled out the possibility that it was the Typhoon who attacked us?" continued Lieutenant Long.

This time it was Commander Walker who answered. "Though such a thing can't be ignored, the sonar operator who first tagged that torpedo doesn't believe that this is the case. The shot seemed to come from an altogether different portion of the sea."

"One thing that's obvious is that until we find this source and negate it, all further rescue attempts will remain on hold," directed the secretary of the Navy. "I'm even considering pulling the *Global Explorer* out of here to safer waters."

"We'd be willing to give it another try," offered the *San Clemente*'s pilot.

Peter Anderson stood firm. "That's not necessary, Lieutenant. We've got too much on the line here. And, after all, I wouldn't want to lose you to a Soviet torpedo while attempting to save the lives of a group of Russian submariners."

"The ironies of war," reflected Richard Walker. "I wonder if the skipper of that suspected Russkie attack boat realizes that he's only putting the lives of his fellow countrymen on the line by opposing us?"

"I doubt that he really cares," said Peter Anderson. "If I know the Soviets, all they really give

339

a damn about is protecting their hardware. Human lives are of secondary importance to them, the interests of the State always coming first."

The metallic sounds of approaching footsteps diverted their attention to the nearby catwalk, where a pert, blond figure dressed in a khaki safari jacket and shorts was visible. The woman continued straight to the platform, where she addressed the only other civilian present. "Did you want to see me, Mr. Secretary?"

"Yes I did, Dr. Patton," answered Peter Anderson. "I'm sure that you're well aware that our current situation has changed radically. Since it looks like we've got a Soviet attack sub in the area to contend with, I think it's best if you return to St. John. It could get awfully messy out here, and there's no reason for you and your assistant to have to needlessly risk your lives for our sake."

"But what about those Soviet sailors trapped below on that disabled submarine?" countered Susan. "Aren't you going to at least attempt to save them?"

"Not until we find the vessel that's responsible for taking that pot shot at Lieutenant Long and his crew," returned Anderson. "Hopefully, we'll be able to do so shortly, and then get on with the rescue."

Susan had little concern about her own safety as she responded, "I appreciate the offer to leave, Mr. Secretary, but are you certain there isn't anything we could do to help out? Both Owen and I understand the risks and want only one thing: to see to it that those Soviet crew members are brought topside before they all suffocate."

Peter Anderson looked to his side for support and found it in the person of Richard Walker. "Thanks for your concern, Susan, but until that Russian attack sub is tracked down, there's nothing much that you can do here except put your life in danger."

"Why can't we help you track down this submarine?" asked Susan.

"And just how do you plan to do that?" countered Walker.

Susan looked to the moonpool, reached into her pocket, and put a silver whistle to her lips. After blowing this high-pitched device a single time, she pointed toward the sleek black dorsal fin of a dolphin just visible beside the *San Clemente*'s stern and curtly answered, "With Sammy, that's how."

Peter Anderson seemed flustered by this response, and quickly replied, "Dr. Patton, I don't think you fully understand the enormity of our problem. That Soviet attack sub could be hiding almost anywhere in this passage, at a depth of only a few inches from the surface, to over three thousand feet below. Since it appears to have arrived here with the express purpose of halting our salvage attempt, they'll obviously go to any extreme to remain undetected. And that includes scramming their reactor and floating noiselessly on the sea floor, all but invisible to even our most sophisticated sensors. So with these sobering facts in mind, what can Sammy possibly do to assist us in finding them?"

Susan's thoughts flowed forth extemporaneously. "My first project for the Navy was to see if dolphins could be trained to repel sharks from beach areas and waters in which naval operatives would be working.

341

I initiated the training process by showing pictures of brown sharks to my dolphins and then conditioning them to attack such creatures should one violate their water space.

"It was common knowledge to me from my previous studies that most dolphins are quick learners and respond well to visual stimuli. This includes both printed matter and video media. In fact, I had one dolphin who seemed particularly enchanted with television reruns of the cowboy show *Bonanza* and never missed a program on the underwater monitor we installed in his tank.

"A few hours after showing my test subjects those shark pictures, a live hammerhead was placed in the tank with them. Yet, much to our dismay, the dolphins showed no signs of aggression, and kept as much distance between the hammerhead and themselves as possible. Only when a brown shark was introduced did their behavior drastically alter. Swimming around in a frenzy, they continued butting the unwary brown with their snouts and bodies until we had to remove the shark for its very safety.

"All this went to show that the dolphins didn't respond to the shark family as a whole, but only to the individual species whose pictures they had been conditioned to attack. Thus I believe that if you were to furnish me a picture of the class of submarine you are after, I can train Sammy to hunt it down, and at the very least utilize his new harness to place an ultrasonic homing beacon on its hull, as he did to that disabled vessel lying on the sea floor beneath us."

As those assembled around Susan absorbed her unorthodox offer, Sammy took this opportunity to steal the spotlight by standing on his tail fin and scooting backward over the entire length of the moonpool.

"It seems that our star of the hour knows that he's being talked about," observed Lieutenant Bill Long. "Though I certainly don't know much about dolphins, Sammy sure made a believer out of me when he tagged that Typhoon for us with that beacon. I can't tell you how much easier that made my whole job."

Looking out to the moonpool, Peter Anderson reflected, "Locating that disabled boomer was one thing, but finding an actual operational vessel is a whole different ball game. Besides, we still don't even know exactly what class of Russian attack sub we're dealing with. It could be any one of several designs, whose individual hulls are as different as night and day."

Following the direction of the secretary's gaze, Richard Walker added, "There's an awful lot of territory for Sammy to cover out there. Yet considering our present circumstances, I don't see any harm in giving him a try. I say if Susan's willing, we should go for it."

"But what about that picture we're going to need to show to the dolphin?" countered Peter Anderson. "Dr. Patton admits that even if he's able to find that attack sub, unless he recognizes its hull design, he'll just pass it right on by."

Grinning, Richard Walker responded, "If I'm not mistaken, I believe that I saw a copy of *Jane's*

Fighting Ships in the *Global Explorer*'s wardroom. Since this whole thing is but a crapshoot anyway, I'd say that we should start at the beginning of the alphabet, and show Sammy the pictures of a Soviet Alfa class attack submarine. Because of their great speed and maneuverability, I'd say that the Alfa wouldn't be such a long shot to begin with."

Peter Anderson answered while watching Sammy swim gracefully around the moonpool's perimeter. "I hope to God that you fully understand what you're getting involved with here, Dr. Patton. Because even if Sammy is able to tag that attack vessel, we still have to somehow eliminate its threat, and that will most likely mean that all hell is going to break out beneath the waters of this passage. Thus there's no guarantee that either Sammy, or us for that matter, will live to survive this fracas."

"That's a risk we're willing to accept," returned Susan, who was absolutely certain that her decision was a correct one.

Deep below the surface of the Anegada Passage, the Alfa class attack sub *Kirov* silently loitered. Protected by the veil of a one-of-a-kind stealth package, the vessel was rendered all but invisible to enemy sensors. An instrumental part of this masking system were the specially designed anechoic tiles that lined the boat's titanium-clad hull. Not only did they serve to muffle interior noise, but they also effectively deflected active sonar scans as well.

In the boat's attack center, the *Kirov*'s captain was in the process of anxiously monitoring the waters

344

that lay above them. Alexander Gnutov initiated this task by clipping on a pair of auxiliary headphones that were plugged into the *Kirov*'s sonar console. Having once been a sonar officer himself, Alexander was most familiar with the variety of sounds presently streaming into his ears.

Only after completing a three-hundred-and-sixty-degree scan of the waters that encircled them did he remove the headphones and hang them back on the console. Quick to approach him at this point was the *Kirov*'s ever-inquisitive political officer. With his beady dark eyes open wide with curiosity, the zampolit nosily questioned, "Well, Captain, what did you hear out there? Has the American rescue submersible returned?"

Alexander halfheartedly answered, "No, Comrade, they haven't."

Relieved by this revelation, the zampolit observed, "Perhaps our torpedo's shockwave somehow damaged the craft. That could account for their non-presence."

"Either that, or we scared them topside," offered Alexander. "Even if our shot was deflected by a decoy, it served its purpose just as well. I guarantee you that they'll think twice before reinitiating another salvage attempt, just knowing that we're lurking somewhere out here in the black depths. And to think that we managed to most likely do this without taking a single life."

"Of course there's still the question of where that decoy came from," reflected the zampolit. "Could the *Global Explorer* possibly have launched it?"

"That's highly unlikely," returned Alexander.

"Such vessels are thought to be unarmed. Besides, they don't have either the sensor or fire-control systems to effect such an intercept. This means that we're not alone in these depths. Somewhere beneath the waters of this passage a Yankee submarine is probably lurking."

The zampolit's upbeat mood noticeably soured. "That's upsetting news, Comrade. Such a vessel could be extremely bothersome. Perhaps we should take this opportunity to finish off the *Global Explorer* once and for all. Since it's clearly evident that they still don't know exactly where we're located, all we have to do is ascend to periscope depth, launch a single weapon, and return to these protective waters. You yourself said that the mother ship is like a sitting duck up there, lying unprotected on the surface as it is."

"I still see no need for such an extreme response," retorted the captain. "Hundreds would die if such an attack succeeded, and the American authorities would be simply outraged. Who knows, it could even very well precipitate the world war all of us have been seeking to prevent these last four decades."

"The imperialists would never go to war over such an incident," returned the zampolit. "Don't forget that it was most likely one of their torpedoes that sealed the *Caspian*'s doom in the first place."

"We still don't know that fact for certain!" shot back Alexander.

Surprised at the emotional force of this response, the political officer calmly continued. "Oh, come now, Captain, what else could have sent the *Caspian* to the bottom, without even giving them time to broadcast a single SOS? The Americans are more than aware of their guilt, and are seeking to salvage the *Caspian* not only for the great secrets that lie within its hull, but to also mask the damage that their torpedo created when it took our ship down. Thus, to even the score and ensure that such a coverup can never take place, I say that we should sink the *Global Explorer* now, while our presence here is still a mystery."

Though he understood the logic of the zampolit's argument, Alexander remained firm. "As long as our sensors indicate that the American salvage effort remains at a standstill, we will initiate no further attack, Comrade Pavlodar. This decision is well within the parameters of Admiral Chimki's latest orders to us."

"So it is, Captain, so it is," mumbled the zampolit, who knew that his suggestion had met with defeat.

Powerless to sway Gnutov's opinion further, the political officer listened as the captain turned to address the *Kirov*'s second-in-command.

"Senior Lieutenant, I'll be down in my quarters if I'm needed."

"Very good, sir," responded Ganady Arbatov, who was huddled over the chart table.

As the captain exited the attack center, the zampolit fought back the urge to follow Gnutov to the deck below. Perhaps within the private confines of the captain's cabin, he'd have a better chance of convincing him to change his mind. But Gnutov seemed to be firm in his convictions, and the zampolit figured that there was little he could say or do to sway him otherwise.

While strolling over to the navigator's station, Ivan Pavlodar reached into his pocket and removed his handkerchief. His forehead was drenched with sweat, and as he patted it dry, he silently cursed his frustrating circumstances.

Though his rank was just as senior as that of the *Kirov*'s captain, he had little say-so when it came down to operational matters. Ivan had always argued that this was a major flaw in the system. As an integral part of the ship's command structure, he felt that his opinion in such matters as strategy and tactics should carry more clout. After all, he was a graduate of the Grechko Academy himself, and though his engineering knowledge was limited, he had a basic understanding of navigation and, more important, an expert grasp on the political concepts that necessitated their going to sea in the first place.

Ivan often knew the moods and capabilities of the ship's complement better than its captain. Not bothered with technical concerns, he was also in a much better position to grasp the big picture. Their current situation was perfect proof of this fact.

To Ivan it was clear as day what needed to be done. Since their mission was to protect the integrity of the *Caspian*'s hull until a proper Soviet rescue flotilla arrived, the American threat that continuously hovered over them had to be eliminated. This was especially the case now that an enemy attack sub was suspected in these same waters. For if this vessel should chance upon the *Kirov* and sink them, the imperialists would be free to get on with their salvage effort without any fear of retribution.

As far as Ivan was concerned, such a thing could not be allowed! The *Caspian* was the pride of their fleet, and was packed with the latest in sophisticated weaponry and software. An examination of the SS-N-20 warheads alone would be an intelligence field day, during which time the CIA would learn the precise makeup of Soviet ballistic missile arms design. Such invaluable knowledge would lead to effective countermeasures, and the strategic advantage that the Motherland had sacrificed so much to achieve would be all but negated.

Ivan shuddered to think what would happen if the Americans were permitted to pick apart the *Caspian*'s highly advanced propulsion system. Not only could they adapt its unique design concepts for their own vessels, but the U.S. Navy could use this knowledge to better prepare its own ASW forces. Since the next war's outcome would inevitably hinge on the battle beneath the planet's oceans, such an ASW breakthrough would be disastrous to the Motherland. Her submarines would be tagged within the first few hours of the conflict, and U.S. attack platforms would swarm in for the easy kill.

Why Alexander Gnutov failed to grasp these points was an enigma to Ivan. In their past conversations, the captain certainly showed few signs of ideological weakness. If anything, his close association with Admiral Chimki put him firmly on the same side as the political hardliners, who promoted a more active role for the Soviet military in countering imperialist aspirations. Since this was the case, the zampolit could see no reason for Gnutov's recalcitrance unless the man was simply a coward and was afraid to initiate an attack of his own.

With this disturbing thought in mind, the zampolit

positioned himself beside the *Kirov*'s senior lieutenant. Peering down at the chart he was intently studying, Ivan took in the now familiar waters of the Anegada Passage. A red X marked their current position, while a blue rectangular box indicated the position of the *Global Explorer*. The giant marine salvage ship lay in the waters almost directly north of them, only a few inviting kilometers distant.

The senior lieutenant was in the process of underscoring the soundings that showed the surrounding sea floor's composition as Ivan cleared his throat and spoke out in greeting, "Well, Comrade Arbatov, have you found any bathymetric features that could be to our advantage should we get ourselves in a scrap?"

The senior lieutenant answered while continuing to focus his attention on the chart. "One thing that's clearly evident is that we have plenty of water beneath us to utilize should we so desire. We currently have well over a thousand meters of water below our hull, with even more depth available in the seas just south of us."

"That's somewhat comforting to know," reflected the zampolit, who decided to test the senior officer's loyalties. "Tell me, Comrade Arbatov, what do you think about our current situation? Should we take advantage of the element of surprise and sink the Yankee salvage vessel while we have this excellent opportunity?"

Looking up to meet the political officer's gaze directly, Ganady Arbatov cautiously responded, "Why do you ask, Comrade Zampolit? Aren't our orders perfectly clear on that matter?"

"Of course they are, my friend. I am speaking completely off the record in this instance, and asking your valued opinion as one citizen of the Motherland to another. How would you handle our situation if you were the *Kirov*'s commanding officer?"

"I imagine exactly like Captain Gnutov has done, Comrade," answered Ganady. "Though I'll be the first to admit that the Yankee salvage ship certainly makes for an inviting target."

"How would you sink her if you were given the chance, my friend?"

The senior lieutenant couldn't resist presenting his already well-thought-out attack plan. "Since the *Global Explorer*'s position is well known to us, as long as they remain at anchor, we could attack from our present submerged position. Such an underwater ambush could be readily accomplished by using one of our wire-guided antiship torpedoes. All we'd have to do is interface the surface vessel's coordinates into our fire-control computers. Then we'd merely have to launch the torpedo and guide it to the point where its on-board 3D sonar homing system can assume autonomous control for the final run to the target. A single proximity-fuse conventional warhead should be more than adequate to crack the salvage ship's hull and send it to the bottom."

"Then we wouldn't have to worry about the Americans initiating further salvage attempts," added the zampolit. "Since they're bound to do so eventually, I wonder why we just don't get on with such an attack, while the element of surprise is still in our favor?"

The senior lieutenant took the bait and answered.

"I was wondering the very same thing. But surely our captain has his just reasons."

The zampolit had the young officer set up to push him further when the concerned voice of the sonar operator interrupted his flow. "Comrade Arbatov, I believe I'm picking up some unusual surface noises."

This was all the two officers had to hear to cause them to cross over hurriedly to the sensor console. As Ganady Arbatov efficiently clipped on the auxiliary headset, Ivan Pavlodar anxiously questioned, "Where is this noise coming from?"

Beckoning the political officer to hold his tongue, Ganady turned up the volume gain and delicately turned the directional finder until the sound's source was definitely pinned down. Only then did he respond.

"It appears to be coming from the direction of the *Global Explorer*. If it is a propulsion signature, it's unlike any prop cavitation that I've ever heard. It's more like the primitive racket produced by some sort of raw machinery."

"Then I bet it's the sound of their salvage retrieval claw being lowered that you're hearing!" exclaimed the zampolit, who reached out for the intercom. "Keep monitoring it, while I notify the captain."

Alexander Gnutov had just sat down at his desk to get to work on some long overdue paperwork when the frantic call from the zampolit arrived. It took the captain a little more than a minute to exit his stateroom and return to the attack center. He entered in a breathless state and immediately proceeded over to the group of officers gathered around the sensor console. Fitting on the headphones that were offered

352

him, he momentarily shut his eyes to focus on the sounds being conveyed from the surface. Above the mad pounding of his own heart rose a throbbing, grinding whine that had a resonance all its own.

"I doubt if it's a propellor wash," he thoughtfully reflected. "It sounds too agitated for that."

"What else would you expect from the noise created by the *Global Explorer*'s retrieval claw being lowered?" observed the excited zampolit. "Just like the stubborn Yankees, they're continuing their greedy salvage efforts oblivious to any outside threat. So before they succeed, it's imperative that we stop them at once!"

"I agree," dared the senior lieutenant. "It's obvious that they've decided to ignore our warning shot. To guarantee the *Caspian*'s integrity, we have no choice but to intercede."

Clearly impressed by this unusual outburst of opinion, Alexander Gnutov caught his senior lieutenant's determined glance.

"So you really think that this noise is the sound of more salvage equipment being lowered, Ganady?" queried the captain. "Launching a torpedo is a serious move, and can you in all honesty really be certain that this is indeed what's occurring topside?"

Without flinching, the senior lieutenant replied, "There's no doubt in my mind that the noise is coming from the machinery associated with the *Global Explorer*'s retrieval claw."

Taking another serious listen to the whining racket being directed into the headphones, Alexander grunted. "It certainly has a unique resonance to it."

"What more proof do you need to order that

attack?'' prompted the zampolit. "Launch that torpedo now, Captain, or the next thing you'll be hearing will be the sickening sound of the *Caspian*'s hull being hauled up from the black depths below!"

Alexander lowered his glance and addressed the seated sonar technician. "What do you think, Lieutenant Kasimov? Is the source of this racket the sound of more salvage equipment being lowered?"

The redheaded sonar operator cautiously expressed himself. "It may very well be, Captain. If it does turn out to be a prop signature, it's unlike any vessel I've ever heard before."

"Don't forget the contents of our current orders, Captain," continued the persistent political officer. "Admiral Chimki expressly directed us to intervene with any means necessary to ensure that the Americans don't get their hands on the *Caspian*. We already warned them of our presence here by attacking their rescue submersible. It's certainly not our fault if their pigheaded leaders ignore the dangers and order yet another salvage attempt."

The whining sound that continued filtering in through his headphones seemed to intensify, and Alexander carefully scanned the somber faces of all those who surrounded him before finally responding. "As you very well know, my greatest fear is that we would somehow misread the situation and initiate a mistaken attack that would develop into a global nuclear exchange. Yet there can be no denying that the continued presence of the American salvage vessel above the remains of the *Caspian* is a clear-cut provocation. Since it appears that the *Global Explorer* is currently attempting yet another effort to

354

illegally seize our warship, I have no choice but to order this ship's immediate destruction.

"Senior Lieutenant Arbatov, load tube number one with a wire-guided, antiship torpedo. Since the enemy's coordinates are well known to us, we can eliminate their threat by following the standard procedural tactics relating to an underwater ambush."

"I will convey this directive to the torpedo room at once, Captain," returned the senior lieutenant.

As Gandy Arbatov eagerly strode off for the fire-control console, Alexander met the zampolit's condescending grin.

"You won't be sorry for making this difficult decision," offered the political officer smugly.

Alexander heavily replied, "Let's hope not, Comrade Pavlodar. Because if I'm wrong, I could be condemning the world to a nuclear apocalypse from which civilization will never return."

Lieutenant John Sher was proud of his career. At thirty-four years of age, he was one of the youngest officers in the U.S. Navy to have a command of his own. This was quite an achievement considering that he had graduated next to last in his Annapolis class and had had more than one superior express serious doubts as to his fitness to even serve in the Navy in the first place.

As fortune would have it, he had been able to come to terms with the weaknesses in his emotional makeup that propelled him toward having a good time at the expense of his studies. His mother had always said he was a late bloomer, and he proved her right shortly after graduation, when he decided to get serious about his chosen profession.

Standing on the glassed-in bridge of the hydrofoil gunship *Pegasus*, with the compact combatant foilborne and doing well over forty knots, Sher knew that his choice had been a wise one. He had really come of age in the years immediately following the receipt of his commission. And as proof of his effort, the destiny of the *Pegasus* and her twenty-three-man crew was in his hands alone.

The one-hundred-and-forty-five-foot vessel skimmed over the calm seas of the Anegada Passage, powered by a single, eighteen thousand shaft horsepower gas turbine engine. Off their port bow, he could clearly see the massive ship that they had been sent down from Key West to escort. The *Global Explorer* was almost five times longer than the *Pegasus*, with a displacement difference of over fifty thousand tons. Yet, unlike the mammoth marine mining ship, the *Pegasus* was armed to do battle with eight harpoon missiles and one 76mm gun.

Until this assignment, most of their operational work involved drug interdiction duty. Only two weeks ago, they had participated in the bust of a Colombian freighter, whose supposed cargo of hardwood was bound for Mobile, Alabama.

Scrambled to intercept the suspected smuggler at the very last minute, they made the three-hundred-mile trip from Key West to the Yucatán Channel in a little more than six hours. Traveling at speeds no other class of U.S. Navy ship could attain, they arrived in time to assist the Coast Guard cutter that had been sent out to board the freighter and inspect its hold.

Though the hardwood looked legitimate, one of the Coast Guardsmen was an experienced logger from Arkansas who spotted what he felt to be an irregularity in some of the wood's grain. With his armed colleagues standing shotgun around him, he proceeded to use an axe to chop one of the preprocessed boards in half, and that's when the real cargo spilled out onto the deck below.

The cocaine was top quality, and had a street value of well over fifty million dollars. Though this was only a bare trickle of the huge amount of illicit drugs entering the U.S. mainland each and every day, Sher and his crew were satisfied that their efforts had been more than worth it.

He was genuinely surprised when they received the orders sending them down to the U.S. Virgin Islands. This cruise took the better part of twenty-four hours to complete, and was a supreme test of the gunship's sea-handling capabilities and range.

It was in the straits of water separating Puerto Rico and St. Thomas that they rendezvoused with the *Global Explorer*. This was Sher's first eyewitness view of the legendary marine mining vessel, and he couldn't help but be impressed by its immense size. Not long after they arrived at their current location in the Anegada Passage, they linked up with yet another unique craft, the catamaran-hulled submarine rescue ship, *Pelican*. This also afforded Sher his first view of the vessel that the *Pelican* was specially built to carry, the DSRV *San Clemente*.

Since this rendezvous, the *Pegasus* had been closely

working with the two one-of-a-kind ships. Their mission was to provide surface cover, while the USS *Swordfish*, a diesel-electric-powered attack submarine patroled the black depths beneath them.

It was already quite obvious that they were sharing these waters with a fully operational Soviet attack submarine. This warship had apparently taken a shot at the DSRV, while it was in the midst of what was to be the first of many trips to the sunken Russian boomer's deck. Hopefully, the *Swordfish* would be able to keep this deadly threat at bay. But for safety's sake, the *Pegasus* had been ordered to initiate almost constant patrols around the area's perimeter.

Though the hydrofoil's ASW capabilities were limited, Sher took his assignment very seriously. No less a figure than the secretary of the Navy was currently stationed aboard the *Global Explorer*, and as long as the *Pegasus* was on duty, no enemy submarine was going to be able to get off a cheap shot at the marine salvage vessel.

To cover as much of the passage as possible, they were currently employing a tactic known as sprint and drift. During this process the *Pegasus* would go foilborne at top speed before its engine was abruptly cut and the gunboat quietly settled back to the surface. At this point a hydrophone would be lowered, and the seas beneath them scanned for the enemy's presence. A negative contact would be the sign to speed off to yet another sector, where the engine would be again cut and the hydrophone lowered. This process would go on indefinitely, until either the Russians were tagged, or the gunboat's limited crew were too exhausted to continue.

They had already made one negative hydrophone scan, and Sher was relying upon his instincts to determine when the next sensor stop would take place. As the *Global Explorer* faded behind the fantail spray left in the hydrofoil's wake, he reached for his Starlight scope binoculars.

The moon had yet to rise, and the Caribbean sky was pitch-black, lit only by a myriad of twinkling stars. Powered by a single, disposable 2.7-volt DC battery, the night vision binoculars allowed him to scan the surrounding waters just as if it was daytime. The foilborne *Pegasus* at full power was far from a stable viewing platform, and since it had been almost five minutes now since their last hydrophone drop, Sher decided that this was as good a time as any to begin the drift portion of their ongoing mission.

"Mr. Moore, you can shut 'em down!" ordered Sher firmly.

As the helmsman nodded and pulled back on the throttle, Sher barked into the intercom, "Prepare to lower the hydrophone."

While the *Pegasus* settled into its new liquid medium, the gunboat's senior officer put the binoculars to his eyes and began scanning the surrounding waters. They were directly south of the *Global Explorer* now, whose deck lights twinkled in the distance.

"The hydrophone has been lowered, sir," barked the coarse voice of the sensor chief from the bulkhead-mounted intercom speaker.

Confident that the sensor equipment was working properly, Sher awaited the results of this scan while

359

continuing his study of the adjoining seas. It was while focusing the binoculars on the southwest horizon that he spotted what appeared to be an anomaly on the water's surface. Only when the sensor operator's voice frantically cried out in warning, did he realize with a start just what this unusual turbulence actually belonged to.

"Incoming torpedo, sir! Bearing two-two-zero."

Instinctively Sher's pulse quickened as every surface sailor's worst nightmare came to fruition before his horrified eyes. Yet from his almost head-on angle, Sher could see that the torpedo wasn't headed toward the *Pegasus* at all. Instead, its target appeared to be the mammoth marine salvage vessel anchored directly north of them. Well aware of the millions of dollars of sophisticated equipment and the hundreds of sailors who manned the *Global Explorer*, Sher could only think of one course of action. Since the immense ship could never have a chance of out-running the rapidly approaching weapon, the *Pegasus* would utilize her superior speed to maneuver in front of the torpedo and take the hit themselves.

Without a second's hesitation, Sher barked out to the helmsman, "Crank 'em up, Mr. Moore! Come around to course two-two-zero. We've got us a date with destiny!"

Completely unaware of the all-important decision that had just been made in the waters south of them, Secretary of the Navy Peter Anderson and Commander Richard Walker stood on the platform directly adjoining the moonpool. Before them in the pool itself, the two wet-suited figures of Dr. Susan Patton and her assistant were completing their last-minute adjustments to the lightweight plastic harness that they had just attached to Sammy's sleek body. Since getting Anderson's somewhat reluctant permission to attempt their unorthodox plan, they had been working nonstop to carry it out.

While the *Global Explorer*'s engineers went to work putting together yet another waterproof, ultra-sonic homing beacon with a magnetic base to it, Sammy's study in Soviet attack sub design began. With the invaluable assistance of a well-worn copy of *Jane's Fighting Ships*, several excellent photographs and sketches of a Russian Alfa class submarine were attained. After being cut out and sealed in a clear plastic sheet protector, the renderings were conveyed down to the moonpool. Here, Susan Patton and Owen initiated the tedious task of conditioning the dolphin to respond to the black-hulled Soviet vessel.

While Owen illuminated the photographs with a powerful, waterproof flashlight, Susan proceeded to hold Sammy's attention on them by using her whistle and a bucket of fat mullets. By using sign language, she attempted to convey to Sammy just what it was they were asking of him. Susan was pretty confident that he understood the part about placing the harness-borne magnetic beacon on the sub-marine's hull. He had already successfully completed a similar task on the sunken Typhoon, and had managed it without a flaw. What bothered her was if he grasped the fact that he was being asked to actively search out this particular vessel that could be loitering almost anywhere in the surrounding waters.

361

To get this point across, she resorted to exaggerated circular hand gestures. She had used such sign language before, when asking Sammy to seek out a hidden object that had been secretly tucked away on the bottom of their lagoon. He had never failed to locate such objects, able to recognize them because of the sketches that they had shared with him beforehand.

The sheltered confines of their lagoon was in vast contrast to the surging depths of the Anegada Passage, and Susan couldn't help but have second doubts as to Sammy's ability to locate what for all effective purposes was a needle in a haystack. Yet because there was always the slimmest chance that he would succeed, she made certain to keep these doubts to herself. Peter Anderson had seemed skeptical of the plan from the very beginning, and in an effort to prove the great potential that dolphin training had for the Navy, she was gambling that Sammy would somehow be able to prove Anderson wrong. Though it was certainly a long shot, it was genuinely exciting working on an actual operational mission. After a lifetime of rote experimentation, this was like a dream come true, even if their lives were endangered by the Soviet attack sub's continued presence.

The lapping waters of the moonpool were illuminated by a series of intense floodlights. Constantly looking down at his watch, Peter Anderson called out to the two researchers visible in the water before him, "How much longer are you going to be?"

Susan Patton answered while helping Owen put the finishing touches on the now-fitted harness. "We're just about through. Do you have the beacon?"

Quick to answer the blond researcher was Richard Walker. "I've got it right here, Susan."

The commander proceeded to bend down at the platform's edge as Susan swam over to meet him. He handed her a fist-sized metallic device, whose flat magnetic shell was specially designed to fit into the harness-borne mount.

"Like the other homing beacon, this one will automatically trigger once Sammy places it on the sub's hull," explained the still-kneeling naval officer. "This will cause its ultrasonic transmitter to activate and it will then be up to the crew of the USS *Swordfish* to take it from there. By the way, is our man of the hour still up to the task at hand?"

"He seems to be ready and willing," returned Susan, who looked on as Peter Anderson kneeled down at the commander's side.

"It's not too late to back out of this crap shoot," observed Anderson. "I'd still feel better if you, Owen, and Sammy were back safely on shore where you belong."

"Thanks for your concern, Mr. Secretary. But Sammy's primed and ready to go, and we actually think that he can pull this mission off."

Meeting Susan's response with a skeptical shake of his head, Peter Anderson somberly reflected, "Well, it won't be much longer until dawn, and there's an awful lot of water out there for Sammy to cover."

"I read you loud and clear, Mr. Secretary," replied Susan as she reached out for her whistle and put it to her lips. The briefest of high-pitched blasts followed, and in the blink of an eye, Sammy swam up to the platform's edge.

Susan clipped the homing beacon firmly in the

mount that was set into the top portion of the harness and then patted the ever-smiling dolphin affectionately on the head. "Go get them, Sammy," she whispered.

In response, the dolphin gently prodded her with his snout. As Owen joined her at the platform's edge, she climbed out of the water and again put the whistle to her lips. Yet this time she blew into it with three sharp blasts, and accompanied this distinctive signal by holding her balled fist high overhead and waving it in a wide circle.

Almost instantaneously, Sammy stood up on his tail and backed into the moonpool's center. Then with a tremendous leap, he soared up into the air and smoothly disappeared beneath the water's surface.

"He's on his way," said Susan thoughtfully.

"May God be with him," added Peter Anderson.

Owen crawled out of the water and joined them on the platform. As all four figures stared out to the glistening surface of the moonpool, a hushed silence filled the air, broken only by the constant sound of the lapping waters. Yet this moment of introspection was all too soon broken by the distant, muted boom of a powerful explosion. No sooner did this mysterious blast fade altogether when the surrounding catwalk filled with the sounds of rapidly approaching footsteps.

Seconds later, the *Global Explorer*'s XO breathlessly climbed down onto the latticed platform. Without taking the time to catch his breath, he faced Peter Anderson and spoke out excitedly. "It's the *Pegasus*, Mr. Secretary. We believe that they just got hit by a torpedo!"

A look of pained concern crossed Anderson's face as he replied, "Are you certain it was the *Pegasus*, Lieutenant?"

The XO nodded. "That's affirmative, sir. One of our lookouts watched the whole thing come down through a night scope. He says that one moment they were foilborne and really trucking, and the next nothing but a ball of flame and smoke. The captain has ordered out the rescue launch, but it doesn't appear that there's going to be much to haul in."

"Damn it to hell!" cursed Anderson angrily. "I should have pulled us all out of here the moment we first got wind of that Soviet attack sub's presence."

"Don't blame yourself, Mr. Secretary," offered Richard Walker. "How were you to know that Ivan was about to go on a shooting rampage?"

Anderson stared out vacantly to the waters of the moonpool. "It should have only been too obvious, Commander. After all, we do have an awfully damn important piece of their property lying on the sea floor beneath us. And who would have ever doubted that they would surrender it without a struggle."

"The *Swordfish* will eventually hunt them down all right," commented Richard Walker. "And besides, now we've got Sammy out there working for us."

The mere mention of the American attack sub caused Peter Anderson to angrily mutter, "Damn it, Ted, find those Red bastards!"

Almost in response to this passionate remark, the *Global Explorer* rocked in the grasp of a sudden swell. Reaching out to the handrail to balance himself, the secretary of the Navy looked out to the surging waters and wondered if his nephew's thirty-year-old command would be able to successfully meet the great challenge that was being asked of them. For American blood had already been shed, and hundreds of other lives, including Peter's own, now lay at risk, unless the *Swordfish* could prove itself this one last, all-important time.

Chapter Fifteen

From a submerged depth of two hundred and fifty feet, the sound of the exploding torpedo was clearly audible. Brad Bodzin listened to this deafening blast, and was also able to hear the gut-wrenching sound of rending metal as the unfortunate vessel hit by this powerful blast split in half and quickly sank into the quiet depths below.

Though his fatigue was starting to catch up with him, the explosion served to cause a new rush of adrenaline to surge through his body. His previously exhausted state was hardly noticeable as he visualized the carnage this thunderous blast had most likely caused.

One noise that was conspicuously absent was the distinctive grinding roar of the foilborne gunship. Brad had been in the process of monitoring the gunship's incredible sprint over the waters lying on the southern portion of their patrol sector when the torpedo took them down.

What made this tragic event even more frustrating

was the disturbing fact that the vessel responsible for launching this attack was still not registering on their sensors. This could only mean that the Russian sub had scrammed its reactor and had activated some sort of novel masking device that made them for all effective purposes invisible to the *Swordfish*'s sonar.

Brad was certain that they'd chance upon the Soviets sooner or later. But they had already managed to carry out two torpedo attacks, and the next one could be directed at either the *Swordfish*, or even worse, the marine salvage vessel they had been sent into these waters to protect.

Stifling a yawn, Bodzin sat up straight in his chair, readjusted his headphones, and reinitiated his intensive scan of the surrounding seas. Since the *Pegasus* got hit, they had moved into the sector that the hydrofoil had been patroling, and he could just make out the sputtering signature of a motor launch topside. This craft was probably sent from the *Global Explorer* to check for survivors. Seriously doubting that there'd be much left to find, the petty officer second class momentarily found himself discouraged with his inability to tag the bastards responsible for this unprovoked carnage.

It proved to be a warm hand on his shoulder that served to redirect his irate ponderings. Looking up to see who this newcomer was, Brad took in the concerned face of their captain.

"How are you holding up, son?" quizzed Ted Anderson somberly.

Genuinely surprised by the officer's presence, Brad quickly responded, "I'm doing just fine, sir. Though I'm afraid I can't say the same for our shipmates topside. It sounds like the *Global Explorer* has sent out a rescue launch, but I'm almost positive that our hydrofoil took a direct hit. It's extremely doubtful that there will be any survivors."

"There's always that one in a million chance," reflected the captain, whose tone suddenly intensified. "Any luck tracking down Ivan?"

"Negative, sir," answered Brad.

"Well, don't lose all hope yet, sailor. I just got the word from the *Global Explorer* that they're trying a little trick that could give us a big hand. As unbelievable as it might sound, they're using that same dolphin who initially chanced upon the disabled Typhoon, to track down our current adversary."

Stunned by this revelation, Bodzin's face lit up with wonder. "That's incredible, Captain. How in the hell are they going about doing it?"

Ted Anderson sardonically grinned. "Though they didn't have the time to share all the juicy details, we've been instructed to be on the lookout for an ultrasonic homing beacon that will be broadcasting on a frequency of about twenty thousand cycles per second. The receipt of this signal will be our invitation to shoot."

"They must be relying on that dolphin to place the beacon on the Soviet vessel's hull," observed Bodzin wonderingly. "But how in the hell is he going to locate Ivan if we can't even find them?"

The captain shook his head. "Ours is not to reason why, sailor. Just be on your toes, and let me know the second that such a frequency is received.

"Now, are you going to be able to remain on duty much longer? If I'm not mistaken, this is the start of

369

your third straight shift. Though I'd hate to lose my best man, you won't be doing me much good if you're too exhausted to properly monitor the equipment."

Brad patted the half-filled mug of black coffee that lay in its holder on the ledge before him. "I'm so flushed with caffeine now that I couldn't sleep even if I wanted to, Captain. So you needn't worry about me. I'll manage, just for the sake of revenging those sailors who didn't make it topside."

"You're a credit to your uniform, Mr. Bodzin. Good hunting!"

Stirred by this brief, unexpected encounter, Brad watched as the captain pivoted and began his way out of the cramped compartment. A new sense of duty guided his movements as he returned his glance to the familiar black plastic knobs and tinted digital readouts of the sonar panel.

With a familiarity born out of thousands of hours of practice, he reinitiated yet another intensive sonar scan. This one was directed into the black depths of the sector they were just entering. As the *Swordfish* continued at quarter speed on a course due southward, they were increasingly moving away from the *Global Explorer*, and into the central portion of the Anegada Passage. Though there was an immense amount of territory to cover, it was most likely somewhere in this sector the Soviets had launched their torpedo from.

To assist in his renewed search effort, Brad tightened the fit of his headphones and turned up the volume gain. The natural surging sounds of the sea met his ears, and he delicately adjusted the angle of each individual, hull-mounted hydrophone to moni-

370

tor each square inch of water that lay before them.

After a quarter of an hour passed, and his monotonous, frustrating duty still failed to show results, Brad issued a wide yawn and allowed his great fatigue to finally get the best of him. Unable to halt the natural movement of his heavy eyelids, he momentarily dozed off, only to reawaken seconds later when his hand dropped the pencil he had been clutching.

Too tired to chastise himself for this brief respite, he reached over to take a sip of coffee. But his bitter drink had long since gone cold, and not bothering to refill it, he turned back to his console, with his intentions set on continuing his duty.

Barely a minute passed before his eyelids once again slammed shut. Yet this time he failed to immediately reawaken. His sleep was sound and deep, his dreams quick in coming. In this vision, he found himself swimming in a calm blue sea, with thousands of gaily frolicking dolphins surrounding him. The excited sounds of their high-pitched clicks, whistles, and groans filled the air like a symphony, and Brad gloried in utter happiness.

It was as he looked to his right that he picked out the sleek body of a particularly beautiful dolphin that had been pacing his own stroke. The glistening marine mammal sported a wide grin, mischievous eyes, and, strangely enough, seemed to be wearing a clear plastic harness of some sort. Disturbed by this realization, Brad impotently looked on as the dolphins suddenly shot away from him, leaving him alone in the water, which had turned cold and agitated. And it was then he felt the malevolent presence, creeping up from the dark depths like a hungry shark in the midst of a feeding frenzy.

Brad snapped from his dream at this point, and awoke with a start. Quickly reorienting himself, he looked to the digital clock that graced the console before him and breathed a sigh of relief upon noting that he had only been asleep less than three minutes. Yet, strangely enough, one element of his recently experienced dream had miraculously returned to haunt him. Flowing into his ears from his head-phones was a boisterous racket of high-pitched clicks, whistles, and groans that could only be originating from an immense herd of passing dolphins!

He efficiently isolated this herd's exact coordinates. The dolphins filled the seas in front of the *Swordfish* for almost a solid square mile. This would indicate that there were literally tens of thousands of animals currently transiting the channel. Such a realization brought a wide grin to Brad's lips, for the playful marine mammals had always been close to his heart.

Wishing that they were at periscope depth so that he could get a look at the leaping herd, Brad momentarily flashed back to his disturbing dream and realized that this was the second time that it had occurred. And now for them to be actually passing through a similar conglomeration of dolphins was absolutely mind boggling!

Was it a strange coincidence, or was his dream but a presentiment of things to come? Though he really couldn't say for sure, the wide-awake Texan reapplied his effort with renewed intensity, concentrating the sub's hydrophones on the black depths below the leaping herd. It was from that direction that the cold, black, evil essence he had sensed in his vision had seemed to emanate.

And from the seas immediately before the *Swordfish*, Sammy was also pondering the incredibly immense herd of dolphins he had just chanced upon. Drawn to these waters by a rumbling explosion, he arrived here with his task firmly in mind. Yet his viewing of thousands of his fellow species had diverted his thoughts away from those of his duty. Caught up in the excitement of the swiftly moving pack, he swam along with his brethren, who were headed toward the open seas to feed and mate.

It was from such a herd that Sammy had been plucked as a youngster. Though he had been confused and frightened at this traumatic time, the humans who had captured him were kind and understanding. They took him from the water, and transferred him to a small tank on dry land. It was here that the humans fed him, taught him tricks, and spoke to him in their strange language. And after he had properly adjusted to his confinement, one of their females joined him in the tank, and for two full moon cycles it wasn't so lonely anymore.

Yet the humans had abruptly left one day after depositing him back into the open seas from which he came. This was a sad time, for he had gotten used to their presence, and he returned to the lagoon from which he used to do tricks for them and receive fat mullets in return. But the shores were empty, and were to stay that way until the yellow-haired human female arrived many moon cycles later. It was this same individual who fitted him with the strange harness that he currently wore, and sent him into the depths to search out the sleek, black-hulled objects that were many times larger than even a full-grown killer whale.

Sammy truly enjoyed his contacts with man, but the call of his fellow dolphins was an overpowering one and he instinctively surrendered to the flow of the herd. Soon to take up a position beside him was a beautiful female. Sighting her caused an alien heaviness to possess him, and he gradually worked his way over to gently touch her smooth flanks with his snout. She seemed to welcome his touch, and after inhaling a full lungful of air, dove downward into the cool depths below. Sammy followed close behind, and as they continued spiraling deeper and deeper, he finally caught up to her. Their bodies again touched, yet before he could finalize their bond, an alien presence drew his attention to the waters beyond. Floating silently here, seemingly filling the entire sea with its immense proportions, was a most familiar sleek black object. Exactly matching the representation shown to him by his new teacher, this sighting caused him to momentarily forget the female dolphin who had led him here.

As she gently nudged him with her snout, Sammy found himself beyond temptation, so strong was the conditioning that guided him. Oblivious to her protests, he continued on to the black behemoth, not stopping until he had delivered the object that he carried above his head to the hard blackness, where it stuck with a soft click.

*   *   *

Lieutenant Igor Kasimov was monitoring the passage of an immense herd of dolphins directly above the loitering *Kirov*, when a sharp metallic tap temporarily diverted his attention. Seeming to come from somewhere on the sub's sail, he intently scanned the adjoining waters. Yet when the brief alien sound failed to repeat itself, he shrugged his shoulders, and deciding that it was a mere anomaly, returned his attention to the passing herd.

Never had he heard such a tremendous concentration of marine mammals before. They seemed to fill the entire passage, their high-pitched whistles and clicks filling the seas with a sonorous resonance.

The redheaded Estonian had always had a genuine dislike for such creatures. Descended from a long line of fishermen, he knew dolphins to be nothing but worthless pests, who stole their catch and fouled their nets. Together with their cousins the whales, the vociferous animals made his current job equally difficult. For how was one to properly listen for the approach of the enemy when the cries of the dolphins filled his headphones with nothing but their incessant chattering?

Making the most out of every filtering device available to him, Kasimov did his best to screen out the high-frequency tones and concentrated his scan on the sound waves occupying the lower portion of the sonic spectrum. No sooner did he initiate this process when an alien, low-pitched throbbing sound emanated from the waters due north of them. Barely audible, this muted hum was disturbingly familiar. Kasimov had heard a similar signature before, when the *Kirov* was participating in combined ASW exercises with one of the many diesel-electric-powered submarines that still served with the Soviet Fleet. Though such vessels didn't need the often noisy coolant pumps that a nuclear vessel relied upon, their propellors still produced a distinctive cavitation signature. Almost certain that this was what he was hearing, the senior sonar technician turned to share his discovery with the attack center's current OOD.

"Senior Lieutenant Arbatov, I believe I've picked up a submerged contact, bearing three-four-zero. The signature is weak, and it appears to be coming from a diesel-electric propulsion system."

Hastily crossing the compartment to join him, the *Kirov*'s second-in-command clipped on the auxiliary headphones. He intently listened for a moment before thoughtfully responding, "That certainly does sound like a diesel-electric, Lieutenant. Yet if that's the case, I wonder who it belongs to? If I'm not mistaken, the American submarine fleet is an all-nuclear one."

Walking over to the nearest vacant computer keyboard, Senior Lieutenant Arbatov entered a single query. He didn't have to wait long until the information he requested flashed onto the monitor.

"Ah, so it appears that I'm mistaken. The Americans indeed have one last diesel-electric-powered vessel in service, the USS *Swordfish*, based out of San Diego. From what it says in the Admiralty files, this same boat is due to be retired sometime this year, and no fossil-fueled replacements are projected to take its place."

"Then perhaps this is the identity of the contact we just picked up," observed the sonar technician.

The senior lieutenant smugly grinned. "If it is, I pity the poor American crew. The *Kirov* will take out the thirty-year-old vessel before they know what hit them."

Reaching out for the nearby intercom handset, he proceeded to page the *Kirov*'s captain, who was last seen headed on his way to the torpedo room.

Alexander Gnutov was immersed in a spirited conversation with both his political officer and his weapons chief when the call from the attack center reached him. Taking in the senior lieutenant's suspicions as to the identity of the submarine that prowled the waters north of them, the captain coolly ordered Ganady Arbatov to continue keeping the *Kirov* sealed in a state of ultra-quiet. After promising to return to the control room shortly, Alexander disconnected the intercom and caught the expectant stares of the two officers who stood anxiously before him.

"Well, Comrades, it appears that we have some additional company in the waters north of us. From its initial signature, it sounds like we've got a diesel-electric submarine on the prowl. Senior Lieutenant Arbatov feels that it could very well be the American ship, USS *Swordfish*, which is the last such vessel in their fleet."

"Will we be engaging it, Captain?" quizzed the weapons officer.

"The answer to that question is only too obvious," interceded the zampolit. "Since our last attack failed to take out its intended target, the American salvage threat is still a very real one. To guarantee the *Caspian*'s continued integrity, we must do everything within our power to keep these waters ours to do with as we please. And that means that no American attack subs must be allowed to interfere, no matter how obsolete they might be. Maybe this will be a target that our torpedoes will be able to accurately hit."

Well aware that the political officer's unfounded innuendo was directed at the *Kirov*'s weapons crew, the burly, mustached chief took immediate offense. "Now hold on a minute, Comrade Pavlodar. You can't blame us for our torpedo's premature detonation. Don't forget that we were utilizing an impact fuse. And how were we to know that our torpedo would end up smacking into an American gunboat instead of the marine salvage vessel?"

Alexander Gnutov spoke up before their spirited discussion got further out of hand. "No one's putting any blame on your crew, Chief. They did their jobs just as ordered. Yet we can all be thankful that our original target remains unscathed. It's now apparent that the noise we assumed to be the reinitiated salvage effort was but the sound of the gunboat's turbojet engines. Thus if our torpedo had run true, hundreds of innocent men could have lost their lives, and the world would be engulfed in a war that would have no winners."

"Did you say innocent men, Captain?" repeated the astounded zampolit. "You've got to be kidding me! How can you hold the imperialists blameless, when it's only too obvious that they were responsible for the *Caspian*'s sinking in the first place? If you ask me, we must eliminate this attack sub at once, and then turn our attentions back to the *Global Explorer*. To do otherwise would be an act of irresponsibility of the first degree!"

This passionate remark was punctuated by the ringing intercom. Quick to answer it, the captain absorbed yet another briefing from his senior lieutenant. Alexander's introspective mood turned increasingly somber as he curtly replied and hung up the handset.

"It appears that our hand is yet again being forced in this matter, Comrades," observed the captain, "for the enemy submarine continues its approach. It will be well within attack range shortly, and even with our masking device in operation, we can't take the chance of escaping its sensors. That means the only prudent course open to us is to eliminate this vessel before its threat intensifies.

"Chief, load tubes three and four with acoustic-homing antisubmarine torpedoes. Interface them with sonar, and transfer their release to the attack center, where I'll personally direct the launch. And this time, I guarantee you that our attack will not fail!"

"For the sake of the Motherland you'd better hope that this is the case," gloomily reflected the zampolit. "Because if the *Kirov* were to be somehow eliminated, there would be absolutely nothing to stand in the way of the *Global Explorer* and the realization of our worst fears. No matter the risks, we must not let such an unthinkable thing happen!"

A tense, dismal mood prevailed as Alexander Gnutov met this disheartening observation with a heavy sigh and unceremoniously pivoted to get on with his all-important duty.

Chapter Sixteen

In the control room of the USS *Swordfish* a mournful mood prevailed. They had just witnessed the sinking of a U.S. Navy warship, and the crew couldn't help but feel somewhat responsible for the hydrofoil's demise.

Nowhere was this depression more noticeable than around the ship's navigation table. Here Ted Anderson, William Abbott, and Ensign Steve Delano, the sub's navigator, huddled around the bathymetric chart of the Anegada Passage. A bright red X showed the spot where the *Pegasus* had gotten hit, while their current course was drawn in blue and occupied the waters directly south of the X.

"I still say that Ivan's original target was the *Global Explorer*," observed William Abbott. "By the grace of God the crew of the *Pegasus* most likely saw the torpedo's wake and nobly sacrificed themselves, saving the lives of over three hundred of their fellow sailors, and the secretary of the Navy as well."

Ted Anderson nodded and pointed to the waters

they were presently penetrating. "If that's the case, the best angle of attack is somewhere in this sector. yet where the hell are they? Except for that herd of dolphins, Sonar has come up with a complete blank. Even if they scrammed, we should be receiving a minimal return of some sort."

"I think that they moved out of here right after they last launched," offered the young navigator. "If their primary target remains the *Global Explorer*, I'd say that the next clearest shot would be attempted from the sector just west of us."

"That could very well be the case, son," returned William Abbott. "But why didn't we hear them high-tailing it out of here at the time? Unless our sonar boys were napping, we were cruising right over the most logical transit lane Ivan would have used to re-position themselves. So unless they moved off to the east, my gut instincts tell me that those Russkies are playing possum, right under our very noses."

Ted Anderson reached down to the chart and pointed out an elongated geological feature that graced that portion of the passage they were currently passing over. "It looks like we've got some kind of elevated shelf beneath us at about a thousand feet. On either side of this ledge, the depth falls off drastically. Not even one of their titanium-hulled Alfas could reach the bottom of those trenches."

"Not in one piece at least," retorted the white-haired veteran with a wise wink.

A sudden commotion broke from that portion of the control room lying immediately behind them, and all three officers looked up in time to see the figure of the rapidly approaching XO.

"Bodzin's tagged them, Skipper!" exclaimed Stan Pukalani. "That ultrasonic homing beacon that we were warned to be on the lookout for just showed up on the oscilloscope. Their range is approximately twenty thousand yards, on a bearing of one-six-five."

William Abbott hurriedly replied, "That would put them in the waters just south of us! I knew I smelled those Red bastards close by. Let's put 'em away, Ted, and show Ivan that Uncle Sam means business."

Not hesitating to ponder what he had to do next, Ted Anderson's voice barked out commandingly, "Sound general quarters, Mr. Pukalani, and have weapons load up a full complement of Mk-48's! Target them to home in on that beacon. We'll launch from up here."

"Aye, aye, Skipper," returned the XO, turning to efficiently relay this directive.

As the muted chimes sending the men scurrying to their battle stations rang throughout the ship, Ted Anderson and William Abbott quickly crossed over to the fire-control console. With an expertise perfected after thousands of hours of rote practice, Anderson primed the system that would allow him to personally coordinate all phases of the attack. All too soon a series of six green lights indicated that the requested torpedo tubes were loaded and ready to fire.

"So we're finally going to actually see what kind of punch this old lady can deliver," remarked Abbott as he watched his protégé complete a final series of last-minute adjustments to the console. "I realize that it's a primitive emotion, but revenge is going to be awfully sweet in this instance, Ted. We've got a crew of damn fine sailors to answer for, and the great sacrifice that the *Pegasus* made mustn't be in vain. So do your duty, son, and damn the frigging consequences!''

Anderson listened to these remarks, and as he armed the warheads of the first four torpedoes, the reality of his actions finally hit home. After almost three decades of intensive training, and so many nerve-wracking close calls, he was finally going in harm's way.

As a veteran cold warrior, he had been ordered to the brink and then called back so many times that he often wondered if his weapons systems even worked. He breathed a sigh of relief when he triggered the first of six toggle switches and watched as the console indicated that torpedo door number one had successfully opened.

"At least we don't have the same problem with this system that plagued your first patrol on the *Swordfish*, Ted," reflected William Abbott.

A nervous tenseness gathered in the pit of Anderson's stomach as he prepared to depress the blinking red launch button.

"Thank goodness for that," he breathlessly managed. "Well, so much for détente. Fire one!"

From the ship's sonar room, the sound of the torpedo leaving its tube in a frothing current of compressed air was magnified a hundred times over. Having had to turn down the sensor array's volume gain significantly to keep from injuring his ears, Brad Bodzin listened as the first of the torpedoes surged off toward its target, its engine whining away with a vengeance. Three other weapons followed, their signatures soon blending into a buzzing cacophony of deadly sound.

Brad closely monitored their progress, and was aware that the *Swordfish* had just made a drastic move that could have consequences far larger than the loss of a single Soviet submarine. The very nature of Brad's daily duty made him no stranger to the tense state of world affairs. He had encountered his share of Russian vessels in his time. And though he never took these confrontations lightly, the possibility of actually becoming involved in a shooting war never really crossed his mind. He had always thought that the two superpowers were too intelligent to participate in such a no-win conflict, especially if nuclear weapons were involved. For he was certain that such an exchange would signal man's extinction as a species.

As he continued monitoring the high-pitched whine of the speeding torpedoes, he sensed the historical significance of this moment. Brave men had already died, and more would soon follow. But unless the Soviet Union and the United States put this tragic encounter in its proper perspective, the lives of hundreds of millions of innocent men, women, and children would be put in jeopardy. The horrors of nuclear war were beyond comprehension. Yet could the ever-spiraling pyramid of military reprisal strike and counterstrike ever hope to be controlled once the nuclear genie had been released from its bottle?

Seriously doubting that it could be, Brad sat

tensely forward, and ever so gradually increased his console's volume gain. The four torpedoes continued onward like a single lethal entity. Yet barely audible in the distance was a radically new signature, almost a twin of the one he had been in the process of monitoring. It was a split second later that a sobering revelation dawned in Brad's consciousness. For this additional racket could only mean but one thing— that they were currently under a torpedo attack themselves! A cold sweat was already forming on his forehead as he reached out for the intercom handset to inform the control room of this terrifying fact.

At about this exact same moment, Lieutenant Igor Kasimov, sonar operator of the Alfa class attack submarine *Kirov*, had made a similar shocking discovery. With his heart beating madly away in his chest, the redheaded Estonian counted four separate torpedoes headed straight for them. Struggling to find the words to express himself, he cried out in alarm, "Incoming torpedoes! I count four of them, coming in at maximum range on bearing zero-five-zero."

"But that can't be!" returned the shocked zampolit, who stood beside the sonar console, monitoring the progress of their own attack. "They could never find us because of our masking system."

Not bothering to respond to this comment, Alexander Gnutov hurried over to Lieutenant Kasimov's side. He threw on the auxiliary headphones, closed his eyes, and attempted to sort out the assortment of audible sounds. Beyond the loud

385

constant grinding roar of their own torpedoes rose a distant, high-pitched whine that seemed to overpower all the other ambient sound. Positive that the sonar operator had properly identified this racket, a cold chill of awareness streaked up Alexander's spine. Ripping off the headphones, he frantically addressed his senior lieutenant.

"Ganady, for our very lives get that reactor back on line and give me speed! We've got an entire Yankee salvo coming our way!"

"But the masking device," protested the zampolit. "How can they attack what they can't see?"

"To hell with that damn masking device!" screamed Alexander. "We need speed and we need it now!"

Rushing over to join the senior lieutenant at the engineering station, Alexander watched as Ganady Arbatov furiously addressed the computer keyboard. His frenzied efforts soon paid off as the *Kirov*'s reactor went critical and they ever so gradually began building a head of steam.

To take advantage of each and every knot of available speed, Alexander next sprinted over to the seated helmsman and pushed the airplanelike steering wheel abruptly downward. While holding it in this position, the captain called out to the sub's diving officer, "Rig the ship for maximum depth and take us down, Comrade Suratov! Our lives are depending upon you."

As the *Kirov* began taking on additional ballast, Alexander handed the wheel back to the helmsman. Slowly the deck began to slope downward stern first, and the captain found himself having to hold on to the adjoining brass handrail to keep from losing his footing. Desperately reaching out to grab this same railing was Ivan Pavlodar. The zampolit's pasty forehead was covered in sweat, his black eyes wide with fear, as he frantically voiced his concern.

"How can this be happening to us, Captain? Surely another submarine almost three times our age couldn't possibly be responsible for this. They must have an accomplice."

With his eyes glued to the digital speed indicator, Alexander responded, "It makes little difference now, Comrade Zampolit. I have only one concern, that being to save this ship and all those inside it. Everything else is meaningless."

Frustrated at their pitiful progress, the captain directed his next blast at his senior lieutenant. "For Lenin's sake, Ganady, give me some speed, man! There's no time for caution. Open those throttles wide, and get us out of these cursed waters!"

The *Kirov*'s angle of descent abruptly steepened, and while struggling to remain standing, Alexander noted a full two-knot increase in their speed indicator. Yet he had little time to celebrate as Lieutenant Kasimov's voice forcefully projected itself for all to hear.

"The torpedoes continue to gain on us, Captain! The range is down to fifteen thousand meters and closing."

Doing his best to will the speed indicator forward, Alexander watched as it began steadily jumping forward in two-knot increments. When it finally passed the fifteen-knot barrier, he knew that the cold engines would either stall at this point, or give them

387

everything they asked for. Only when they broke the twenty-knot threshold was he absolutely certain that the *Kirov*'s remarkable propulsion plant was not going to fail them.

Quickly now, the digital counter began progressively increasing. The deck beneath them seemed to shudder in response to this incredibly sudden burst of speed, and Alexander momentarily found his gloom dissipating. New hope surged through his being, as he called out to the navigator, "Lieutenant Natya, what does it look like beneath us?"

Hurriedly scanning his instruments, the navigator answered, "The bathymeter indicates a deep trench over three thousand meters below us, Captain."

Though the *Kirov*'s titanium hull could only withstand but a third of this depth, Alexander's spirits further lightened. "That's excellent news, Comrade. With plenty of water beneath us to work with, and our forward speed already on the increase, we just might yet escape this snare."

"But how are we ever going to do that?" questioned the trembling political officer.

Making the most out of the zampolit's panic, Alexander took his time voicing a response. "We will escape the Yankee torpedoes by merely outdiving and outrunning them, Comrade Pavlodar. Have you already forgotten the remarkable nature of this vessel? For what other submarine on this planet can run faster than even the speediest of torpedoes?"

A look of utter confidence masked the captain's face as he returned his glance to the helm. Here the bulkhead-mounted speed indicator showed a digital readout of twenty-seven knots. They were already traveling at a speed that the majority of submariners would be most satisfied with. Yet to effect their escape, the *Kirov* would almost double this figure, putting them in a realm all their own.

"The torpedoes continue to close, Captain. Range is 11,500 meters."

Calmly absorbing the sonar technician's observation, Alexander mentally calculated that they still had plenty of time to reach full speed before the torpedoes would catch up with them. And once this velocity was achieved, no underwater weapon on the planet would be able to reach them.

In a nearby portion of the passage, the USS *Swordfish* was in the midst of its own desperate escape attempt. From the vessel's hushed control room its captain was also in the process of mentally calculating how much time they had left before the torpedoes reached them. Unfortunately, Ted Anderson's command could only hope to attain but a fraction of the forward velocity that the nuclear-powered *Kirov* was capable of reaching. That meant that merely attempting to outrun the two weapons headed their way would be but a wasted effort.

Solemnly gathered beside the chart table, with William Abbott and his XO close beside him, Anderson listened as the latest update arrived over the mounted intercom speakers from Sonar.

"The torpedoes have just broken the ten-thousand-yard threshold, Captain. Their course and speed remain true and constant."

Glancing over to the helm, Ted took in their

current speed of thirty knots. This was just about at the limit of their propulsion plant's capacity. Though such a velocity was certainly nothing to be ashamed of, it merely acted to postpone the inevitable temporarily.

"If only we were carrying another Mk-70 decoy," reflected the XO. "At least that would give us a decent chance of making good an escape."

The captain somberly nodded. "Right now, I'd just settle for a decent thermocline, or another school of squid for that matter. Because we need something to help get those two fish off our tail."

"Why don't you try another series of evasive maneuvers, Ted?" offered William Abbott. "It sure as hell beats doing nothing."

"I guess you're right, Admiral," replied Anderson as he directed his next remark to the helmsman. "Bring us hard aport, Mr. Conlin, on bearing one-zero-zero."

The alert helmsman repeated this order and turned the rudder abuptly to the left. In response, the *Swordfish* canted over hard on its side, its hull groaning and creaking with the ensuing strain.

Forced to grab a handrail tightly to keep from tumbling over, Anderson waited until their new course was reached before addressing the helmsman once again. "Bring us around to bearing two-eight-zero, Mr. Conlin. And make it crisp!"

This time turning the wheel in the opposite direction, the helmsman guided the *Swordfish* in a tight turn to the starboard. The hull once more moaned in protest as the angle of the deck pitched hard on its right side, and those not secured by seat harnesses found themselves fighting to keep their balance.

With the slim hope that the resulting turbulence would throw the torpedoes off course, Ted Anderson anxiously listened as the intercom filled with the cool voice of Brad Bodzin.

"The range is down to seven thousand yards, Captain. Our last maneuver didn't seem to fool 'em in the least."

"Damn it!" cursed Anderson, whose rising frustration was rapidly leading him to the breaking point.

"Easy now, son," softly cautioned the white-haired veteran who stood close at the captain's side. "If we can't out turn them, maybe we can lose them by putting a little knuckle in the water."

Briefly catching Abbott's unruffled glance, Ted turned to check out the chart table. It was as he scanned the bathymetric chart to see what the surrounding depths had in store for them that a familiar subterranean feature suddenly caught his attention.

"That submerged ridge below us!" he excitedly observed. "If we can dive straight for it and then manage to pull up at the last second, maybe we can lead those torpedoes smack into it."

"Sounds good to me, Ted," retorted Abbott. "Let's do it."

Hastily calculating a new course, Anderson barked out to the helmsman, "Take us down, Mr. Conlin, to nine hundred and fifty feet, on bearing zero-two-zero."

"But that's below our maximum test depth!" countered the perplexed XO.

Meeting the Hawaiian's concerned stare, Ted Anderson emotionally responded, "If you can offer any alternatives, I'm more than willing to listen, Stan. But right now, this is the only way I see to shake those torpedoes. So if we want to live to fight another day, we'd better seal up this old lady good and tight and see what this hull is really made out of."

"She can make it, all right," added a very confident William Abbott. "Don't forget, they don't make them like this anymore."

This remark was met by a sudden downward pitch of the deck. Tightening their grasps to keep from sliding forward, the three senior officers looked out to the diving console, where the two seated helmsmen were pushing down on their steering columns. In response, the vessel's hydroplanes bit into the surrounding seawater, and the ship's bow angled down into the black, cold depths below.

As they passed the four-hundred-foot level, the sub's valves, seals, and other vulnerable fittings began to strain under a pressure of over three hunded and fifty pounds per square inch. Yet ever deeper they went, until the hull itself was groaning in protest.

The depth indicator had just clicked off seven hundred and fifty-three feet when the voice of sonarman Brad Bodzin broke over the intercom. "The range is down to 4,500 yards, Captain. The torpedoes are coming right down after us."

"It's going to be close, my friends," reflected William Abbott stoically.

A thin band of sweat had formed on Ted Anderson's forehead as he ardently commented, "Come on, *Swordfish*, hold together just a little bit longer. You can do it."

The captain's XO fingered the golden crucifix that hung from his neck, while throughout the ship, similar silent petitions were being offered. These prayers intensified as the *Swordfish* plunged beneath the nine-hundred-foot level and entered a heretofore unvisited realm where the sub's hull could rip wide open at any moment.

"We're doing it, Captain Gnutov! We're actually outrunning the Yankee torpedoes! The latest range is two thousand meters and constantly falling."

The spirited report of the joyous sonar operator was met by a round of relieved sighs from the attack center's complement. Nowhere was this relief more apparent than on the face of the *Kirov*'s zampolit. Wiping his fat cheeks dry with his already soaked handkerchief, Ivan Pavlodar looked like a man on death row who had unexpectedly received a reprieve. Though the sub's continued abrupt angle of descent necessitated that he tightly grasp the brass handrail to keep from sliding into the forward bulkhead, the zampolit managed to voice his relief. "It appears that you were correct, Comrade Gnutov. In my moment of doubt and panic, I forgot the remarkable nature of the vessel I've been assigned to serve on. The *Kirov* is truly the most incredible attack platform ever to sail the seas, and all of us owe the ingenious engineers who designed her a hearty round of thanks."

"There'll hopefully be plenty of time for that later, Comrade Zampolit," returned the captain, who hung onto an adjoining portion of the handrail.

"But right now, there are much more important concerns for us to focus on, for as long as those torpedoes remain on our tail, we are not yet out of danger."

Glancing over to the helm, Alexander efficiently scanned the instruments. The velocity indicator showed an unprecedented fifty-three knots of forward speed, while the depth gauge put them eight hundred and seventy-five meters beneath the water's surface. Even the *Kirov* would be forced to break from this dive shortly as they entered a portion of the sea three times deeper than the average submarine could ever hope to safely visit.

"Something's happening to the Yankee torpedoes, Captain!" screamed the sonar officer from his harness-mounted chair. "They've either run out of fuel, or perhaps it's the great depth, but they seem to have halted their pursuit."

Tightly pressing his headphones over his ears, the redheaded Estonian triumphantly added, "That's affirmative, Captain, their engines have stopped altogether! We've done it, sir, we've escaped them!"

As an excited chorus of relieved cheers rose from all those assembled in the attack center, Alexander Gnutov barked out forcefully, "Lieutenant Suratov, remove our diving angle. Senior Lieutenant Arbatov, reverse engines, back emergency. It's time to ascend from these depths and make sure that the bastards responsible for this attack are properly taken care of!"

Briefly meeting the zampolit's respectful gaze, Alexander found his thoughts unexpectedly returning back in time, to his recent hunt in the hills of his

394

birthplace. It was during his confrontation with the Ural brown bear that he had become aware of a primal secret of life he could readily apply to their present circumstances. For it was technological brilliance, high intellect, and sheer cunning that had allowed the crew of the *Kirov* to survive, while their weaker adversary would surely perish.

To guarantee this, the captain decided that once the American attack sub was finished, the *Kirov* would turn its attentions back to the *Global Explorer*. And the United States would all too soon be forced to pay the ultimate price for their greedy, imperialistic ambitions. Relishing these events to come, Alexander was abruptly forced to turn his attention back to the helm, when the diving officer's voice cried out frantically, "I'm unable to reverse the diving angle, Captain! We seem to have lost all of our hydraulics!"

This shocking revelation was reinforced by the equally horrified voice of the *Kirov*'s senior lieutenant. "The engines aren't responding to my back bell, Captain! It must be a result of that quick start, but the throttle seems to be frozen wide open!"

"But that's impossible!" retorted the captain. "Override the computer, and reverse the engines manually if necessary, but cut our forward speed this instant, Comrade Arbatov! And Lieutenant Suratov, you must do the same to our hydraulics system. If we can't pull out of this dive, we'll be doomed!"

The depth gauge had already registered nine hundred and fifty meters. And with their propulsion plant continuing to spew out a furious fifty-three knots of forward velocity, the *Kirov* was entering a portion of the ocean that not even its titanium-reinforced hull could protect them from. Unable to let go of the handrail for fear of crashing into the forward bulkhead, Alexander could only watch as his subordinates frantically addressed their individual consoles.

As the *Kirov*'s hull began to ominously moan and creak around them, the ship's zampolit cleared his dry throat and managed to timidly express himself. "And to think that we came so very close to succeeding, Comrade. Will our end be quick?"

Somberly nodding that it would, Alexander Gnutov returned the political officer's horror-filled gaze, as the *Kirov*'s depth gauge broke the one thousand meter mark.

Petty Officer Second Class Brad Bodzin continued monitoring the approach of the two Russian torpedoes and figured that it would be three minutes at the very most before the *Swordfish* would be hit. Having long ago lost the signature of the vessel responsible for launching this attack, Brad's headphones were filled with a sickening metallic whine that reminded him of the cries of a frenzied banshee from another realm.

From the steep pitch of the deck and the throbbing hum of the *Swordfish*'s engines, it was apparent that their skipper was valiantly trying to outrun the torpedoes. But this was a losing cause, and the two weapons easily kept up with them, all the while increasingly closing the distance between the primed warheads and the vessel's stern.

The Texan accepted their fate and found himself unusually calm. Death had always seemed unreal to him, and now that its grim specter was only minutes away, his purpose in life was suddenly clear. They would take the wrath of the Russian torpedoes, and the world would somehow react to this wasteful tragedy by demanding that their leaders return to their senses and bilaterally disarm. Only then would their sacrifice be a worthy one.

With this hope in mind, he picked up the intercom handset and dully spoke into its transmitter. "The torpedoes continue closing, Captain. Range is down to one thousand yards."

In the ship's control room on the deck above, this emotionless observation was received with an anxious sigh. Perched behind the bathymeter, Ted Anderson watched as the distance between the *Swordfish* and their goal continually decreased. The subterranean ridge toward which they were plunging through the depths lay barely seventy-five feet away, and as the captain monitored its approach, his XO nervously commented, "Skipper, we've already exceeded our crush depth. Isn't this far enough for us to go?"

Without taking his eyes off the bathymeter, Ted Anderson beckoned the Hawaiian to be patient. The groaning hull seemed to underscore the urgency of the XO's remarks, as William Abbott added, "I think he's right, Ted. Let's turn this rust bucket topside before we tear apart from the sheer pressure of the surrounding sea."

Taking a last long look at the bathymeter, Anderson forcefully cried out, "Mr. Conlin, remove the diving angle, right full rudder! Engineering, reverse engines, back emergency! Full rise both planes. Blow the forward group. Vent the forward tanks when you get an up angle!"

As the seated helmsmen pulled back on their steering columns, the planes bit into the icy depths and the *Swordfish* moaned in protest as its angle of descent was negated. The compartment filled with the raucous roar of venting ballast, and the now-lightened submarine reversed its previous course and began ascending.

They had been able to rise to a depth of eight hundred and fifty feet when a pair of thunderous explosions sounded from the depths beneath them. Seconds later, the vessel was engulfed by a massive shock wave. Rocking violently from side to side, the twenty-eight-hundred ton vessel was tossed to and fro like a feather on the wind. Inside the ship's steel hull, loose equipment clattered to the deck, along with those unfortunate sailors who didn't have the benefit of a seatbelt or a sturdy handhold to keep them in place.

As the lights blinked off, then on again, another shock wave hit. This one was noticeably weaker than its predecessor, and all too soon the *Swordfish* was able to stabilize itself. And only then did the relieved crew cry out in triumphant joy.

Ted Anderson and William Abbott joined in on this brief celebration. As they vented their anxieties, the white-haired veteran patted his blond protégé on his back and remarked sincerely, "Congratulations, Captain. You and your crew did this old man proud."

"We couldn't have done it without you, Skipper,"

retorted Ted Anderson emotionally. "And, of course, the *Swordfish* sure cooperated. This old lady deserves to retire after the scare she just went through."

"Speaking of the devil, I wonder what the hell ever happened to Ivan?" quizzed Abbott.

It proved to be the XO who attempted to answer him. "The last we heard from them, they were plunging off into the depths with our four fish on their tail. Maybe Bodzin can give us an update."

Oblivious to the XO's remark, Brad Bodzin sat at his console on the deck below, monitoring a sickening sound that was emanating from deep within the subterranean trench lying to the immediate south of them. His headphones had picked up this distinctive racket soon after the last of the shock waves had passed. Though he had no past experience to compare it with, the intuitive Texan could only assume that the rending, screeching noise he was hearing was the sound of a submarine imploding.

Strangely saddened by this realization, Brad closed his eyes. And as this mournful cry of the deep gradually faded in the distance, the great tension that had previously wracked his body miraculously dissipated.

Chapter Seventeen

The excited call from the deputy director of the KGB sent Admiral Viktor Chimki scurrying from his Kremlin office. With his faithful assistant Katya at his side, the silver-haired veteran breathlessly climbed into the backseat of his awaiting Zil limousine. Having already been informed of their destination, the chauffeur wasted no time driving them out of Red Square and southward down Leninski Prospekt.

"Is the KGB certain that the fellow they have cornered is Premier Ivanov's assassin?" questioned Katya as tree-lined Gorky Park passed on their left.

"Absolutely," answered Chimki. "On his way to the dormitory room where he's currently barricaded, he took several shots at the agents sent to apprehend him. One of our men was injured, and a cursory ballistics check on the bullet dug from his shoulder showed an exact match to the slug pulled out of the premier's skull. He's the bloodthirsty bastard all right, and soon the whole world will know it was the CIA that hired him to kill our beloved leader."

The chauffeur had guided the limo onto the left-most lane, which was marked off with a solid yellow line. Specially reserved for VIP traffic, it allowed them instant relief from the congested mass of diesel-belching trucks, buses, and automobiles that blocked the rest of the roadway in a virtual gridlock.

The Lenin stadium passed on their right, and all too soon the lofty tower of the University of Moscow's main administration building beckoned in the distance. It was a dismal, overcast afternoon, and Viktor Chimki's sullen mood seemed a perfect match to the weather. Yet as he looked out to the rapidly approaching university grounds, the spotting of two circling helicopters brought a slight grin to his lips.

"Excellent. I see that the militia has provided some air support. We've got him now, dearest Katya. And with his capture and subsequent interrogation, the Motherland can get on with the all-important task of choosing its new direction."

Katya anxiously sat forward as a police roadblock obstructed the street before them. "From the idle chatter I've been picking up in the halls of the Kremlin, your name is being frequently mentioned as Premier Ivanov's successor. I'm so excited for you, Viktor! You've worked so hard for so many years, and finally your selfless effort is being recognized."

Chimki answered as the limo braked to a stop before the police barricade, "Your kind words are most flattering, my dearest. But it's not gossip that chooses our country's supreme leader, it's the votes of the politburo. And right now, we are at an impasse."

"But surely all that will change once the assassin is apprehended and admits both his guilt and his connection with the moderate CIA faction," observed Katya shrewdly.

Keeping Viktor from answering her was the sudden appearance at the limo's passenger window of a uniformed militia officer. As the man rapped on the bulletproof glass, Chimki lowered the window and accepted a somber greeting.

"Good afternoon, Admiral. Captain Sergei Nagorny of the MVD at your service. Colonel Lykov is waiting for you outside the dormitory where the suspect still lies barricaded. I'm afraid, though, that the only way to get there is by foot."

"These old legs are still quite capable of getting me around, Captain," said Chimki, who turned to address his escort. "Now are you sure that you won't reconsider and stay here in the car, Katya? The suspect is armed and the situation is still quite dangerous."

Without a second's hesitation, Katya responded, "I wouldn't miss this historic moment for a trip to America. So if I won't be a burden, I'd like to accompany you."

"As you wish, my dearest," returned Viktor as he opened the door and beckoned Katya to join him outside.

With the militia captain leading the way, they crossed over the university's parklike grounds. The oaks were just starting to bud, and the humid air was filled with the ripe rich scent of spring. The students who normally packed these pathways were noticeably absent, replaced instead by dozens of stern-faced, uniformed policemen, most of whom had light-weight machine guns draped over their shoulders.

The chopping clatter of the circling helicopters intensified as they broke out into a broad clearing dominated by a massive brick high-rise. Surrounding the entrance to this building were even more uniformed soldiers, and a group of plain-clothed figures whom Viktor recognized as being from the KGB. As they approached this structure, a tall, middle-aged, brown-haired individual dressed in an indistinct black suit and red tie stepped forward to greet them.

"You got here quicker than I expected, Admiral," remarked Colonel Yuri Lykov, deputy director of the KGB.

As the two men exchanged handshakes, Viktor introduced his attractive associate. "Colonel Lykov, I'd like you to meet my administrative assistant, Miss Katya Markova."

"Ah, so I finally get to see the face that goes along with your voice," offered the KGB agent with a polite nod. "We've been on the phone together quite often lately, and your efficient manner is most appreciated."

Katya noted the sincere spark that momentarily gleamed from his cold black eyes. "Thank you, Colonel. Is the suspect still trapped inside?"

Yuri Lykov looked upward and pointed to the building's third floor. "That he is, Comrade. As I promised the admiral here, we have been waiting for you before moving in to apprehend him. Since he's still believed to be heavily armed, I hope you don't mind wearing helmets and bulletproof vests as we make our final assault. Even though my men are experts at this kind of thing, one never knows what to expect when dealing with such madmen."

Nodding that this was fine with them, both Viktor and Katya donned the protective gear that was handed to them by an alert militiaman. Only then did Colonel Lykov lead them into the building's interior.

They continued on to the dormitory's third floor by way of a wide interior stairway. Chimki accomplished this climb without faltering and reached their final destination fully ready to get on with the task at hand.

Waiting outside the suspect's shut door was a squad of five burly KGB operatives. This elite, specially trained unit was dressed in green fatigues and armed with a variety of weapons and assault hardware. Silently signaling the blond leader of this detachment that he was free to proceed, Colonel Lykov stood in the adjoining hallway, with his two guests huddled protectively behind him.

With a minimum of fanfare, the assault team's leader positioned himself before the doorway and kicked it open with a single, powerful blow from the sole of his booted foot. Like a well-choreographed ballet, his men raised their weapons, and seemingly oblivious to any awaiting danger, stormed into the dorm room one after the other.

Viktor Chimki watched this assault, and while pondering the team's bravado, anticipated the exploding blast of gunshots. Yet, strangely enough, not even the sounds of a struggle followed. Moments later, the unit's leader poked his blond head out of the doorway and merely beckoned them to enter.

Colonel Lykov led the way inside, with Katya close on his heels. Viktor entered last, and would take to his grave the macabre scene that awaited them there. Hanging limply from the room's ceiling-mounted light fixture was the lifeless body of a young man. It was obvious from the crude noose wrapped around his neck that he had committed suicide by hanging himself. Taking in the victim's bulging eyes, swarthy good looks, curly head of black hair, and full mustache, Viktor angrily cursed. "Damn, I wanted so to take this bastard alive!"

It proved to be Katya's gasps of horror that served to divert his attention away from the body. Turning to scan the rest of the room, Viktor soon saw for himself the reason for his secretary's upset. Lining the room's walls were dozens of poster-size photographs showing literally thousands of corpses. Many of these cadavers were emaciated beyond belief, merely skeletons covered by a thin layer of skin. Other photos displayed huge burial pits lined with body after body, whose bloodstained torsos were clearly scarred by bullet holes.

"What kind of ghastly nightmare have we managed to stumble upon?" questioned the shocked Navy veteran.

It was the icy voice of Colonel Lykov that answered him. "I believe that this suicide note left on the victim's desk can answer your question, Admiral. It seems that our suspect's name was Kevork Bagdarian. He was a student here, and an Armenian by birth. Not only does he admit to assassinating Premier Ivanov, but he also explains his motivation. It says

405

here that he went on his rampage solely in response to Ivanov's failure to sign a proclamation that would officially blame the Azerbaijanian Moslems for the killing of over a million of his Christian Armenian ancestors in 1915."

"But that can't be true!" protested Viktor. "I tell you, it's Yakov Rosenstein and his CIA-influenced moderate lackeys who are responsible for this deception."

From the blank look on the KGB colonel's face, Viktor could tell that not even the intelligence specialist was buying his continued suspicions. Suddenly doubting his beliefs himself, Chimki sighed heavily. As his shoulders slumped forward, he made his way over to the room's only window. The chopping clatter of the circling helicopters sounded from overhead as he focused his weary gaze on the skyline that formed the northern horizon.

The new glass-and-steel face of Moscow lay in the distance, and Viktor suddenly felt very old and very tired. Well aware that his great vision for the Motherland's future would never reach fruition after all, he pondered the consequences that would result when news of their gruesome discovery was made public. The hard-liners would be handed a devastating setback. Certain now to wrest away the reins of government, the moderates would rise victorious, and the Motherland's great socialist experiment would be all but doomed.

One of the first things that Yakov Rosenstein and his cowardly cohorts would demand would be the immediate release of the American Elint ship, the USS *Turner*. Then Viktor would most likely be held personally accountable for an even greater loss. Once again sighing heavily, the seventy-seven-year-old veteran couldn't help but wonder if he had needlessly condemned the brave crews of the *Caspian* and the *Kirov* to their deaths because of his groundless suspicions. If this turned out to be the case, he knew that he would never be able to live such a tragic waste down!

Susan Patton stood on the dive boat's wide transom, gazing out to the glistening black seas beyond. The eastern horizon was just beginning to lighten with the first hint of dawn, and Susan continued her lonely vigil, as she had done throughout the entire night.

In the distance she could clearly hear the persistent, deep grinding roar of the *Global Explorer*'s drilling rig. Such a muted sound had accompanied her entire watch, and she knew that the mammoth marine salvage vessel would soon be reaching its goal on the sea floor, eight hundred and seventy-three feet below.

The crew of the disabled Soviet ballistic-missile-carrying submarine had long since been rescued. This recovery included the body of the ship's captain, who had blown his brains out with a single pistol shot the moment that the DSRV *San Clemente* had attached itself to his sub's main access trunk.

Unfortunately, the crew of the other Russian sub they had encountered would not be as lucky. This warship had split in half, and had sunk to the bottom of a nearby trench, resulting in the certain loss of all aboard.

The one indirectly responsible for this vessel's demise had yet to show himself. Ever since releasing him out of the moonpool of the *Global Explorer* with the harness-mounted, ultrasonic homing beacon on his head, Sammy had been conspicuously absent. This was the first time since the dolphin had originally arrived in their lagoon at Hurricane Hole that he had failed to return from a mission, and Susan couldn't help but be seriously concerned. Thus the reason for her current all-night vigil, as she patiently waited for the lovable marine mammal to show himself.

The night wind blew in a warm, southerly gust, and the blond marine biologist redirected her gaze to the shadowy landmass that could just be seen on the northeastern horizon. Norman Island loomed like a silent sentinel, its mountainous terrain barely visible in the dim light of dawn. Between the dive boat and this isolated mass of rock and tropical scrub lay the wide expanse of shallow water known as Lucifer's Seat. It was the razor-sharp reef that gave birth to this descriptive name that was the apparent reason for the Typhoon class vessel's sinking. The mysterious buoy that drew the Russian warship to its doom lay only a few dozen feet off the dive boat's stern. Susan knew that with the dawn a Coast Guard cutter would be arriving on the scene to determine why the official channel beacon had been painted over and this new buoy situated in its place.

A sudden slapping sound diverted Susan's attention, and she anxiously scanned the waters to identify its source. A leaping mullet broke the surface of the seas, and she dejectedly shook her head in disappointment.

The longer Sammy remained away, the greater the chances were that he would never return to her. Of course, she could never discount the possibility that he had been killed during the furious underwater battle that followed his placing of the beacon on the Soviet attack sub's hull. It was apparent that both Commander Walker and Secretary of the Navy Anderson felt that this had been Sammy's fate. They had taken the time to express their condolences before returning to the massive salvage job that lay before them.

Susan failed to share their pessimism. With the slim hope that Sammy had survived the fracas and was merely wandering the seas disoriented, she called in the dive boat and began her current twenty-four-hour-a-day watch.

So far, she had been met with nothing but disappointment. While wondering if her efforts would all be in vain, Susan issued a wide yawn. Her eyelids were heavy, and just planning to catch but a brief catnap, she sat down heavily on a nearby deck chair and fell almost instantly into a deep, dreamless sleep.

The oars bit into the warm waters of the Caribbean Sea with a bare splash. There was a muted squeal as Egbert pulled the rough wooden handles up toward his chest before lifting up the oar heads and extending his long arms to once again repeat the monotonous process. There was a familiar tightness in his upper arms and shoulders, and the palms of his hands had long since callused over. Yet because their skiff's engine had once again conked out soon after they reached Norman Island, he would have to put up with this physical discomfort if they intended to reach their goal as planned.

The blinking red strobe light of the channel buoy they were headed toward invitingly shone on the horizon, while behind them, the lights of St. John had long since faded.

As a gentle swell rocked the battered wooden vessel, Egbert heard the voice of his brother bark out behind him. "There's a boat out there all right. Though it's not the cruise liner that I was hoping for, it's a good fifty-footer."

"Shit, it looks to me like nothin' but a dive boat," reflected Stanley Wilkes.

"And what's wrong with that?" returned Delbert. "There'll be a load of tourists in its hold all the same. And even if they don't have all that much cash and jewelry, we can make up our expenses just by ripping off their diving equipment and fencing it in Charlotte Amalie."

"I still don't see how these plastic pistols are going to fool 'em," added Stanley.

A disgusted tone flavored Delbert's voice as he responded, "Don't tell me that you were expecting me to come up with the real thing, Stanley? Though I don't mind being involved in a little redistribution of wealth, accidentally killing an innocent tourist isn't in my book of tricks."

Egbert listened to this pointless discussion and silently shook his head. As far as he was concerned, this entire idea was idiotic. Not only were they risking prison for such a crime, but there was no telling if their efforts would even pay off. What if the occupants of the dive boat didn't buy their ploy and resisted. Never known for their fighting abilities, they'd end up tossing their plastic handguns into the water and rowing off back to St. John with their tails between their legs.

"How are you holding up, little brother?" questioned Delbert.

"I'll make it, Del," answered Egbert in between strokes.

"Well, just know that we appreciate your muscle, Egbert. I still can't understand why that engine failed on us again. I could have sworn that I completely cleaned up that blocked fuel line that caused our last breakdown."

"I guess that we're just not cut out to be mechanics," returned Egbert. "Otherwise, we'd both be back in Cruz Bay working with Father."

"That's no life for us, little brother. Just you watch. This caper will go off without a snag, and we'll make more money in a single evening than we could in an entire month."

"I hope it's more than that," added Stanley Wilkes. "Maybe that dive boat belongs to a bunch of treasure hunters, and we'll chance upon a fortune in golden loot."

Delbert chuckled. "That's what I like about you, Stanley, always a positive outlook. But if you don't stop dreamin' and start bailing, we're never going to live long enough to see one of your damn dreams come true!"

411

Egbert soon heard the characteristic sound of water being scooped from the bottom of their boat and poured out into the sea. Doing his best to concentrate solely on his rowing, Egbert gradually increased the pace of his strokes until the flashing red beacon of the channel buoy was practically right before their bow. This put their desired goal less than one hundred yards distant.

Also conscious of their excellent progress was his brother, who softly whispered, "Easy now, Egbert. We're close enough to be heard now, and from the lack of lights on board, I'd say that there's a good chance we'll catch them napping. And that will only make our job that much easier."

Silently drawing in the oars, Egbert carefully turned around and spotted the wooden vessel bobbing on the nearby sea. His brother caught his gaze and winked. "We're about to take that first big step, little brother. From now on, life's only going to get sweeter and sweeter."

Trying hard to ignore the gnawing tension deep in his gut, Egbert nodded, and watched as Delbert reached into the sack that lay at his side. He pulled out three plastic toy handguns and a trio of rubberized Halloween masks, that had been purchased to ensure their anonymity. As Delbert passed them out, Stanley Wilkes annoyingly protested, "Hey, you said that I could be Spiderman!"

"Damn you, Stanley, keep that fool mouth of yours shut!" whispered Delbert forcefully as he turned to exchange masks with Stanley.

Shaking his head in disgust, Delbert pulled on the mask of Frankenstein, while Egbert became the infamous Count Dracula. With their disguises now in place and their authentically crafted toy handguns ready for action, Delbert signaled his brother to begin rowing once again.

Careful to proceed as silently as possible, Egbert dipped the oars in the water and the launch jerked forward. Guessing that it would take a mere dozen strokes to reach the dive boat's side, Egbert extended his arms before him and pulled the oar handles up to his chest. But strangely enough, the boat failed to respond. When he repeated this process and the launch still remained motionless, he raised his voice in concern. "Hey, Del, I think that we're stuck on something."

Scanning the surrounding waters, Delbert responded, "It doesn't look like we're caught up on the reef, little brother. But since these waters can fool the best of sailors, you never know. Stanley, reach overboard and see if you can feel any obstructions beneath our hull."

Quick to carry out this direction, the lanky teenager scooted up to the rowboat's bow and cautiously leaned over its gunwales. He was in the process of dipping his long arms into the warm sea when a sleek, black-skinned creature came surging up from the depths below, leaped out of the water, and ended up with half of its nine-foot-long, four-hundred-pound body actually inside the rocking launch, directly beside the startled figure of Stanley Wilkes.

"It's Jaws!" cried Stanley at the top of his lungs.

Though Egbert was able to identify this creature as a dolphin immediately, he had no time to share this information with his startled friend. It was a combination of Stanley's unwarranted panic and the dolphin's great weight that proceeded to overturn the rowboat and send the three of them crashing out into the black water.

From the transom of the dive boat, Susan Patton heard this commotion and instantly snapped from her brief slumber. Realizing it wasn't a dream that had awakened her, she grabbed for the flashlight that lay at her feet and directed its wide beam into the surrounding sea. Quick to meet her eyes was the rounded hull of an overturned rowboat, while its three soaked occupants struggled to make their way to the shelter of the nearby buoy.

Below deck, her assistant Owen had also been awakened by this racket, and came sprinting topside dressed only in a pair of ragged cut-offs. It was just as he reached Susan's side that her flashlight picked out yet another object in the water beside the capsized launch. This sighting caused a scream of pure joy to flow forth from the lips of the two marine biologists, for innocently swimming in the seas before them was Sammy! They were able to instantly verify this fact by the distinctive clear plastic harness that still lay attached to his body and the mischievous black eyes that glowed from his ever-smiling face.

Oblivious to the frantic efforts of the three soaked Rastafarians, who were in the process of climbing onto the bobbing channel marker, both Owen and Susan leaped into the water themselves. Between the two of them they readily removed the harness, and as

414

Susan stroked Sammy's smooth flanks and accepted some gentle prodding from his snout, she realized that he wasn't alone. For floating nearby was yet another dolphin.

From her small size, she was surely a female, and a shy one at that. Unwilling to approach the two joyous humans, she watched from afar as Sammy stood on his tail and initiated a complete backward flip. Then to a chorus of high-pitched clicks and whistles, Sammy swam over to the other dolphin's side apparently to reassure her.

Certain now that Sammy had indeed found himself a girlfriend, Susan watched as the two dolphins sensually rubbed up against each other. Then, with a swift movement of his tail, Sammy returned to Susan. He surfaced close beside her, and while chattering away in yet another burst of unintelligible dolphinese, looked her straight in the eye. This glance brought with it a sudden warmth, and Susan found her soul touched by a language that needed no words with which to convey itself. And the last she ever saw of Sammy was as he gracefully swam off toward the open sea, with his new mate close beside him.

Myrtle Hall awoke from her trance with a start, called back into waking consciousness by the shrill crowings of a distant rooster. As her eyes popped open, she found herself staring at her makeshift altar and breathlessly watched as the red candle that had been burning on the coral ledge was snuffed out by an invisible breath. And it was at this very moment

415

that her recently experienced vision returned to her.

Once more she had been mounted by the spirit of Baron Samedi, and transferred back to the crossroads, where the ghostly figure of Miss Sarah was waiting for her. Speaking with the deep, hoarse voice of Damballah the serpent, her spiritual mentor conveyed to her a joyful report of the great victory that the forces of light had just won over the black tide of evil. Yet Sarah's blissful mood was short-lived as she left Myrtle with a strict warning. For although their recent triumph was responsible for sending the blackness back to the pit from which it had crawled, it was destined to reemerge, at which time mankind would once again be put to the test.

Praying that this wouldn't happen in her lifetime, Myrtle stiffly rose from the dusty floor of her hounfour. As the sound of the crowing cock again sounded from the jungle, she made her way over to the extreme edge of the volcanic promontory. With her glance now directed to the east, she took in the spellbinding sight of the sun breaking the distant horizon.

Aglow in the vibrant colors of this spectacular dawn was the surging Caribbean. Stretching for as far as the eye could see, the glistening waters beckoned like a long-lost lover. For it was from these very depths that their savior had come, only to be called back in preparation for his next destined return.